Green Eye
The Dominion Falls Series 4

Sarah Cass

Historical Romance
Romantic Suspense
Historical Western Romance

A Divine Roses Ink Book
Historical Romance
Romantic Suspense
Historical Western Romance

PUBLISHER
Divine Roses Ink
http://www.divinerosesink.com

Other Books in
The Dominion Falls Series

Independent Brake
Changing Tracks
Derailed
Dark Territory
Runaway Train
Home Signal
Red Zone

Coming Soon in
The Dominion Falls Series

Dust Raiser
Chase the Red
Blizzard Lights
Dead Man's Switch
Bird Cage
A Highball Arrangement
Douse the Glim
Blood
Grave Digger
Bad Order

Books by Sarah Cass

The Tribe Series
The Tribe
The Wolf
The Chief
The Raven
The Lake Point Series
Santa, Maybe
Deep-Fried Sweethearts
Stalled Independence
Witch Way
A Thorough Thanksgiving
Eve's New Year
Heartstrings & Hockey Pucks
Luck of the Cowgirl
Stars, Stripes & Motorbikes
Free Falling
Love for Hire
Haunted Hearts
Stand Alone Novels
Masked Hearts
Leap

Dedication

To my newest Beta Reader, Annette.
Thank you for your honest feedback and advice.
The series has gotten better thanks to
your input and excitement!

Here's to many more to come!

Table of Contents

*True friendship is a plant of slow growth,
and must undergo and withstand the shocks
of adversity before it is entitled to
the appellation.
-George Washington*

Jane unlocked the library in a rush. She'd stayed at her ex-husband, David's, homestead the night before on her son Jesse's request. As usual, Cole had joined her there, leaving the saloon in his partner Graham Cooke's hands.

While they'd had great fun making popcorn and telling stories, they'd stayed up far too late. The morning had been rushed and busy, until Jane and Cole were both late. Him, to open the saloon, and she to open the library.

As they'd sped through town to their respective businesses, she'd spotted Hammy pouting on the porch of the saloon. Gilbert Hamm, the failed miner turned successful carpenter, was like clockwork when it came to getting his beer. Jane did hate to disappoint him and knew Cole did as well.

That meant their parting had been rushed and brusque, rather than enthusiastic enough to delay her further. It was likely for the best, though Jane could have used another enthusiastic moment or two with Cole.

She could hardly believe it had been two years since she'd first fallen into Cole's saloon near-dead. Though their first year together had been difficult, what with the mad man out for her death, and the mystery of her missing years thanks to her amnesia.

Once the man had been first arrested, and then died, her life had fallen into a wonderful routine. She'd finally confessed her love to Cole. Though he hadn't been able to say the words back, he proved his affections many times over.

Her skin flushed with the memory of the day before when he'd come to visit her at the library to prove his affections once again. They'd nearly been caught when a patron had entered as they were in the former kitchen of the building. She'd had to rush to resituate herself and greet the patron, leaving Cole behind.

As if he'd read her mind, the man himself strode into the library. The bright sun behind him darkened his visage from her view. Rather than say hello, he went to her desk and grabbed a book off it.

Knowing that while he could read, he wasn't one to, she pondered the meaning. She studied him as he leafed through the book without reading one word.

The tension in his back was plain through his tight shirt worn by years of wear. Something had happened.

Jane drew close to Cole, setting her hand on his spine. The tension ramped through his muscles before dissipating. "What's wrong? I know it can't be Mr. Hamm."

"Nah. He's fine. Got Chauncey taking care of him." He tossed the book back onto her desk without care.

"Then what could it be?"

"What do ya think?"

"Ah. Graham?" Jane gathered the book he'd tossed to return it to the shelves. She'd finished it the evening before, but Cole had swept her out in a rush. A grunt was her sole reply, so she pondered. "What did he damage this time?"

"The mirror. Three bottles of whiskey."

Jane mentally calculated the cost, though she imagined Cole had done so quite quickly. "Is that all?"

"A hundred dollars' worth what with the mirror. Took us six months to replace the last one." He perched on the edge of her desk, his attention now full on her.

"I was being facetious."

"What?"

"Indecorous."

"Huh?"

"Now you're deliberately being obtuse." She met his gaze to scold further to find his lips quirked in a sexy smirk. "As I said, you're being deliberately obtuse."

"Maybe."

"When are you going to talk to him about his behavior?" She moved about the library, cleaning as she always did. "Or, even better, buy him out? He only participates in the business now to get drunk and start fights."

"I can't afford that. Would if I could." Cole glared out the door where they could see the back side of the saloon. "I've talked to him."

"You've fought with him, certainly. Had yelling matches to rival ours. That doesn't mean you've talked."

"Can't talk to him no more. Not since Becky snared him for good."

"It was a shame for us all when she did."

"Ain't that the truth?"

"There is little we can do about his marriage or the fact she drove his paramour out of town. However, you could try to sit and carry on a real discussion with him about his disruptive behavior."

"Won't do no good. He'll be itching for a fight, always is anymore. First I say something it'll be fists first, words never."

"I can't argue your logic."

"You could." He snatched her hand to draw her close. "Then we could fight."

"Why on earth would we do that?" Though she knew where he was going with his line of thinking, she wasn't about to make it easy for him.

"So's we can make up real nice in the back there again."

"Funny you should mention that. I was thinking about it right before you came in here all chuffed."

"Were you now?" He pulled her even closer until their bodies were flush. "That mean you're interested?"

"For the sole purpose of easing your upset?"

"Been for less reason before."

"Hmmm." She pondered the definite temptation of his proposal. Even as she considered, someone stepped into the library. "Oh, too bad for you Cole. Good afternoon Mrs. Henry."

Cole grumbled a complaint but released her without argument. While she dealt with Mrs. Henry, he did her the kindness of getting her stove lit.

Though already late April, the chill of the harsh winter they'd suffered lingered in the valley. He even performed an additional thoughtfulness of setting a kettle of water to heat for her tea. By the time she returned to her desk to send off Mrs. Henry, her favorite orange tea sat steeping before her.

Her heart warmed at his thoughtfulness. Once again, he proved their couplings weren't the only way he displayed his affection for her. The little things such as this proved them over and over. Even if no one else saw, she knew.

His strong arms circled her waist from behind. A gentle kiss landed on her neck. "You're going to insist on working, aren't you?"

"You do know me."

"I know when you're ready for a go and when you're not, at least."

"That could come from your years upon years of experience in the sex trade."

"Nah. That comes from two years getting to know ya. Every inch."

"Ah, but the first two months you only knew what my body was like broken and bleeding. You, sir, got to know my mind and temper first."

"Definitely your temper. Ya had plenty of tempers."

"All around you." She pursed her lips against her burgeoning laughter. "Even today you tend to spark that as much as any other emotions."

"Ya look better when you're mad. Well, that and when you're expecting something."

"Which is why you're always expecting something when I get mad."

"Not gonna lie and say no."

"Hmmm." She turned to face him. "Now, go make nice with Mr. Hamm. You probably hurt his feelings by being grumpy about his beer because of the mirror."

"Hammy will live."

"You be nice to him."

"Yes, ma'am." He leaned closer. Lips hovering close to hers, a smile made his ice blue eyes twinkle. "Any other orders for me?"

"Come find me for supper."

His smile faltered into a grimace. "Can't. Won't let Graham watch tonight and Cuddy's off. I could have him come in to help out."

"No. He's been working his tail off because you can't trust Graham alone."

"Can't trust him period. Cuddy was there last night, couldn't stop it. Should make him come in just to ask him what in blazes he was doing."

"It's not Cuddy's fault Graham is impossible any longer. No punishing him for being unable to stop a running locomotive when it gets going."

"There you go, giving orders again."

To soothe his renewed temper, she pressed into him. Her hand slipped between them. Her voluminous skirts hid the way she traced her fingertips along his length from anyone who might approach. "You liked when I was ordering you yesterday. Or did you forget?"

He groaned until his forehead dropped to press to hers. "You don't play fair. Grope me and send me off."

"What if I promise to make it up to you soon as the saloon closes?"

"Promise?"

"Always."

A throat cleared behind them. The familiar titter of her best friend's laughter preceded Kat's words. "You two will never cease, will you? I swear everyone in town has caught you in compromising positions at least once. Myself, I've caught you far too many times for comfort."

"Compromising positions are the best ones to be in." Cole winked at Jane before lifting his grin to the person behind her. "You should know that Kathy."

Jane chuckled low under Kat's continued laughter. "Unfortunately, though she married a man whose skills she swears by, he's not one for public displays."

"Too bad for her." Cole kissed Jane boldly. "I'll go make nice with Hammy. Happy?"

"Infinitely," she concurred. Soon as he parted her company, she sighed at the loss. With that mood passed for the moment, she turned to face Katherine Daugherty.

The woman's vibrant red curls were contained rather nicely for once. A jaunty hat perched precariously on her head. Jane wondered at how many pins Kat used to keep the blasted thing in place.

One thing Jane loved about Kat is though Jane did much to cause scandal and rumor, Kat did just as much by the simple matter of the trousers she always wore. Though now married and with a daughter, all the most decent folks were infinitely scandalized by the trousers she wore.

Of course, Kat had caused plenty of scandal on her own in the years before her marriage. From running away from an arranged marriage to a dalliance with Cole, and her involvement with the suffrage movement. It was good to have a friend all too familiar with the life of scandal and rumors.

Kat embraced Jane in a warm hug. "What was all that about? I thought you two just parted a few minutes ago."

"We did, however he returned to the saloon to find new damage done by his irascible partner." Jane poured a second tea for her friend. With it deposited on the desk, Jane resumed her seat. "He rarely bothers to go into the saloon, and when he does there's always damage and loss of plenty of alcohol."

"Oh, that cannot possibly be." Kat gasped, pressing her hand to her chest to add flair to her mocking surprise. "The good Rebecca Cooke swears her husband is sober as the day is long and despises the saloon any longer."

"He despises something," Jane concurred.

"It's not the saloon or alcohol."

"Not even close. Some days he acts as though it's me."

"I sometimes wonder if he suffered temporary insanity when he saved your life."

"I believe that was actually temporary sanity. His kindness and humor only lasted a month into his miserable marriage of convenience."

"That's why I'm well-pleased I didn't marry for convenience, only love."

"May we all hold the example of Graham and his sham of a marriage up to remind us of what not to look for in a lifetime mate."

"Money."

"Money." Jane shook her head. "Common as it might be, it doesn't often lead to a life of happiness. Perhaps contentment, but not happiness."

"Speaking of contentment." Kat leaned forward, a familiar wicked gleam in her eyes. "Despite your scandalizing level of public disputes."

Jane laughed when Kat wagged her brows at the feigned reprimand. Kat alone knew that despite the frequency and volume of their arguments, Jane and Cole no longer remained mad at each other for long. Many missteps in their early days had led to a commitment to talk through their problems. Even if arguing first was fun, because making up was so much better, their anger blew hot but quick.

"Have you had any thoughts of marriage?"

"Oh, please. You know I haven't. I'm rather content in my life as it is. It's simple but filled with passion that I will not contest with marriage."

"Marriage hasn't rid me of my passions."

"I'm well aware."

"It seems as though you and Cole haven't been able to get quite as much time together lately, though. What with Graham and his indelicacy."

"This is very much true."

"When will your brother arrive?"

"Which one? Clara had six, remember? Although one is dead. Two live here now. So, I suppose I should say which of the other three?"

Kat fixed her with a dark look. "Don't be contentious."

"It's fun. We just expounded on my enjoyment of contention with Cole."

"Jane Spencer. When is Thomas arriving?"

"I don't have an exact date at the moment." Jane sipped her tea. "I am quite relieved that Cole took Thomas up on his offer to manage the hotel. That means we'll have more time, and perhaps Cole's tempers will only be caused by myself."

"What?"

"Well, I do prefer his tempers come from me. It's difficult to make up after a fit of temper if you aren't part of the cause."

"Then this is about you making nice?"

"Always. It is the best part, after all."

"No. Not on your life." Graham glowered at Jane. His hands rested on the back of a chair, the muscles in his meaty forearms twitched as he clenched tighter.

Jane sighed and straightened the rest of the chairs around the ramshackle table. Perhaps she should have been scared, but she'd long been threatened by Graham and had grown tired of it.

As she tried to pass him to straighten the next table, his proximity made his large stomach shift her bustle off-kilter. She tried to straighten the damnable contraption while moving away from the cross man. "Don't shoot the messenger. I am simply sharing the news as I heard it."

"Bull. It was your idea, wasn't it?"

She bit down on her tongue to keep the initial harsh retort to herself. In the year since Graham married Becky for her dowry, and her dowry alone, his moods had become increasingly dark and angry.

For a few fleeting months Graham had been funny, kind, and sometimes even helpful to Jane. She began to see why Cole had ever called him friend in the first place. At one point she'd even dared to call him a friend. After all, he'd helped to save her life, rather than let her be buried alive after a botched hanging. To her, that earned him the right of friendship.

Unfortunately, he'd gone ahead and married Becky. Over the course of several months, he'd returned to the intolerable brutish idiot he'd been when she'd met him. "No. I had no involvement in the matter at all. I am rather upset to be honest, Cole managed to come up with the idea all on his lonesome."

"Liar. You don't want me here." He tossed back a glass of whiskey. Three months into his sham of a marriage he'd caved and had his first drink, which ruined a solid six months of sobriety. Worse, his drinking led to regular fights during the few hours he actually bothered to come work at the Hangman's Inn anymore.

"It seems to me you are the one that doesn't want to be here." She grabbed the cleaning rag off the table. Rather than respond to his renewed glare, she moved behind the bar. They'd received a new shipment of whiskey that needed put away. It would be better for her to focus on that then the increasingly volatile temper of Graham. Maybe she'd not been scared at first but the more he snarled and hovered close to her, the more her nerves shook. "I have a job elsewhere. I can't always be here, and when I am I would like to relax."

"So it was your idea."

"No. It wasn't. I think Tommy made the offer before he went to New York to wrap up his affairs there." She turned a bottle straight, taking a peek in the newly replaced mirror above the bar. Against Cole's better judgement they'd bought it on credit, but within a week and a few five dollar poker games, he was close to paying it off. She was pleased to find Graham remained seated on the other side of the bar.

Her brother, Tommy Young, had offered to be manager for the saloon and hotel. While Jane had every capability of taking on such a job, as she'd done it before a couple years before, she refused to work for Cole.

The mere thought of Cole replaced her frown with a smile. The mental image of him sleeping sprawled on their bed when she'd slipped from the room earlier made her whole body tingle with excitement.

"Well, he doesn't have the right, neither."

"Tommy has every right to make whatever offers he wants to. Cole has every right to make the decisions." The pleasant tingles dissipated into her annoyance with Graham. "Cole owns over half the business. He can do whatever he wants toward its betterment."

"I got us an investor!"

"Of course, you did—and then you promptly turned around and destroyed the bar so Cole had to use every bit of that money on repairs instead of improvement." She cursed inwardly when she realized he'd circled the bar to block the only exit. Trapped by an angry bear of a man could never be called a smart idea. Now she had to come up with some sort of escape. "It doesn't matter. It wasn't my idea."

"You talked to him about it, convinced him how good it was. Didn't you?"

"To be perfectly clear, he spoke to me. I did not tell him what to do. We discussed it. I counseled him on his options. The decision was his and his alone. The Hangman's Inn is over half his. Despite your so-called help in the form of an investor, you have done nothing to improve the place since Cole changed the name."

"You counseled him, eh?"

The hair on the back of her neck stood when he drew closer still, and bile threatened to rise as her stomach churned. When he wasn't an angry drunk, she knew Graham could be tolerable—even likable. However, at the moment she wanted to punch him in the nose. "Yes."

"Considering how Cole's changed since you got to town, you must give some awful good counsel." His hands planted on either side of her. "Maybe I should see how well it works. You sure got Cole's head spinning. You must be right good."

She tried to ignore the large, very strong body which held her pinned to the back counter. Rather than look in the mirror, she set her hands on the edge of the counter and gripped it. Her knuckles turned white before she felt in control of her temper. "I wouldn't."

"Why not?"

"I will rip your prick off if you even think about touching me."

"Would like to see you try." He all but growled, but at least he pushed off her. One of the bottles she'd put away ended up in his hands. "Why do you keep hanging around anyhow? You know he's gonna get bored eventually."

Two years ago that statement would have worried her. Before everything she'd gone through with Cole, every step he'd taken to help her find the truth of her past and, in the end, save her life. Now and then Cole might get bored, but together they enjoyed finding fun ways to make things exciting again.

"Oh, don't tell me." His low chuckle breached the silence she'd let linger. "You don't really think he loves you, do you?"

"I know how Cole feels." Even if he'd never said he loved her, he didn't need to. Cole excelled with actions over words. She didn't need to hear it, as long as she was free to say it to him often, without worry he'd run.

"Feels?" Graham snorted, and it quickly dissolved into a grating chortle. "Cole don't feel nothing. Ever. That's why I like him. Still not sure why he's hung on for so long. You must be pretty damn good."

"Oh, I am." A momentary flutter of pride squelched her nerves for all too brief a second. She finished putting away the bottles. Next she had to figure out her escape from her continued entrapment. Graham blocked the one exit unless she wanted to take an undignified, and most likely awkward, leap over the bar.

"Minute he hears what Hammy calls you, you'll be out of here."

Hammy. Despite her trapped state and high level of annoyance, Jane cracked a smile at the mere mention of the name. Gilbert Hamm, a scruffy old man with a deep love of beer, ran the local carpentry business. From the day she'd met him, he'd been nothing but sweet. In recent months he'd taken to calling her 'Mrs. Mitchell', as if she was Cole's wife. Far as she knew, Cole hadn't heard it yet. To be honest, she didn't know how he'd react. "Maybe I will. It's not like it means anything. I'm certainly not calling myself Mrs. Mitchell."

"You're acting like you do."

She pursed her lips to suppress a grin. To buy time she wiped the counter. The more she thought about it, the more she believed Cole would only be annoyed Hammy called her his wife publicly. Truth be told, in ways no one knew, she was closer to being his wife than one would expect.

When she'd first arrived in Dominion Falls with amnesia, she'd taken on the name Jane Doe. However, after a year and her own death, she'd taken on a new surname. Jane Spencer. No one else knew that Cole's birth name was Colton Spencer but her. While she'd felt good to no longer be going by Jane Doe, she never would have taken on the name Spencer without Cole's blessing. Cole had made sure she knew he wanted her to use his real surname.

Graham seemed to decide she'd been quiet too long and bumped into her hard enough to cause her to stumble. "You listening to me?"

"Not particularly. You might be able to ruffle Cole's feathers with all your bluster on a regular basis. I, however, find you no more annoying than a gnat buzzing in my ear."

"You'll find me more annoying than that." He gripped her wrist tight enough to smart. When she winced, unable to fight her reaction he yanked her hard enough to turn her. He grabbed her other wrist before she could pull it away.

It took every ounce of control she had to not fight his hold. A fight would only serve to spur him on, and likely cause her worse pain. Her hands flexed against the discomfort, a natural instinct to free themselves. She kept her face as neutral as possible. "If you hurt me, Cole will feed you to Soong's pigs."

"Think so, do you?" With a sharp tug he had them nose to nose. His forehead scrunched in deep lines. He bared his teeth in a snarl. "Stop interfering."

"Tell that to your wife, not me." The attempt to keep her voice level wavered when he twisted one of her wrists. Her pulse raced until it pounded in her ears. Fear that he might actually hurt her rose close to the surface. "Becky is who you're mad at."

"Presumptuous bitch."

"Graham," Cole's rich baritone voice cracked with ferocity. "Ya best let her go or I will shoot you where you stand."

The click of his Colt Walker cocking echoed through the empty saloon. Jane swallowed against the lump in her throat. Tensions what they were, Cole could see through on his threat. The only solution to avoiding an all-out brawl, or worse, an actual gun fight between the two would be to diffuse the friction.

She dug past the pain of another harsh twist to her wrist and somehow managed to force forward a smile. To take her gaze off the furious man holding her hostage seemed stupid, but she lifted her gaze to the angrier man standing on the balcony above their heads. She couldn't see Cole, only the barrel of the gun he had pointed downward. Her mind scrambled for something to lighten the state of things. "But Cole, if you shoot him, you'll ruin my brand-new dress with his blood."

"Not now Janey." Cole had to be pissed if he used the familiar nickname half the men of the town used on her. His eyes were impossible to see in the shadow of his Stetson, but not even the corner of his lip twitched in amusement. The level of his anger made her wonder how long he'd stood there above them listening to the conversation.

"She's a nosy little bitch." Graham shoved her backward. He held on until her arms jerked painfully straight before he released his grip.

Jane bit through her lip to keep from crying out as her back hit the bar. At the same time the blood rushed back into her hands with sharp tingling spikes of agony. She shut her lips and licked at the blood that trickled into her mouth and rubbed her wrists and hands until the feeling eased from them.

"You let her run this saloon and walk all over you." Graham, not smart enough to shut his trap, glared up at the weapon still aimed at him. "Now you let her talk you into bringing in that brute Tommy. You're letting her push me right out of here."

"You all right Jane?" Cole's aim didn't waver, he didn't even glance at her. The barrel remained pointed down at his shiny bald target.

"I'm fine," she admitted. Though there was damage, Graham had done nothing that would leave a permanent mark. At most she'd suffer a bruise or two from the abuse. She'd faced far worse pain than this. Her ankle alone still ached when it rained from an old break.

"Jane." Cole's head tilted enough she thought he might have actually looked at her. She knew he was all too aware of the brute strength that lay beneath Graham's beefy exterior.

"Really." She did her best to reassure him, not wishing any bloodshed spilled between the two, despite Graham's behavior. "My wrists are a little sore, but it's nothing I can't handle. He's drunk again, and I imagine his wife gave him another earful today."

Graham raged forward again; his hand outstretched to grab her. "You don't know nothing—"

The crack of the gun interrupted his tirade and forward motion. The wood of the bar to Graham's left splintered at the impact of the bullet. Jane couldn't stop her small shriek of surprise and ducked behind her arm to avoid the rush of wood splinters.

In the back rooms a racket started. The shot must have startled the whores awake.

"I told ya to leave her be." Cole cocked the gun again. "Now let her out. She's gotta get to work and I gotta deal with you."

Jane gripped the edge of the bar to steady herself. Even as the ruckus of ten whores rushing into the bar to find the reason behind the gunshot created enough distraction for Graham she might have slipped past. The shock of the situation left her trembling in her bones, and she had to pull herself together.

Graham's fists clenched, and he turned to glare at her again. He lowered his voice so she barely heard it. "See what you done? I knew you were nothing but trouble."

"Graham," Cole warned again.

"I'm not the drunk," Jane muttered.

Graham stepped aside against the back counter. His nostrils flared, but he waved her in front of him. "Get. Before I change my mind."

Grateful for the brief reprieve, she didn't wait another second to rush out from behind the bar into the open floor of the saloon. The moment she was no longer trapped, the knot in her stomach eased and she took a deep breath.

As her nerves eased, she sought out distraction, and found it in the gaggle of whores gaping at the scene before them. "Get on back to your rooms and get cleaned up. I smelled you coming down the hall. I imagine Cole will be opening soon enough. Don't worry yourself about this. Go on. Get."

Graham blustered and surged forward fast enough to make her back up a few steps. "You aren't the boss—"

"Shut up." Cole's long, muscular legs appeared at the top of the steps to distract her from the tense situation. One by one they moved down to the first floor.

Inappropriate or not, Jane didn't stop herself from admiring the flex and stretch of his thighs against his trousers. The mere image of her man eased her enough to sigh and allow steamy imaginings forward again. A smile formed despite her earlier tension. The ache in her wrists didn't affect her as bad now that she wasn't trapped, and Cole was almost close enough to touch.

"You'd best get to the library." Cole didn't turn his attention from Graham, his pistol leveled at his business partner. If Jane didn't know better, she'd have found it hard to believe they were once great friends.

"Don't kill him."

"After what he done? Give me one good reason not to." Cole's lip curled in a sneer. He stepped to block Jane when Graham moved.

"Because David would take great pleasure in hanging you." Jane set her hand on his arm, her inner tension easing more at the amused twitch of his lips. At least he wasn't too far gone in anger. "Don't give my ex-husband a reason to hang you. I'd never hear the end of it."

"I ain't allowed to shoot this bastard because you don't wanna be annoyed?" In the shadow of his hat brim his eyebrow arched.

"Exactly. I do hate being annoyed, it messes with my libido. And neither of us wants that." She patted his arm and slipped toward the door. Even with the aching in her wrists, she knew Cole wouldn't shoot Graham in cold blood. Problem would be how to diffuse the situation going forward—more specifically how to deal with Graham.

Once she'd left the building she automatically turned right to head to the library. Her mind on the problem of Graham, she moved more on instinct than actual attention.

Graham had always been difficult, and a drunk, but for a brief time he'd been helpful. She'd seen hints of humor and friendliness in the giant boor of a man when he wasn't a drunk, angry bastard.

"You aren't supposed to have problems anymore. Remember?" The voice that cut through her thoughts belonged to none other than the ex-husband she'd just spoken of. David Schaffer hopped off his horse, his sheriff badge gleamed in the sunshine. A cockeyed grin spread across his handsome features. "Or did you forget again?"

She jabbed his ribs with her elbow. "Shouldn't you be off wooing the exceptionally lovely and kind Widow Dynan instead of teasing me?" For over a year David had been courting the young widow, Lee Dynan, with Jane's full blessing.

While she'd once been married to David when she'd lived as Clara Young in her pre-amnesia life, in the time since she'd woken without her memories and become Jane, she hadn't found herself with the same deep love for him as Clara had felt.

Still, she cared for him and held him in deep respect. They even shared a son they'd created when she'd been Clara. As she'd moved on and become happy with Cole, she truly wished David every happiness, and Lee appeared to make him very happy.

"Don't you worry yourself about Lee. She's working right now." He looped the reins of his horse around the hitching post and followed her into the library. "So why, may I ask, do you look fit to be tied?"

"No, you may not."

"Too bad. I'm asking anyway."

"I can't imagine what you could mean." She flipped the lock on the window's interior shutters and pushed open the top two. Light streamed in across the book spines to her right. The glimmer of dust floated through as it always did in the library, no matter how she might clean. The lazy drifting soothed some of her nerves. "I'm perfectly fine."

A soft snort reached her ears, loud enough to pull her attention from her distraction. "Of course you are. Might as well tell me now. I'm going to pester you until you do." He leaned against the open door; a grin plastered firmly across his face. "If that fails, I'll go find Mike."

Jane gasped at the mere suggestion. "Don't you dare. I have enough hassle with so many of the Young boys around these parts now. Clara's brothers—"

"Your brothers, you mean."

"Fine. My brothers are quite annoying and nosy."

"So, in other words, they're just like you."

"I told you to hush. Now the last thing I need is you calling one of my brothers in on the simple fact that you are in a fit."

He chuckled. "So then tell me what has you cackling at me like an old hen."

She clenched her fists in an effort to stay mad, but the grin he kept giving her diffused any whiff of anger into simple annoyance. "Oh. You silly man."

"Never could stay mad at me as Clara. Good to know it still stands as such with Jane here." He perched on the edge of her desk and pulled off his leather gloves. "Are you talking or am I pestering more?"

"For the simple satisfaction of having you hush, I suppose I have no choice in the matter except to talk now, do I?" She opened the bottom shutters to let in as much light as possible. As she crossed to the desk she chided, "I do have plenty of work to do, David."

"Nice try. You can talk and work. Seen you do it enough times."

"Fine. What on earth do you think could be bothering me?" With a stack of books returned the previous day in her hand, she crossed to the shelves. Perhaps if she worked and kept busy enough he'd give up and leave.

"Could be any number of things. One of your brothers, perhaps, since you were complaining about them. Mack could be acting like a rake again. Of course, if I really think about it, the favorite in the battle for your annoyance lately is Graham Cooke."

"And there you have it. Are you happy? Will you leave me be now?" A strong urge to take her annoyance out on the books caused her to hesitate. She breathed in a few deep breaths until she felt calm enough to slip a copy of Dangerous Liaisons in its place.

"What did the idiot do this time?"

"What does the idiot always do?" She perched on the desk beside him with the two remaining books from her stack clutched to her chest. "If he isn't attacking me for daring to exist, he's doing everything in his power to get under Cole's skin."

"Did he succeed today?"

"Well, when I left the hotel Cole had his gun cocked and ready."

"What?" He flew to his feet, hand already on his holster.

"Relax. Cole won't shoot him; he won't give you the pleasure of hanging him."

His face twisted in an odd mix of laughter, frustration, and pain. "Hanging is never a pleasure, in some case it's the worst…however in others…"

"Exactly. Anyhow, Cole won't shoot Graham, even if he was being rather…" She rubbed her sore wrist. "Let's say aggressive."

"He's a nasty bastard." His hand left his holster, but he didn't relax.

"He's angry at the world. Despite my suggestion to get out of his engagement, he followed through and married Becky, a woman he can barely stand. She promptly went and ran the woman I think Graham may actually have had real feelings for out of town."

David snorted. "What? Feelings? Graham?"

"People used to say that about Cole."

"I still say it about him."

"I know, and I am serious about Graham. I think he is not only capable of real feelings; I also believe he actually had them for Linh. Can't say I understand it, but I do know that by the time Becky ran her out of town, Linh spoke better English than she did the day I met her."

Before his sham of a marriage Graham took up with a young Chinese woman whose family ran the laundry for most of the businesses in town. With Becky less than thrilled about his relations with Linh, she'd seen fit to destroy the family's business and sent them packing.

David frowned. "Where'd she go?"

"I'm not certain. Becky's father made sure her whole family packed up and left town. Wouldn't have his daughter embarrassed by such a scandal once they were married. I imagine Becky isn't making Graham's home life much fun."

"Is he still dipping into the talent pool at Cole's place?"

"Hasn't touched a whore in the months since the wedding." She set the books she still held on the desk. "Of course, he spends what time he's in the saloon taunting Cole about me. About the way I, as he puts it, 'moon' over Cole. He insists I'm trying to take the business away and run it like my own."

"Are you?"

"No." The idea hadn't even crossed her mind, to be honest. Graham's constant berating is the only thing that made her think of such a silly thing. "I'm trying to help it make money. Cole happy makes me happy. Cole making money means Cole is happy."

"I see. Would think Graham would want the same thing."

"Ah, but my bigger question is why does he care? He spends so little time there now, anyhow. If he comes in twice a week it's a miracle. The few times he bothers to show up he gets drunk and incites fights. Cole hardly ever has a night off because Graham cannot be trusted behind the bar."

"Which again makes Cole unhappy, and therefore you as well." He chuckled. "Poor grumpy Jane."

"Very grumpy Jane." She shrugged. "So, when Graham heard Cole hired Tommy as a manager so he could get some time off…"

"Graham took it as an insult?"

"You could say that." The memory made her wrists smart again. She wrapped her arms around herself to shake it off. "He made out like it was my fault. I'm sure that right now if Cole hasn't managed to kick him out, Graham is getting him all riled up again about what he claims I want out of the relationship."

His brow furrowed. "What?"

"Graham is convinced I want marriage, children, and everything a proper woman should want in life. To hear him tell it, I'm manipulating Cole into these things."

"Has he heard what Hammy calls you?"

"Cole or Graham?"

"Either."

"Graham certainly has." Heat flooded her cheeks, and she shook her head. "I can't imagine Cole hasn't. I think everyone has heard Hammy call me Mrs. Mitchell on one occasion or another. He means no harm by it of course, but I'm sure Graham will take the chance to twist it into me wanting marriage."

"Jane Mitchell. No. Can't see it. That doesn't roll off the tongue." David returned to sit beside her again. "Does any part of you want that?"

She blinked in surprise at the question. Did she ever want to be married again? As much as she loved Cole, she didn't need a wedding to confirm what they had for nothing more than propriety and prying eyes. "If I ever wanted to be married again, it wouldn't be for the reasons Graham is suggesting, or many of the townsfolk would like to see."

"Could you clarify that for me?"

"I don't wish to be married for expectations or propriety. I don't want to be a doting wife, or use my marriage to influence my husband. Or for children. Or to make people happy because I'm such a sinful, scandalous human. I don't want to do it for anyone else."

"All right."

"If I were to ever be married again, I would want to married for the sake of love. As it stands right now though, I am quite content in my life as it is. I rather enjoy living in scandal. Who else in this town will give old women something to gossip about over their tea?"

"I'm certain they'd find plenty to gossip about if you ever dared to dream of a quiet and content life. No one would blame you for wanting such a thing."

"Just because you are a hopeless romantic does not mean I hold any such notions." With a bright laugh she nudged him on the shoulder. "You are confusing me with your ex-wife, the late Clara Young."

He chuckled and draped his arm around her shoulders. "No. I think you have more of Clara's romantic spirit in you than you think. I just keep hoping you'll admit it."

"If I ever admitted any such nonsense, it wouldn't be to you."

"So long as you admit it to someone." He winked and gave her shoulders a squeeze. As he released her from the embrace, he rose. "Don't let Graham get to you. He's no more than a worthless drunk."

"If I believed that, he wouldn't be able to get to me. I've seen different. Don't forget, he did help save my life once."

"Circumstance."

"Circumstance or not, he did have a choice in the matter." She pushed off the desk. "Now off with you, Sheriff. I have work to do and in about an hour the library will be overrun by annoying children."

"Our son is not annoying, and you like Arthur. Not to mention you adore Kat's girl Cindy. I think you're even starting to enjoy Isaac's company."

She kept her back to him in order to keep her smile hidden. There was no reason to let him see he was right. While in general she still wasn't comfortable with children as a whole, a few select children had slipped through into her heart.

Of course, Jesse was different. He was Clara's son. While Jane might not remember being Clara or giving birth, she felt every bit the part of Jesse's Ma.

"Jane?"

"Be gone with you, Sheriff. You should probably make sure blood wasn't spilled at the Hangman's Inn." She chuckled and turned toward him. "I'll see you at supper tonight. Jesse invited me to join you, I do hope he made sure you knew."

"Was my and Lee's idea. We noticed you've been eating alone most nights with Cole so busy. If Tommy's going to be working at the hotel, I'm sure our chances for supper together will soon diminish."

"I certainly hope so." Her laughter grew stronger when his ears turned red. "I'll see you at supper, David."

"See you at supper."

*Cease to inquire what the future has in store,
and take as a gift whatever the day
brings forth.
—Horace*

"Mrs. Mitchell."

"Not now Mr. Hamm," Jane snapped. In the corner of the saloon a heated argument raged. The discussion needed her full attention to be sure it didn't come to fisticuffs, so she slammed a beer down in front of Hammy without asking what he wanted.

"Sorry Miss Spencer." Hammy stared into his beer without touching it. The normally smiling features of the scruffy old man sagged in sadness.

With a start, Jane realized she'd snapped at one of the kindest men she'd ever met. She reached across the bar and set her hand on his shaky one. "Mr. Hamm. Don't apologize. You owe me no such thing. I am the one that owes you an apology. In my distraction I was rude and thoughtless. I hope you'll find it in your heart to forgive me."

Hammy's ruddy features darkened even more. He tucked his chin down toward his chest. "Aw, shucks Lady Jane."

"Please. Enjoy your beer. It's on the house."

A wide, gap-toothed grin spread across his lips. His head popped up and he lifted the beer in a toast, "Good on ya, Jane."

"So long as my rudeness is forgiven."

"Sure is." He drank down half the glass in a long gulp. After a long sigh, he set the glass on the bar. "Ya said Cole might be building on. Any word on when it might happen?"

The heated discussion in the corner pulled Jane's attention away. She drew her lips down in a frown. "Unfortunately, that may be put on hold, Mr. Hamm."

"Too bad. I could use another big job."

"I imagine with construction on Mike's new hotel finally complete, you could." Her brother's initial plans for a hotel had expanded exponentially with a boom of visitors to the Sage Brush Resort and Spa. He'd advertised as far away as their hometown of Buffalo, New York, and then even further to the likes of Boston.

"And we finished with the settlement way back before winter." Hammy kept nursing his beer, oblivious to Jane's repeated glances toward the corner.

"Which the occupants are ever grateful for. Even the ones that have since left after the great Crime Act ripped their jobs away." Back in February, President Grant had signed the sham of a bill, The Coinage Act, into law, irreparably harming the livelihoods of many of the mines, and the men that worked them in the town. Jane's own uneasiness about what the Act would mean long term had caused her to withdraw all her investments and savings. She had a feeling the worst was yet to come.

"Yup." Hammy wiped some foam from his lip with his sleeve. "Thank ya kindly for getting the town to pay me for it. I didn't ask for no money."

"I know you didn't. And there's no need to thank me. I merely made a suggestion to the town council. You worked for over a year to provide every family with a home again after the Indian attacks, without charging a soul a dime. You should receive some compensation for your kind deed."

"Much obliged."

"Think nothing of it—"

"Devil." Cole's shout rang through the saloon as his chair clattered across the floor. The patrons of the saloon stilled as another curse echoed through the room. Cole leaned in close to mutter something unintelligible to Graham. He shoved the table hard enough that it rammed into Graham's stomach before he stormed from the building.

Graham slouched guiltily in his chair. Jane narrowed her eyes with a frown. She waved Mel over to watch the bar. Soon as the bar was handled, she crossed to the table where Graham slouched. He remained silent, so she took a seat prepared to draw it out of him.

"Didn't think he'd take it that bad," Graham muttered.

She quirked a brow at his quiet demeanor. The venom of several days before had dissipated into whatever he'd told Cole. "Would you mind telling what exactly you think he's handling poorly?"

"Becky wants a baby. Now."

"All right. So what does that have to do with Cole?"

"Since we haven't had any luck trying, she wants to adopt. Her pa has a friend at the orphanage in Denver." His jaw clenched. The muscles along his jaw twitched as he dug at a sliver in the table top.

"You haven't been married that long."

"Don't matter, she wants one now."

"She wants one. I'm guessing you don't."

"Don't matter none." His large hands ran over his bald head, tugging the skin into wrinkles under the force of the motion. "So we're going to have a baby now. Probably another one if I manage to do my job as a husband."

"All right. I understand all of that, well, as much as a sane human can. However I don't understand what your virility, or lack thereof, has to do with Cole storming out of here looking like he could have ripped the hinges off the door if I hadn't propped them open this morning."

"I'm selling my half of the business."

The words hit Jane with such impact her mouth dropped open. After a few moments of stunned silence she managed to close it. "You…are selling?"

"Yeah. With the help of Becky's pa I already found a couple of interested parties." His small eyes disappeared in his grimace.

"What?" The shock dropped away in a burst of anger so rapid her teeth ground together. "You went so far as to make inquiries to outside parties before you even bothered to tell Cole? How long ago did Becky order you to sell?"

"Been talking about it since before the wedding. I agreed maybe three months ago."

"You should have told Cole first, before ever looking for a buyer. At best you could have given him a chance to come up with the funds first. We've already got an investor."

"We?" His fists clenched. He jerked closer. "What the hell do you mean, we?"

She pursed her lips in an attempt to avoid the impulse to shrink away from his vitriol. She knew he was only talking to her because he wanted help. So she turned it back against him. "This is not the way to get me to talk to him."

His fists relaxed, but his jaw remained tense and twitchy. "You know Becky hasn't ever liked me owning this place, especially since I've got to work here regular shifts behind the bar. What with my…issues."

"Issues? Is that what we're calling them now?"

"You know what I mean."

"I do know quite well. You're a blinding drunk without the faintest clue how to keep your mouth shut when you're behind the bar. Eight months' worth of a marriage to a woman you dislike, and a father-in-law that's helping her control you, only makes you want to drink more."

He shuddered and clenched his glass.

She shook her head. "Your promises to stop drinking both to her and Cole are now worthless because you weren't man enough to walk away."

"What did you expect me to do? Go on off with all them Chinese people?"

An unladylike snort slipped out from under Jane's waning hold on decorum. "Linh is Chinese. You cared for her a great deal, but hated when someone picked on you for being with someone like her. She's probably better off without you—but you could have stayed with Linh and broken off the engagement."

"Just like that? It isn't that easy." Graham's lips twisted in a sneer. "Not everyone wants to live the way you do."

"The way I do? Oh, you mean being insanely happy."

"That isn't what I mean and you know it."

"Of course not, you mean living in scandal and surrounded by gossip. No, such a life isn't for everyone. Some days I wonder if I am even cut out for this existence. Of course, I lose my doubts when I think about how good I have it in the end."

He glowered into the coffee cup before him.

She took the risk to set her hand on his. The action caused the sleeve of her dress to pull up enough to reveal the lingering bruises from their last encounter. The reminder of the risk she took in even this simple conversation made her cautious, but didn't make her stop. "This marriage you've landed yourself in has made you miserable."

"My business is doing good. I like the thought of being a pa."

"Maybe you do, maybe being a pa will make you happy. But, you hate your wife and the growing noose of restrictions she's placing on you. It's made you not only miserable, but bitter, and mean. I know that you aren't always this way. I've seen you be a different sort of man than the one you've been lately."

"Becky makes sense." The words choked out of him under brute force.

"Who are you trying to convince?"

"Hey, being a pa—well, it wouldn't make sense to keep the saloon. It's better this way. Our house is almost done. Being undertaker keeps me earning a good living without having to use her pa's money."

"You still don't get it. This hotel is all Cole has. It's his only business, his livelihood. This place was all his until you two decided to be business partners ten years ago. You remember that, right? You were friends then."

"He was different then, too."

"Apparently there's a lot of that going around." Jane pulled her hand back. With a sigh, she tugged her sleeves back down. "Think about it. Now you want to sell part of the business to some stranger, one who may not want the same things Cole wants. Someone Cole might not even get along with, not that the two of you have gotten along much at all lately."

"He can't afford to buy me out."

"If you'd told him when you first started thinking of this, he might have had a chance. He could have at least tried. You didn't even give him a fighting chance. You're selling off half of all he has. The one thing that you and I both can agree means a lot to him. He's worked hard to build this place from a saloon and brothel to a halfway viable hotel."

"When you put it like that—"

"How would you put it?"

"I'm trying to help him out. Yeah, we got that investor a couple years back, but we've been The Hangman's Inn for a year now and it hasn't helped business much. We keep losing money hand over fist."

She bit her cheek hard to keep her retort at bay. The cause of their money loss had much to do with his drinking and temper.

"Selling would take some of the weight off."

"It would take the weight off of you. Not only the money, but your wife would stop nagging you daily about the saloon." She rose, letting loose a great sigh. "Think about it, Graham. No matter your reasons, you should have talked to him first. You shouldn't have gone sneaking around behind his back using your father-in-law's connections, using the excuse you were helping him out when all you were helping was yourself. You should've been upfront the minute you agreed to your wife's demands. You're yellow."

"Will you talk to him or not?"

She snatched the coffee mug from his grasp and took a sip. Pure whiskey burned down her throat instead of the coffee he pretended was there. She wrinkled her nose and turned over the cup above his head. The liquid splashed against his bald head. "You want me to talk to him get back behind the bar and fill this with coffee next time."

Graham leaped to his feet. "What the devil?"

"Tell me, Graham. What exactly do you expect me to say to Cole? I am in complete agreement with his side of things, and understand his anger. You've been backing off of this business for months. Cole noticed. Everyone did. All you had to do was offer and he would have found a way to come up with the money."

"I'm selling my half. Maybe I did it wrong by your way of thinking, but it's happening. Don't want it to end ugly."

"You should have thought of that long ago." She leaned on the table to meet his gaze. Her frown drew deeper as the idea came to her head. "Not that it matters much anyway. Since you've been married you're hardly here. Maybe that's how I should lead off when I talk to him, hmm?"

"So you'll talk to him?"

"For my sake. Certainly not for yours."

"Thanks, Jane."

"Yellow. From your shiny pate to your rotted toes you are nothing but a coward. I liked you better before you were married. Back then I thought you had a shot at being a decent human being." She shoved her chair into the table and stormed to the doors. If they'd not been propped open, she might have released some of her frustration shoving them open, but she didn't have such luck. She stepped onto the porch outside into the bright sunshine.

While her eyes adjusted to the change, she brushed her fingers across her forehead.

A whistle drew her attention across the street and down a couple of buildings. Through the passing pedestrians and horses in the street she found Charlie Young, another of her brothers, on the porch of the clinic. He pointed to her right and shouted over the crowd. "Library."

Surely he couldn't be talking about Cole. She furrowed her brow as she glanced to her right. Though she couldn't see the building sitting just out of sight around the corner, but she couldn't imagine Cole had voluntarily gone there when she wasn't present. She turned back to her brother and shook her head.

Charlie popped his cigarette in his mouth before he quick-stepped across the street. As he approached he tipped his bowler hat the passing form of Mrs. Kennedy. His mustache twitched and he winked at Jane. "Everything all right? Cole looked mad as a March hare."

Her jaw remained locked up tight, so mad she wasn't sure she could explain. Instead, she managed to spit out one word, "Graham."

"What's he done now?"

"Just being his general idiot self, as he has been for some time. Did Cole really go to the library? On his own?" The man could read well enough, but held no compulsion to seek out something to read, especially when angry.

"You know he's probably waiting on you. Might be angry you didn't follow sooner."

"I was trying to find out what had happened." She lifted the bangs off her forehead as a cool breeze passed through. The heat seemed worse in the fit of tempers lately.

"Clara!" Charlie grabbed her arms. "What happened to your wrist?"

"It's nothing. I am fine."

"I'm the doctor here. Let me be the judge."

She yanked her arm free in a fit of exasperation. "They're nothing more than bruises. It's simply another example of Graham being a drunken idiot. Cole about shot his head off for it. Everything has been handled and I am fine. The bruises are already healing."

"Graham did this?"

"Who else?" She clasped her hands behind her back to keep him from staring. "I should probably go find Cole. Thank you, Charlie."

She nodded to the tip of his hat before rushing around the corner to the library. Inside, her best friend Katherine sat behind the desk. Kat continued working, making notes in the library ledger despite the sullen Cole sitting across from her.

Jane walked up behind Cole. When Kat looked up from her work she smiled. "Has it been busy today?"

"Not at all." Kat gave a nod toward Cole. "Cole's been the first one in here in a couple of hours. I don't believe he's looking for a book, though."

Cole remained sullen and silent, not even rising to the challenge of Kat's teasing.

Jane squeezed his shoulder. The concerned frown Kat cast his way didn't help ease Jane's worries in the least. She leaned down near his ear. "Bottom drawer on the left. Behind Poe."

Cole rose without a word and went to the drawer she mentioned. After he rummaged for a moment he stood with a flask in hand. He continued to otherwise ignore them both. Instead of speaking, he crossed the library. He tilted his head back to take a long swig in the lingering silence.

Jane turned back to Kat. "Thank you for minding the library for me this morning. I know it was a last minute request."

"No problem. I told you I'm happy to help out in the library as often as you need. Ask any time." Kat embraced her in a warm hug. She held on longer than necessary and spoke low, "Think you can talk him down?"

"No. Not yet. He needs to release his anger first. He has the right to every bit of fury right now, so I'm going to let him." She kissed Kat's cheek and shooed her from the building. Once her friend had left, she leaned against her desk to study the tall man glowering in the corner.

He polished off the flask quick as a wink. Without even asking he returned to her desk. He tossed the near-empty flask on her desk with little regard to the books sitting there. Despite her quiet protest to his action, he yanked open her drawer where the flasks were hidden.

"I've only got three. Slow down or go back to the saloon."

"Did he tell ya?"

"Yes. That's why it took me a few minutes to get here." She pressed the heels of her hands against the desk to slide herself up on it. Feet hooked together, she swung them without a care, as if she wasn't nearly as upset as he was. In this situation the last thing she needed to do was feed the beast. "He explained how much of an idiot he is. Of course, I was already well aware of that fact—but yes. He told me."

"Some strangers are gonna buy my—"

"I think you should buy it." She sucked her lips between her teeth to hide the smirk at his reaction. His pacing had ceased, the flask poised near his lips. Once sure she had her amusement under control she spoke again, "Then you wouldn't have to worry about strangers."

His eyes widened, and his arm went lax. The flask hung precariously in his slack fingers. "Excuse me?"

"I said that you should buy his half of the business. I'm quite certain I did not speak in French there. Nor are you deaf. So what is the problem?"

"Just how would I do that?" His fingers clasped the flask tight again as the energy of frustration returned to his limbs. Another swig and he wiped his mouth with the back of his hand. "I ain't got that kind of money."

"Of course. Besides, you and Graham are supposed to be partners. Without him the loss would be all your own if things went wrong." She ticked off the possible problems on her fingers as she said them aloud. "Also you'd have no more excuses like Graham for profit losses. Etcetera, etcetera, etcetera. Plenty of reason not to. I understand."

He turned his back on her. At the window he propped his elbow against the glass and rested his forehead on the back of his wrist.

She knew she had his attention now, so she stilled her legs. "The thing is, the loss has been all yours from the beginning. Graham has never been as invested in the saloon as you were. In the past year it's been even less if that's possible. He's always had another business to fall back on. The destruction from the renegades never bothered him as much as it did you."

Cole stared out the window without moving.

"He's your friend."

"No. He ain't."

"Well, he was. Once upon a time. Back before you tried to be business partners. Maybe now you can be friends again once he's done lousing up the business."

"That ain't all he's lousing up. What about what he did to you?"

"I am not what we are discussing right now. He's always been an ass toward me. I'm used to it, and I knew you were there the whole time."

"Liar. You don't lie, so don't start now."

She pursed her lips, unable to argue his point. So she returned to her original point. "You should do this, Cole. Buy his half. Make the Inn yours again."

He resumed his stony silence. Once again he tipped back the flask. The amber liquid poured into his mouth until only drips remained.

"It's no bigger risk for you without a partner. The hotel will mean as much to you with or without one. All it means is that it's your say and your say alone. No one to argue with over what goes, like it was before Graham." Rather than face his doubt or attempts at argument, she focused on the tips of her toes where they peeked out from under her dress.

He maintained his silence, but at least he didn't run for her third flask of whiskey.

She straightened her legs to reveal more of her feet. The idea came to her so sudden she had to force herself to not jump in excitement. If she was going to present the idea, she couldn't be too eager. "Find out how much Graham is wanting. I still have a decent amount of money left over from the investments and savings I withdrew after the Coinage Act. I need something to do with that money so it isn't just sitting hidden away."

"No. I ain't gonna…"

When his words trailed off she focused on him again over her shoes. She frowned and narrowed her eyes at his back. He couldn't be implying what it seemed he was. "What? You aren't going to borrow money from a woman?"

He spun to sneer at her. "No. I ain't taking your money. You need it for your boy."

"I already gave David all the money I wanted set aside for Jesse. He's well taken care of. This is my money, and it's yours if you want it."

"Not taking money from you."

She pinched her tongue between her teeth to hide her giggle over the idea she'd had. One thing she did allow was a slow grin to rise. "Well, then how about this? Look at it as a loan. A loan with a very—generous—interest rate."

He turned to face her at this, his icy blue eyes focused intent on her. Slow steps brought him nearer, like a tiger stalking its prey. Some of his anger disappeared, replaced with the familiar smoldering smirk. The flask thumped on the desk before his hands came to rest on either side of her hips. He hovered close, his face inches from hers as his brow rose. "Generous?"

Her pulse raced at his proximity. An excited tingle of anticipation shot right to her core. All she could manage in response at first was a small nod. The man could drive her to insanity so easily she might have been embarrassed if the knowledge of his skilled attentions weren't so damned exciting. "You would be the one that would need to be generous."

"Is that so?"

A hum of agreement preceded her own smile. She leaned closer still. "Do you think you can handle being…generous?"

Her skirts shifted. Within moments his hand circled her ankle. Inch by inch his hand crept along her calf. His sly smile grew while his fingers danced along her thigh. He focused on her lips at her gasp the moment he reached his destination. Skilled fingers slipped along her folds until they drove her distraction with their teasing. He chuckled when she moaned low and deep. "That generous enough for you?"

She bit her lip and attempted to keep her breathing even. Somehow she managed a small nod. A squeaky gasp slipped free when he rewarded her with a forceful thrust of his fingers. The shudder that coursed through her was unavoidable and she whispered his name. She dug her fingers into his biceps as he tugged her to the edge of the desk.

The brush of his lips against hers drew her eyes open again. Her attempts to deepen the kiss were thwarted by him as he pulled back with a cocky grin. The weak whimper of protest turned into a sigh as he trailed his lips in a feather-light path along her jaw line.

She tried to keep somewhat collected, but his insistent touch drew out a soft cry of passion. The few thoughts she had in her head scattered as he drove her closer to the edge of passion over and over, each time retreating just enough to make her want to scream for me.

She slid her hands along his arms far enough to rake her nails back down them. His growl of approval sent a ripple of pleasure through her. The increased drive of his fingers sent her body racing toward the edge. Muscles tensed, small pants escaped her weak grasp of control.

So close, she pleaded for release.

"Ma!" Jesse's excited call came far too close for comfort or decency.

Cole froze and muttered a curse under his breath.

A cross between a moan and a sob crossed her lips. She dropped her head to his shoulder to try to collect herself. He straightened her skirts for her, for which she had infinite gratitude as she didn't think she could even speak yet.

How on earth could she have forgotten to shut the door? And how close was her son? She tried to get a grip on her quivering muscles before she'd need them.

When Jesse's feet pounded the floorboards of the library Cole squeezed her arms gently. He rested his chin on her head. "Hey there, Jesse."

"Hi, Cole. Ma." Jesse paused nearby. "Ma? You all right?"

Jane managed to straighten her back, glad to find her muscles once again obeyed her command. After a small glare at Cole's barely hidden laughter, she smiled at Jesse. "Yes, Jesse. I'm fine. Cole was just giving me a hug."

Cole snorted. "Yup. A real big hug."

Jane couldn't stop her grin if she wanted to—and she really didn't want to. By all accounts, Jesse had no idea what had happened, and David's unamused stare only bolstered her humor. Not because she enjoyed upsetting him, but because she had a vital weapon in her arsenal against any ire he might carry for how they'd been caught.

"Jane." David nodded, his lips barely moving through their tension. "Are you still planning to have supper with Jesse or should I find someone else?"

"Of course I am." Somehow she managed to gather the last of her wits about her and hopped off the desk. "I wouldn't miss supper with my little man."

David cast a glare at Cole. "That so?"

"Jesse." She chuckled and knelt in front of her son. David's indignation still fueled her amusement, and Cole's from what she could tell by his now outright laughter. "Do you have homework from Miss Fine?"

"I got a test tomorrow. Maf." Jesse wrinkled his nose.

"Math." Jane did her best to not flinch at her automatic correction of his verbiage. After he'd been silent for so long, she should simply be happy to have him talking as much as he now did. Still, there was an automatic response that made her correct grammar. She had no doubt it came from Clara's past as a school teacher, the other half from being around the miner's that didn't care much for proper etiquette.

Jesse heaved a great sigh. His hands fisted at his sides as he carefully took time to form the word. "Math. Can ya help me with it?"

Since he'd taken such care to correct math she didn't correct the ya, which she knew he had adopted from his best friend, Isaac. "In a few minutes. Right now, put away the book you borrowed last week and get a new one." She ruffled his hair and gave him a grin. Once he ran off she rose to face David. "So you're—"

"The library? In the open? Jane." David's brows knit together.

She had enough dignity to blush at his statement, though part from excitement rather than embarrassment. "It wasn't something I planned on. We were talking and I got caught up in the moment before I remembered to shut the door."

"I thought we talked about—"

"And you have no room for so much righteous indignation, Mr. Schaffer. If I remember correctly I read something about you and Clara."

Cole grinned and folded his arms across his chest. He turned to face David expectantly. The excitement of hearing whatever morsel she held onto set him almost bursting. "You remember everything you read, so don't play coy. Spill it. What's Davie guilty of?"

"According to Clara's letters to Michael you weren't much better when it came to Clara, David. There's some mention of a coupling behind the church after services on Sunday morning as I recall?" She grinned when David's ears turned bright red. Cole's bark of laughter brought a curious Jesse closer.

"Jane." David's mouth opened and closed like a fish in his protest.

"So you'll be staying at the jail tonight after your picnic with Lee?" She kept her smile pleasant when Jesse leaned up against her. She ran her fingers through his hair and hugged him against her hip. "Cole will be joining Jesse and me for supper, and will stay at the homestead once the saloon is closed."

David nodded, "Yes. I'll be staying at the jail."

"Good. Give my best to Lee. I hope to see her soon." Jane smiled warmly, letting it grow when Jesse darted out from under her arm to hug David before returning to the books. Within seconds the boy was lost in the spines, searching for the perfect book.

A slight frown remained when David leaned in to kiss her on the cheek. Most likely Cole's continued laughter added to his consternation. "I'll tell her you send your regards."

"Behind the church? Even I ain't that bold. Bully for you, Sheriff." Cole grinned his most wicked grin and held out his hand.

Red still darkened the tops of David's ears, but Cole's bit of praise drew a halfway sly grin from David. "Cole." He shook Cole's hand and strode from the library.

Jane sucked her lips between her teeth to keep her laughter back. When Cole's arms went around her she chuckled, "You're terrible."

"I know."

"You're going to finish what you started."

"Plan on it."

You cannot teach a man anything, you can only help him discover it in himself.
—Galileo Galilei

Another hand groped Jane through her skirts. She slapped the intrusive hand away out of habit. Business in town had increased over the previous year, meaning the business in the saloon portion of the hotel which remained its forefront attraction had grown. If it wasn't for Graham's tendency for fights, Cole might be able to earn a tidy profit.

On the other hand, the rise in business also meant the rise in strangers without the faintest idea of her status within the confines of the saloon. Which equated to regular, inappropriate groping and offers. Such events had become so commonplace, she hardly noticed unless someone became far too insistent.

She didn't mind so much, but it bothered Cole to no end. The man had a jealous streak ten miles wide, to be sure. A smile tugged her lips wider at the thought, but she made herself keep about her business.

The drinks she carried got dispersed to a table of men deep in a game of poker. As a standard practice she took a good look around the table to see who was doing poorly. Once she'd established the loser she waved Pansy over and directed her to Mr. Burke's side. As Pansy followed her direction and plopped into the man's lap, Jane took a pause. As had happened many times in the months Pansy had been a whore in the saloon, the girl appeared much younger than her claimed eighteen years of age.

She brushed it off as a trick of the lighting and makeup when the man on her right nudged her with his elbow. He smiled brightly up at her. "Janey! How the hell are ya?"

"Not as good as you are, Clive. You're cleaning up." Jane squeezed his shoulder. "Do me a favor and don't break the house tonight, all right? I have my eye on a new dress."

Clive returned his cigar to his mouth and offered a wink. He granted her a peak at the flush he held. "Can't make any promises!"

Her laughter carried her all the way back behind the bar where she set down her tray. She grabbed some glasses to fill. As she poured the whiskey, a warm body pressed against her back. Cole's hands leaned on the bar. He nuzzled the back of her neck until pleasant tingles pulsed along her skin.

The action was a definite pleasure, and a complete distraction. She sighed. "You are so predictable, Mr. Mitchell."

"I can get rid of him for ya." The way his rich baritone rumbled in her ear sent a shiver down her spine. Every time he spoke in such a way the promise of more excitement seemed to bubble under every syllable.

Her attempts to convey annoyance were fleeting. His mere presence caused far more pleasurable thoughts than angry ones. "Which one?"

"You saying there's more than one? I just saw that new one right there."

She rolled her eyes and kept at her task. If she rose to his anger, he might act on it. "You cannot throw out every single man that gropes me. You'd have no customers left."

"I don't like it when they got their hands on you."

"Your jealousy is flattering, but you're forgetting one thing."

"What's that?"

"They can grope all they want, because there is only one man I grope in return." She tilted her head enough to catch his gaze out of the corner of her eye. With one hand she reached behind her to demonstrate her point with a good firm grope of her own.

His cock twitched in response. When his forehead dropped on the top of her head and her name left him in a low growl, she giggled.

She edged the tray down the bar before dropping straight down to scoot under his arm. A mutter of *'ya don't play fair'* reached her ears when she darted out from behind the bar with the tray. Still, he didn't move from the spot, most likely getting a grip on his now uncomfortable, and unsatisfied, state.

The moment she started to weave between the tables someone grabbed her hand.

"Janey."

"Yes?" She smiled down at the large man. "What did you need Wills?"

Built like a locomotive, the man wore a friendly smile and sheen of sweat on his forehead. He crooked his finger to draw her closer. "Dahlia. Think she's open?"

The man had been trying for months to get up the nerve to ask for one of their newest whores. Dahlia and Pansy were both new contracts within the past year, Dahlia was pretty enough to make Jane a little jealous. She spoke quietly. "I think it can be arranged. Let me see for you."

"Good on ya, Janey." Wills tossed back his drink. One knee bounced rapidly under the table in his fit of nerves.

She set her full tray back on the bar to find the whore in question. In the corner, she spotted two whores lounging about like they didn't have a bar full. She approached them, ready to yell when she realized Dahlia was one of them. "Dahlia."

Dahlia lifted her head in a slow, lazy manner. A sloppy smile creased her painted lips. "Oh. Well. Hey there, Jane." The words drawled out so slow, Jane could hardly understand them. Within moments the whores head lolled back against the wall again.

"What the devil?" Jane grabbed Dahlia's chin and snapped her head upright. "What are you on? Dahlia. We've told you time and again we don't want you high. *Primmy*."

Primrose, who sat next to Dahlia, jumped at her name. She swallowed heavy, her hands shook as she gripped the edge of her bloomers. Rather than look at Jane, despite her name being barked, Primmy kept focused on the bloomers she now twisted between her fingers. "Yeah?"

"Get Dahlia in the back immediately. Make sure she stays back in that room. Tie her to the bed if you have to. Damn girl dosed up on the opium again. I thought you said she was off."

"I thought she was." Primmy leaped to her feet. "I swear it."

Jane let her struggle to lift the girl to her feet. "If you're covering for her, you're both going to be out on your scantily clad asses." Jane hauled Dahlia to her feet.

Primmy dragged Dahlia to the back as fast as she could pull the woman.

After a long exhale to release her anger at the disruption, Jane returned to one of the two tables where poker games ran. She stepped next to a man with a large pile of winnings and a whore on his lap. She leaned down next to him. "Are you planning to enjoy her company this evening?"

He turned a surly eye on her. "What business is it of yours?"

"I'm good luck." Heather offered a bright smile.

"Good luck doesn't pay the house. Sorry, but we have someone that's actually looking for a little more than luck." Jane gestured Heather to her feet. Over the man's protest she patted his shoulder. "The next five drinks will be on the house, after which you pay for your luck like everyone else."

Wills frowned when she approached with Heather. "What about Dahlia?"

"Trust me, Wills. Right now Heather is the far better option." Jane gave him a peck on the temple. He'd always been a decent guy to her, so she hated to disappoint him. Despite his grumble of disappointment, Wills pulled Heather close and settled her on his lap. After another scan of the saloon, she turned to wind her way through the tables.

She kept her eyes peeled for men needing drinks or whores, with a final destination of Mel's game in mind. Halfway to her final destination an arm snaked around her waist. Over her protest she found herself yanked into a strangers lap.

"Well, what do we have here?" A slim man with a blond handlebar mustache and a bowler hat wagged his brows. "From what I could tell, this Inn only had bottom of the barrel."

"There is nothing for you here, sir." She shoved herself off his lap. His renewed attempt to snag her received a harsh slap.

"Wait just a second." He managed to grab her wrist to yank her back to his side. "You know, I've heard the fancier the dress, the more wild the time is spent. I sure wouldn't mind testing that theory with you."

"You'll never know. I'm not for sale."

"Everything, and everyone, is for sale." With an unyielding grasp he dragged her closer. "For the right price."

She clenched her jaw. This one would need some special convincing in order to avoid the approach of the possessive man behind the bar. "You could never afford me."

"I think you'd be surprised."

A deep, bracing breath tamped down her anger enough to help her hatch a plan. She allowed a smile to curve slowly across her features. With a side step to sidle closer, she leaned toward him. As expected he settled back, and the hold on her wrist eased. She propped her knee on the chair between his legs, then settled her hands on his shoulders. "Do you really think I would be the one surprised?"

The saloon had quieted some around them. Several chairs in the vicinity creaked under the weight of bodies turning to watch the show. Men that knew her well chuckled and whispered among each other in the edges of her vision. The man beneath her remained oblivious enough to grin in triumph. His hands dared settled on her waist. "Yeah. I do."

She turned as if to sit on his lap. Before she could settle there, she hooked her foot around the leg of his chair. The man didn't have time for a moment of concern, she yanked her foot backward too fast. His chair creaked and wobbled before toppling to the floor.

The guy's head hit the floor with a satisfying crack. She set her foot firm on his chest. "A piece of advice for you, stranger. When you are told *not for sale*, listen."

He groaned and lifted a hand to his head. When he withdrew it, there was blood on it. He held it in front of his face and cursed.

"Here." She tossed three dollars on his chest. "Go across the street to the clinic to get stitched up. Don't bother coming back until you realize not everything is yours for the taking."

Pulling back, she snapped her skirts close to his face when she turned back toward the bar. Cole's amused, proud smile brought a grin back to her own lips. Two steps toward the bar the man's voice hit her ears.

"Bitch."

She froze. Her temper flared up to prepare her for another round. Before she could react, Hammy and two other men headed their way. She skimmed through the middle of them to get back to the bar.

Cole leaned back against the bar as she circled behind it. He wiped down a glass even as his eyes raked her body. "I said it before, and I'll say it again. My kind of woman."

With a chuckle she twirled his tie around her finger for a moment before she yanked him close. Her lips claimed his for a deep kiss, erasing the slimy feel of any other man's hands with his heat and passion.

He winked when she released him from the embrace. "That's the first time ya ever drew blood."

"Well, it didn't help that I was already in a rotten mood."

"I noticed. What the hell happened?"

"Dahlia took some opium again tonight."

Every inch of humor and pride dripped from Cole's features quick as she'd ever seen. "What did you say?"

"I haven't the faintest idea who keeps supplying her with it. I told Primrose she's out too if she's been covering for Dahlia. Cole, wait—"

Too late. She'd never had a chance to stop him, and he disappeared down the back hall to the room where the whores stayed. A heavy sigh pushed away the last of her decent mood. The three men who took a seat at the bar managed to bring her amusement back. "Mr. Hamm. Mr. Berman. Mr. Tyler. Thank you all very much for your help dispensing with the trash. Can I offer you a beer for your trouble?"

"Nah, Lady Jane. That one was on me." Hammy lifted his glass. His gap-toothed grin grew ever broader. "Always a pleasure to see ya take someone down."

Jane bowed her head, touched that the men thought so highly of her. Without hesitation she pushed herself up onto the bar. She leaned in to give him a kiss on the cheek.

From there the crowd kept her busy so long, the time to close the saloon came before she had a chance to wonder where Cole had disappeared to. A frown tugged at her lips and she made her way down to the whores' room to poke her head inside.

No sign of Cole in there, so she took a moment to remind them all to bathe and closed the door on the room. Not only had Cole not been in there, but neither had Dahlia or Primmy.

She pursed her lips and went back into the saloon to clean up some more.

"No Mel. Thank you. I just have a few glasses left to wipe down." She waved toward the door. "Go on home. I'll see you tomorrow night."

"Good night, then." He rolled down his sleeves and grabbed his jacket. On his way out he closed the large outer doors so the town would be shut out. Within a minute he was long gone into the silent town.

After he left she pulled the pins from her hair and let the curls free. She shook them out and scratched her scalp to relieve the pressure of the night. The buttons of her bodice were next to be released, and she peeled off the top and set it on the bar.

The heat of summer mixed with the chaos of the saloon always made her overheated by nights end. She fanned herself with the towel before dabbing at the perspiration dotting her forehead.

Suddenly she was pressed against the counter without ever hearing a footstep. A gasp escaped and she started to fight.

"I told ya to stop buttoning up so tight when you're in here." Cole chuckled warm in her ear. His nose brushed her earlobe and sent a shiver down her spine, effectively ending her struggle. "Not that I mind what you do to ease the heat once the saloon is clear."

Her flesh pebbled under his wandering fingertips. She bit her lip and arched back against him, her bustle interrupting any pleasure-worthy wiggling. "You're not exactly cooling me down, Mr. Mitchell."

"Don't plan on it, neither." His lips brushed along her shoulder. "Still say you should change your clothes on account of the heat."

"And give all those men even more reason to think they can grope me?" A sigh escaped when her skirts dropped to the floor. The man had little patience, thank the heavens. "Are you going to tell me where you disappeared to? With you gone, Hammy thought he had to stand guard. It took me forever to get him out of here."

"Made sure those two were gone. Got them to tell me who was giving 'em the opium." He tugged on her corset laces. The strings hummed as he pulled them out slow, sending tiny vibrations along the fabric.

Her breath rasped and she licked her lips against her dry mouth. "Who was it?" She braced her hands on the counter he had her pinned against. The moment his lips touched her neck she tilted her head to give him better access.

Heat trickled along her nerves with every hot kiss against her flesh and every tremble of her corset laces. "Some new guy in town. Gus…something or other."

"Warren?"

He hummed against her neck, sending a jolt of energy right to her core. The laces tugged free of her corset at the same time she whimpered.

"He's a man of business." She sighed, losing her will to keep her wits about her. After all, his touch was far more pleasurable. "What purpose is there in—"

Strong, calloused hands ran along her stomach, down toward her center. Her thoughts fluttered away as he teased her, not quite giving her the satisfaction she craved.

"Don't know his game." He could've been reciting a recipe and she wouldn't have cared or bothered to think about it. Finally he let his fingers skim the flesh between her thighs, eliciting a whimper out of her. "Gonna talk to him tomorrow."

"You were already down three whores." She really didn't know why she kept the conversation up. All she craved was his touch. He was so good with actions. She yelped when he spun her around. Warm hands slid up under her chemise, cupping and kneading her breasts. "Now…two more."

"They'll get replaced." He bent down and bit her nipple through the thin fabric of her chemise. Not stopping there, he dropped down to his knees in front of her to lift the fabric. Teasing, grating tingles ran along her flesh from the mix of stubble and lips he used against the sensitive skin. "Always do. You're the one that said I need to get a higher class anyhow."

A soft moan escaped when he took advantage of his position. A jolt of pleasure made her grip the edge of the bar again as his fingers drove her rising passion. "Guess I did…"

"Don't ya worry." His breath was hot and moist against her stomach; one hand gripped her hip tight enough to mingle a hint of pain into the pleasure. It also served to keep her standing as her knees wobbled. "We'll get 'em replaced. Maybe get more. Only problem with that…"

She hummed, any attempt to stay in the conversation long gone.

"I'll have to make a couple trips outta town." His low chuckle carried under her moans.

"Cole." She managed to gasp.

"What?"

"Shut up."

"Thought ya liked talking."

She braced her hands on his shoulders and pushed him back to the floor. Once she straddled him, she let her lips hover above his. Her breath came in ragged gasps and she met his eyes. "Just shut up."

"Yes, ma'am." He flipped her over and followed her order without a lick of argument.

I have found you an argument, I am not obliged to find you an understanding.
—James Boswell

Cole leaned on the bar, his full attention on the conversation in the corner. He'd just returned from a short trip to Pueblo. While his initial intention had been to head further south to see what girls he could find to replace those lost, he'd lucked upon a couple of girls in Pueblo ripe for the job.

Now Jane sat with them to go over the rules. As always, he enjoyed the way she stood out among the soiled doves like a brightly colored and proud peacock. His woman dominated the conversation, took charge, and laid down the law with the girls. There was no arguing with Jane when she was in this frame of mind.

After two years of her taking the lead on the girls, he knew the rules like the back of his hand, and agreed with every one of them. Regular baths, increased checkups with Daisy, no drugs, and she monitored every one of their womanly schedules, plus made sure they were amply supplied with whatever protection she could get her hands on.

He had no idea why it had taken him so long to see it, but six months ago he took notice of how much the girls business had increased. Once he'd noticed that, it hadn't taken him long to realize that Graham's accusations were correct in a lot of ways. Jane had stepped in and taken charge, but Cole couldn't be happier to not only let her, but encourage her.

The way Jane got on the whores about their sobriety, cleanliness and appearance couldn't have come at a better time. The increase in their profits coincided with Graham's rise in temper. The bump in profits had gone a long way to covering the man's drunken antics.

The whores were Jane's least favorite part of his business, yet she still did all she could to make sure they worked well for him and turned a tidy profit. Not once had she talked to him about it or given a reason for her behavior, but he didn't bother asking either. He happily let her be and now she handled most of the whores as well as any madam he'd known.

Her biggest hitch with all of the girls was sobriety. If one of the girls got caught in the throws of opium or whatever they got their hands on not even he was able to avoid her temper. In recent months the problem had gotten worse than he'd ever had.

Movement at the door pulled Cole from his musings. He frowned at the large form shadowing the doorway. "What are you doing here?"

"I'm still part owner since you asked for a month. That makes it my day," Graham snapped. He glowered toward the counter as he moved behind the bar. "What the hell is she doing?"

"Talking to the new girls I brung in." Cole bristled, prepared for Graham's usual battle stance. Whether or not Graham's beef about Jane taking charge happened to be right,

Cole didn't like being ridiculed. Or for Graham to think Cole was whipped because it wasn't anything of the sort. He knew that, and Jane knew that, or at least she should.

"Why do you let her do that? You know she's always acted like she was the one that owned this place instead of me. Ever since you first brought her here."

Cole chewed the inside of his cheek. His knuckles turned white, he gripped the counter hard in an effort to control himself. It wouldn't do him any good to punch Graham right then. "Is that so?"

"Yeah. Bossing me around left and right. Not to mention the girls, Mel, Chauncey, and Cuddy. Like you don't have any say anymore. Can't believe you let her walk on you like that."

"She does plenty of things to me, Graham. A great many things." Cole curled the corner of his lip in a smirk. "A lot of them are way beyond anything your priss of a wife would do for you. Of all the things she does for me? Not a one of them is walk on me."

"Don't you speak of my wife!" Graham's nostrils flared.

"Someone should," Cole retorted. "You sure don't like to speak about her."

Graham narrowed his eyes. "Well everyone around here knows Jane's got you wrapped around her finger. They all talk about it. Especially Hammy."

"Watch it, Graham."

"You're so damn blind. Do you know what Hammy calls her? He calls her Mrs. Mitchell—like the two of you are married or something." Graham snorted. His deep, grating chortle shook his round stomach. "How rich is that? *You.*

Married. You got no reason to let her walk on you. No reason to keep her around running the show. You just do."

"I already told ya, and I'll say it again since ya didn't hear me the first time. She don't walk on me." Cole leaned toward him. No one knew the truth of Jane's name, not even Cole's best friend, Graham. Truthfully, Cole was prouder than hell she used his birth surname, Spencer, but only they had to know it. It was how they both liked it. Unfortunately, not knowing made Graham think he was wiser and had something over Cole. When in the end Graham was the one playing whipping boy to his woman. "Now get the hell outta my hotel."

"No."

"Graham…"

Michael's voice echoed into the saloon, catching both men off guard. "Jane!"

Cole allowed the fight to dissipate when Jane's boy Jesse bounce in the doorway of the inn. "Ma! Look, Ma."

Jane's attention diverted from the whores to her son in an instant. A bright grin lit her features. After another couple of words to the girls she rose and raced across the floor. At the door she stopped short with a loud gasp. "Oh, my."

"Ain't it neat?" Jesse bounced and tugged on her hand. "Come see. Come see."

"Isn't it, Jesse. Isn't. And yes, it is. Michael, where did that come from?"

Cole didn't bother to waste another moment on Graham. He strode to the door to see what the fuss was about. Soon as he saw the piano sitting in the wagon, tension raced back through his limbs. After many fights about it, Cole thought for sure Jane had gotten the message. He was not getting a piano in the inn. Ever.

The last thing he wanted in his place of business was music, especially piano music. Too many bad memories centered around piano music. "What the hell?"

"Nick sent it." Mike handed Jane a letter. His broad smile irked Cole even more. "Look."

Jane scanned the letter, her free hand smoothing Jesse's unruly hair. "He says, 'My wife is terrible at playing. I must get the atrocity out of my home before my ears bleed. Please find better use for it at the saloon. Tell that louse to listen to you—you are not a total idiot'."

"No." Cole all but barked the word, arms folded across his chest. "Let your kid have it. We don't got the room and I ain't having no loud, obnoxious piano in my saloon. We've done fine without it, and will continue to do so."

"Cole," Jane's harsh whisper carried under Jesse's excited squeal. Her deep blue eyes turned stormy gray. She huffed at him, about to blow from what he could tell. The ramblings of her son begging to have the piano saved him from her tirade. Jane narrowed her eyes at him before she knelt before her son. "I don't know that your pa would agree. We'll have to discuss where this piano is going to go."

"Well what should I do with it, then?" Mike glared down at Cole.

Cole snapped back, "I got a suggestion."

"*Cole*." Jane flew to her feet, but instead of yelling more, she turned her back on him. She grasped Jesse's hand and tugged him toward the wagon. "Why don't we squeeze it in the library for now? I haven't the faintest idea where else we could store it."

"We'll need help to move this out of the wagon." Mike hopped out of the wagon. He bent down to Jesse. "Why don't we go get some help, then we'll come back for the wagon and meet your ma at the library. All right?"

"Sure Uncle Mike!" Jesse raced ahead of Mike toward the clinic catty corner from the saloon.

Jane's back remained tense, straight as a rod when he approached.

"I told you. I ain't gonna—"

"I am *not* deaf." She spun fast. Cheeks flushed, fists clenched. "You've more than made your point on many occasions. Now if you'll excuse me, I have to go to work. Deal with your own girls. I told them the rules *Mister* Mitchell."

He glared at her retreating back as if the action would pass along every nasty reply in his head. Once she turned the corner out of sight, he spun on his heel to storm back into the saloon. "Get the hell out, Graham. You ain't welcome here no more." Cole waved toward the two new whores. "You two, get on outta here. Get yourselves cleaned up. I want ya ready to work by shift end at the mines."

Graham didn't budge, despite Cole's order. He just wiped the counter with a sickening sneer, and his disgusting chortle filled the empty saloon. "Don't be sore at me for being right. She'll win. She'll cut you off at the prick until you cave, just like you always do."

"Thought I told ya to get the hell out."

"Wonder just how she managed to swing it, though. Been pestering you about a piano for over a year. And now this one just fell into her lap? Seems unlikely." Graham sneered toward the door. "Gotta give her credit. Knew she was a good liar, but she really managed to act surprised."

Cole lunged across the bar to grab him by the collar. He hauled the large man right over the top of the counter until he toppled to the ground. "Shut up. Get outta my hotel."

Graham flew to his feet, fists clenched for a fight. If Graham could do anything well, it was fight. "Sure you don't want me to watch the bar so you can go apologize right proper? Maybe get a good, relaxing apology from her? I'm sure she'll make it all better so we can get that piano in here like she wants."

This time Cole was prepared for a fight as he shoved Graham toward the door. Despite the shorter man's brute strength, Cole had spent years learning how to subdue his business partner. He moved quick to pin Graham's big arms behind his back. It took all his strength against the fight, but he pushed the man to the doors and right out onto the porch.

Cole kicked him for good measure when he stumbled, and Graham toppled into the dirt road. "Just stay the hell out." He grabbed the doors and slammed them shut. One click of the clock meant Graham would stay out. Cole paced in front of the doors for a minute.

To go after Jane right then would be stupid. They both needed to calm down before that could happen. He might have been out of line snapping at her like he had, but he wasn't about to apologize for it. Not yet.

He poured himself a big glass of whiskey. His jaw worked in tight circles as the arguments replayed themselves in his head. Up until Graham had come in he'd been fine. In minutes his anger at Graham turned into annoyance with Jane when she'd done nothing.

Over the past year, Jane's declarations of love had begun to worry him. Not once had he been able to say it back, and that had to bother her. All her tempers at him happened when someone brought it up and said as much. Especially Graham.

And today, the mention of what Hammy tended to call her? Of course he knew, he'd always known. Hammy could be called many things, but discreet was not one of them. Cole hadn't ever been bothered by it, after all Jane did carry his real surname.

Jane had to know how Cole felt anyhow, didn't she? He'd let her take his real name, told her to take it when she'd hesitated. She already had his name. Did she need more?

Whether she said as much or not, he hated himself sometimes for not giving her more, for not giving her all she deserved. After everything that had happened to him in the past, most of the time he didn't think he could. Sometimes, though, when she looked at him—in those moments he almost believed he could.

The slam of the back door snapped him out of his thoughts and he straightened. Mel's arrival signaled time to open for business.

Time to forget about Jane for a while.

Then he'd go apologize and they'd make up.

After all, making up was what they did best.

*Love is a battle, love is a war,
love is a growing up.
-James Arthur Baldwin*

Several hours passed by where Cole saw neither hide nor tail of Jane. Already the time creeped past seven-fifteen, and she always closed the library at seven to return to the Inn. Like clockwork she always came around.

Her absence meant she had to be real mad. After all, he'd already calmed down. Determined to end their latest quarrel with is usual skill, he told Mel to keep an eye on things while he went to see her.

Around the corner lamplight poured from the library onto its porch before it spilled into the street. The whisper of a shadow teased the edges of the squares of light, then her shadow passed by clear and strong.

He drew close. Nothing could be heard from inside but the familiar *thump* of each book as she set it in its place. He stepped inside to face the situation. For several minutes he waited for a greeting, any response at all. Though he went so far as to clear his throat, she went about her business like he wasn't there at all.

She scratched entries into her ledger and pulled another stack of books out of a crate next to the desk. To his left, the piano sat crammed in the small space between the door and the shelves, positioned right in front of the window. Where it sat several shelves of books were blocked from view.

"Thought you'd be fiddlin' on that damn thing."

"I'm tone deaf." Not a hint of humor, not even a whisper of a smile graced her features. She carried another few books toward a shelf where she shifted around the existing books to accommodate those in her arms.

He didn't bother to cover his laughter. "Is that so?"

"Yes." She walked past him twice more without acknowledging him or sharing in his humor. Her features remained emotionless, stoic.

His own amusement faded into a frown. "Jane."

"Did you need something? I'm really quite busy. I received a new shipment of books that I must put away. Not to mention I promised Jesse I'd stay at the homestead tonight."

He didn't remember hearing her mention that before. She always told him when she wouldn't be sleeping in their bed. Without a doubt the woman before him was beyond mad. He straightened, not sure whether to be upset or downright angry over her continued temper. "You're staying at the homestead? But I thought we—"

"I asked if there was something you needed." Back at her desk now she lifted her chin to face him for the first time since he'd entered the library. Her jaw set, eyes dark, her luscious lips pressed into a thin, uninviting line.

"It's a library. What's so damn important?"

She narrowed her eyes. Her mouth opened to reply, but shut just as quick. After another few notes in her ledger she gathered two more books and moved to a shelf near where he stood.

Cole remained at a loss, and she gave him nothing on how to resolve his situation. Always before she let him know he had a way to fix things. Anger rushed forward to heat his blood again, but he grinned. He knew one way to resolve their argument, the same way they always got through their fights.

The moment she turned to head back to her desk he stepped in front of her. He used his whole body to press her back into the shelves and crushed his lips to hers. Her lips tensed against his at first, her fists shoved into his shoulders in a brief, silent protest.

One swipe of his tongue across the seam of her lips made her melt in his arms with a moan. She opened up to him, and he eagerly brushed his tongue along hers. The familiar sensations heated his passion. He slid his hands along her sides to her rump, which he squeezed gently through her skirts.

A gasp erupted from her like a shot. Her eyes flew open and she shoved him back hard. Frustration stung against his fired nerves, and she made it worse by slapping him hard across the face.

"I'm not in the mood to be manhandled tonight. If you want to blow off steam, find someone else to do the blowing." Her cheeks flushed, hair mussed until unruly curls topped over her forehead. She stood before him all beauty and vexation.

"What the hell?" He rubbed his cheek. Anger and frustration bubbled in confusing burning mass in his belly. "You loony cun—"

"*Don't* you dare."

Yeah, he was definitely angry. How dare she get mad at him? They always ended their arguments quick and efficient-like with a hotter than hell make-up session. "What the devil is your problem?"

"The problem is that I won't be your personal punching bag, no matter what form the punching takes. Even if you want to resolve your anger with sex, I refuse to be your tool of release." She shoved him away hard enough to make him stumble a step. While he recovered she moved to the desk. Somehow her fury always made her beautiful. Fire lit her eyes, pinked her cheeks, and tossed numerous curls free of the bindings she kept them in. "I also will not have you yell at me for something that isn't even *my* fault because Graham is getting under your skin telling you I want things I have no interest in."

"Ya don't have any idea what—"

"I am *not* deaf, and neither is Graham quiet. I heard everything Graham and his big mouth sat over there spouting off to you. I always do when I'm in the room or anywhere nearby. He is loud and brash, and infinitely obnoxious." She threw her hands in the air. "I didn't ask for the damn piano. *You* did not even give me a chance to object before you threw your little fit."

"My little fit? Me? You're the one slapping me."

"Because you assumed that a mere few hours would be enough for you to come in here and work me over. Without my permission or any inclination that I had the slightest bit of interest."

"You saying I was forcing ya?"

"No, but you wouldn't have listened without some shock factor. You assumed I'd cooled enough and all would be forgiven and forgotten like it always has been. This time it's not good enough, not even close."

"Never bothered you before. Maybe Graham *is* right." Damn. The minute he said the words he wanted to take them back. They'd been the wrong thing to say. He hadn't even meant it.

Her nostrils flared and her fingers flexed over the ink bottle, almost like she had designs on throwing it at him. "I *am* staying at the homestead tonight. I told Jesse you were working so you are not expected. Do not come."

"Jane."

"I've already spoken to Rusty and I am running an ad in the paper to sell that damn thing. I will be more than happy to never see it again."

"All right. I'll admit I—"

"Don't bother. I'm not interested in *any* form you may choose to apologize." Damn woman wouldn't let him get a word in for nothing. Her whole face flushed, her hands shook when she snapped up another two books. "Not once in the past year have I asked you for more than you were willing to give. I have been quite content. I'm growing tired of you acting insane every time someone even hints that I might want something more."

"Graham's—"

"He is trying to get on your last nerve and you are letting him every time." Her dark glare and constant interruptions worked on his last nerve without any help from Graham. A curl to her lips preceded a disgusted scoff and shake of her head. "You go one of two ways whenever he or anyone else manages to get under your skin with their insinuations and assumptions. You either get possessive and handsy or you get crazy and cut off all public displays of any semblance of a relationship whatsoever."

He shook with his last semblance of restraint. Every fiber of his being wanted to snap back and set her straight, but he was damn tired of getting cut off every time he spoke.

"I love you, but I will not live like this any longer. I thought you knew me well enough to know that what people say means *nothing*. But since it seems to bother you so much, maybe it is time that we defined this thing we have."

The shaking stopped. His body numbed at the pure venom beneath her suggestion. Angry as she was, he was loathed to ask. A sick roiling in his belly took over. "What do ya mean?"

"This. Us. I mean that it is no longer clear to me where I am welcome and where I'm not. Perhaps I should only see the Inn long enough to pass through and give you a good screw before I go about my business. At least I know we agree on that. As for the rest, I have no idea. You asked me for my honesty, but maybe you no longer want that."

"Course I do. That's what I…" Devil if he didn't freeze again. The words he needed to say, the words she deserved to hear got stuck in his craw like a bad piece of meat. He could feel his nose wrinkle before he could stop it.

Her brow rose as she waited him to finish. Not that he expected her to miss the implication of the missing words. The silence lingered as his sentence remained painfully unfinished and dropped like a dead bird between them.

A sharp bark of laughter from her cut through the tension. "You know what? I am right. It's beyond time we defined this once and for all. No need for further argument or discussion. I'll make it real simple. It's *nothing*."

Numbness coursed through him until his jaw went slack. He stared at her with wide eyes for almost a full minute. After the two years they'd gone through, this was her conclusion?

The shock wore off into a driving pain around his heart. Old habit helped him grab hold of that pain and turn it around into a hot ball of anger. "You're really are going to act like a loon over a damn piano?"

"If you truly believe this is about that stupid piano you're a bigger idiot than I thought." She blinked fast, but not fast enough for him to miss the tear that slipped down her cheek. "You'd better get back to the inn. The saloon won't run itself."

"Yeah. Best get back to it." He sneered. "It's been fine for years. I ain't needed help before. I sure don't need it now."

"Good."

"Loon."

"Bastard."

The greatest griefs are those we cause
ourselves.
-Sophocles

"Sorry I'm late!" Jane pulled out a chair and plopped down with her plate. Relieved to have lunch with her friends, a solid distraction from her grief and anger, her excitement was only half-forced. "I had to drop off a letter before the train got here. I about didn't make it."

Silence greeted her proclamation, so Jane indulged in a few bites before bothering to figure out what her silent companions were up to. Kat and Norman both leaned toward the window. They leered through the panes with surprising intensity.

Jane chuckled at the sight. "What on earth are you two doing?"

"Watching." Kat finally acknowledged Jane with a giggle. "Isaac's been telling Mike and Norman about a girl he likes. We're trying to see if she likes him back."

"You're spying on a child?" Jane wanted to frown, or even laugh, but her curiosity piqued. She rose to move behind them to survey the scene herself.

Isaac sat beside a young girl, their lunch pals on either side of them. The girl with bright red curls reached into her bucket, but handed Isaac the prize.

Jane gasped. "Oh. Did she just give him her apple?"

Both women turned to each other and simultaneously clasped their hands to their chests. "It's true love."

Norman returned his seat to its normal position. He scoffed. "It's just an apple."

"Oh, it's more than an apple. It always is." Kat gave a serious nod. "You just don't understand, Norman."

"Sure he does." Jane mouthed the words *bed warmer* before dissolving into a fit of giggles. For Christmas two years back Norman had given Kat a bed warmer for Christmas when she'd been hoping for an engagement ring.

Kat burst into laughter, and soon she and Jane leaned against each other to keep from toppling in their amusement. Once she'd wiped the tears from her eyes, Kat clasped Jane's hand. "That was not nice."

Jane shrugged with a grin before taking a bite of meatloaf. "I wouldn't be nearly as much fun if I were nice all the time."

"So." Kat scooted her chair closer. When Jane paid her little mind, she persisted by leaning on the table next to Jane. "What is going on? David said you were miserable when you went to the homestead last night—and that your overnight visit was rather unplanned."

Jane choked on her food at the suddenness of the conversation change, and how fast word had spread. After coughing and sputtering for a minute, she took a drink of water to swallow down the now heavy lump of food. All she offered Kat in response was a sideways glance and a turned down mouth. Rather than get prompted for more she shoved another large bite of the once delicious meal that had become unappetizing in a heartbeat.

"Jane."

"Cole and I had an argument." Jane dabbed her mouth with a napkin. After another sip of water, she cleared her throat. "It isn't as if this has never happened before."

"But you always reconcile within a few hours at most. Usually at the drop of a hat."

Heat flooded Jane's cheeks. She turned her attention to carefully placing her napkin in her lap to avoid Kat's smirk.

"I swear I thought Edna Monroe about gave herself a heart attack rushing to whisper the rumors the last time you two so abruptly made up."

Her jaw strained against the amusement rising and the attempt to smile. Jane kept her eyes downcast and pushed her food around her plate with her fork. Every ounce of focus poured into not reacting.

"You're just lucky it seemed too fantastical to be true. I mean if I didn't know you so well I might have doubted it myself."

A giggle escaped her waning control over her emotions. "It's not my fault she interrupted us. Then again—we didn't consider it an interruption—we didn't stop."

"Middle of the day." Kat's mocked admonishment took her voice up an octave. "Practically in the middle of the street, like heathens."

"We were not in the middle of the street. It was a secluded spot against the lean-to behind the old cooper shop. No one ever goes there. Besides, the day was overcast."

Kat laughed outright. "That's your defense? The sky was overcast?"

"It is not my fault Edna felt it necessary to poke her nose out of that window. No one else in town saw. I don't even know why she happened to be in the closed cooper shop anyhow."

"She claims she thought someone was being accosted."

"Oh, she did not. The nosy old biddy knows what a beating sounds like—and what sex sounds like."

"What?" Norman's head popped up at the word *sex.* "What in blazes are the two of you hens clucking about?"

Again they spoke in unison. "Nothing Norman." Their attempts to remain straight faced failed the moment they looked at each other.

"Go back to your lunch, Norman." Jane gasped through her laughter. "No need to worry. We only talk about decent, proper things in public. You know that."

"Yeah. Sure." Norman grumbled. "It's usually easier to ignore you two when I got Cole to talk to."

Jane's happy mood faded. She poked at her potatoes again. "Then go to the saloon. I am quite certain he'll be there. As for myself, I hate to eat and run but I need to go out to Michael's hotel for a visit. I promised."

"Jane…"

Kat's grasp on her hand drew her to a stop. Jane sighed and met her friend's gaze. "Yes?"

"Are you sure you're all right? This is a long time for the two of you. You haven't been apart this long because of an argument since…" Thankfully Kat's voice trailed off rather than speak of the baby Jane had lost when her relationship had been new and unsure.

For the first time in well over a year things felt that shaky again. Still, she had to believe things would improve again. Too much had happened, and while Cole wasn't good at words so she'd never heard the three words he couldn't say—she knew how he felt by his actions.

"Jane?"

"That was a long time ago, Kat." Jane set her hand on Katherine's and tried to smile. "A different life—quite literally. I am fine. I will be. It's an argument, simple as that. The matter will be resolved or it won't."

"I'm sure it will. You two can't keep your hands off each other."

Though Jane knew it to be unintentional, the words cut deep. They rang with the reminder that almost everyone thought her relationship with Cole was purely physical. This time she couldn't even muster a smile. She wrenched her hand free. "Yes. I supposed we can't. Excuse me."

"Jane! Wait. I didn't mean…"

Kat's protest got lost behind Jane as she raced outside. Without stopping to check for traffic, she tore down the steps of Cora's café and store. She slowed across the street to a virtual stop. With a groan, she pinched the bridge of her nose at the first stinging hint of tears. She wouldn't shed them. Not here, not now.

"Jane?" A voice she hadn't heard in over a year carried over the sound of the crowd. One she'd thought she wouldn't ever hear again. Al Webb, a former major in the Army. "Jane Spencer, there you are."

"Al?" An entirely undignified squeal slipped free as she raced into the street to throw her arms around the neck of her old friend. "I didn't think I'd see you again, Major."

"Please. It's not Major any longer. Hasn't been for a while now." He chuckled as he returned her hug with one as tight. "It's good to see you too."

"I thought you said you were returning to North Carolina." Jane clasped his hand in hers, unable to keep the grin from her features. Al had been in Dominion Falls, tasked with the management of the Renegade problem they'd had before the railroad came. The two of them had formed an instant friendship, after a failed attempt at wooing Jane never ceased to tease him about in her frequent letters.

"I'm planning to. You didn't think I'd pass through Colorado without stopping to see you again, did you?" He grunted, and moved to protect her when he got bumped from behind. Al's brow furrowed as Cole stormed passed without a word. "Jane?"

"Why didn't you tell me you were going to stop?" Jane urged the conversation in any other direction than the angry man that had passed them. "Your last letter said you were leaving San Francisco and going home. You didn't have to stop off here just to see me."

"Of course I did. Letters just aren't the same. You censor yourself."

"I do not." She gave an indignant lift of her chin. The frequent peeks Al kept making behind her weren't needed to let her know they were being watched. She could practically feel holes burning in her back from Cole's stare. "How long are you staying?"

"A couple of days."

"Excellent. Plenty of time to catch up. Let's start with a walk. Away." She looped her arm with his, half dragging him down the street. As they walked, most of the bustle of people remained on the boardwalks and in the stores. She had to admit she missed the carts that once lined the streets to show off their wares. Now all the wares were displayed in shop windows and on porches. Interaction with the shop keepers wasn't as frequent this way.

"Jane?"

"Hmm? Oh, I apologize. My mind wandered again."

"It's not that. Take it easy, will you? I'll walk with you nice and easy. There is no need to drag me through town."

"Sorry."

"What's going on? Cole sure didn't seem thrilled to see me, and you ignored him. In fact, you rather nearly ran away." He nudged her shoulder. "Cole is not usually a person you've been known to run from."

"Do you ever stop observing?"

"Do you ever stop talking?"

Her jaw dropped, a stuttering protest tumbled through her lips. "I—how dare—you really—Al!"

He flinched away when she slugged his arm. His laughter flowed free. "Hey now."

"You are terrible. You might as well get back on that train if you're going to continue to behave in such a manner."

"Na. You wouldn't kick me out. You missed me too much."

Laughter filled the air between them. She wrapped her arm around his waist as his draped across her shoulders. "I have missed you, this is true."

"Told you."

"I cannot begin to tell you how glad I have been that you've continued to send me letters. I've enjoyed the tales of your travels since your retirement. Are you feeling better about retiring your commission now?"

"It wasn't an easy decision." A frown tugged down his lips, a damper on his previous amusement. "But you can only be ineffectual in the grand scheme of things for so long before the truth begins to wear on you."

"I wouldn't say you were completely ineffectual." Jane paused their walk so she could turn to face him. "You did a lot of good here in Dominion Falls. You saved many lives because you were willing to listen and compromise."

"Thank you for saying so. I'm not so sure it's as simple as all that, but I did try." His arm returned to her shoulders and he resumed their slow pace. "Now would you care to tell me why I feel as though it would be wise to sleep with one eye open at the Hangman's Inn tonight?"

"Don't be ridiculous," she admonished. "Pay Cole no mind."

"So you don't want to talk about it?"

With a gentle squeeze to his waist, she shook her head. "Certainly in this vast world we can find many other more interesting things to discuss. Such as your plans now."

"Not certain that I have plans, so much. I'm just going back home and seeing where life takes me."

"Of course." The volume of her scoff startled a bird out of a nearby bush. "Because you aren't the type of person to plan anything. Please, Al. Don't try to act coy with me. I think you'll find my response unpleasant."

"And this would be different in what way?"

Jealousy is the injured lover's hell.
—John Milton

After a pleasant afternoon of laughter and catching up on what they'd left out of their letters, Jane and Al returned to Cora's for supper in good spirits. Jane hadn't realized how much she'd missed her friend until he filled her afternoon with cheer enough to distract her from her worries.

Almost every table in Cora's sat full with patrons for supper. Toward the back at a large table Mike studied a book while he ate. Jane pulled Al over with her. "Mike. I'm sorry I forgot to stop by today. Look who showed up to surprise me. Do you think you can forgive me this transgression in the name of friendship?"

Mike pulled his eyes from his book, a smile lit his features. He'd recently shaved off his mustache and now looked even younger. Jane had a sneaking suspicion it had much to do with a certain woman doctor in town. "I suppose I can forgive you. Major Webb. It's good to see you again."

"It's just Al now." Al shook Mike's hand and took a seat. "How'd you end up at this table all by yourself with this place so full?"

"I think everyone else was afraid to take it with a small party. I figured I'd have stragglers join me after a time, so I sat. With your arrival, my figuring proved right." Mike chuckled. "So what brings you to town?"

"I was passing through Colorado on my way back east. I figured I'd take a detour and stop by to see Jane before I headed home. My biggest fear is she wouldn't recognize me out of uniform." Al flashed his teeth in a wicked grin.

Jane snorted. "According to rumors I've seen you well out of uniform."

"Ah yes, the rumors. Have they ceased with the towns growing numbers?" Al's brows rose at Jane's firm shake of her head. "No?"

"If you can believe it, it's worse. Horrible gossips in this town, men, and women alike. What's more, some of them have found friends." The rest of her commentary got interrupted by the waitress. Once they'd ordered, she leaned on her hand, her elbow propped rudely on the table. "To tell the truth, I wasn't certain I'd ever see Al again."

"Well, you know—"

Norman's gruff voice interrupted Al's statement. "There ain't nowhere else to sit. You wanna starve?"

Jane straightened in surprise, a smile placed firm on her face in expectation of Kat joining him. Instead, the tall figure next to Norman wiped the smile clear off her face. Every muscle tensed at her warring emotions over the sight of Cole. She shifted in her seat. Rather than face Cole's angry features, she dropped her gaze to the table.

"Mind if we sit?" Norman didn't wait for approval before he dropped into a seat next to Al. That left only the other seat on Al's right, and the one beside her as options for Cole.

Her mouth went dry in the eternity it took for him to take the seat beside her. She snatched her water to gulp it down. The curious stare from her brother didn't help her tension in the least. To push any questions or her own distress aside she forced a bright smile as she turned to her brother. "Did you get a letter from Thomas today too?"

"Yes I did." While the curious tilt of his brow didn't waver, Mike's smile returned. "He said James would be returning with him for a visit. I guess Ida wanted to see where we lived."

Al shook his head. He looked between the two in confused. "Wait. What?"

"Mike's brother—" An elbow to her ribs cut her off. She groaned at the reproachful frown Mike wore. After a retaliating jab at his ribs she corrected herself. "My brother James came out last summer with his—our—parents once he'd healed from the poisoning. His wife Ida was quite nonplussed that she was left out of the adventure west."

"I thought you'd said they were just here." Al leaned back when their food was brought to the table. Silence fell when everyone dove into their food. After a few hearty bites, Al resumed the conversation. "And Tommy is coming back?"

"He took a job as hotel manager at the Hangman's Inn." She tried to keep her expression neutral. Mike made her fully aware of her failure by poking her arm with his fork.

"Tommy's not one to sit still long." Mike pushed the conversation forward when she failed to continue her thought process. "He tried settling down and farming like our brothers, even tried marriage once. None of it worked for him."

The chair next to her scraped the floor so abrupt everyone jumped. Cole strode away without a word. He'd not even touched a bite of his food. Jane's fingers tightened around her fork. At the curious looks from Al and Mike she cleared her throat to return the subject to anything else. "So from what Tommy's told me, he hasn't sat still much since. He's been a deputy out in New York for some time, but I think coming out here is his way of finding something else to do."

"I think you're right." Mike nodded agreement. "He's been itching to find a reason to move again. Coming out here is perfect for him."

"So he'll be working for Cole then?" Al quirked a brow. A smile tugged the corner of his lips. "Should be fun."

"Shockingly, Cole and Tommy get along really well. I'd say it's rather scary." Mike grinned. "Then again, Tommy and Jane have a lot in common too."

"If you'll excuse me." Jane rose. Her appetite gone, she shoved her half-eaten meal away. "I think I'm going to call it a night."

"I was just heading back myself." Al wiped his mouth with his napkin. He rose and offered his arm. "If you'll allow me to escort you again. I don't wish to intrude."

"You aren't, and I'd be happy to allow you to escort me." A quick grab of her wrist made Jane hesitate. She turned to Mike, who had a firm grip on her wrist.

He leaned in close and spoke under the din. "Where are you staying tonight?"

"Don't you worry about me." She patted his arm in her best attempt at reassurance. "I'll try to come by the hotel tomorrow for the visit I keep promising. I'd like a cooling dip in your swimming hole."

Al nodded to Mike before he fell into step beside Jane. "Why did he ask where you're staying? I thought I was escorting you back to the hotel."

"I told you. Cole and I are having a disagreement. I'm going a bit further than the Inn, but I'll walk with you that far." Jane smiled best as she could. "Don't look so concerned. I'll still have a place to rest my head."

"That isn't why I'm concerned," Al muttered.

They were at the Inn before she could ruminate over his meaning long. The scene on the porch of the establishment sent Jane's heart into a panicked thumping. Her lips trembled when she tried to offer a strong smile to hide the painful sinking of her heart. "I believe this is where we'll part company, Al. Thank you for a pleasant afternoon."

Al's dark eyes focused on her, concern puckering his brow. "Jane."

Rather than face his weak attempt at comfort, she raced around the corner to the library. She fumbled the keys out of her pocket, flipping through them with shaky hands. When she found the right one the lock fought her attempts to open it. When the door finally flew open, she rushed inside.

She slammed the door shut. One quick motion locked it tight. The air grew thin under her short gasping attempts to breathe. She grabbed at her bodice and popped it open before releasing the busks of her corset to draw a deep breath.

The image of Cole cozied up to one of the new whores seared itself in her brain. Tears smarted in her eyes. All her burgeoning anger burst into pain. Somehow she had to erase the image from her thoughts. She had to forget.

She raced for the desk and tore open the bottom drawer. Five full flasks clanked together. She grabbed them all.

Without another moment's hesitation she unscrewed the first flask. The whiskey burned down her throat, but she chugged it. Anything to make her forget her pain.

If the headache would only precede the intoxication, alcohol would be a virtue.
–Samuel Butler

Charlie tapped his finger on the center glass pane of the library door. No response emanated from within even though he'd knocked three times already. He frowned deeper. Nerves made him draw on his nervous habit of running his fingers along his mustache. Jane had to be inside because he'd been unable to locate her anywhere else.

Again he raised his hand to rap harder on the pane. A soft shuffling reached his ears through the door. "Jane? Is that you? Are you all right?"

A hand appeared between the curtain and glass to wave at him. After a click the door opened slow as molasses. "Shhh. Stop making so much noise." Jane opened the door a crack further. By doing so she revealed her disheveled state.

The woman that was his sister, and the woman she'd become, would never let herself be seen as she appeared at the moment. Hair stuck out at odd angles from a bun she'd never taken down. The curls twisted into a rat's nest of a mess on the right side of her head.

She wore no bodice, and her corset sat wide open to reveal her chemise. From the look of her skirts she'd even removed her petticoats at some juncture. Her blue eyes were bloodshot and disappeared between her squinting lids. She pinched her fingers across the bridge of her nose.

The Jane he knew could only be called fastidious. Despite her reputation, she always dressed well and put her hair up neat as a pin. Nothing ever found its way out of place.

"Jane."

"Shhh." She waved sharply at him.

Five empty flasks haphazardly spread across the desk caught his eye. "Are you—Jane, did you drink all of those?"

"Shush." She blinked a few times. After hazarding a glance at the desk she winced. The nod she gave was miniscule but sent her groaning and covering her mouth.

"You hate drinking that much. Even when you were Clara you had a firm grasp on how much you could drink without causing this sort of ailment." Concern knotted his belly. Mike had been worried enough to have them both out looking for her the night before, and all morning. Now to find her like this? "Why the hell would you do that?"

"Go away." Her body convulsed and she covered her mouth again. After a shaky breath she seemed to steady herself. She muttered, "Go, Charlie."

He ignored her to move into the dimly lit library. Behind the desk he found a rolled-up ball of fabrics. The petticoats he'd suspected were missing. "Did you sleep on the floor in here? Mike and I were looking for you for hours last night. Didn't you hear us knocking?"

All he got in reply was a tiny shrug. Her head rested against the door frame. Eyes closed, she hand one hand on her stomach and the other shielding her eyes.

"Whatever your argument with Cole, this is ridiculous. It's the middle of the day and we've been looking for you most of the morning. You've been sulking in here like an insolent child, drinking yourself sick, sleeping off the whiskey with your head on a rolled-up petticoat? Damn it Jane, you're better than that."

"I said go—oh—oh—" She turned and stumbled out onto the porch. Before she'd reached the alley he heard her retching.

Charlie sighed and gathered the petticoats along with a shawl she had hanging on a hook behind her desk. It might be hot outside, but Jane would be embarrassed to be seen like this once she got back to normal.

Since he could still hear her voiding her stomach's contents he took the time to clean up the pile of flasks on the desk. He tossed the petticoats over his shoulder and walked outside. Once he'd made sure the door locked thanks to the keys she'd left on the desk, he moved over to where Jane had managed to control her heaves.

He set the shawl gingerly over her head. As she tugged it closer he braced his arm around her waist. "Come with me. Let's get you to the clinic where you can sleep this off in peace."

"Can't sleep…my head…can't…"

"I'll give you something for the headache." He stooped to pick her up when she groaned.

Her whole body went stiff and she set her hand on his shoulder. "No. I'll walk on my own two feet. Thank you." A gray tinge lingered on her skin, but her jaw set in a determined line.

Charlie imagined she'd rather suffer the pain of the long walk to the clinic over the embarrassment of being carried.

Especially as their trail would take them right past the inn. "Stubborn, proud fool."

"Perhaps."

"All right," he agreed begrudgingly. Once again he braced his arm around her waist. "You know what Tommy would say to you right now?"

"That I'm an idiot?" At least now that she'd gotten sick she sounded more like herself. Though she still squinted against the sunlight and gripped his waist as if she might collapse without his support she had some bite to her speech.

"Sounds about right. Know what I say?"

"'Man, being reasonable, must get drunk. The best of life is but intoxication'. Lord Byron."

"Not quite. I was going to say 'A drunkard is like a whiskey bottle, all neck and belly—no head'. Austin O'Malley."

"'There are more old drunkards than old doctors'," she muttered. "Ben Franklin."

"'To debate with a drunkard is to debate with an empty house'. Syrus."

Jane groaned and her hand once again flew to her mouth. He tightened his arm around her waist. They stopped walking while she gathered herself. After a ragged breath she offered a nod and they resumed their pace.

"I thought you and Cole were well past the point of acting stupid after your fights. Last I recalled you had a well-planned execution of making up, after which you'd discuss the problem like adults. It feels to me like we've gone back in time."

"I wish we had. You wouldn't be here yapping in my ear." She kept her free hand pressed hard against her forehead between her eyes. "Giving me a headache."

"The headache is not my fault—the whiskey is solely to blame. You're being childish, although I imagine Cole isn't behaving any better. In a normal argument I'd say you are the better behaved of the two of you which, at this point, frightens me a bit. Honestly, Jane. What were you thinking?"

"I'm not up for a lecture."

"Too bad. As your older brother, it's my obligation."

"You were Clara's older…"

He chuckled when her argument was cut off by another groan. At least they'd arrived at the clinic without her getting ill again. With just a little bit of effort he helped her onto the porch and inside before closing the door behind them. He led her into his office where she dropped on the bench. He sighed and tossed her petticoats onto his chair. "Really, Jane. Getting drunk? You hate getting drunk. What on earth convinced you this would be a good idea?"

"I told you. I am not up for a lecture."

Charlie shook his head against his own urge to continue to scold. Without a doubt she'd suffer enough without his help. He pulled medicine for her headache from the cabinet. While he worked, he kept an eye on her. Somehow she'd managed to gather herself together, and with the shawl covering her hair now only appeared to have a megrim.

Once the medicine dissolved into the glass of water he handed it to her. He tried to soften his tone as he spoke again, "Drink this. It will help with the headache. Would you mind telling me why you let this happen?"

"I just wanted to shut my mind up for a while." Delicate sips gave way to a quick chug to get the medicine down. For a moment she looked almost green, but it passed. She handed the glass back to him. "Do you have a dark room I can lie in? Please."

"Fine. But once your head stops pounding we will discuss this."

"Then my head will never cease pounding because we aren't discussing anything. I got drunk. It's all over but the recovery. If it eases your mind, I sincerely doubt I will be doing any such thing for a very long time."

He helped her to her feet while he considered his argument. Right then she wouldn't put up much of a fight, but from what he could tell she was punishing herself enough.

Rather than take her upstairs, he led her to the closest room. Usually used for operating, the windows were always covered to avoid people peeking in on operations. He guided her to the bed near the wall they used for recovery. As she got settled in, he went so far as to tuck her in.

While she snuggled under the covers he pulled a second layer of curtains over the window to make the room darker. "Need anything else, Jane?"

"Would you get me a dress, please? When I get up I'll need to change."

"Of course. I'll head over to the Inn and get one soon as Daisy arrives. Get some rest."

"Charlie. Tell Cole…" Her voice trailed off. The silence lingered long enough that he drew closer, only to spot a tear on her cheek.

He resisted the urge to wipe it away. "What Jane?"

"Tell him I want my books back."

Shock cooled Charlie's blood, confusion furrowed his brow. Books meant everything to Jane. No matter where she ended up, if there were books she was comfortable. If she wanted her books back, that could only mean she was leaving. That couldn't be, though. She loved the bastard. "What, Jane? Why would I tell him that?"

"Just do it," she mumbled before she buried her head under the covers.

He lingered near the door, but she didn't speak again. While he had plenty of paperwork to do and the occasional patient to occupy his time over the next few hours, his mind continued to wander back to Jane's request.

Mike had mentioned tension between Cole and Jane at supper the night before. The pair who usually didn't care who saw their open affection, or rather desire, hadn't even looked at each other for the few minutes Cole had been at the table.

Now this.

None of it bode well. Maybe he could get some answers from Cole as it seemed Jane didn't care to talk. Stubborn woman.

When Daisy arrived Charlie took the time to fill her in on the day's patients and Jane's presence in the surgery room. Soon as he'd caught up Daisy, Charlie grabbed his hat and set out for a dress—and answers.

Raucous laughter and cheers hit his ears before he made it to the door of the inn. From the sounds of it business as usual had returned. Charlie wondered what that meant for any guests the Inn might have.

Inside the doors he paused long enough to let his eyes adjust to the change in lighting. He scanned the saloon and its occupants, finally finding Cole at the poker table. The reasons behind Jane's anger, distress, and night of drinking were easy to spot as it draped around him like a wet blanket in the form of a pretty, young whore.

Fire burned through Charlie's veins. He stormed across the room. Cole hadn't notice his arrival. "I'm getting some of Jane's things. I'm sure you don't care."

Cole's eyes narrowed as he turned his gaze to Charlie. He leaned back in his seat. A sneer tugged the corner of his lip. "Get the hell out. I'm busy."

"Not until I get her things." Charlie ignored Cole's protest as he strode to the stairs in the back of the room. By the time he got to the top of the stairs, he could hear Cole stomping behind him hot on his heels.

"It's locked, 'cause no one goes in there. I ain't letting you in." Cole snarled behind him.

Charlie smirked, still about ten feet from Cole's door at the end of the hall. "I didn't expect you to." Without another word he stopped short and drew his pistol from its holster. The crack of gunfire stilled all activity in the saloon for a minute, and busted the door wide open in a splinter of wood.

"What the devil?"

"I told you. I'm getting some of Jane's things, like she asked me to." Charlie happily took advantage of Cole's stunned silence to enter the room without the full-on fight he'd expected.

Cole recovered quickly. He charged forward to try to block Charlie. "No. You ain't taking her things."

"She asked for them. Are you going to prevent her from getting the things she owns?"

"She can get them herself. Not that she will. She'll be back."

"You are a stupid bastard, aren't you? With the show you're putting on with that whore do you really think she'll come back here?"

Cole's chin lifted in defiance. "She's putting on a good show herself."

"She put on a show? You mean Al? That was in no way the sort of show you're putting on. It wasn't a show at all. They're friends. Jane has made it exceedingly clear whom it is she loves. Unfortunately for her, it's you."

"I've been plenty clear too." Eyes narrowed, Cole still didn't budge.

"Jane tolerates a lot. More than she should, in my opinion. But not—"

"Cole?" The girl that had been sitting on his lap hovered near the door. She half curtsied at Charlie. "Pardon me. They're waiting on you, Cole."

"Be there in a minute, Belladonna." Cole's lip twisted. "Don't you go far."

"Like I said," Charlie spoke quiet. His body tensed, more than ready for a fight now. "You are a stupid bastard."

"I'm just doing what she told me to."

"You know, I didn't understand why she asked me to relay this message. After this display it's all crystal clear."

"What the devil do ya mean?"

"She asked for her books back," Charlie snapped.

The red hue of fury seeped from Cole's features. The words had their intended impact. It appeared not even Cole's thick brain missed the implication of her request.

"Books have always been the first thing Clara packed, and from what I've heard and seen Jane is no different. In fact, it may be even more true of her. Clara was just a teacher,

Jane lives and breathes books as they are her one solid connection to Clara." Charlie plucked a dress off a hook and grabbed clean petticoats from the next hook. "I see you actually understand the gravity of what I'm saying here."

"You're lying." Cole licked his lips like they had gone dry. After a second he grabbed a bottle of whiskey and poured himself a glass. He tossed it back. When he finished, he slammed down the glass. "She didn't say that."

Charlie snorted. "I personally don't care how far you took your performance with the whore, because it doesn't matter with the level of damage you've done. If you were trying to make Jane jealous you failed miserably. If you were trying to hurt her, congratulations. You succeeded in spades."

"You don't got any idea."

"To be honest, all I've been told is you two argued. Despite the gossip flying about this town, Jane does not divulge much in the way of intimate details about your relationship. She leaves it at the simple fact that she loves you. Up until now, it's been enough for us."

"Yeah, we argued. It ain't none of your business."

"You're right. It wasn't. You two hot-heads argue all the time, we've grown accustomed to it. Until you go hurting my sister, I stay the hell out of it." Charlie headed toward the door. "Intentionally causing pain is beyond what either of you have done before. Pack up her books. Mike and I will be by for them later."

"She ain't faultless."

"She never is, and doesn't claim to be." Leaving the broken door hanging wide open, Charlie called back on his way down the hall, "'How quickly love makes fools of us'. Moliere."

"Words. Damn words." The door slammed with a crack of wood.

From the top of the stairs, Charlie could see the broken door swinging on its hinges. Inside the room, Cole stood stock still. The only movement came from the clenching and unclenching of his fists.

Without another word, Charlie descended the stairs to return to the clinic. Truth be told, he knew Jane still loved the guy, and up until this action none of the Young brothers cared. After all, they had all witnessed how much Cole cared for Jane when he'd done everything he could to save her from the clutches of a madman. From risking his own life as a target, to trusting the brothers as he left her behind.

If tempers were already high, he imagined Jane's innocent excitement at seeing Al had sparked some hurt and jealousy within the numbskull. Two wrongs sure didn't make a right, but when it came to love it had been more than evident that neither Jane nor Cole were particularly good at handling themselves.

Back at the clinic he sought out Daisy, only to find her examining a patient. So Charlie went right back to the room he'd put Jane in. He pushed open the door slow and tapped with a gentle knock. "Jane? Are you awake?"

"Yes." Her voice barely above a whisper, she sat slowly. "I feel horrible, but I'm awake."

"Well you should."

"I know." The weak laugh she offered got marred by her flinches of pain. "I think it's safe to say that I now know for certain why I prefer to not get drunk."

He dropped the clothing into her lap. Unable to stop himself, he chuckled. "Does that mean I can trust that you won't be such an idiot about drinking again?"

"I'll always be a bit of an idiot, just not about drinking ever again."

Amusement bubbled up enough to push aside his earlier anger. "You are definitely feeling better."

"Just be nice. I could still throw up on you, you know."

"It wouldn't be the first time. Get dressed. I think you need some food in your belly to help get rid of the last of the alcohol."

"Food does not sound in the least bit appealing," she muttered on her way back behind the screen. "However, if you really think it will help me feel better."

"It will." He let the silence linger for a few moments. After just a little time, he felt compelled to put in his two cents on the matter. "Jane. About Cole—"

"It's all right, Charles." She stepped out from behind the screen. The shaky smile she wore barely covered her still-pained eyes and shaky hands. "Yes. I love him. I won't deny it. I also don't think it's particularly logical to wallow. I've told him from day one that I only want what he can give. If he's no longer willing to—or wants to find it elsewhere I can't stop him."

"Logic? What place does logic have when it comes to love?"

Her smile faltered further. "In this situation I must cling to logic. It is not easy."

"'No mistake is more common and fatuous than appealing to logic in cases which are beyond her jurisdiction'." Charlie chuckled when she scoffed. "Samuel Butler."

"'Our affections, however laudable, should never master us; we should guide them'. Dickens." Jane quirked a brow. "I really don't want to do this with a headache. Could we adjourn until I'm more reasonably equipped for this debate?"

"You're just saying that because you know you'll lose."

"I know no such thing. I won't lose."

"Oh, but you will." He gave her a hug and threw in a kiss to her forehead for good measure. "Your fights have never been strong when they involve matters of the heart. You feel too strongly. Always have, always will."

The stiffness with which she'd received the kiss melted away until she sagged against him. Her face buried in his shoulder. Arms wrapped around him as her first sob erupted. For a few minutes her body quaked with tears, and he let her have the privacy of silence.

He ran his hand along her back. With patience, he waited for her to find the strength to gather herself together. Somehow he suspected both she and Cole were realizing what fools they were, and perhaps wouldn't have to suffer the pain of a fool long.

"Sorry." She took several deep, ragged breaths. Her body stilled enough to show she'd collected herself. "It must be the headache making me weak."

"Don't apologize. You're allowed to be an emotional idiot."

This time her laughter was heartier. She smacked him hard in the chest. Wiping the tears from her cheeks, she straightened. "You said I needed to eat."

"Yes you do." He held out his arm. When she took it he patted her hand.

"Thank you for taking care of me today. Sleeping on the floor was not very comfortable. Not to mention how sick I felt this morning."

"I'll always take care of you. It's what brothers do, you know. Especially brothers that happen to be doctors." He offered a wink. "Besides, you didn't get sick on me, so there's nothing to thank me for."

"Such an event is still not out of the realm of possibility." Once they stepped outside into the open air she paused to set a hand to her forehead.

With her attempt to gather herself, she missed spotting Cole's approach like Charlie did. Cole leaned against the post at the end of the porch. Charlie thought he caught a hint of regret before the man shut down to his usual stoic expression. To get her attention Charlie tapped the back of her hand. As Cole approached Charlie slipped his arm free.

"No," she managed to squeak. However she didn't immediately reach for Charlie to support her or move his way.

Cole glared down at her. "We gotta talk."

"No. I need to eat." Her hand still hadn't left her belly, but her color had returned even more at the sight of Cole. Whether relief or anger caused her energy boost, Charlie couldn't be sure. Despite that, she stepped back from Cole's reaching hand. "I mean it. I am not in the mood for talking, not with you."

"Why don't you take her to Cora's, Cole?" Charlie interrupted. After the past night and morning, the last thing he would let Jane do was be stubborn. Someone had to force both of their hands and throw them together. It could all blow up, or maybe they'd actually make up. It was anyone's guess. He spoke over Jane's protest. "Millie is expecting me for lunch anyhow, Jane. I do best to not annoy my wife."

"Charlie." Jane visibly bristled.

Charlie stepped closer to her again. He spoke quietly, "He's been a stupid bastard, but you love him. And let's not forget you haven't been too brilliant yourself."

It looked like she'd bust him in the nose for a minute, but then the tension left her shoulders. She gave him a sharp jab to the ribs. "Go home."

Cole's eyes narrowed when Jane didn't acknowledge him and started toward Turner's alone. "Charlie."

"Go on ahead. I think you'll both find crow goes down easier if you share it."

Let us forgive each other–only then will we live in peace.
–Leo Nikolayevich Tolstoy

Cole's smooth voice broke through the silence that had filled Jane's lunch time. "Can we go back to our room now?"

Jane's fork clattered to the plate. She gripped her skirts with her free hand. The lump lodged in her throat held on tight through her surprise. After a few deep breaths she considered herself steady enough to reply. "*Our* room?"

"Yeah, our room. It's been your room since ya first left *Leaves of Grass* in it. That ain't changed."

Inwardly she cursed herself for the rush of relief his voice, and what he'd said, caused within. Unbidden, her mouth twitched in its attempt to smile without her permission. After their fight and ensuing silence, to attempt a conversation seemed odd, but she had to try. He'd made the first effort. She forced herself to meet his gaze. "I don't know. Certainly not if you expect this to be over simple as that."

"Just wanna get away from prying eyes."

Sure enough, now that he'd pointed it out, she found curious glances turned toward their table from all sides. Her brow furrowed at their captive audience. "So I see."

"Much as we keep 'em talking, don't need to add to it by having it out right here."

"Oh, I don't know." She smoothed the crease in her napkin in a slow, meticulous manner. With a great effort she managed to swallow her laughter before she spoke again. "If we made up right here on this table it might give us some privacy. Or it could bring more interested onlookers."

That brought his attention back to her, his wide eyes scanned her face. By now her laughter had almost escaped her hold. He chuckled low and leaned closer. "I'd say we'd lose a few, but most would stay for the show."

With the tension lessened, she leaned back. Her renewed relaxation allowed the lump in her throat to dissipate. She nodded. "I suppose we can go back, then. If worse comes to worst, I can get a few of my things."

That wiped the smile right off his handsome face. The loss of the smile saddened her in a way, but she wouldn't deny she was still hurt by his actions. Not to say her own behavior hadn't been poor as well, but she hadn't…

No. She wouldn't go into deep speculation about what occurred between him and the whore. If she did, she'd never hear him out. Instead, she rose to her feet. After another deep breath, she focused on him. "Shall we then?"

"Right."

The tension so recently released returned. Her lips tightened until she'd sucked them between her teeth. The touch of his hand to her lower back left her heart beating double time. In her heart she knew he'd never betray her, but seeing the whore draped all over him had hurt deeper than she'd expected.

She supposed she wasn't faultless, either. In her own head and heart, Al could never be more than a friend, but Cole had always been even more jealous of Al than he'd ever been of David.

With every step closer to the Inn, Cole remained beside her. Through the crowded streets, his hand never left her back. The gesture might have been small, but its possessive hold was one he'd adopted early on in their relationship. He didn't seem near as tense as she, but he never did.

On their way down the street a few more curious glances turned their way, but they both ignored them. Jane tried to keep her eyes focused straight ahead and not look at him again until they talked. She couldn't be sure what direction her thoughts would take if she did.

Once inside the Inn, Cole's hand left her back. "Gonna grab a new bottle of whiskey. Think I'll need it. I'll get you a glass."

Her stomach churned at the mere idea of more alcohol. The blood drained from her face. With a sharp shake of her head she held up her hand. "No. Thank you. I can't tonight."

His brow rose in curiosity, but he didn't question. After a simple nod he moved behind the bar.

"Lady Jane." Hammy waved from his bar stool.

"*Jane.*" Iris rushed forward to clasp Jane's hands.

Confused, Jane furrowed her brow at Iris before offering a polite nod to Hammy. She gasped when Iris tugged her violently toward the back of the building. "Iris? Wait."

"I gotta talk to you. It's urgent," Iris whispered. She snuck a furtive, fearful glance in Cole's direction.

Cole frowned at the scene. Then he surprised her by jerking his head toward the back. "Deal with it, please. Damn loon's been a wreck all day and won't tell me why. I'd like to be done with it, whatever it is. I'll meet you upstairs."

Jane gave him a smile, but didn't feel so certain she should follow his instructions. Iris didn't appear to have the same hesitation as she dragged her all the way toward the back where the whore's rooms were.

Since Cole had given his blessing, Jane followed with no external argument. The moment the door opened the stench of sweat and unclean women hit her. She plugged her nose. "I've only been gone three days and you have all gone against the rules. You've had men back here, haven't you?"

Irish shifted her feet without answering. She stared at the floor rather than meet Jane's gaze.

"This is not a good way to start. What else is going on, Iris? What has you frantic?"

"You ain't gonna like it, Jane."

Jane pursed her lips, her arms folded across her chest. "You have made that quite clear already. Out with it. Who is it?"

"Which part?" Iris twisted her hands in front of her. She still refused to meet Jane's eyes. "Rose, Heather, or Violet?"

Jane pressed her fingers to her forehead to try to stem the headache that had returned with a vengeance. "Before you tell me, why didn't you tell Cole?"

"He's been so mad these past few days, don't know what he'd do. We'd lose them all, and be short again. We're already working ourselves dry." Iris paced the floor. "Cole don't look for solutions like ya do. He just sends us away with nothing."

"You have five minutes, and make it fast before my headache gets too loud to hear you."

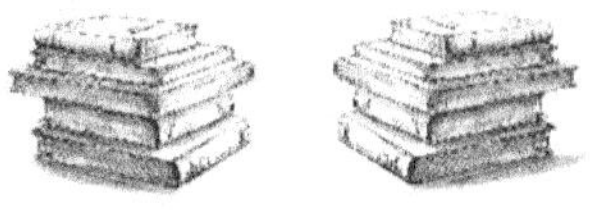

Liars when they speak the truth are not to be believed.
—Aristotle

Iris sat on the edge of a bed, hands clasped tight in her lap. "What are you gonna do, Jane?"

"It may not be up to me, Iris. Just because I walked in that door today doesn't mean I have any control over what's going to happen." Jane still didn't know where she stood, as she and Cole had yet to speak. Even if she did have say, Cole would likely have a fit of temper over all she'd learned. "I'll speak to Cole and let him know what's going on. I'll try to make sure no one is put out."

"Thank you."

"Don't thank me yet." Jane pulled open the door. "There may be nothing to thank me for in the end. Keep Rose and Heather where they are and get back on the floor to work. Violet can still work for now—but that situation will be dealt with. If I have any luck speaking with Cole I'll expect to talk to each of them myself."

"Of course. Yes. I'll get back to work. Thank you."

Jane wrinkled her nose. "And get this room and the girls cleaned up straight away. It smells like Soong's pig farm in here."

If it hadn't been for her headache, Jane would have slammed the door. Instead she just pulled it closed with a heavy sigh. Now she had even more to confront Cole with, she just hoped that first they were able to work out their own issues.

Dealing with the whores wasn't for the faint of heart, and often required a firm hand. She didn't envy Cole his years of working with them. Of course, before she'd come into his life he'd had plenty of side benefits. A shudder ran through her at the implication of her own thoughts. She took a deep breath to try to still them.

On that note, she had to get herself upstairs to see him before her imagination made everything worse than it was.

She darted up the stairs to head for the room she'd shared with Cole for over a year. Near the top she passed a gentleman and one of the girls, Pansy. Out of habit, Jane calculated the date. A realization stopped her short. She spun. "Pansy!"

"Yeah, Jane?" Pansy turned around. She wore a lazy smile and rested a hand on her hip. "Did ya need something?"

"Aren't you supposed to be off this week? No company of any sort?" To cover her rising anger, Jane pulled out a smile that might have been pleasant. Then again, it might not have. "I do believe we spoke on the same subject last month. I am certain Mr. Warren could have found other suitable company."

"I asked for Miss Pansy." Warren's smirk was as slimy as his hair when he removed his hat. Man of business, her left foot. There was something off about that man. "I do believe when they are on the floor it's my preference."

"Well, Mr. Warren. We'll have to make sure Pansy isn't on the floor when she's not supposed to be keeping company. Good day." She tilted her head barely enough to acknowledge the tip of his hat. Silence fell between Jane and Pansy while Warren departed. The man hopped down the stairs, whistling.

Jane moved closer to Pansy. The whole situation reeked of deception. Right down to the fact she knew Warren had given the last two whores their stash of opium in the days before Cole had kicked them out. "Give it to me, Pansy."

"What?" Wide brown doe eyes met her gaze. Pansy blinked, the false innocence adding to her young appearance. "I don't know what you mean."

"The last thing you want to do right now is lie to me, Pansy." Jane held out her hand. After the past several days, not to mention the talk she'd just had with Iris, Jane's nerves were about ready to snap. Everything was falling apart, and she didn't know how to fix it.

Pansy straightened her shoulders. Defiance lit her eyes. "Don't gotta. You and Cole are on the outs. He said we—"

"Do what she says," Cole interrupted from somewhere very close by. His voice held a dark note belying his anger. Jane wondered how long he'd been standing there.

Unable to see him, Jane had no idea what he was thinking or feeling. It bothered her, but she had to finish this. Pansy, of all the girls, had always given Jane as much trouble as a surly child. It was time to end that once and for all, whether Jane had any say after today or not. "Give it to me now."

Pansy huffed, but shoved her hand down the front of her bodice. She slapped a small pouch into Jane's hand and glared at her. For a split second she looked all of twelve years old in the heat of her tantrum.

It struck Jane as odd, but she didn't have the time to think on it long. There was more of the dope, and she knew it. "The rest."

"There—there's no more." Pansy's jaw dropped. She took a step back, hands shaking as they reached for the railing.

Jane reached out and grabbed her ear, using it to drag her up the few steps to the top. Once the girl was against the wall, she leaned close. She released the ear and snarled. "Give me the rest now or I will let Cole search for it—and I am *quite* convinced you will not enjoy it."

A string of curses erupted from Pansy's lips. The flash of venom and curl of her lip effectively erased the illusion of teenager. Without shame she hauled up her skirts and pulled another bag from her garter. "There. Happy?"

"You don't use this." Jane shook the bags in front of her face. "You never have once. Why bother obtaining it?"

"Iris wanted it."

"Bull. Iris doesn't use either. Try again."

"The girls were lookin' for some. Ya know, to relax at the end of the night. They still work. It don't do no harm."

"It does now. Get downstairs and in the room with Rose and Heather. Stay there or expect to be on the streets with nothing but the flimsy clothes you're wearing. I need to speak with Cole."

"Ya don't own me."

Jane smirked. "Look behind me. Do you think that *he* gives two figs about where you end up? I don't think you have any ground here. The rules are simple, and I would suggest not breaking them again."

With a huff, Pansy turned to walk away.

She didn't get far as Jane grabbed her arm to pull her back close. "And if you ever screw out of the approved dates again, you won't have a penny when you and whatever spawn you produce are tossed into the street. Accidents happen. This was intentional."

The second Jane released her arm, Pansy ran down the stairs.

What she'd just done sickened Jane because she hated the thought of abusing any of them, or tossing them out with nothing. How often had she chastised Cole for the same threat?

"I told ya long ago, sometimes you gotta be the bad guy. You know I never hurt any of them, but that don't mean the threat ain't been there." Cole now stood right behind her. His familiar heat washed over her until her shoulders slumped. His hands rubbed along them briefly. Then he gave her a gentle squeeze and turned her around.

She sighed. "You've got a damn big mess on your hands, Mr. Mitchell."

"So I'm gathering."

Hesitation and fear mingled to keep her eyes cast downward. She gathered her strength to meet his gaze. The admiration she found there surprised her. She swallowed down the rising lump of emotion. "Which mess are you dealing with first?"

His hands slipped down her arms to cup her elbows in a gentle grasp. "Let get in our room." He released an elbow and guided her down the hall into their room.

Once through the door, she rushed forward out of his grasp. She came to a dead stop in the middle of the room. Her body trembled when he rested his hands on her shoulders again and she closed her eyes to try to ease the emotions. After a long sigh slipped free, she dropped her head. "I'm sorry."

"Thought ya said it wasn't over."

"It isn't. However, I am sorry." For her part in the whole mess, she was. He had to know that.

"What now?"

"Words over action. Right now I need words over action."

"Damn words."

A slow smile rose over his frustration. She chuckled low. "I know."

"Jane." His body pressed flush against her back. Either his chin or possibly his nose rested on the crown of her head. Warm breath tickled the loose hair at the nape of her neck. One hand slid around her waist and held her tight. "Ya can't think I been with her, or any of 'em. It was all for show. I didn't need the riff raff thinking I'm no good with a woman. What use do I got for a whore anyhow?"

Hope stirred in her belly to counteract the tears that slipped down her cheeks. She feared her knees might go weak, but they were far from done. Somehow she gathered her wits, but her voice was shaky as she whispered, "I told you we were nothing. I spoke out of such anger, I wouldn't blame you if…"

"Ain't no whore alive that could compare to what you got. Only use I got for them now is to make me money. I knew you'd come back—least-wise I thought I did. I didn't like what you said none, and I wanted to make you mad."

"You hurt me."

"You and soldier boy," His words choked in his throat.

She set her hand on his, and managed to contain her laughter at the absurdity of the idea. Clearly he'd been hurt too. "Al? How many times have I told you there is nothing to worry about? He and I will never be more than friends."

"He had his hands all over ya."

"No. He had his arm around my shoulders. I gave him a hug. That's all. You were the one with hands all over you."

"Thought we were making up, not fighting again."

She leaned into his warmth, eager to put things behind them. The mere happenstance of being close to him made her realize more than ever how much she'd missed him. "You're right. Then let me say that you never have had, and never will have, anything to worry about where Al is concerned. He is a good man, and a good friend—but he is not the man I love."

"I don't like the way he looks at ya. Never have. Hard to believe I got nothing to worry about there."

"You have as little to worry about with Al as you ever did with David."

"I don't trust him."

"Then trust me." She slid her hand along his arm where it remained wrapped tight around her waist. "Trust me. You know who I love, and despite my harsh words the other day that has never changed."

"Good." Hair stirred near her ear when he leaned his cheek against her head. "There ain't ever been a woman like you. Not even Ella made me feel what you do."

Heat flooded her cheeks at his bold statement. To hear such words from his mouth set her stomach aflutter. She had no idea how to take the comparison to his late wife, a wife no one knew existed but her. "I don't ask you to compare me to her. She was the woman you loved."

"The girl. We were nothing more than kids ourselves."

She smiled as she remembered the woman she'd been before amnesia. "Much like Clara and David were."

"He let Clara go."

"Yes. After a few years, he did let her go."

Close as they were, Cole just stood there holding her. No words, and no actions either. Maybe he was enjoying being close again as much as she was. After several moments of silence he took a shaky breath. "I let her go a long time ago. But I ain't ever forgot."

"I know." She closed her eyes and laced her fingers with his. "You tried to forget. You put them in a box and tried hard as you could."

"Thought I had to. You helped me see I don't."

"Forgetting never helps, it often makes things worse." Of all people, she knew that truth all too well. Forgetting an entire lifetime made you all too aware of how detrimental it can be to forget anything about your past.

"I ain't been fair to you."

"Balderdash." She tried to turn to face him, but he held her tight where she was.

"Let me talk. Please. Before you start arguing again."

The tone had become so serious, she worried over the direction it took. She tried to lighten the mood a little. "You hate words."

"Please."

"All right."

He gave her another squeeze before he released his hold on her.

The suddenness of his absence inched her panic forward more. She wrung her hands until the creak of the bed ropes pulled her gaze his direction. Their apologies were made, he didn't have to say more. She opened her mouth, but her promise to let him speak kept her silent.

"There's something ya need. Something you deserve to hear."

She shook her head so fast she thought it might spin off. "Cole. Don't. You don't have to say anything more."

"Shut up."

Shock stilled her nervous tics and froze her to the spot. "Excuse me?"

"You wanted words. If you wanna hear them you damn well better shut your mouth so's I can talk for a change."

The nervous flutter returned to her hands, but a smile crept its way out from his bold insistence. When he held out his hand she moved closer to take it. Rather than sit next to him, she knelt in front of him where she could see him.

"You're impossible. You're infuriating. Ya get far too fond of the sound of your own voice." He grinned and set his finger on her lips when she opened them to speak. "You never know when to shut up."

She scrunched up her nose. Before he could react, she snapped at his finger and managed to catch it between her teeth. She grinned and held on tight when he tried to pull free. After a minute's struggle she set it free.

He chuckled. "Behave."

She sank back onto her ankles and snorted a reply. Somehow she managed to settle her amusement to sit quiet enough to appease him.

"Ya don't deserve something so one-sided."

All amusement faded over his words. He couldn't really think their relationship was one sided. Another attempt at protest got cut off by his finger again. This time she pushed it aside and rose to her knees. She pressed her forehead to his. Her fingers slipped through his hair before she brushed her lips across his.

How he could believe that their relationship was one-sided, or worry she might feel that way, was well beyond her comprehension. He gave her so much. She longed to say it all, but he'd forbade her to speak.

Long fingers twined through her hair and kept her close. A shuddering breath escaped him.

She couldn't let him suffer. "I know it is not all me, Cole. I've known for a long time. That's all that matters."

"Sometimes ya need the words too."

"Cole. With everything you've done for me, all you went through for me, I couldn't ever doubt it. Words can lie. What you are, what you do? None of that lies."

"I love you." His voice was gruff, and his fingers flexed against her scalp. "Shoulda told you long ago."

A tear slipped down her cheek, salty evidence of her overflowing heart. Her hands slipped along his arms to the hands he still clenched in her hair. She laced her fingers with his. When he opened his eyes, his gaze met hers with intensity she felt down to her toes. She smiled. "You did. Often. In actions."

"Sometimes actions ain't enough."

"Sometimes it's just what I need."

A smile teased the corner of his lips. He finally relaxed enough to respond to the way her fingers laced with his. His grip on her hair lessened so his fingers curled with hers.

"I've never wanted more than you could give. Are you sure you're ready for this?"

This time the smile took full form and he chuckled. Once he'd brushed the tear from her cheek he gave her a soft kiss. "I don't do nothing I don't mean. Thought you knew that by now."

"I do. I just wanted to make sure."

"We done with words now?"

She grinned. "Say it again."

"I love you."

"I love you too. And we are very much done with words."

*There is only one happiness in this life:
to love and be loved.
-George Sand*

"You do still give the best apologies." Jane smiled. Cole lay with his head on her belly, his body still damp with sweat. She trailed her fingers in lazy circles along his back.

"That felt more like you apologizing to me." Cole chuckled warm against her belly.

"Maybe I was a little bit." She giggled. "Of course, I like your responses to my apologies too, so it's a no-lose situation."

"Damn straight." He hauled himself up the bed to lie even with her. One brow quirked, a sexy slow smile forming. "All your apologies almost made me forget what else I wanted to say to you."

"There's more? Oh no, Cole. You really should quit while you're ahead. You can live many years off my apologies after that revelation." The laughter that rose up only got a gentle smack on the ass from him.

He shook his head. "You behave, wicked woman."

"But I prefer actions right now." She thrust her lip out in an attempt at a pout.

"Jane."

She groaned acquiescence. Her body aches made themselves known so she stretched herself from tip to toes. With a heavy sigh she turned toward him, propped on her elbow. "Are you certain? As a man that's better at actions, you must be positive you want to risk attempting more words. It could be detrimental to your health."

"You done?"

"Never."

He pinched her lips shut. "Jane."

"Mmf mmf fmmfmm." She narrowed her eyes over her contained words. The infuriating man only kept her lips pinched shut. "Mmmf!"

"Only if you're nice." At her nod he released his grip.

"I'm not certain I can handle more today. Our argument seems to have spawned some deep thoughts for you. I believe I can only handle one such revelation a day."

"You're gonna have to handle two."

Clearly he wouldn't let things lie nice and easy as they were, no matter how much she begged. With a resigned sigh, she nodded. "Fine. What else do you have to tell me?"

"It's about Graham. The things he said."

She pinched her brows together, unsure whether to be incensed or laugh. "Are you serious? You want to discuss Graham and his idiocy? While we're in bed?"

"No, not him. About what he said. What you say he's doing."

"You mean that he is needling you until you become a bastard? Of course."

The bed creaked when he pushed himself to sit. His back to her, he rested his forearms on his knees. "I ain't stupid."

"I'm sorry. I didn't mean to imply you were."

"Not you. I just—I know what ya do around here. What you've always done. I know what you do for me. I know that everyone in town knows it."

"I don't care what they think they know. I never have." She rose to sit beside him. When she set her hand on his back the tense twitch of his muscles relaxed under her touch.

"I know."

Silence lingered long enough to work her nerves. She pursed her lips against annoyance at the unfinished conversation. "Where are you going with this, Cole?"

"I ain't dumb."

"I know. You've already said that. Like I said, I never thought you were. I believe you're an impossibly mule-headed male at times, but that can't be helped."

"You do all of this. The saloon, the hotel, the girls…me."

"Cole." She leaned in to kiss his shoulder. "I don't mind doing any of those things. If it helps you, that's all that matters."

"That's my point. Ya do it all, and you don't ask for nothing."

"Yes I do."

"No. You really don't."

"I ask for you. All of you. Anything you are willing to give me. It's all I've ever wanted."

She squeezed his arm. His hand covered hers, only to rub along it gently. He met her gaze steady as a rock. "No, it ain't."

"No more than you can give."

"No more lies."

She moved so they were hip to hip, face to face. With a gentle touch, she traced the line of his jaw. She gave him a soft smile. "It's not a lie. I am content. Being with you, fighting with you, making up, and helping out at the saloon and hotel. Knowing that you are happy is enough for me."

"I ain't doing it."

The words could mean so much, she didn't know what to think yet again. Confusion furrowed her brow. If he thought she was telling him she wanted marriage, he was wrong. He'd just spoken his feelings aloud; she wouldn't dare push for me. It wasn't even a factor, as she didn't know if she even wanted such a thing. "I'm sorry. What are you not doing? I haven't asked you to do anything."

"I ain't taking your money. I'm not borrowing it, and I'm not taking it."

Relief flooded her that he hadn't misread her intentions. Then the meaning of what he'd said hit her. "What? What will you do if you can't buy Graham's half of the Inn? It means so much to you. Cole. Don't be foolish."

"I think if it's your money," Cole interrupted her tirade. "It should be you that's doing the buying."

"I…what?"

"I was talking to Mike. He told me about how Nick's his silent partner at the hotel. That he owns most of it, but to help him fund it, Nick put money in." He played with her fingers, lifting them one by one off his arm. "I think we could make it work."

"You do?" She might be capable of a more intelligent answer on a normal today, but the newest revelation stunned her.

"Well, not the silent part. You ain't ever gonna be good at that."

Her protest was quelled by his trailing fingers. Gooseflesh rose as they brushed feather-light up her arm and over her shoulder. She calmed her brain, if not her libido to think about his suggestion. "I don't know if it's a good idea."

"I told ya. I know what you do. I'm not gonna ignore it."

The finger teased along the top of her breast, inching toward her nipple, which peaked in anticipation of his touch. "Business partners." Damn, he'd made her breathless already. "That could muck up…"

His teasing paused. A frown creased his features. "Muck it up? Doubt it."

"Why?"

"Because Graham was right about one thing." He smirked. "A first for him, no doubt."

A snort found its way through the haze of his touch now that it had stopped. "They do say there is a first time for everything."

"He said you've been running this place since you first stepped in. You have. I ain't ever stopped you before."

She dropped back onto her elbows. With the shock worn off, amusement found its way back into her heart. "I wouldn't exactly say *never*."

"What I mean is, we don't fight no more or less when you're helping me out than when you're not. That's all." He resumed his teasing touch, this time along her thigh. Gentle tingles of pleasure swept right up to her core. "Being partner now, I'd have more reason to listen—after all, you'd need it to work as much as I do."

"I'll have to think about it." She certainly couldn't think about it now. Not with his touch burning her libido more than her brain cells.

"You still want words? Or do you want my points made in actions?"

"Actions, please." Every nerve ending sprang to life as he responded to her request with fingers and lips. She sought purchase and dug her nails into his shoulders as her body trembled under the onslaught of pleasure.

Experience gave him intimate knowledge of every spot that inflamed her passion, and he made good use of each of them until her head spun and moans filled the room. By the time his lips found hers she felt intoxicated again, but this time by desire.

A familiar, unrushed rhythm took hold as they joined together again.

Someone pounded on the door with enough force to make the wood crack. The building flame cooled into annoyance at the interruption.

Cole practically growled. "Go away."

"Cole." Graham's voice boomed through the door. "Get on outta your woman and get out here. We got big trouble."

Jane's fists clenched as they both tensed under the intrusion. "Graham, go away."

A loud crash followed by a gunshot made them both jump. Cole snarled. He grasped her closer as if to protect her. "Damn it."

"Go." She pushed on his chest. "You can be down there faster. I'll be right behind you."

Cole sprang from the bed. He cursed as he shoved his feet into trousers. In under a minute, he stormed toward the door, sans shirt. Soon as he wrenched it open, Graham stood on the other side. He leaned in far enough Jane could see him, unusual for the way the room was situated, and obviously intentional.

Jane snapped the sheet around her to cover up under Graham's leer.

"What's going on?" Cole leaned toward Graham until the man moved back into the hall.

"What did I tell you? I knew you'd cave." There was a scuffle and a loud thump.

Jane grabbed some clothes and rushed behind the curtain they used as a closet. Despite her speed, she managed to catch a glimpse of Graham shoved into the wall, Cole's hands tight on his collar.

By the time she stepped out from behind the curtain, Cole had disappeared. Graham remained in the hallway, though. Somehow the man didn't seem to hear, or care about, the cacophony of yells, shouts, and screams from the floor below.

On the way past Graham, she stopped to face him. The second he opened his mouth, she slapped him before he could emit whatever insult his pea-sized brain had come up with. "I hope I never have a friend like you. You're a jackass."

He rubbed his face with his beefy hand. Though his gaze was dark, he nodded behind her. "Think there's bigger problems to be worrying about."

She spun in time to see a couple leaving their room, bags in hand. That didn't bode well. Not that she blamed them with the chaos that had erupted downstairs. She rushed forward, determined to make it right. "Folks. Please. It's awful late to be checking out."

"We will not be staying where guns are fired off at all hours," the gentleman snapped as he ushered his wife past Jane. "This is supposed to be a hotel."

"I apologize. Sometimes the gentlemen in the saloon get a little overzealous. We usually do everything we can to prevent such occurrences, but tonight our…staff proved incapable. Mr. Mitchell is taking care of the situation right now. Things are calming down."

"It shouldn't have happened at all. We'll be finding a real hotel. One without any likelihood of such events."

Out of habit, Jane smiled as bright as possible to mask her burgeoning anger. If Graham had taken action instead of chasing after Cole, this might never have happened. "That isn't necessary. I assure you it won't happen again. To make up for your fright, we'll cover your meals at Cora's for the rest of your stay."

They both hesitated at the added incentive. The wife elbowed the husband gently. The eyed each other for a long moment. He frowned at her miniscule nod. "It won't happen again?"

"On my honor. If it does—we'll cover your room at the Sage Brush Hotel or the boarding house." Jane barely managed to keep from flinching at the expensive promise and hoped her bother Mike would cut her a deal if it became necessary. Holding steady, she let them discuss it between themselves for a few minutes. Her shoulders relaxed at their nod. She shook their hands and guided them back to their room.

Once their door closed, Graham came up behind her. "Sure didn't take you long to start acting like you own the place again."

She straightened her shoulders. His proximity and the alcohol on his breath caused a sliver of fear down her back. "You are the one choosing to sell. I don't care for your opinions any longer, Graham. Every day you're proving a bigger idiot."

"Jane," Cole called from the now almost silent room below.

She rushed to the railing to find a frightening sight. Cole stood there covered in blood, she gasped at the rush of fear that filled her. Panic sped her feet until she'd rushed downstairs into the saloon in no time flat. "Cole!"

"It's Mel's, not mine." He wiped his forehead with the back of his wrist. "They got him over at the clinic now."

"Heavens, no. What the hell is going on?"

"Someone claimed Mel was stacking the deck." Graham made his way through the tables and chairs toward them. "Started fighting. That's when I came up to get you."

"You didn't think to stop the fight?" Jane narrowed her eyes. "Maybe protect the bar and its patrons, rather than trying to stir up more trouble with Cole?"

"Eddie was helping. I thought Cole might want to know what was going on." Graham folded his arms across his chest.

Cole shook his head. He uselessly wiped the blood on his hands on his trousers. "As usual, you're useless. Get out, Graham."

"I still own—"

"Jane!" Iris sobbed in her rush across the room. Her clothes were disheveled, her eyes wide with shock. "Mel?"

"Oh heavens. Iris. Of course, go on. Go be with him." Jane waved her toward the door. "Go ahead. Let us know what's going on."

Iris threw her arms around Jane in a tight hug. After a second, she darted out of the saloon.

Both Graham and Cole stared slack-jawed after the departing whore.

Jane set her hands on her hips. "What?"

"What the hell was that about?" Graham's scowl deepened. "Where's she going?"

"She's going to wait on word about Mel, of course." If the situation were different, Jane might have been amused by the complete lack of comprehension on the men's features. "Don't tell me you two are so blind you didn't know."

Cole's lips pursed. "Apparently we are."

"They've been all-but courting for months now. I told them it was fine if it did nothing to disrupt business as usual. Iris has no desire to get out of her contract—but they appear to care for each other. I'm not about to—"

"What gives you the right?" Graham took a threatening step toward her. "You never had that kind of say."

"She sure did. You said so yourself." Cole set one hand on his hip, but in his rush to leave the room he'd left his holster behind. After he grasped for the missing gun, he took a step closer to Jane. "She's been acting like she was partner since she got here. I sure ain't about to tell her she can't do nothing so long as it's good for business."

Graham snorted. "No account woman whipped you."

Jane rolled her eyes when Cole grabbed Graham and shoved him against the bar. "Would the two of you knock it off? Graham—you want out for the same reason Cole wants me in. Your woman has you as hog-tied as you claim Cole is. Big difference is, I don't make him do something he doesn't want to."

Graham shoved off Cole and stormed toward Jane. "You stupid cunt."

She punched him in the nose without even thinking. The whole thing happened so fast; she'd only had the thought to stop him. The crack of impact in her hand made her wince. She bit her lip to cover the whimper.

With a glare at Graham, she pulled her left hand close against her chest. The change in position eased the waves of pain. "Just because you didn't want to sell in the first place is no reason to attack Cole or I at every opportunity. If you're that mad, tell your wife. If you're too yellow to tell your woman how you really feel, it's you that's been whipped by a woman, not Cole."

Blood poured from Graham's nose. He wiped it away with his arm. "You stupid little—"

"Get the *hell* out." Cole didn't move, his voice darker than it had been in weeks. He moved in a protective stance in front of Jane. "We've got more than enough chaos around here tonight. Don't need no more of your lip adding to it."

Jane clenched her jaw and returned Graham's glare. Once he'd turned to storm off, she sagged in relief. The throbbing in her hand eased so long as she kept it clutched to her chest. "That was not my most intelligent move."

"It was too little too late." Cole wrapped his arm around her waist. They walked through the saloon to the bar amid the staff cleaning up the mess. "We should have Charlie or Daisy come check on your hand."

"No. They have to worry about Mel. I can wait, he can't." She sat with a sigh; her hand pressed against her chest. "It doesn't hurt so much, really. It was just really stupid."

"But funny."

She slapped him with her right hand in an attempt at offense. Her own humor drew a snort anyway. "I still have another hand. I could punch you too."

"Nah. You need at least one good hand." He stepped closer still. His hand slipped around her waist to draw her tight against him. "At least I'd appreciate it if ya had one good hand."

"Cole Mitchell."

"You're smiling." He tapped her gently on the ass. "That means you're gonna live. I'm gonna go wash off the blood, get my weapon, and check on the cleanup. Then we'll see about getting that hand looked at."

"It can wait. You have more pressing matters." With a nod to the upper level, she frowned. "The couple you have in room four almost left. I had to promise free meals at Cora's, and that if a weapon discharged again, to pay for a room elsewhere."

"Well. Ain't that dandy."

She flinched. "Sorry. I thought it was better to keep them around than lose them."

"Nah. Not mad at you. It's just that we get someone in here for a room instead of just time with a whore for once— and almost lose 'em over a poker game."

"That's not all." She clutched her arm beneath the wrist to stem the ache traveling down. A deep sigh wrenched from her belly as she brought up the courage to state her fears. "Something is going on here. I have no idea what, but it's like someone is out to shut this place down."

"Why would you say that?"

"Just think about all we're dealing with here. You lost three whores last month. Two so far this month. While you managed to obtain new ones, we have three more issues. Not to mention Pansy."

The open concern and curiosity in his features hardened to anger in less than a heartbeat. "What do you mean, issues?"

Jane pinched her lip between her teeth. Knowing it would be best to say it fast and have it over, and actually doing it were two different things. With a deep breath she barreled forward. "Rose and Heather have been on the opium, heavy handed with it, even. Violet's pregnant. Pansy didn't just acquire opium tonight; she spent time with Gus Warren. She's supposed to be abstaining right now. I'd hedge my bets that she didn't use her veil."

Stock still, not even an eyelid twitched on Cole's face.

She reached out a hesitant hand to touch his. "Cole?"

"*What*?"

"Shh," Jane snapped. She clutched his hand to keep him where he was. After one deep, long exhale, she released her grip. "We'll talk about it more once the saloon is closed. Don't do anything rash. We have more to deal with right now."

His jaw clenched, but he nodded. "If we're gonna wrap that hand, you need a drink."

"I don't believe I could right now if I wanted to." The simple suggestion made her stomach turn. "If I had a drink right now I'd likely throw it up all over you."

"Why would ya do that? You can handle a drink."

"I can. However, last night I tried to handle too much." Heat flooded her cheeks under his blatant stare. She turned her attention to the cleanup as if it were the most interesting thing in the world. "I got drunk."

"You don't get drunk."

"I did last night."

He touched her chin gently to pull her gaze back to his furrowed brow. "Why?"

"I was upset." She wanted to lower her eyes but kept them steady right where they were. "Which, I believe, was your intention."

"What?" His eyes widened. For the first time she could remember, his cheeks obtained a ruddy hue. "Oh. Right."

"Yes. Right."

"I knew you'd be back. Leastwise, I thought I did until your brother came in here shooting my damn door open."

She blinked to cover her shock. "I'm sorry. I don't think I heard you correctly. My brother did what?"

"Charlie. Damn fool came in here shooting the door down to get your stuff. He called me a damn fool."

"You are."

A chuckle preceded his pinch to her thigh. "Behave."

"You don't like it when I behave."

"Anyhow, he got me thinking maybe you might not come back. Said you asked for your books back and all. I sure didn't want that." For a second his expression softened to one usually reserved to private moments. An expression that bespoke of the love he'd only just managed to express in words. He brushed a curl from her cheek. "Figured I'd best try to make it right."

"I'd say you succeeded."

"What happened here?" Al's surprised voice carried easily through the half empty saloon. Like magic it worked to tense Cole right back up.

Jane kicked Cole in the shin. When he frowned, she stuck her tongue out at him. She spoke in his silence, "Someone didn't appreciate losing. They shot Mel."

Cole stepped closer to Jane, one arm possessively behind her. With the arrival of Al, he seemed to have forgotten he needed to get cleaned up. "We're waiting on word from the docs."

"Your hand." Al's brow furrowed. "Jane. It's swollen. Is that a bruise?"

"Hmm?" She looked down in surprise. Sure enough her hand had swelled quite a bit and darkened to a deep shade of purple. "Well, look at that—it is swollen. It hardly hurts at all."

"She finally gave Graham what-for." Cole managed a chuckle. "He sure as hell deserved it. Think she broke his nose."

"I hope I did." When Al stepped closer, she shook her head. "Never you mind, it's nothing to worry about. I've been through worse. I told you, it doesn't hurt at the moment. I'm quite certain I'll live."

Al frowned. "What about the shooter?"

"Davie already took him in." Cole tapped his fingers on the bar. "He was drunk as all get out. Kept saying someone told him Mel was fixing the game."

"I should check on Iris." Jane slipped off the stool. "We should probably do something about the stragglers. Send them home."

"No. People want a drink after something like this." Cole rubbed her arm. "I should get changed and get behind the bar. You rest that hand."

"I told you it's fine." Jane's protest got interrupted by a loud sob at the door. All three of them turned to find Charlie supporting Iris as they entered the bar. He offered a solemn shake of his head and Jane's heart sank. "Oh no."

"He was shot point blank." Charlie kept guiding Iris through the tables toward the back. "There wasn't anything Daisy and I could do."

"Oh, Iris." Jane slid off the stool and crossed to the pair. With her good hand, she offered as much support as she could when Iris transferred her grief to Jane's shoulder. At Charlie's offer to keep helping, Jane only shook her head. She led Iris back to the whores' room, where the rest of the girls met them.

Before long, Jane could be assured Iris was being seen to and comforted, so Jane returned to the saloon. She sat at the bar, vaguely noticing Cole now wore a shirt and his holster. Her mind had turned into a blurry haze. A glass of whiskey was pushed into her hands, but she just stared at the amber liquid.

A flash of pain shot up her arm, disrupting her stupor. She let out a surprised yelp. "Ow. Damn it, Charles. What are you doing?"

"All I did was pull your arm away from your chest. I hear you punched a no-good bastard in the nose tonight." Charlie's mustache twitched. "I see the hand is swollen, and that bruise is looking relatively nasty."

"It was fine until you started messing with, *ow*." She sucked air in through her teeth when he moved her thumb. The hand hadn't hurt her much at all while she'd kept it close. Now every time he moved it a little it throbbed more.

"Of all the things you forgot, you had to forget how to throw a punch without breaking your hand?" Charlie tsked. "Careless."

"I don't choose which memor—ow, ow, ow, ow, *ow.*" She gritted her teeth as he worked his way through her fingers, moving each one. "One insult at a time, please. Physical or verbal."

Charlie chuckled. "Cole says you worked things out. What happened to wanting your books back?"

"I think I'd prefer the insults," Jane muttered. Her teeth clenched in a weak attempt to keep from flinching. "Over this brotherly crap."

"You sure about this?" His gaze carried across the saloon where Cole worked to direct the cleanup operation.

Heat rose to her cheeks, but she smiled as Cole managed to handle cleanup and entertaining the remaining customers to keep them where they were. Grateful for the distraction from the influx of pain Charlie appeared content to foist on her, she sighed. "I'm sure. I've known I loved him for a long time."

"What about his latest fit of temperament?"

"It wasn't about what I thought it was. Now that I know what it *was* about…" Yes, having him upset at himself over his own limitations and taking it out on her wasn't her favorite thing—however, the resolution to that matter definitely was. "Well, I'm quite certain."

"Now you've got me curious."

"'Curiosity is only vanity. Most frequently we wish not to know, but to talk'. Blaise Pascal." Jane pulled her hand back to her chest when he released it, and little by little the throbbing started to subside. "So brush it aside."

Charlie pulled a roll of bandages from his medical bag. "'Curiosity is one of the permanent and certain characteristics of a'—"

"*Ow.*" She jumped when he pulled her hand back and straightened her thumb.

"'Vigorous mind'." Charlie grinned and began to wrap her hand through her winces of pain. Not even her string of strong curses made him blink. "Samuel Johnson."

"What's the word doc?" Cole walked up in the middle of Jane's colorful protest. "Sounds like you're torturing her over here."

"He is." Jane groaned. She dropped her head back on Cole's chest with a heavy sigh. Once again the pain had reached levels that brought tears to her eyes, but Charlie didn't stop wrapping for a second. He worked fast, but not fast enough to make it not hurt.

"She managed to break her hand. If she's careful, and allows regular medical care by myself or Daisy, she should heal in some weeks." Charlie made one last wrap around the wrist, and braced the bandage with a knot.

"Some weeks?" Jane frowned and yanked her hand close again.

"It depends. It'll be at least a month, probably more. Used to treat these all the time, with the fools that thought boxing a good sport. Most of the time they didn't know how to punch right." Charlie squeezed her shoulder, "That means you'll have to write as Clara did for a while—with your right hand."

She wrinkled her nose and groaned. "Oh, that's awful."

"For those of us trying to read it, it is." Cole grunted when she elbowed him in the stomach. "Any other restrictions?"

"Just don't hurt her again." Charlie's features lost all hint of humor when he snapped the medical bag shut. He put his hat back on and kissed Jane's cheek. "I know it's unappealing after your bout last night, but take a shot of whiskey. It'll help with the pain. I know me playing with it hurt."

"Damn straight." Jane pursed her lips, and pulled her hand closer like he might try again. "Go away, you horrible doctor. I'll go see Daisy, thank you very much. She's a doctor I trust."

"Love you too, Jane."

She sighed and set her hand on Cole's where it rested on her shoulder. "Well, wasn't this a wonderful night?"

"Wasn't all bad."

"No. I guess it wasn't." A small smile broke through the pain and sorrow. She tilted her neck to look up at him. "I know we still have a lot to talk about, but please, no more hell tonight."

"No more hell."

*Love is composed of a single soul
inhabiting two bodies.
—Aristotle*

"Jane?" David sounded far away, muffled and dim. That didn't make any sense.

She jolted awake with a start. Her hands pressed into the hard wood of a table. She used it to push herself upright. Sleep clung to her like a blanket. "What?'

A warm hand settled on her shoulder. "Jane. Are you all right?"

Jane tried to laugh off the incident, but had to wipe a spot of drool from the corner of her lip before she adjusted herself in her chair. "I apologize, David. I fell asleep. I'm afraid my night was far from restful."

"I'm well aware of what happened last night." David laughed. "There's no need for concern. Although Cora might take it as an insult that you fell asleep without eating her delicious lunch."

Of all the places to fall asleep, she'd done so in the middle of Cora's restaurant. Several quiet snickers came from a nearby table of saloon patrons. She hushed them best as she could.

"May we join you?"

"We?" Jane managed to wake up even more and noticed the pretty young woman beside David. She smiled at the blonde and nodded. "Of course. I'd love the company to help me keep awake. How are you, Lee?"

Lee took the chair Jane gestured to. "Good afternoon, Jane. I'm well."

"I'm pleased to hear it. I heard Cora say you aren't going to be working in the restaurant any longer." Jane smiled. "Does that mean you found another job?"

"I did, actually. I'll be assisting—oh my, what happened to your hand?" Lee reached toward the bandaged hand. Before she actually touched it, she stopped short.

David sat down with coffee for both himself and Lee. A frown creased his features. "Jane? What's this?"

"It's nothing." Jane tugged her hand back to her lap, even though keeping it there hurt the worst. "Nothing at all. Lee, you were telling me about your new job."

David's eyes grew wide. "Wait a minute. If I'm not mistaken, we spotted Graham looking rather like a raccoon this morning. Does that have anything to do with this?"

"You're right. Graham did have two black eyes this morning." Lee gasped and turned to Jane again. "Did you break his nose?"

"And my hand," Jane admitted ruefully.

David started laughing too hard to even speak. Lee merely shook her head. "What happened? From all I've heard, he may have had it coming."

"I was getting…I was…" Every attempt at explanation got punctuated by another loud guffaw from David. Jane reached across herself to smack his leg. "David, would you hush?"

At another admonishment from Lee, David made some attempt to gather himself together.

Jane frowned. "I grew tired of Graham's incredibly small grasp of the English language when it came to describing his opinion of me."

Lee's brow puckered. "What?"

"He was cursing at her." David's laughter eased into a chuckle. "If my guess is correct, he was most likely calling her all sorts of unseemly names."

"He certainly tried to." Jane shrugged. "But besides that, I was tired of him being an idiot about giving up the Hangman's Inn. He doesn't want to sell out his shares, his hand is being forced, and I understand that—but he's blaming Cole and myself, or at least using us as a target for his anger."

"So." Lee's valiant attempt to conceal her grin failed. Her bright smile flashed as she leaned closer. "You punched him? That's so scandalous."

"She should have done so a long time ago, by my way of thinking." David snorted when Jane did a double take. "I give him all the credit in the world for saving you from being buried alive. However, when it comes to the Hangman's Inn, he's never been exactly…"

"He despises the way Cole lets me have any say in the business when he is supposed to be partner," Jane finished for him. "And he *really* hates that even though it's been well over a year since he destroyed the place, Cole still doesn't trust him. Graham sees me as the cause of their friendship weakening. I make a very good target."

"Apparently not as good a target as Graham's nose." Lee covered her mouth as soon as the words had left it. As she lowered them, a sheepish smile remained in reaction to Jane's outright laughter. "Sorry. I had no intention of saying such a thing out loud."

"Don't apologize." Jane pressed her hand to her side as her corset made the depth of her laughter uncomfortable. Despite her pain, it felt damn good to laugh. "I've said far worse with far less regret. I'm only upset that I didn't think of it first."

"She means that, too." David chuckled. He nodded at Jane's hand. "So, what are you going to tell Jesse about this?"

"I hadn't thought about that yet, to be honest. I'm still surprised it's happened." Jane brought her hand close to her chest again to ease the ache. Now confronted with the problem, she found herself torn. "I, um…I supposed I could tell him I fell. I'd rather be honest—but I know you wouldn't want him thinking it's all right to walk around punching people."

"You don't do it *all* the time." Lee grinned. "Only on special occasions. At least, this is the first I've heard of you doing such a thing."

"She does have a point." David nodded. "I suppose you'll know what to say when he does ask what happened."

"Speaking of Jesse, where is he?" Jane straightened. "I thought he'd be with you today."

"He was. He'd planned to join us, but Isaac wanted to go fishing. Arthur got a basket of food together and took Jesse and Cindy along. I dare say Cindy is quite a bit like Kat. I think she was actually excited to dig up the worms." David sighed. "I wanted to go, but I had to be at the jail."

"And Norman wanted to go, but Kat's working at the library this morning and couldn't watch the depot," Lee added. "Not that the boys mind. If they've got a fish hook and a creek filled with fish, they're thrilled."

Jane gasped and flew to her feet. "Drat! Katherine. I was supposed to be at the library by now. I'm sorry, I have to run."

David half rose, but sank back down when Jane waved off the polite gesture. "I'm sure Kat will understand."

"I know she will." Jane pushed her chair back in place. She leaned in with a conspiratorial grin. "She'll not be upset I'm late, she'll be upset because she's waiting for details about what happened last night and I've kept her waiting for several hours. Sorry to rush off. You two enjoy your lunch."

Without another word, Jane darted from the restaurant. She only waved in passing to greetings from others until a sharp whistle stopped her short right outside the Inn. One brow rose when Cole crooked a finger at her. She smirked. "What?"

"Come here."

"It will take much more than that magnificent digit to get me over there."

"Magnificent?"

"Well. It certainly was last night."

Cole burst into laughter, the loud chortle only barely covered the horrified gasp beside Jane. His head tilted and he offered a wicked grin and a wink to whomever had gasped. "Something wrong, Mrs. Garrett?"

"Only that her husband isn't as generous as you are." Jane tried to contain her own wicked enjoyment, but knew she failed miserably. "Or have such talented hands."

"Indecent." Mrs. Garrett lifted her nose in a haughty glare.

"Sorry to have insulted your husband and his attendance to marital matters, Mrs. Garrett. The truth can be painful, I know." Jane leaned closer to the woman. She meant to whisper, but her glee made her voice louder than intended. "Have your husband ask Cole for advice. I promise you won't regret it."

Red rushed into Mrs. Garrett's cheeks so fast Jane feared she might have forgotten to breathe. Her mouth opened and closed several times like a fish out of water before she turned away. "I never!"

"It's nothing to be ashamed of, Mrs. Garrett. Pleasures should be enjoyed. Have a lovely afternoon." Jane shrugged. When she turned back she spotted Cole stepping off the porch. Every step he took she mirrored with one of her own until they were in each other's arms.

He half-lifted her off the ground in his enthusiasm.

Despite the heat and fire they each poured into the kiss, by the time they separated they were both chuckling.

"You're downright wicked, you know that?" Cole's blue eyes shone with laughter.

"I most certainly do. Do you mind?"

"Hell, no."

"Mrs. Garrett is new in town. It's only appropriate that introduce myself properly." She stood on tip toe to brush her lips across his again. "That means adding enough just enough lecherous and scandalous activity to make her giddy."

"That didn't look giddy."

"Of course it was. Didn't you know? As Josh Billings said – 'old maids sweeten their tea with scandal'." She giggled at the doubt lining his brow. "It's important to look offended so they might properly revel in the depths of the gossip at a later time. Only proper women are offended enough to balk and then turn around and talk about it."

"That ain't what you do, though." He tugged her tight against him. "Seem like you and Kathy only gossip 'bout me and Norman."

"I am no old maid, no matter my age. I'd much rather be upfront about my opinions of people than to gossip behind their back. The expression on their faces when you tell them how you truly feel is far more fun."

He laughed again. "Wicked."

"I've heard no complaints from you in regards to my wickedness."

"Why don't you come in and remind me how much I appreciate it?"

"Nice try, Mr. Mitchell, but I am supposed to be at the library. What's more, you can't leave the bar unmanaged."

"Who says I'd be leaving the bar?"

She smacked him in the chest, doing her best to emit a shocked gasp through her laughter. The blast of pain that shot through her hand wiped away the amusement. She winced and groaned. Instinct had led to her hitting him with her injured hand. "Oh, ow. Look what you made me do. Shame on you."

"You ain't supposed to be using that hand."

"Gee. Thank you for the advice." She pursed her lips and smacked him with her uninjured hand. "Get yourself back to work. I have to work as well. I promise that tonight we will have plenty of time to be wicked together."

"That's a promise I'm gonna see you keep."

She wrapped her arms around his waist. When he did the same, she pressed into him. "You'd better."

"If you really meant to leave, you'd better stop rubbing against me and do it now. Or we'll end up beyond indecent right here in the middle of the street."

"And that pushes even my rather broad limits of decency." She stepped away with a small sigh. Before she'd gone two steps he grabbed her wrist and yanked her close. She yelped as he held her tight. "Cole."

He cut her off with his lips, plunging his tongue into her still-open mouth. Tugging her even closer, he dragged out the kiss until her body trembled and a deep moan escaped.

When he pulled away she found herself gasping for air. She stared up at him with wide eyes. His thumb brushed along her lips and her eyes fluttered shut. She managed to find a whisper of a voice, "Not fair."

"It ain't just you that wasn't fair to." He turned her away, but she didn't miss his groan. With a smack to her ass that made her yelp, he grinned. "Get outta here. I'm supposed to be working, you wicked woman."

She adjusted the bustle he'd shifted with the slap and muttered, "Right. I'm going."

The rest of the way to the library she fought with the bustle using her less-capable, but uninjured hand. Right at the door it felt straight again so she smoothed her overskirt and opened the door.

"*Where* have you been? I've been waiting." Kat rose, her laughter erasing her attempts at scolding. "You appear to be in an even better mood than when I saw you this morning, and that's saying something."

"I fell asleep in Cora's and then got stopped by Cole on my way here." Even Jane could feel how deep the fire red heat burned her cheeks when Kat's eyes widened.

"Jane Doe Spencer! Just now?"

"No." Jane shook her head with a laugh. "Not that. We just—well. We were in the street so we didn't get quite so far as a complete public display."

Kat waved her closer, still shaking her head. She offered Jane her chair and took the one on the other side of the desk. "All right. Sit. Tell me everything. All you told me this morning was that you made up and left me knowing you had big news. So please, don't keep me waiting any longer."

"I hardly know where to begin." Jane fiddled with the bandage on her hand, honestly flummoxed at which part to tell Kat first. So much had happened. The smile she tried to contain refused to budge an inch. "I guess first we'll talk business, then pleasure."

"Business?"

"He told me he wouldn't borrow the money from me."

"What? But why in heavens not? Because you're a woman?"

"Because he wants me to buy Graham out and become his business partner."

Kat didn't budge. Her mouth sat open, her eyes wide.

"Are you trying to catch flies?"

After a quick shake of her head, Kat smiled. "I'm just—I guess—I'm surprised. Cole really suggested you buy Graham's part of the business?"

"I couldn't believe it either, but he said he wouldn't ignore what I do at the Inn any longer. He wants to acknowledge it for what it is, and what I am to the business."

"Of course, all of this was said in Cole-speak. Yes?"

Jane snorted. "Yes. In Cole-speak."

"Partners?"

"Yes. Business partners. I told him I'd think about it."

"Hogwash."

"Katherine."

"You're already picking out new curtains for the rooms and dresses for the whores. I know you, Jane."

Jane focused on her hands rather than acknowledge her friends spot-on guess. Her smile tried to force its way out, despite her efforts.

"I knew it." Kat's laughter showed how much Jane had failed to hide it.

"All right, all right." Jane shook her head, but joined in Kat's vocal amusement. "So I've been thinking about how to class up the girls. I was doing that long before he asked me to be a partner, so that doesn't count."

"Of course not. Whatever you say." Kat left the chair to perch on the desk. She focused on Jane with a calculating eye. "So, keep going. What else is there? You said business and then pleasure. Just what pleasure are you talking about? And please don't be too explicit, I do have the most delicate ears."

Jane guffawed. "Of course you do."

"So?"

Leaning in close, Jane lowered her voice. "First off he said it wasn't fair that things were so one-sided. And then he said—oh, good afternoon Mrs. Cooke." Jane rose when Graham's wife entered the library.

"Good afternoon." Becky disregarded them immediately to focus on the shelves.

Jane squeezed Kat's hand and whispered, "Sorry. It's going to have to wait."

Kat murmured, "Great timing. Somehow I think you were just getting to the good part of the story."

"Oh, it was all good." Jane chuckled, but then sighed. "At least for a couple hours."

Kat frowned and took the seat across the desk from Jane. "It's just awful what happened. I can't believe that man shot Mel. It wasn't even true."

"Iris is distraught." Jane leaned back in her chair and tapped her finger on the arm. "I couldn't imagine if that had happened to Cole."

When she shuddered, Kat leaned forward. "It didn't."

"I know. I just—I don't know how to help her."

"She'll get through it, I'm sure. Now what in heavens happened to your hand? You didn't have time to explain this morning, and I'm really dying to know."

Jane glanced at Becky and bit her lip. Unsure how much Graham might have told his wife, Jane decided to downplay the incident. She lowered her voice and shrugged. "I broke it when I hit something hard."

"What? What on earth would you hit that was that hard?"

"A hard head."

Kat's brow furrowed. "Who's hard head?"

Becky froze with a book half pulled from a shelf when Kat's voice echoed through the small library.

Jane groaned and gave Kat a pointed look. She forced a smile on her face and stood when Becky took a few steps toward the desk. "Was there something I could help you find, Mrs. Cooke?"

"No. I've found what I need, thank you." Becky set the book on the desk, eying Jane's hand when she kept it close to her chest. She frowned. "I wasn't trying to eavesdrop—"

"I'm quite certain you weren't. After all, you are above such activities, are you not?" Jane clenched her jaw at her own seething sarcasm. She finished checking the book out. There was no smile to be found, even a forced one, when she handed the book to Becky. "Here you go. Please have it back in two weeks. If you wish to keep it longer, please let me know."

"You're the one that injured my husband?"

She'd said it so formal Jane almost laughed.

Becky had always been proper, painfully so. When Cole had bothered to spend time with the woman to learn how to read, she'd almost died of embarrassment when he'd asked her to teach him using Leaves of Grass.

Still, just like Graham, since the wedding there'd been a change in Becky as well. She'd become even more proper, haughtier.

Beside the woman, Kat hid her grin behind her hand.

Jane didn't crack a smile, even at Kat's amusement. She stood tall and met Becky's disapproving gaze without hesitation. After a nod, she held the book out further to encourage the woman to take it. "Yes. Did he not tell you?"

Becky took the book finally. She hesitated with it in mid-air as she glanced at Jane's injured hand again. Then she drew up tall and lifted her chin. "I heard there was an incident."

"By that I gather he told you he was injured during the tragic events that occurred at the saloon last night. Perhaps he told you he made a valiant effort to stop the man that shot Mel?" Jane somehow found a smile, though there was no joy or humor behind it. "Or did he just mention the incident and let you draw your own conclusions?"

"He didn't correct me." Becky drew the book close to her chest.

"Or course he didn't. Why would he?" Jane shook her head. "He'd rather you didn't know that I am the one that broke his nose, and he certainly wouldn't want you to know why it happened."

"You actually broke his nose?" Kat's eyes grew wide and she sat straighter.

"Why would you do such a thing?" Becky's eyes narrowed. "It isn't your place."

"Is it *his* place to insult me at every turn? To call me names that I'm sure are above your tolerance level?" Jane leaned on the desk with a smirk. "Of course, it's easier to blame me because I'm such a soiled and sinful creature. I couldn't possibly be anything else than a wretch, could I?"

"You broke his nose."

"Mrs. Cooke. I had no problems with Graham for a long time after we met. Once I started staying at the saloon and helping Cole out more, I dare say we even became friendly, right up until about eight months ago, coincidentally." The insinuation was a low blow, but Jane couldn't help herself. "I suppose the stipulation for the wedding must have been that he had to end his business partnership."

"Our private life is none of your concern."

"It is when he uses it to add onto his anger at me and then insult me at every turn. I am not perfect, and I've never claimed to be. My faults are many, but so are Graham's. I imagine you have a few faults of your own."

Becky's nostrils flared. "Some of your flaws are more like sins."

Jane's smile grew tight. "I'm a tolerant person and I put up with Graham's insults for a long time. I put up with his threats to make my hanging more painful and lingering. I abide his continuing drunken behavior after swearing to Cole he wouldn't drink while working behind the bar again."

"He doesn't still drink." Becky's eyes widened. "He promised."

"He still drinks." Jane sighed. "I wish I could tell you different. I understand why you want him out of the business and away from the saloon, but you and your father are forcing him to do it. No man likes being forced to do anything, especially one with a temper like Graham's. So he's taking out all of his anger on myself, and on Cole—who was his best friend for many years."

"It is best that he gets away from that negative influence."

"I do hope you mean the alcohol."

"I don't."

"Me? Or Cole?" Jane guffawed and shook her head. "Oh, of course. The combination of the two of us is so much more powerful. There's something you just don't understand, Becky."

"I believe I understand enough. You and Cole live in sin, and with sin. It's immorality that causes the soul to weaken."

"You believe my soul is weak?"

"I believe that is between you and God."

"God and I are fine. Thank you." Jane straightened again. The state of her soul had been something she'd struggled with for too long for Becky's words to have any painful meaning to her. "I'm used to being judged for my choices in life, but even those that judge me don't act as condemnatory as you and have come to see that despite where I live and with whom I live, I am not a devil."

Jane raised her hand at Becky's gasped protest. "You and your husband can't even be honest with each other, how is that a strong marriage? How will your soul fare after years of lies?"

"I am honest with my husband."

"You manipulate your husband. You use your father to do it, to make choices for him and force his hand when he doesn't behave to your standards. Cole and I may not be married, but I would never do that to him."

"The things you do. In the open. You help him sell those women. You."

Kat had fallen silent, looking between the women with wide eyes. This time she ended on Jane, blinking in surprise.

"I don't care for that aspect of the business, but the fact is, it's a reality. Men are allowed their pleasures, and they take them when they can get them. If at all possible, I send them home to their wives, but many of those miners have no wives." Jane shrugged. "I'd rather be rid of all the whores, but the hotel can't seem to reach that point since it keeps losing any profit to repairs."

"Graham needs to be far from that depravity. We are going to start a family."

"I heard. You told him so, and that's why the sudden rush to sell after six months of waffling. I wholeheartedly agree that Graham should be away from the temptation of the liquor since he can't seem to control himself, but has he ever told you how much he *hates* selling out?"

"He'll be better for it in the end."

"An angry and bitter man doesn't make a better man." Jane frowned and looked down at the desk. "Cole and I may not be married, but we care deeply for each other. We're beyond honest—there is no deception, no covering who we are. All of our faults are revealed; we do not cover them in the belief that our bond isn't enough to conquer them. Your husband is too afraid to tell you that he still craves alcohol, that he misses the friend he had in Cole, and that he doesn't want to leave the inn."

Becky straightened her shoulders. "Sin is sin."

"'Above all, love each other deeply, because love conquers a multitude of sins. Offer hospitality to one another without grumbling'. First Peter, Chapter four, verses eight and nine." Jane quirked a brow when Becky startled. "I am intelligent, I'm loving, and generally I am a very accepting person. I don't have room to judge others, and I would rather leave the final judgment up to God."

Jane took a deep, bracing breath. "I don't know if you love your husband, but you're asking him to give up more than a business partnership. You're asking him to give up a friendship he's had for years."

"I gave up teaching to be his wife. If he gives up a friendship that has not benefited his life in any way, that's his choice."

"Fine." Jane nodded quietly. "But do not judge me again. I would rather live as I am with my family and many friendships all filled with love than isolated with just one whom I might not even love."

Becky turned and left the library without another word. Silence fell, drifting between the remaining friends like the dust motes catching the sunlight.

"He told me he loved me." Jane whispered. "He actually said the words."

"Damn."

"Yes. Damn."

*The most thoroughly wasted of all days is
that on which one has not laughed.
-Chamfort*

Cole's loud laughter greeted Jane as soon as she stepped out of their room. The annoyance that had formed upon waking to see the late hour only grew at his apparent glee. She stomped down the walkway and maintained the childish stride all the way down the stairs.

Since he hadn't stopped laughing despite her clear fit of temper she glared him down. She poured herself a glass of water while she waited for him to show some signs of calm. "How could you let me sleep so late? I'm going to be late for the train."

"All day yesterday you complained that ya didn't get enough sleep." Cole's mirth continued to remain untouched by her irked attitude. "Since we stayed up most of the night again last night, I figured you'd wanna get some shut eye."

She narrowed her eyes. "You figured wrong, then. I'm never going to be able to eat before the train gets here. Which means I won't be able to eat until this afternoon because I have things to do today. And what in hell are you still finding funny?"

The man hadn't stopped chuckling through her tirade. He leaned on the bar next to her, his grin broad as could be.

"You'll never guess who I was just talking to. It's the reason I ain't been up to wake you proper yet."

At his continued silence, she huffed her exasperation. He was clearly determined to work her last nerve. She set down the water she'd been sipping to face him dead on. "Damn it, Cole. Just tell me who it was. Mike will be here any second.

"Mr. Garrett."

Jane snorted and slapped her hands over her mouth and nose in shock. The action made her wince in pain but she couldn't stop her laughter from escaping. Only three days before she'd told Mrs. Garrett to send her husband to speak to Cole, and the woman had actually done so?

Once again Cole burst into loud laughter. She could swore she saw tears in his eyes as he slapped the bar. It took several minutes for him to get enough control to speak. "It took all I had not to yell at ya to get your ass down here. I got no doubt he would have enjoyed a thorough demonstration."

She choked on the water she'd just raised to drink again. In retaliation, she threw the cup at him. She had to grip the edge of the bar in her efforts to steady the uncontrollable coughing. Laughter interrupted each cough in a rather staccato bark. It wasn't long before tears slipped down her cheeks from her own pained amusement. "Rake!"

Cole wiped himself off with a towel, still laughing. A wicked grin formed as he finished. The towel lowered toward the wash basin. Before she could think or truly believe that he might dare, he submerged the towel. She hadn't time to duck before he flung the sopping wet mass toward her.

"*Cole*," she shrieked. Somehow she managed to catch the wet mass before it dropped to the floor. A large wet spot covered the front of her dress, her hand ached from catching the towel. She scowled at him as she allowed the towel to drop to the floor.

Nearby on the bar sat a full pitcher, and she snatched it fast to toss it his way. While the water soared toward him, he lunged for another pitcher at the other side of the bar.

She backed up a few steps, and then darted out from behind the bar with a squeal. Moments before she made it to the doors water doused her from head to foot. Sputtering, she wiped the water from her eyes and turned slowly to face him.

"Always did like ya wet."

Her ragged breathing barely evened out under her attempts to gain some cool. Mouth open, and for the briefest moment at a loss for words, she could only blink in shock.

"Just wish you didn't have so many layers to peel off."

The words she'd lost flooded forward, but she retained control of them. Behind Cole there was movement, movement in her defense, so she didn't stop it. She curled her lips into a smirk and quirked a brow. Her mood significantly bolstered, she chuckled low. "I'm afraid you picked the wrong woman to mess with, Mr. Mitchell."

"That so?"

"Oh yes. See, you forgot—now that you aren't sleeping with your girls, they're not necessarily on your side any longer." Before he could process her meaning, two buckets of water dumped over his head. Jane snickered and gave the girls a nod. The buckets crashed to the ground while they darted into hiding. "Oops."

His long fingers wiped the water from his forehead and flung it aside. Bit by bit his head lifted until he glared at her sideways. "How in hell did you manage that?"

"I always have a backup plan."

"For a water fight we just started?"

She shrugged, glad for the summer heat that kept her from freezing under so much water. "Well, to be fair, those buckets were sitting out waiting for the daily mopping. The girls saw your little game and came to my defense. So it wasn't so much a plan—and don't you dare yell at them for it."

"Oh, I ain't gonna yell at them." An evil leer overtook his smirk.

She backed up a step and shook her head. "Oh no. No, you don't."

"Hope you're fast."

The shriek rose before she could stop it and she turned to race from the inn. She never had a chance, as Cole and his long legs caught up to her easily barely halfway across the street.

He grabbed her tight around her waist and started to pull her back toward the inn.

"Cole. *Don't.*"

He laughed when her protests were punctuated by her own laughter. "Don't what?"

Jane gasped when he stopped and spun her around. Through her own laughter she fought against his grip and tried to kick at him. "Just don't. Whatever it is you're planning, don't do it."

"Don't what?" He flung her over his shoulder and smacked her ass. For several feet, and amid growing calls of amusement from the gathering crowd, he carried her. When he stopped short, she saw the edge of the trough.

"Cole Mitchell. Don't you—" The end of the statement was cut off as she fell backward and landed with a splash in the trough. Sputtering, she pulled herself up to sit. Water dripped down her face, and she did her best to free her eyes from the annoyance. She still couldn't believe he'd done such a thing. "You…you…"

"Jane? You ain't at a loss for words are ya? That's not like you. Did you hit your head?" Cole leaned a foot on the edge of the trough. He grinned down at her bigger than anything. That wouldn't do.

She flew to her knees and grabbed his wrist with her good hand. With one good yank before he had a chance to react, they both toppled back into the water. She wasn't able to get a decent breath before he had her pinned. Worse, he started tickling her until she sank down under the water in her attempts to fight him off.

When she burst out of the water for another breath, he laughed. "Give up."

"Ow." She clutched her arm to her chest. As she'd done for days, she cradled it close. She even added in a wince for good measure. "Damn it."

"Jane?"

With a weak laugh, she leaned against the edge of the trough. She pushed out her lower lip in a pout. "Damn hand."

"Jesus, Jane…"

He picked up the hand to check it over, now ignorant of the cat calls and enjoyment surrounding them. Concern puckered his brow, and she almost felt guilty for faking her current level of pain. Almost.

Soon as he was good and distracted, she reached up with her good hand. A grin replaced her recent pout. She grabbed a handful of his hair and tugged hard, using his surprise to flip them both so he was now the one on his back in the water.

Just as he came up for air, she braced her legs tight against the sides of the trough. "Never trust a woman, Cole. I thought you of all people knew that best."

Cheers and hollers went up all around them. Men called out for Cole to not let her best him, while some cheered her on instead. A rueful grin creased his handsome, if wet, features. "You gonna let me get my pride stepped on like this?"

"Oh, you've got enough pride—a little stepping won't hurt it none."

"At least make losing worth my while."

"And theirs?"

He shrugged, still grinning. Uselessly he tried to blow the wet hair off his forehead. When it didn't work, he chuckled. "More concerned 'bout me."

With a giggle, she leaned in to press her lips to his. She gave into the kiss eagerly, but suspected shenanigans and so kept her legs tense against the sides of the trough. The cheers of the crowd grew raucous enough to infringe on even Jane's decency she tried to pull back. Before she got far he gripped her around the waist and tried to flip them.

She winked when his valiant attempt only moved her a smidgeon. "Did you really think I didn't expect you to try that?"

"Kinda hoped you wouldn't."

"My legs are good and pinned to the sides of the trough. I'm not moving unless I relax them, and I think you know they are plenty strong." The train whistle disrupted her amusement. "Oh dear! I don't have time to change now."

"You should've thought of that earlier." Mike pushed his way through the crowd. A frustrated wrinkle in his brow didn't match his crooked grin. He held out his hand to her. "If you two are done with your show, I think the wives would like to drag their husbands back to everyday business."

"Aw, but this is so much more fun." Jane stuck her tongue out at her brother. "And it is wonderful to see you as well, Michael."

"It's good to see the pair of you no longer acting like strangers, but you and I have a train to meet." Mike glanced toward Cole. "That is, if Cole is willing to let you go."

Cole shook his head, his arm still planted firm around her waist. "I owe her one."

"Don't worry, Cole. I'll definitely make it up to you." She offered a wink to Cole, but her arm to Mike. It wasn't until Mike had a good hold of her arm and waist that she relaxed enough to allow her brother to haul her out of the water. "I promise."

"Get her outta here." Cole groaned when she slipped away. He dropped his head back against the side of the trough. All around the area the crowd began to dissipate, though a few curious onlookers stuck around. "I got a business to run and she's disrupting it."

"Jane." Daisy stood nearby, her hands on her hips. A disapproving wrinkle in her brow helped along the deep frown.

"Daisy? How are you today? Is it too warm? I thought so. I'd suggest a dip in the trough, it's rather refreshing."

All of Daisy's attempts at being stern faltered. She cracked a smile. "I'm fine, thank you. The question is how are you? The two of you could have hurt yourselves."

"We could have, I'm afraid we weren't thinking that far." Jane nodded. "However, we fortunately came out of this all unharmed. I do think, well, I'm rather certain I'll need my hand rewrapped after I've met the train. Would you mind assisting me with that?"

"Of course not." Daisy looked between Jane and Cole for a moment before she burst out laughing. "Cole, you were never this fun before."

"I was always this fun," Cole protested. "Just no whore would ever dare to try some of the stuff Jane does."

"You mean we weren't that stupid." Daisy's attention turned back to Jane. She took in Jane's appearance, her laughter slightly contained. "Please tell me you aren't meeting the train like that?"

"It's just our brothers, Daisy." Michael stepped closer to her. "I am quite sure they will have a good idea why Jane's appearance is so—why it is the way it is."

"You have a very good point, Mike." Daisy shook her head. "I should return to the clinic now. I'll be sure to have everything set to rewrap your hand."

"Thank you." Jane waved over her shoulder to begin her walk to the station. Rather than linger longer so she might tease Michael for taking an extra minute to say goodbye to the doctor, she kept a slow pace and her eyes forward on her way toward the depot. None the less, when Mike managed to catch up, she couldn't prevent her grin.

"Hush."

"I said nothing." Jane nodded to a passerby who had gone so far as to stop and stare at her drowned rat appearance. "However, if I had—"

"But you won't."

"I see. We can discuss my relationship until you're blue in the face. When it comes to you, heaven forbid I even dare to hint that you and Daisy are anything more than friends."

"We are just friends. Now what the hell happened with you and Cole? You didn't speak for days if the rumors are true."

She shrugged. "For once the gossips in this town had things right. There were a few days where we fought."

"That must have been quite a fight. Several days apart is like years for the two of you." Mike chuckled when she elbowed him. "It's the truth and you know it."

"I suppose our fights are not usually quite so long anymore. Not as they once were."

"Was this one about anything in particular?"

"The usual. Graham. The Hangman's Inn. Our relationship."

"Ah. So, in other words, everything, and anything."

"'Here's a matter to vex you, and matter to grieve you. Here's doubt to distrust you, and faith to believe you—I am all as you see, common earth, common dew'."

Mike's lower jaw jutted out. He narrowed his eyes toward the sky, clearly trying to remember. "'Look close on my heart—see the worst of its shining—it is not yours today for the yesterday's winning. The past is not mine, I am too proud to borrow. You must grow to new heights if I love you tomorrow'."

"Well done. I am pleased to see you remember Alice Carey's words since you struggle with so many others."

"Funny, really. The question is, have you grown to new heights?"

"Oh goodness yes." Jane grinned. "But alas, I am sworn to secrecy."

"You can't keep a secret. To you it is akin to lying."

"Not exactly as such." She hefted her soaked skirts upward to climb the steps onto the train platform. Every step she took dripped along the boards. Several heads turned her way, humor and scorn mixing among her reception. "My goodness, I am drawing some attention. Whatever shall I do?"

"Same as you always do." He laughed. "Revel in it. Poke fun at what they could possibly be whispering about you."

"Well whispering and gossip are senseless. Rumors always return to the person you're gossiping about, so why bother with such subterfuge? Just tell me to my face you believe I'm no better than a soiled dove and that I'd do well to keep my behavior within the proper restrictions of society—"

"*Lou*. What in blazes happened to you?" Tommy's jovial voice boomed across the crowded platform. His nickname for her had once annoyed her as the shortening of her former middle name when she'd been Clara Louise. That is, until he'd explained how different he'd found her from Clara.

"*Thomas*." Jane hopped in excitement before darting across the platform to throw her arms around her large brother's neck. Of all her living brothers, Tommy was the only one that wasn't lean. He was tall, as they all were, but had more bulk on him; with a round belly that was deceptive to the amount of speed and strength he possessed. His protests over her wet clothes sent her chuckling again. "Oh, please. You could use a bath anyhow."

"Hey now." Tommy nudged her. "Be nice."

"Always." Jane turned her attention to the man behind Tommy. She approached, her smile well in place. "James."

"Don't you dare approach me like that." James held up his hands before she could get too close to him. "Contrary to our brother, I do not need a bath and neither does Ida. You may give me a proper hug once you are decent. What were you thinking Clara?"

Jane rolled her eyes at his prissy behavior over a little water. "Oh, drop the act. Number one, my name is Jane. Number two, don't act like my father. Number three, I do not care what you need or want."

James groaned when she hugged him tight. "You've always been a spoiled brat."

"You deserve it, acting all delicate and proper. I did meet you last year, and know what you're really like under that pomp and circumstance. You might clean up well but you still act like a mudsill in the right company." Jane gave him another squeeze for good measure before she stepped back. "You are looking much better, James. I hope the effects of the poison were not terribly long lasting."

"No, I'm pretty much back to normal." James had been poisoned by the same man that had once tried to kill Jane, along with everyone she held dear. In a ploy to draw her out and exact his revenge, Alan had killed one of her brothers and poisoned James repeatedly.

"I'm glad to hear it. I'd never forgive Clara if there had been any permanent damage." Jane leaned into Tommy when his arm draped around her shoulders.

Tommy snorted. "You are Clara."

"No, she is not." The woman next to James stepped into his extended arm. She smiled warmly at Jane. "I have met

Clara, but I have not met Jane. They certainly appear similar enough, but you yourself has said they weren't the same, Thomas."

"My apologies." Tommy bowed his head with an air of polite humor.

Ida chuckled and shook her head at him before turning her attention back to Jane. She held out her hand. "It is nice to finally meet you. I hope I won't offend if I inquire as to your current state of—um—"

Jane shook her hand in return. At the sweep of her current state of doused dress by Ida, Jane giggled. "I was running late this morning already, and Cole decided I wasn't late enough for his satisfaction. The end result is he saw fit to dunk me in the horse trough."

"I highly doubt that is precisely what happened." Mike folded his arms across his chest and quirked a brow. "From where I stood you appeared to share the responsibility."

Charlie rushed toward the group. "So sorry to be late. I was helping a patient—Jane? What the devil?" He eyed her from top to bottom.

"I believe she was reveling in the sin of frivolity this morning." Tommy gave her a wink.

"No. I reveled in that for quite some time last night." Jane bumped Tommy's hip with her own. "Of course, there is not a thing wrong with frivolity. 'There is always some frivolity in excellent minds; they have wings to rise, but also stray'. Joseph Joubert."

"Excellent minds?" Tommy guffawed. "This from the mouth of the amnesiac?"

Jane scoffed. At his continued laughter she jabbed her elbow into his side. "You'd best behave yourself. Otherwise

I will force you to take residence at Michael's fancy hotel and become his hotel manager."

Tommy's eyes grew wide as saucers. He went slack-jawed in mock horror. "Oh balls. You wouldn't dare."

"Some things never change." James shook his head. "I, however, promised Ida we would stay at Mike's and enjoy a little luxury while we're here. She heard Nick talk of the fancy bath houses he built, not to mention the waterfall swimming hole."

"I think you just don't wish to hear Michael complain that everyone is staying at the Hangman's Inn." Ida cast her husband a pointed look. "Perhaps we'll spend a night or two at the Hangman's Inn later in the week to divide the business between."

"Then it's settled." Jane pushed Tommy toward the edge of the platform. "Come along, Thomas. Norman will see your things get to the inn. I'll show you the room we picked for you. Ida and James can take some time to make themselves comfortable at the Sage Brush. I'll don some dry clothes and perhaps later we'll meet at Cora's for supper?"

"Sounds like a delicious plan." James stopped her long enough to kiss her cheek. "Just please show up dry this time, would you?"

"I'd rather not make a promise I cannot be certain I'll be able to keep." Jane waved her goodbyes before jumping off the platform beside Tommy. "Shall we?"

"Of course." Tommy offered her an elaborate scrape-and-bow before extending his arm for her to take. "I am honored."

"Boor."

"All the best men are, Lou."

"I'm glad you decided to be manager of the inn. I do hope the change in management doesn't disrupt your plans. Graham is selling his half, and there's already a buyer. I hear they're a real beast, too."

Tommy stopped short. His jovial gaze turned calculating and focused right on her. "I've been gone for just a few weeks and Graham is selling out?"

"Apparently you becoming manager because he couldn't bother to be around really was the last straw." Jane bit her lip. "Of course, there's a lot more that happened that you haven't the faintest idea about."

"Like what happened to your hand? And why you're grinning like a Cheshire cat?"

"I hardly know where to begin. Let's see. Oh yes, Al came back to town last week. He's passing through on his way back home and wanted to visit."

"Al? As in Major Webb? The same Major you were making time with?"

"Men. I swear you are all the same. Yes, Major Webb, my *friend*. The one I was rumored to be making time with along with his entire camp. However he is nothing more than a friend. Cole accepts it somewhat—of course, if he didn't he'd have a very cold bed at night."

"Uh-huh. In other words, he keeps his mouth shut so you don't yell at him." Tommy shook his head at her shrug. "What else? Tell me more about this new owner of the inn?"

"Oh, we'll get there. May I continue?" She laced her arm with his to continue their trek back to the inn. "Graham was furious when he learned that Cole had asked you to be manager of the inn, and you'd accepted, and he'd had no say in the matter."

"I didn't see him for a full week before I headed back to Buffalo to take care of my final business so that I might move." Tommy's brow furrowed under his Stetson. "It's difficult to speak to someone that isn't present."

"You'll get no argument from me on that. It's all too true. None of that mattered to Graham. Then a few days later he informed Cole that he was selling his half of the business." Jane pursed her lips at the memory. "Worse than that, the bastard had already located a couple of interested parties to purchase his half."

"You mean Becky's pa found a couple of interested parties."

"Precisely." Jane found it difficult to keep her grin concealed any longer. "Once Cole stopped being furious long enough to think, he eventually found a buyer all on his own. Then the other day there was an incident with Mel—"

"Wait a minute, there. You skipped something."

"Did I?"

"Who's the buyer?"

"Oh, hush. I'll get there. I'm trying to tell you about Mel. He was shot at close range by an angry patron. He didn't survive." The familiar sadness returned and lingered for a minute while they stood on the porch of the saloon. "In the chaos following, Graham made some choice comments to me. Fed up, I reacted. I did break his nose—and unfortunately my hand as well."

"About damn time," Tommy muttered. "But you went and broke your hand doing it? We taught you better than that."

"Lessons I don't remember." Jane sighed and pulled her hand close to her chest again. "Believe me, with how much this hurts I really wish I did.'

"You haven't remembered anything new since I left?"

"You've been gone three weeks. I've had amnesia for over two years. What did you expect?"

"I dunno. Maybe you hit your head again." He laughed as he pushed her into the inn. "Go get yourself dressed into a somewhat proper person again. I'm getting a drink. It was a very long train ride with only James and Ida for conversation. Boring."

"Mean." Jane hightailed it up the stairs, still chuckling. By the time she'd peeled off her wet clothes and changed, not to mention fixing her hair, half an hour had passed. Downstairs she found Tommy and Cole in high spirits. "You boys having fun?"

"Cole was just filling me in on what you left out of your story." Tommy held up his glass. "And keeping me happy, too."

"How hospitable," Jane muttered in as droll a tone as she could manage.

Cole gave her a wicked smirk. "Still prefer ya wet."

"Quiet." Jane blew a raspberry before she took the stood beside Tommy. "How far did Cole get in the goings on around here?"

"He told me more about Mel, the whores." Tommy leaned close. "And what is this business about *you* being the one buying Graham's part of the business?"

"Well then, you are fully filled in. I guess that means I can go."

"Hold up." Tommy grabbed her arm. "You don't get off that easy. Cole also tells me you think there's something else going on with the business?"

"I suppose you could say such a thing, although I wouldn't have put it in those words. It really is more that I am not sure that any of these events are unrelated." Jane turned in her stool to lean against the bar. Her foot bounced a slow rhythm as she surveyed the saloon. "I can't put my finger on it, something just doesn't sit right. The girls, who have been relatively sober since I put my foot down and Cole told them to listen, are now regularly getting opium and other recreations at an alarming rate."

Cole's voice broached into the conversation near her ear like he'd leaned on the bar. His voice was dark with frustration. "We got one pregnant and at least one more keeping company when she ain't supposed to. Jane's sure she isn't using the protection we give them."

Jane rubbed her hand over her face as if it would wipe away her own burgeoning frown. She sighed. "This Gus Warren has been helping them get the opium. I also know for a fact he was with, and asked for, Pansy both this month and last—"

"Did you say Gus Warren?" Tommy sat straighter. His brow wrinkled in thought as his knee bounced a rapid pace.

"Yeah." Cole came around the bar and stood next to Jane. "Why do ya ask?"

"The name rings a bell. I'll send a telegram or two, figure out what's so familiar."

"Tommy?" Jane narrowed her eyes and tilted her head to study him. His knee kept bouncing and he was chewing on his cheeks. "What is it?"

"I think you might be right, Jane." Tommy rubbed his hand over his beard. "I don't think any of it is unrelated."

"How?"

"So now you need a dealer too?"

Cole blinked at the change of subject. "Sure do. And a bartender. Not to mention a few more girls that don't mind sobriety."

"Can't help with the girls, but as I'm already going to be managing for you, I can add in dealing and tending bar."

Jane grinned, "You still have to pay rent."

"But not for my whiskey."

She pondered and glanced at Cole. After a minute she nodded, "Fine, but your rent is five dollars more a month than you and Cole agreed on."

"I'm going to hate having you as boss."

"Love you too, Tommy. Is it a deal?"

"Deal."

A friend should bear his friend's infirmities.
-William Shakespeare

"You've *got* to be kidding me." Graham's round face was beet red. The color spread all the way up to his bald head.

"Do I look like I'm kidding?" With Graham on the receiving end of his glare, Cole tensed for a fight. He'd expected this reaction, but that didn't mean he'd put up with it long. "Already talked to Lloyd. You agreed to the price, she's got the money. She's buying it."

"You're letting that woman—"

"What? What is it I'm doing? Letting her do what she's already been doing? What you've been harping on me about letting her do for months? Nothing's gonna change. I'm just making it legal, oh, and you'll be outta here.

"Might as well make something legal." Graham smirked. "Guess business is the best she'll get out of you."

"You really want another broken nose?" Cole leaned close until they were almost nose to nose. "Unlike Jane, I ain't likely to break my hand doing it."

"What is it with men?" The very woman he spoke of breezed through the saloon, calm and relaxed despite the men's state of near fisticuffs. Cole would dare say he heard a hint of humor in Jane's tone. "I could practically hear your entire conversation from the street."

And here Cole thought he'd been real nice and quiet. Apparently they'd been shouting by her take on it. He shrugged when she moved behind him to grab a mug of coffee. "I wasn't yelling."

"You most certainly were. Thomas and I were betting on who would draw the attention of Mr. Hamm enough to make him think the saloon was open and serving already."

Cole shook his head. "We woulda set him straight."

"Not the point." Jane poured a second mug of coffee. "You were both yelling. Graham is stirring the pot for no good reason again. You're letting him."

"Not so much." Cole smirked. "Not like ya think."

"Funny. You say that a lot." She glanced between the pair of them, a frown setting firm in place of the humor she had employed. "*Must* you both continue to play 'who's the real man'? I think we have already settled that. I am. So put your pricks away and talk like human beings. I'm going to sit a spell with Thomas on the porch."

Cole chuckled as she carried two mugs out onto the porch. After she'd handed one to Tommy, they both took a seat on the bench right outside the window.

"She's got a real mouth on her." Graham grumbled. All his vigor left at the statement, which left him sagging in his seat.

"Boy does she ever. She sure knows how to use it, too."

Graham lifted his head, a hint of a smirk on his features. He shook his head, blowing out a gust of air. "I don't get it."

"What do ya find so confusing?"

"You get in a snit any time someone steps foot over your lines. For years. Then one day you just let her barge on in here and take over. You didn't even put up a fight."

"She ain't barging in. I want her here." Cole leaned on bar. Motion outside drew his eye, where he spotted Al join Jane and Tommy. He curled his lip at the sight, but kept going on with the conversation in front of him. "You're a fine one to talk. You're selling this place to keep your woman happy. Gave up that little wash-girl for her too."

Graham's fist clenched at the mention of Linh. For once, the man didn't snap. "So you're just doing it to keep her happy."

"Nah. Not her. It's to keep me happy." Cole downed his glass of whiskey. He shrugged. "It ain't such a bad thing to be. You should try it sometime."

"I am happy," Graham blustered. Even through the false words he grimaced. "With Becky."

"Ain't seen you happy since last year this time, before Becky done run Linh right outta town." Cole shook his head. There wasn't a soul alive that hadn't noticed the change in Graham. "Shouldn't matter to you none who buys this Inn if you're happy as ya say. So stop pitching a fit over it already."

Graham frowned deeper. When Cole tossed back another whiskey, Graham pulled his mug of coffee closer. He stared down the whiskey bottle hard and licked his lips. After a second he shook himself and turned back to Cole. "Next thing you know, you're gonna be marrying her. Then it'll be all over."

"Jane and I both agree with don't want that. We like things how they are." Cole wouldn't admit to anyone that once in a while his thoughts turned to making it legal, just like he wanted to do for the Inn and her part in it. Every time he started to think real serious about it though, memories came back to haunt him strong enough he backed off.

"What was that you said? About doing what you've already been doing—just making it legal?" Graham chortled. "Only applies to matters of business, I guess."

Cole pursed his lips when Graham voiced some of Cole's own thoughts. He pushed forward with a smirk instead of letting on the truth of the matter. "Ain't no union here that could be blessed by God."

"Good point." Graham's laughter burst free. His turned his attention to the window Jane where Jane sat. "You really want to keep her around here for that long?"

Rather than answer, Cole picked up a glass to clean.

"Just because she's a good screw?"

"If that was the only reason, she'd be gone already." Not that he hadn't tried to get rid of her a time or two in the past. For that matter, they both had. In the end he couldn't get rid of her. He liked it more than he would ever admit.

"Huh." Graham shrugged. "Guess you could do worse."

"Couldn't do no better."

"She don't like me."

"Neither do I." Cole snorted when Graham cut him a glare. "And yet, ya still come around here. Unless it's for the girls.'

"Ain't been in for the girls in a while. Think they're grumpy since we stopped using the talent pool?"

"Miserable. Probably why they started doping." Cole snickered. Graham joined in a few seconds later. The tension between them dissipated further in their laughter, and within minutes both were laughing full volume.

Jane entered the saloon, a sly smile on her tempting lips. She slipped behind him to set down the coffee mugs. "I'm not here to interrupt the two of you. I just wanted to let you know

Kat's here. The wagon is all loaded and Reverend Greene is ready to go. I'll see you for supper."

Cole snaked his arm around her waist to stop her attempt at departure. He frowned when she tried to slip away. One tug brought her tight against him. "Why do ya still go out there every week? There's far more exciting—"

She clamped her hand over his mouth before he could finish. "Don't you ever get tired of spending every week trying to convince me to waste away my afternoon upstairs with you? I do this because not everyone is as fortunate as you and I are to have such a luxury."

Cole nipped her hand until she snatched it away. "Fine. Get on outta here. Don't you go taking all that stuff out of the wagon. Charlie says you ain't supposed to use that hand."

Graham's snort cut off Cole's statement. While he cleared his throat and took an innocent sip of his coffee, a wicked gleam remained.

"I don't see what's so funny. There are some things I don't need my hand for. I have other body parts capable of performing the task." Jane wagged her eyebrows at Graham. When the man busted a gut laughing, she turned her attention back to Cole. She gripped his shirt to yank him into a kiss. "Now both of you behave or Thomas will deal with your obnoxiousness in ways my broken hand won't allow me to."

"Yes ma'am." Cole smacked her ass the moment she turned her back on him. "You'd best be good and quick today. Can't guarantee I'm gonna stay behaved for long."

"You never do."

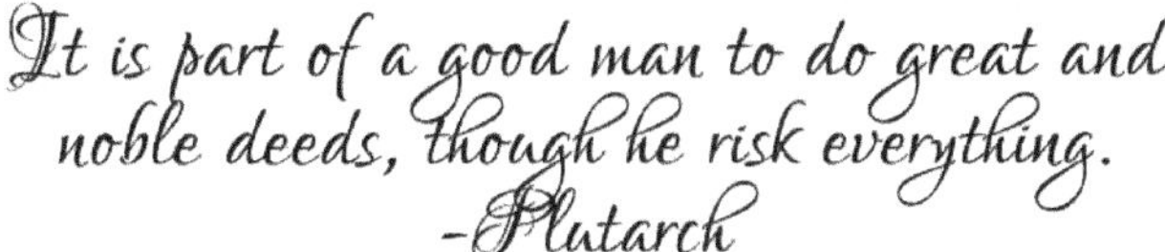

It is part of a good man to do great and noble deeds, though he risk everything.
—Plutarch

"Hello, Jane." Reverend Greene greeted her with a smile. "Are you ready for our run to the settlement?"

"I am." Jane had to shift to pull herself into the wagon seat with her good hand. The help Kat offered was gratefully accepted. "I don't know how I'm going to keep this up for weeks. I cannot wait to regain the use of my hand."

The reverend hopped up into the wagon. "Patience, Jane. Perhaps this is God's way of telling you to slow down."

"I think it's God's way of telling her to watch her temper." Kat squeaked at Jane's harsh nudge to her side. "Well, it's true."

"I have not punched another living soul before. It's not like I don't know how to control my temper." Heat rose to Jane's cheeks. If she were honest, that wasn't always the case. She demurred, "Except when it comes to Cole, of course."

Reverend slapped the reins and the wagon took off. Once they'd reached a good pace, he rested back against the seat, the reins held in his hands casually. "The Porters left this week. Mr. Porter found a job on a ranch in Wyoming."

"I really wish David could convince his friend to bring his ranch here. There is land for it, and it could help give jobs to the men still looking." Jane sighed. The Coinage Act had sent the cost of silver down and left quite a few men without jobs. Those without families had simply left town. Those with families had tried to stay on, but it had been just two years since the Indian attacks had robbed them of homes.

While the town had come together and managed to get everyone back in homes, the loss of jobs so soon after losing their homes was a harsh blow. Still, Reverend Greene worked every week to get donations to help out the families. Along with that, Jane and Kat went with him every week to deliver all the donations.

"I suppose it's for the better, donations were a little thin this week." Kat broke the silence with a glance into the wagon. "So if the Porters aren't here any longer, where are we heading first?"

"The Broder's missed church on Sunday." Reverend Greene frowned. "I'd like to head to their homestead to check on them first."

"It isn't like Mrs. Broder to miss church." Jane liked Mrs. Broder, and thought her daughter Lizzie was a beautiful, smart little girl. One of the few children Jane didn't mind.

"Exactly. If it had been Mr. Broder that missed church, I wouldn't have been surprised. He's been picking up odd jobs all around town, which leaves little time to take care of the homestead and animals. Sometimes he uses Sundays for it." The reverend turned the wagon toward a house just northeast of them. "Which I understand and the good Lord forgives, I'm sure. However, Mrs. Broder hasn't missed a Sunday in all the years I've been here."

"She was even at church the day after the renegades burned down their original home," Jane agreed. When she'd been injured a couple of years ago, Mrs. Broder and Lizzie had cared for her while Cole had been busy letting the town use the saloon like a hospital. "I do wish Mr. Broder could find more regular work. I'd hate to see them leave."

"That reminds me." Reverend Greene brightened. "I spoke to Hammy and he's agreed to hire a few of the men. He said with the town's current rate of growth, he'll need the help for the construction boom he's seeing."

"That's wonderful of him. Good for Hammy. I'll make sure he gets an extra beer when he stops in tonight." The wagon hit a large bump in the ground, which caused Jane to grip the back of the seat.

"I can't believe that even with all the men fired from the mines, the town is still growing like it is." Kat shook her head. "It has to be those advertisements of your brothers."

"Fresh, clean mountain air for your consumption. It's certainly tempting enough, I suppose. His touted health spa is certainly flourishing." Jane pursed her lips. While the Hangman's Inn struggled by with only a few actual guests each month, Mike had added months onto construction to build his hotel bigger to accommodate his rush of guests.

"Well, maybe your changes will help the Hangman's Inn to grow, too." Kat patted her arm and leaned over to speak to the reverend. "Did you know Jane is buying Graham's half of the business, Reverend?"

"I hadn't heard." He tugged on the reins to slow the wagon.

Jane sat straighter as she took in the small homestead. Her frown grew deeper. With the exception of the cow mooing pitifully in the barn, everything else sat eerily silent. Jane didn't wait, but scrambled over Kat's legs to leap down.

A breeze stirred across the homestead, setting the corn in the garden rustling. Another long moo punctuated the silence. Jane turned back to the wagon where Kat was following her lead to get out of the wagon fast. "Why don't you two check on that cow and their horses?"

"What's that? Do you hear that?" Reverend Greene leaned forward, his head turned toward the house. "I think someone is crying."

Jane strained to hear it, and there it was. She met Kat's gaze, her own heart pounding in concern. There was something wrong here for certain. "Get that cow milked before the pain is unbearable. I'll check on the family."

As Kat and the reverend headed for the barn, Jane gathered her skirts. She darted to the house to knock firmly on the door. "Mrs. Broder? Mr. Broder? It's Jane. Are you in there?"

Silence echoed back. Out of the corner of her eye she saw the others enter the barn. She knew they had to be as curious as she was as to whether thieves had come and taken the horses or worse.

Jane pounded harder on the door. "Please, Mrs. Broder. I know you're in there, I can hear you crying."

The door cracked open slowly. Mrs. Broder peeked through the opening. Her skin was waxy and pale, dark circles lingered under her red eyes. "I'm sorry, Jane. I'm afraid we aren't up for visiting today."

"We brought you some supplies. I'm sure you need them." Jane slipped her foot in the opening of the door. "You don't look well. Is everything all right?"

"You'd best go now."

"Mrs. Broder, please." Jane clamped her hand on the door when she heard a pained cry in the house. "Was that Lizzie? Does she need a doctor?"

"Please. It's best you…go." Mrs. Broder swayed, her firm hold on the door loosened. Her hand went to her forehead.

Jane pushed the door open a little more. "If you're sick, you should all get to the clinic."

"I don't know how to hook up the wagon." Mrs. Broder's eyes fluttered shut. Her forehead rested against the door. A shallow sigh slipped free. "I couldn't pay."

"I'll pay." Jane touched Mrs. Broder's forehead only to find it hot as fire. She took her hand from the woman's forehead and pushed the door open further. "Please, let me in."

"We can't…pay." Mrs. Broder collapsed.

Jane slipped into the house and shut the door behind her. She pulled the latch string in to lock the door so Kat and the reverend didn't enter until she was certain what was going on.

She knelt next to Caroline and set her hand to her forehead again. Another pained cry from the back drew her attention. She rushed through the house to the first bedroom.

Sprawled on the bed, a basin and sponge beside him lay Mr. Broder. Jane quickly went to his side to check his temperature, but stopped short. A rash covered Mr. Broder's chest, a telling rash that rang alarm bells in Jane's head.

She backed away from the bed, although she knew at this point there was nothing she could do. She'd already been exposed to the illness by being in the house. Rather than linger in that worrying thought, she ran to Lizzie's room.

On her own small bed Lizzie laid with sweat beaded on her forehead. Her eyes lingered half-open, her mouth moving as if to speak.

Jane didn't hesitate to move to Lizzie's side. She clutched the girls hand as she reached out to brush her fingers across the burning hot forehead. "Easy, Lizzie. Try to sleep. Don't try to talk. That's good. Shhh."

Once Lizzie's eyes fluttered shut, Jane moved aside the collar of her nightgown to check for the tell-tale rash she'd seen on Mr. Broder. With a shuddering breath, she grabbed the sponge next to the bed and brushed it along Lizzie's forehead in an attempt to cool her down.

"Jane." Kat's voice breached the silence of the house, accompanied by loud pounding on the door.

"I'm coming," Jane called back. The noise startled Lizzie, so Jane soothed her once more before she rose. She moved back through the house quick as she could to the door. "Kat, stop. I can't open the door, it isn't safe. Stay outside, please."

Kat stopped knocking. "Jane? What is it? What's going on?"

"I can't be certain. I'm not a doctor." Jane eyed Caroline on the floor. She knelt beside the woman slowly. With a quiet apology, she unbuttoned the top of the woman's bodice. She found the rash there as well. To be sure, Jane pulled open her mouth to see if the ulcers were inside.

"Jane?"

"Based on what I've read in those medical texts, I think it's Scarlet Fever."

"Jane!"

"I've already been exposed. It isn't wise for me to leave, or you to come in. We need Charles and Daisy both, if possible. There are three of them, and having two doctors would be far better than one. I can't move Mrs. Broder; she's collapsed on the floor. Mr. Broder is in bed as is Lizzie." Jane spotted Kat at the window and went over to where she had her hand pressed on the glass. "Go on. Get whomever is at the clinic. I'll be all right."

"You should come back as well." Kat's hand didn't leave the glass.

"No. I've already been exposed. I should remain here to help them. They all need to be cooled down, the fever is quite severe. I'm not even certain Dorsey is still alive." Jane stepped back from the window. "Hurry."

"All right. I'll go get Daisy and Charlie." Kat patted the window before she disappeared from view.

Jane took a deep breath before she surveyed the house. She had to come up with a plan, no matter her fear. She wasn't ill at the moment, and wouldn't be for days if she were to find she had contracted the illness.

First, she had to see if Mr. Broder lived. After that, she'd tend to them all as best she could until help arrived.

It was the best she could do, so it would have to do.

*Let fear of the danger be a spur to prevent
it; he that fears not, gives advantage
to the danger.
-Francis Quarles*

Dorsey was dead.

When she'd returned to the bedroom, he'd breathed his last breath. She hadn't known how to help, if she even would have been able to stop his death if she had known. She'd returned the latch string through its hole in the door and gone on to tend to Caroline and Lizzie as best she could.

At the moment she sat and ran the sponge along Lizzie's forehead, neck, and hands. It wouldn't do any of them any good for her to cry. Not yet anyhow.

"Jane." Charlie spoke quietly from the door.

"Hello. Did you see to Caroline and Dorsey?" Jane didn't let her attention waver from the small child before her.

"Yes. Daisy is attending to Caroline now. I've been in to see Dorsey. He didn't survive the fever." Charlie set his hand on her shoulder and his medical bag on the spare chair beside the bed Jane had abandoned. "How is Lizzie?"

"She hasn't done much but cry since I got here. She's so feverish, I'm not certain she understands anything that's going on."

Charlie slipped his arms under Jane's. He lifted her to move her to the chair beside the bed. "Let me have a look." He gathered supplies from his bag before he leaned over to examine Lizzie.

Jane twisted her hand in her skirts. The silence lingered interminably long until it became unbearable. "I read the symptoms in one of the medical texts in the library. I wasn't certain if I was right."

"You suspected correct." He put away his stethoscope. "It is Scarlet Fever."

"What are her chances?"

"They both have a very pronounced case. If she survives the fever, her chances are good. The same goes for Mrs. Broder. Daisy?"

Daisy stepped into the room and offered a nod to Jane. "Mrs. Broder is holding on right now. I can't give any promises for the future. How is Lizzie?"

"Her fever is quite high. I've given her some quinine to try to ease it." Charlie frowned. "We have a decision to make."

Jane straightened. "What decision is that?"

"We're already in quarantine right where we are, and that is the safest measure to take." Charlie moved to allow Jane access to the child again. "However, I don't like being this far from needed supplies. A good bath, an ice house, our surgical supplies."

"Should anyone else get sick we'll need the space the clinic provides," Daisy agreed. "We aren't sure how they contracted it, or who they might have passed it on to. We should be prepared for the worst."

Charlie rose. "It is best that we are prepared. This house isn't large enough in the case this were to become an epidemic. We'll just have to make certain to tell people not to come in until we've seen it cleaned of infection."

"Of course. Now for the most important matter at hand beyond these two. Has Jane been exposed before?" Daisy moved to Jane's side. "Or should we be prepared?"

Jane lifted her head from her task in search of Charlie. Her brother had his back to her as he packed up her supplies. "I have no idea. Charlie?"

"No." Charlie kept his back to them both. A gruff note had seeped into his tone. "She and Mike weren't born yet when Thomas and James had it. She's never been exposed."

"How long until we know if I've got it?" Jane rose. The idea was terrifying, but she'd rather be prepared. "Will it take long?"

"It could be a day, or a week." Daisy wrapped her arms around her own waist. "Some people are naturally resistant— others don't become resistant until they've had it. We won't know for at least a week."

Her throat tight, Jane could only nod. She was surprised by how much her hand shook when she lifted it to smooth back her hair. "Well, then. I suppose I'll need Thomas to obtain some of my books and clothes. I'll remain at the clinic and assist you with Lizzie."

After the decision was made, everything happened too quickly for Jane to think too hard about her current situation. They prepared the family for transport, and Dorsey Broder for burial. Jane wasn't even sure when Tommy arrived, but there he was, helping to carry Mrs. Broder to the wagon.

Jane tried to insist on carrying Lizzie herself, but Tommy wouldn't hear of it considering her injured hand. In the end, she gave up the fight when she realized how much it did hurt after she'd ignored it for most of the afternoon.

Once she'd taken her seat in the wagon, Tommy sidled his horse beside her. "Hey, Lou. Any special books you want?"

Jane shook her head. "No. Nothing special. I'd just like enough to keep me occupied for a little while."

"I'd need the whole library for that." Tommy laughed. He gave her a wink and tipped his hat to her. With a loud whoop, he spurred his horse into a full gallop back toward down.

The wagon travelled far slower, creaking and bumping along the road. Jane's nose burned with her effort to keep the tears at bay. Already the Broder family had lost so much, and now she was faced with what remained of the small family. A mother and daughter, both with hair as pure white as the moon.

"How did you know, Jane?" Daisy sat in the wagon bed with her, attending to Caroline. She turned her gaze toward Jane. "I mean, how did you know it was likely Scarlet Fever?"

"Oh." Jane shook her head from her dark thoughts at the question. Grateful for the distraction, she shrugged. "I was just telling Charles that back at the homestead. I'd read the symptoms in one of the medical texts in the library. I remembered them."

Daisy's brows rose. "You read medical texts?"

"I was waiting on a new shipment of books. I had little else to read, so I perused some of the medical texts." Jane turned her gaze toward town. "I might have been trying to get some information on amnesia as well. Out of curiosity, of course."

"You don't seem to forget anything you've read." Daisy studied her.

"I'm not certain how or why, honestly. It just seems to happen that way." Jane pursed her lips. "I don't imagine I truly remember everything I've read. That doesn't seem quite possible."

"First Peter chapter four, verse five." Charlie piped up, his attention on the road.

"'But they will give account to him who is ready to judge the living and the dead'." Without hesitation, the words spilled from Jane's lips. Her brows drew together and she glared at the back of Charlie's head. "What are you doing?"

"Der Erklönig."

"'Wer reitet so spät durch nacht und wind? Es ist der vater mit seinem kind; er hat den knaben wohl in dem arm, er faßt ihn sicher, er hält ihn warm'." Jane pressed her hand to her forehead and tried to figure out what she'd just said. "Charles."

"In German, even." Charlie laughed. "Very good. How about this? *Last of the Mohicans*. Chapter twenty-nine, Cora's speech to the Huron chief."

"'Just and venerable Delaware, on thy wisdom and power we lean for mercy! Be deaf to yonder artful and remorseless monster, who poisons thy ears with falsehoods'..." Jane clenched her jaw together. "I'm not a parlor trick."

Charlie grinned at Daisy. "Just proving a point. Clara could always do that, from the time she was very little. We never could explain it. My own memory is quite good, but I can't compete with Jane's. I had to pick text and verse I already knew."

Daisy paused to wipe her brow and offered Jane a smile. "I've never seen anything like it."

"And yet she can't remember her own name." Charlie hooted. "The most ironic case of amnesia I've ever seen."

"You are not amusing and this is not an amusing situation." Jane chastised.

"What is that proverb, Jane? 'Joy and sorrow are next door neighbors'?" Charlie didn't turn back again as he maneuvered into the silent town. "The next week is going to be difficult, we have to keep finding joy. You should know that, you managed quite well to find joy when facing death yourself."

"I'd rather not have to face it again." Jane gripped the edge of the wagon. The town around them was the emptiest she'd ever seen it. Not a soul walked the streets. A few horses remained tied up, but windows and doors were shut tight. Jane thought she heard a scuffle at the saloon as they passed, but she couldn't be certain. "Looks like they knew we were coming."

Tommy waved from the porch of the clinic. "Let's get them inside. Glad this place has been fixed up into more of a hospital than hotel."

"Me too. We can isolate them well in the rooms upstairs." Charlie hopped down. In the past year he and Daisy had taken great pains to make sure they would have a functional clinic in place of the old Silver Saddle hotel.

"Let's get them inside. Lou, I already got your things upstairs in that front room. You can't actually go out on the balcony, but I thought if you could at least see what was going on in the town, you wouldn't feel so isolated." Tommy helped Jane out of the wagon before hopping into it to get Caroline.

"Thank you. Let's put Lizzie in there with me. I've already been exposed; I want to help take care of her. She should have a familiar person nearby." Jane followed Charlie through the doors of the clinic.

They bypassed the waiting room and went right up the stairs. The two halves of the building had been divided by a thick wall, with the intention of separating patients in case of an epidemic. Jane hadn't imagined they'd ever use it.

Now she stepped through the wall as a possible victim of a possible full blown epidemic. She shook off the dark thoughts and strode into the room Tommy had set up for her. A few minutes later Tommy appeared lugging a trundle bed into the room.

"Here you go, Lou. Charlie will bring her in shortly." He walked over and gripped her shoulders. "No getting sick, understood?"

A smile tugged at her features, and she chuckled. "From your lips to God's ears, Thomas. I think we'll need a little help on this one."

"Reverend's already praying." He nodded. "Don't you worry none about Cole. I'll make sure he doesn't act foolish."

"Good luck. Most days he acts foolish." Jane smiled and looked toward the door. "Might not have been smart to put me in this room."

Before Tommy could answer, Charlie brought in Lizzie. Jane spent the next several hours wrapped up in taking care of the girl, and was surprised to find she had to light the lamp. With a long exhale, she leaned back in the chair she'd put next to the trundle.

She picked up a book and flipped it open. "'I see the better in the dark, I do not need a light. The love of thee, a prism be'…"

Lizzie's moan pulled her away again and Jane grabbed the sponge from the basin. She wiped at Lizzie's brow and sighed when she settled again. Jane picked up the book and rose. Halfway to the pile of books on the large table in the room a tapping reached her ears.

She froze and listened, her gaze falling on the door to the balcony.

Cole stood on the other side, his palm now flat on the glass. Thankfully he made no attempts to breach the lock, or storm in.

Jane swallowed against the sudden lump that had formed in her throat. Her guilt nagged at her, and she crossed to the window, setting her palm where his lay.

The inch of glass might as well have been ten feet thick for all the closeness they were able to share. She sighed and lifted her eyes to his gaze. Unsure whether he'd hear her, she spoke anyway. "I might not get sick. They just want to be sure."

"Ya better not." His voice carried through the door, muffled but strong. "Girls won't listen to no one but you."

"That's why I need to stay healthy?"

"Nah. There are plenty of reasons." A frown flickered across his features and his hand dropped from the door. "I prefer a warning when you aren't gonna be coming back to the room."

"There is something to be said for spontaneity. Although, I'd prefer to not hear it right now." Jane smiled as strong as she could. "Guess you've never been exposed?"

"There's only one thing stopping me from breaking in there."

"Don't even think of it. I don't want you risking yourself, especially when I'm not even sick." She set her hands on her hips, stopping her tirade at his amused expression. "What's the one thing stopping you, then?"

"I brung you something, and I'd be in trouble if I didn't take it back."

"What?"

"*Ma*." Jesse pounded on the pane at Cole's waist. "Hi, Ma."

Jane gasped and dropped down to her knees. Through the door she could hear mumbles of Cole's grumbling when Jesse shoved him out of the way. She wiped at her tears and set her hand on the pane again. "Jesse. How are you doing?"

"Good. Cole tooked me to—"

"Took me."

"*Ma*." Jesse's brow furrowed.

"I'm sorry. Go on with your story." She glanced up at Cole while Jesse started the story of his evening. Once Jesse was done, she smiled. "Sounds like you and Cole had lots of fun."

"Yeah. He said he had to take me 'cause you're sick." Jesse's forehead hit the glass.

"Well it was nice of Cole to take you riding. Did you thank him?" At his nod, she smiled. "Good. Now does your pa know you're here?"

"I told him." Cole spoke up. "He said he'll be stopping by himself tomorrow."

Jane sighed and nodded. "Thank you, Cole. For everything."

"Is Lizzie gonna be all right, Ma?" Jesse pressed his face to the pane, trying to see past Jane to the girl in the bed. "Cole says she's real sick."

"If I have anything to say about it, she will get better." She sighed. "But you know what? As much as I have loved seeing you, Lizzie is all by herself. You be a good boy for Cole and your pa for me, all right? I'm going to take real good care of Lizzie so you can see her again."

"All right. Miss you." Jesse's shoulders slumped and he backed away from the pane.

"Miss you too." Jane stood and met Cole's gaze. "Thank you. I can't believe you did this for me."

"You planned on taking him on a ride. I just made sure he got it. Figured you'd wanna see him before he went back to his pa."

"God I love you."

"I know."

The melancholy days are come, the saddest of the year, of wailing winds, and naked woods, and meadows brown and sear.
-William Cullen Bryant

"Morning Charlie." Tommy pushed his way into Charlie's office using the large basket he had carried in.

"Thomas." Charlie rubbed his hands over his face. He took the cup of coffee Tommy poured for him gratefully. After a big drink, he sighed. "Caroline took a turn for the worse last night. I believe the infection has traveled to her brain."

"That's too bad. I checked their family out. If Caroline is lost, that little girl doesn't have any other family to take her in." Tommy set the basket on the floor. "I brought some food for you and Lou. How's she doing? Still looking healthy?"

"As of last night she was still pretty strong. I haven't seen her yet this morning." Charlie rubbed the tense muscles on the back of his neck. "I stopped by, but she asked for some more sleep before she broke her fast. She hasn't left that child's side for a week, so I thought more sleep wouldn't hurt."

"You're actually letting her get by without an exam?"

"I most certainly am not." Charlie chuckled. "I'll be going up with her breakfast soon. After the night I've had, I needed a good strong cup of coffee before I checked on Lizzie. I have little doubt Jane would let me know if she felt worse. You can come with me when I go up to check on her if you want."

A bell rang Charlie's head. The cord on it tugged again and again, the insistent ring grew stronger with each pull. Tommy smirked. "So much for your coffee."

They both rose together to rush out of the office toward the stairs. Charlie ran faster, his concern for Lizzie after the turn her mother had taken far too strong to allow him to dawdle. He burst into the room, stopping short when he found Jane near the balcony doors, and the child sound asleep in her bed. "Jane?"

She'd barely budged when he'd stormed in, but now remained still for a few moments. Then her weight shifted and she turned slowly. A handkerchief pressed to the throat. She clutched it tight in her uninjured hand. With the bright morning light behind her, he couldn't make out her features. Her head bobbed in a small nod. "Charles."

His fist clenched at the weakness of her voice. "Is it Lizzie?"

"No. I'm afraid not." Jane stepped forward. "Lizzie seems to be improving. As much as I'd like to continue to help care for her, it might be best to move her from my room. I'm sorry."

Tommy's voice erupted in a gravelly grow. "You got it?"

"I'm not entirely certain, but it seems as though I do. I probably should not have sent you away this morning,

Charles." Her voice cracked. The kerchief pressed to her lips as her eyes fluttered closed. After several moments she spoke again. "I was comfortable asleep, but the more I woke the more I realized how cold I was. When I tried to swallow—my throat is so raw."

Charlie moved next to her. He touched her forehead with the back of his fingers. Even without the thermometer he could tell she was on fire. "Clara."

"At least now we know." Her smile was as weak as her voice.

"Thomas, move the child please. Come and sit down, Clara. I'll do an exam and get you some medicine. You're going to be fine." He had to believe it, because the alternative was unacceptable. When Jane swayed, he wrapped his arm around her waist to lead her back to the bed. "I have to say I'm proud of you."

"For what?" She let him guide her to the bed. Immediately upon getting in, she tugged the covers up to her chin.

Charlie opened the medical bag he'd left on her bedside table. "For telling me straight away. I thought you might try to hide it."

"How could I? You checked on me every ten minutes." She managed a small laugh, though it quickly dissolved into a cough. Once she had it under control, she leaned her head back against the headboard. "Except when I'm sleeping. That's the only reason I didn't get up when you knocked. I wanted a few more minutes."

Tommy stomped back into the room. He dropped heavily onto the side of Jane's bed. "What's the word, Charlie?" He took Jane's hand in his and cradled it gently.

When Charlie held up his finger and remained focused on his pocket watch while he checked her pulse, Jane took a shaky breath. "Don't let Cole risk himself over this."

"Like I could stop him." Tommy scoffed. "It's been difficult enough with you healthy and strong. I'll do whatever I can, but don't count on it."

Charlie cut off her protest with a thermometer. He kept as stern an expression as he could when she glared at him. "Stop your talking immediately. In case you hadn't noticed, us Young boys aren't idiots. We know how you feel on this matter. Right now all you need to do is focus on staying strong and fighting this with all your might."

Jane's shoulders sagged. She lowered her defiant glare to frown at her hand.

Tommy squeezed the hand he held. "Hey. I was your boy's age when I got it and I made it through all right. So will you and that little girl."

Jane's brow furrowed and she opened her mouth to speak. Charlie raised his hand to stop her in her tracks. Arms folded across her chest, she glared at Charlie until he removed the thermometer. "Her mother?"

Charlie hazarded a glance at Tommy. Rather than answer, he lifted the thermometer to read it. "One-oh-two point three. Clara."

"I understand, Charles. I'm sick. I figured that out all on my own. Now tell me. What about Caroline?" Jane's free hand clutched her throat, her eyes fluttered shut again.

"She isn't doing well. Charlie says he thinks it went to her brain," Tommy said quietly. "We don't yet know what'll happen."

A shudder tore through Jane's body hard enough to make the bed creak. Her head lolled to the side. Charlie cupped her face in his hands. "Clara? Clara, look at me."

Her eyes remained hooded, though she tried to follow through on his demand. "I don't feel so well."

"When it starts, it comes on strong. I need to check your throat first and then you can rest, all right?" Charlie furrowed his brow at her weak nod. He nudged his chin toward Tommy and whispered, "Get me the acetate of ammonia, and the nitrate, just in case she needs it."

Once Tommy crossed the room to fetch the medicine, Charlie pulled open Jane's mouth. With the candle held close, he frowned. Already several ulcers were visible in her throat. "And what about the rash, Jane?"

Jane didn't reply, and her shrug dissolved into tremors.

"It's been awful quiet around the saloon." Tommy sat on the bed and handed Charlie the medicine. "All except for that damn piano."

That got Jane's eyes open, and Charlie was grateful for that. He knew his brother was doing exactly what he was, trying to keep her awake. Not that it mattered; the fever would take her soon.

She blinked slowly. "Piano?"

"Cole had it moved over from the library when you left with Kat and the rev. He wanted to surprise you." Tommy nudged her.

"You ruined the…" Jane groaned.

Tommy grabbed a nearby basin and held it under her so she could get sick. He ran his hand along her hair as she made use of it. "I'm horrible at keeping secrets."

"Liar." She pressed her handkerchief to her lips.

When she groaned again, Tommy frowned. He turned his attention to Charlie. "We'll need to find someone to stay with the girl that's been exposed. Has Ida?"

"I'll ask." Charlie waited until Jane finished before handing her the medicine he'd mixed for her. "Drink slowly."

"Kat insisted she's been exposed, but Daisy reminded her Jane was watching over Lizzie. I'm sure she's not going to want to stay away now that she knows Jane's sick." Tommy carried the basin away from the bed.

Jane held out the glass. "All gone."

"Now I know you're sick. You're being far too complacent." Charlie smiled. While she sank lower in the covers he put the medicine away. "Go ahead and rest now."

"If you insist." She mumbled, her head dropped to the side.

Tommy rubbed the back of his neck. With a wave, he moved into the hall and stood silent until Charlie joined him. The minute the door shut he spoke. "So?"

"It took a few days, but once it came on it came on strong. I can't begin to predict what's going to happen." Charlie pressed his fingers to his forehead. Concern and fear colored every sane thought. "Everyone in our family that's gotten it has come out the other end without any serious lasting effects. I have faith she'll be the same."

"What about Uncle Clay?" Tommy folded his arms across his chest.

A laugh threatened to disrupt the concern and Charlie's lips twitched. "He was just an idiot. Before or after Scarlet Fever made no difference."

"Good point." Tommy did let his laughter out. It didn't last long and he took a big breath. "Now for the fun part. I get to try to make Cole stay put."

"You'll need luck on your side for that one."

"Luck doesn't seem to be with us today."

Refuse to be ill. Never tell people you are ill; never own it yourself. Illness is one of of those things which a man should resist on principle.
—Edward Butler-Lytton

Cole wiped down the bar. A figure entering caught his attention. Before Hammy could make it to a stool, Cole set down a beer for him. "Jane keeps sending word for me to give you free beer. What sort of game are you playing, Hammy?"

The scruffy old man gave him a gap-toothed grin. "Ain't sure what you're talking 'bout. I ain't doing nothing special."

"Jane must think you are. She don't give free beer to all the old fogeys that come into this place." Cole tapped the bar as the old man chuckled. The chances he'd had to talk with Jane had been few and far between while she'd been cooped up in the clinic. It drove him to distraction to not have her in his bed. He'd gotten so used to her being there.

"Don't rightly know what ya mean." Hammy practically buried his face in his mug. A bright red hue took over his usually ruddy complexion.

"What're ya up to, Hammy?"

"Just nothin'." Hammy shrugged. "I only asked Miss Cora to order her a book every day so she'd have somethin' new all the time. I don't read much, but I think it might get borin' for her readin' the same books all the time. Used the money the town gave me for them homes. I don't need it anyhow. Books'll stop comin' when the money's gone, I suspect."

"If you don't keep putting money in." Cole smirked. He knew the old bastard had more money that he let on. Hammy was the one that had loaned Cole enough money to buy the saloon years ago when he'd first come to town. While Cole had managed to pay back the money years ago, he was one of the few that knew what deep pockets Hammy had thanks to an early gold find and subsequent sale of most of his claims to the Daugherty's for a hefty sum.

"Ain't sure what you mean." Hammy was also more crafty than most suspected. They all thought the stroke he'd had some time back had addled his brain more than he'd been addled before. Cole knew Hammy just preferred being happy, and making those he cared about happy. Including Jane, whom Hammy had been sweet on near as long as Cole himself.

"Of course you don't."

"How's she doing? Any sign of the fever?" Hammy wiped at the foam on his mustache. The hopeful face betrayed how sweet Hammy was on Jane.

"I haven't heard word today. I talked to her a bit yesterday. She was tired, and annoyed with her brother, but in good spirits." Cole frowned. "Tommy went by today. I expect word soon."

The piano sat silent across the room. The day Jane had gone out to deliver supplies he'd moved it in as a surprise. Just like always, Jane's advice had proved sound and the saloon was livelier than it had been in years. Despite Cole's personal issues with the piano being there, he couldn't deny it turned out to be a good thing.

When word arrived of Jane's trouble, the whole building had gone silent for almost an hour. Unable to bear the new levels of silence, he'd pushed Chauncey back to the piano and made sure things got good and riled up again.

After that, he'd followed through on her promise to take her kid for a ride out to Mike's place. They'd gone to visit her so Jesse could see his Ma looking good and strong. Seeing her in that room had ripped up Cole's insides something fierce.

Just when he'd managed to admit how he felt she was torn away from him. It felt like a cruel joke.

"Cole?" Hammy savored a sip of beer. Once he'd licked the foam from his mustache he turned his attention away to stare at himself in the mirror rather than face Cole. "Lady Jane said maybe you'd be building on."

The man wasn't hurting for work, but Cole had promised he'd get the job if the expansion ever happened. Jane's suggestion must have been made in the excitement of her buying Graham's part of the business. Cole frowned. "Ain't sure yet, Hammy. Jane hasn't even bought in yet. Then she's gonna have to work her magic with investors. She's hoping it'll be easier to get an investor than a loan since she said something about banks being nervous since the silver went down."

Hammy's brow pursed. "What?"

"Just means times are gonna be tough."

"Ain't they always?" Hammy shrugged and finished off his beer. "So then you won't mind if I take on another big job? Mrs. Daugherty wants to build a theater and a big dress shop. Think they might move back now that the town's growing."

"That so?" Cole straightened. That nugget of information could mean anything. Any fool could see the town was growing fast, but as Jane had said, the drop of silver prices had scared most people. Didn't help that quite a few lost their jobs at the silver mines because of it.

It was something Jane might not even know yet. He doubted anyone did, but Hammy never could keep a secret. Cole smirked and gave Hammy another beer. "You know what? They want to build up a theater and dress shop, I say it might as well be the best. Go right ahead, Hammy. Hopefully Jane'll be out and we can see about those investors soon, but don't keep yourself from work on our account."

"Right good of ya, Cole." Hammy lifted his glass in salute.

The door swung open and Tommy strolled in. Without any haste he made his way through the thin crowd. Much like Jane, the man already knew most of the regulars and called them by name, asked after their families. It was all very normal, but Cole's whole body went tense.

His gut told him something was wrong.

Tommy stepped behind the bar. After a quick greeting, he poured himself a drink. While he gulped on his whisky, he leaned back casually on the counter. The casual position put most of his bulk in front of Cole's only exit.

Cole ground his teeth together. The towel he'd been wiping the counter with felt heavy in his hands. He tossed it aside to face his friend. "Tommy. What's the latest? Is the girl getting better finally?"

"Yup." Tommy downed the whiskey quickly. He set it aside. One hand braced on the bar, the other on the back counter.

"And Jane?"

"She don't want you risking yourself. Remember that." Tommy didn't budge, a stern furrow to his brow. "She's got it."

Cole's stomach fell through the floor when Tommy confirmed his greatest fear. In a heartbeat it jolted back, twisted so tight he had to grip the bar to steady himself. "Ya sure? She's been fine all this time."

"Charlie examined her a little while ago. Fever, chills, throat is red as an apple."

The whole time Tommy spoke, Cole considered his limited options. He could fight his way past Tommy, but that would waste valuable time. He had one option left, so he took it. He gripped the edge of the bar and launched himself over it.

"Cole! Damn it." Tommy stomped behind him.

Cole didn't give him a chance to catch up, no matter if the man was surprisingly fast for such a large man. Using every inch of his long stride, Cole ran across the street all the way down to the clinic. He burst inside without hesitation. "Where is she doc?"

"You shouldn't be here." Charlie moved to block him. "There's still time to leave without worrying about infection. She wouldn't want you putting yourself at risk. She specifically told us not to let you."

"I didn't ask ya that. Where is she? Same room?" At Charlie's nod, Cole raced up the steps two at a time. He shoved open the door separating the two halves of the building and stormed down the hall right into Jane's room. "Jane?"

Curled up under layers of blankets she slept, just one arm on top of the blankets. A faint gleam of sweat shimmered on her brow, her mouth parted slightly. She didn't move an inch when he pulled the chair close to the bed.

Cole sighed and set his hand in hers. A crinkle of paper drew his attention to her palm. He slipped a slightly damp slip of paper free of her loose grasp. One brow rose at the discovery. He glanced at her before pulling open the paper.

The moment he read the words, he threw his head back in laughter. He didn't bother to try to be quiet, almost hoping she'd wake up to curse him.

"What the hell are you doing? She's supposed to be resting." Charlie set a fresh basin of water next to the bed along with a sponge. "Waking her up is not part of what needs to be done to help her."

"Sorry Doc." Cole kept chuckling. "Guess she figured Tommy wouldn't have any luck keeping me away."

Charlie took the piece of paper he offered. "It just says 'Damn fool'."

"Yup. That's all it needs to say. She knew I'd be here." Cole grinned and snatched it back, putting it in his breast pocket. "That's her way of yelling at me."

"She's right, you know. If you get sick—you'll be useless by the time she comes out of it. You'll be the first one she'd want to see. She feels guilty as hell for not being able to take care of Lizzie anymore."

"I ain't gonna wait around the saloon."

"Not anymore you're not." Charlie pressed the damp sponge against Jane's forehead. With a sigh, he handed it to

Cole. "She's had the chills, but we need to cool down her fever as much as we can. If it gets too high, she'll be in real trouble."

"Just tell me what to do. We'll be fine. I know you got other patients." Cole remained quiet and listened to Charlie's instructions on sponging her down carefully. At this point he'd do whatever it took.

Once Charlie had left, Cole set about removing her nightgown and corset so that all she wore was the chemise. The tremors that ran through her and left her teeth chattering made his stomach turn, but he still did as instructed.

In the hall he could hear Charlie, Tommy and what he guessed was James in a brief argument before their steps receded and silence fell.

He stopped what he was doing to lean close. "You gotta get better. I'm not the only damn fool here. I got plenty to be yelling at you for, so you wake up. Understood?"

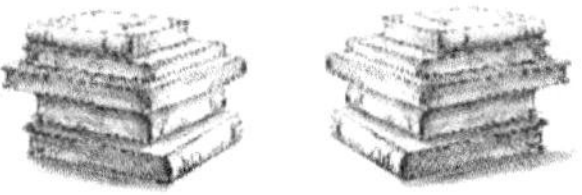

Laughter is the sun that drives winter from the human face.
—Victor Hugo

Kat touched her fingers to Lizzie's forehead. The girl no longer felt like fire to the touch, so she released a sigh of relief. With any luck the fever would be completely gone soon.

When she'd received word Jane had fallen ill two days before, her first instinct had been to come and help Lizzie. She and Jane had both promised Caroline Broder well over a year ago they'd take care of the girl should anything happen to the Broder's. Still, she had her own daughter Cindy to worry about as well.

It was Cindy herself that told Kat to go help her friend. Since Kat had been exposed when she was younger, her risk was minimal, and Cindy wanted to be sure her good friend Lizzie was well cared for. Even with the presence of Ida in the clinic, Lizzie had never met James' wife, and Cindy didn't want Lizzie to wake to a stranger.

Daisy might have been there too, but Lizzie didn't know her all that well, and Daisy had other patients. In fact, the female doctor had been spending most of her time caring for the lesser ills of the town out at the hotel since so many were afraid to set foot in the clinic.

Kat sighed and rose. She crossed the room to look out the window. Lizzie's room looked onto not much of anything. She had a good view of the alley below, and a partial view of the street over the next rooftop. The alley was quiet, but the street itself bustled with life and activity, which Kat knew most everyone in the clinic wanted to be a part of. Once the scare was over, Kat would take Norman and Cindy on a picnic out in the wide open.

"Here you go, Katherine." Ida carried a tray of food into the room and set it on the table. As always, the elegant woman had her hair pinned in proper, well tamed curls and a thick knot. Not a hair sat out of place. "You slept through breakfast. I thought you might want some food."

"I do, actually." Kat didn't often feel self-conscious, but she tapped her own unruly red curls before taking a seat. Ida had never looked down her nose at Kat's wild appearance with her untamed hair and the pants she wore, but something about the woman's easy elegance and quiet demeanor made Kat keenly aware of their differences. "I'm rather hungry. It's easy to lose track of time when you're locked in this place."

"I know. I think Charles keeps checking his watch so he doesn't lose track. James and Tommy are picking on him incessantly for it." Ida smiled brightly. While Kat started eating, she crossed to the bed. Just as Kat had done, Ida smoothed her fingers across Lizzie's forehead. "How is the little one doing?"

"Charlie was in here a little while ago. He says the infection has spread to her ears, that's why she's still a little warm." Kat sipped her tea to wash down the food she was shoveling in. She hadn't realized she was so hungry until the food was in front of her. Once she was able to slow down and eat with some decorum, she let out a heavy sigh. "By and large, it's far better than her parents fared, but I do wish she'd recover enough for more than a few minutes of wakefulness at a time."

Ida took a seat at the table, a small frown teasing her dainty lips. "Charlie said Caroline's stroke was quite severe. If she does wake, she may be unable to function. Such tragedy for this poor family. I hear it isn't their first, either."

"It isn't. First their home, then Dorsey lost his job at the mines, and now this."

"I'll never understand such suffering."

Kat couldn't stop her laughter from bubbling until it erupted. Ida's confused glance only bolstered her amusement.

She held up her hands and shook her head. "I'm sorry, I don't mean to sound callous. It isn't like that at all. I completely agree with you. It is almost too much to bear, but I just had to wonder what Jane would say if she heard our conversation. She'd likely cite some great mind with a perfectly fitting statement."

"'You must submit to supreme suffering in order to discover the completion of joy'. John Calvin." Charlie smiled from the doorway. "I brought Lizzie's medicine. I didn't mean to interrupt, I just happened to overhear."

Ida laughed, a delightful tinkling sound that brightened the atmosphere in the room. "You don't need to apologize. How is Jane this morning?"

Charlie's smile faded into deep lines of concern across his forehead. He set the medicine down next to Lizzie's bed and wiped his palms on his trousers. "Her fever isn't breaking. In fact, it's getting worse. When she does wake, which is rare, she's always in some state of delirium."

The booming voice of Tommy chimed in from the door, breaking through the somberness. "Delirium is her natural state."

The lump that had begun to lodge its way into Kat's throat dissolved under Tommy's humor. She grinned, letting it erupt into a bright smile at Charlie's exasperated sigh.

"I meant beyond her usual delirium." A droll smirk broke Charlie's frown. "What are you doing here, Thomas?"

"Wanted to stop by and see Lou. Edgar's got the saloon for now, and I got a lead on some more help for Cole." Tommy nodded toward the table. "Ladies. I hope I didn't interrupt your gossip session. Just heard Charlie jawing off."

Kat gave up on decorum to set her laughter free. "You didn't interrupt, Tommy. You're welcome to join us if you'd like. Although, if you're looking for good gossip, you might have tea with the widow Swearengen. She always seems to have her ear placed firmly to the ground."

A great shudder ran through Tommy that he took the step to kick out from his toes. "No thank you. I'll get my gossip elsewhere if I want it. Alcohol tends to loosen tongues, don't you know?"

Ida snorted when he tipped his hat and left. She leaned across the table toward Kat. "He failed to mention that men tend to be bigger gossips than women."

"No wonder Jane likes spending so much time in that saloon, then." Kat giggled at Charlie's amused smirk. "And here we all thought it was Cole. Silly us, right Charlie?"

"Of course." Charlie chuckled, the tense lines on his forehead softened under his laughter. "Now finish your lunch. You need to keep your strength up as much as the little one does. It's only been one day. We have a very long week ahead of us."

"I know." Kat sighed and obliged him by eating her food as quick as she could.

"Why don't you go with Charlie for a bit? Get out and see something other than this room for a few minutes. I'll sit with Lizzie." Ida rose and headed for the bed.

Kat pondered for a minute, then pushed out of the chair. "I think I will. This room doesn't have the doors to look out of like Jane's room. A change of scenery might do me good for a few minutes. If she wakes—"

"I'll ring the bell the minute she starts to stir." Ida pointed toward the pull-string just above the headboard. "Don't you worry."

"Thank you." Kat smiled and followed Charlie from the room. Halfway down the stairs they heard a door close above them and both froze. It wasn't until Tommy appeared at the top of the stairs without any trace of panic that they resumed their path.

Tommy nudged his brother when they got to the waiting room. "Get yourself in a bed, Charlie. The world isn't going to end if you catch a few winks."

"With three sick patients upstairs you can't say that." Charlie glared. "It might just for one or all of them."

"Just stopped in on Caroline." Tommy boosted himself to sit on the desk. "She's the same. Catatonic."

Kat sighed. "And Jane?"

"Cole's sleeping finally. Jane's fitful with the heat, but didn't wake up when I was in there at all. Did hit me a few times, though."

"Well." Charlie brightened. "Maybe she isn't delirious, then."

"You're funny." Tommy's lip curled. "Real funny."

"I know."

"Boys." Kat laughed. "You're as bad as the Turner boys and you don't have the excuse of youth. Behave yourselves."

"I'm afraid I don't have the discipline of the great Charles Emerson Young, my dear." Tommy hopped off the desk. "But I do have to get back to the inn. Need to make sure it keeps running smooth without Cole or Jane there."

"I'll make sure everyone stays updated." Charlie nodded.

Tommy threw open the door, and froze right at the entrance. "Sorry about that Dr. Pearson. Always lovely to see you." He hopped out of the way and dipped into an elegant bow despite his girth.

"As it is with you, Tommy." Daisy couldn't hide her flustered blush. "How is everything at the Hangman's Inn?"

"Running smooth as it can without Jane there to keep them lot of ruffians in line." Tommy smirked. After another bow, he left the clinic.

Kat nodded to Daisy. "Afternoon, Daisy. How's the rest of the town faring?"

"Well enough. I saw Cindy this morning. Arthur is taking her and the boys fishing today." Daisy set down her bag and cast a stern eye on Charlie. "How are you holding up, Charlie?"

"About as well as can be expected." Charlie rested his chin on his hand. The man looked about ready to fall asleep right there.

"And our patients?" Daisy set her bag on a side table and her hat on a hook. In the past two years, after finally returning to her position as town doctor, and both the friendship of a colleague like Charlie and the caring friendship of Mike, Daisy had once again become the woman she'd come to town as. The whore she'd been for three years only made itself known through her continual use of powders and the way she left her hair fly loose unless in surgery.

"Caroline is catatonic." Charlie rubbed his hand over his face. "Lizzie is improving. She's maintained a temperature, but I believe it's because the infection has settled in her ears."

"We'll have to keep an eye on that." Daisy sat on the chair next to Kat. "And Jane?"

"The rash set in last night. It wasn't a peaceful night for her or Cole. I don't like how high her fever is, and have been checking her often. I'm concerned it will get too high." Charlie tapped his thumb on the desk, a nervous habit Kat had noticed he shared with Jane. "Her tonsils might need to come out at the rate they've swollen."

"Hopefully surgery won't be required. Her body couldn't take it right now." Daisy bit her lip.

Before Kat could ask any of the questions brewing in her head, one of the bells over Charlie's head started to ring frantically. Every head turned toward it and Kat gasped. "That's Lizzie's room."

All three of them leaped to their feet and rushed up the stairs. Before they'd arrived at the door separating the halves of the building they could hear Lizzie's cries. Panic gripped Kat's heart and froze it until Charlie shoved open the door.

Her heart resumed beating, but pounded fast in her chest and she raced down the hall, beating Charlie to the room. Inside she found Ida trying to calm down Lizzie, who'd hidden in a corner.

Kat touched Ida on the shoulder and moved around her. She fought down the erratic heartbeat of panic and dug deep to find a smile. It never helped a child's fear to see an adult just as scared. "Hi, Lizzie. Sweetie, it's all right."

Lizzie stared up at her with wide eyes and shook her head viciously. After a few heaving breaths she released another loud wail. Her hands flew to cover her eyes once again.

"All right, Lizzie." Kat moved in front of the child to kneel down. Once Lizzie peeked at her, she held out her hand. "You're going to be fine. I'm here. I'm here."

Lizzie sobbed and scrambled into Kat's lap. She threw her arms around Kat's neck with a low whimper.

Kat sat on the floor with a sigh and held her close.

"I'm not sure she heard you." Ida whispered.

"Neither am I." Kat rubbed Lizzie's back and rocked her gently. "But we won't know for sure until she calms down."

"We'll let you do that." Daisy waved everyone else toward the door. "She knows you best. If you need me, ring the bell. I'm sending Charlie to take a nap."

Kat nodded. "I will, Daisy. Thank you."

Once they left, she sighed and rested her cheek on the top of Lizzie's head. "Don't you worry, little one. I'll take care of you. For your ma and for Cindy."

Hope is necessary in every condition.
The miseries of poverty, sickness, of captivity
would, without this comfort,
be insupportable.
-Samuel Johnson

Cole remained still when the door creaked closed and shut with a solid click after Charlie poked his head in the room. The chaos with the girl in the next room had woken Cole, but he wasn't ready for visitors and was glad the doctor didn't enter. After all, he'd just been in to check on Jane two hours before.

Sleep hadn't been easy. Partly because Charlie checked on Jane every few hours. Mostly because he'd been so worried for Jane that he'd caught only a few minutes of sleep here and there.

Every time she moved or groaned; he woke. Charlie's increasing visits to check her fever and rash didn't help Cole's state of mind. The doc couldn't hide his intense worry. Daisy's recent visits to the room as well proved she was aware of the issue.

All night long Cole had remained a foot away from Jane's feverish form. He'd been under strict orders to not add to her temperature if he could help it, and for her alone he'd behaved. Even now his fingers stayed inches from hers, though he longed to take her hand and offer some form of comfort.

His whole body ached from the tense vigil he'd kept, from his unwillingness to get more comfortable even in sleep. Half the night he'd spent sponging her down, the other half pretending to sleep when it was impossible.

This last bout of pretending to sleep had somehow led to a small amount of actual sleep. Not enough to ease his tired mind, but he'd managed to doze. Maybe because Jane had been the quietest she'd been all night.

The realization struck him like a lightning bolt. Cole's eyes flew open fast. He flew to sit beside her so he could actually see her. His breath came in short bursts as he slipped off the edge of the bed. "Jane."

The second he regained his bearings, he leaned over to study her face. Her skin remained pale, her normally pink lips hinted toward blue. Her chest rose in a painfully slow, weak breath before growing still again.

"Jane!" With a panicked, sharp movement, he yanked on the bell string. It snapped off in his hands. He let out a string of curses. "*Charlie.*"

Cole flew to the door and threw it open. "*Charlie. Doc. Hurry.*"

Once footsteps pounded up the stairs, Cole ran back to her side. He set his hand on hers, finding it to be the hottest it had been yet. He grabbed a sponge to wipe her down again. "Come on, Jane. I told you, you ain't allowed to do this."

"Cole?" Charlie flew to the other side of the bed. After a brief exam, he cursed. "That's not going to be enough, Cole."

Cole stumbled out of the way when Charlie shoved him aside. "What the hell?"

Charlie lifted the whole basin of water and dumped it on Jane. "We've got to cool her down now. Fast. Pick her up; we need to get her downstairs. I'm going to need help."

Without hesitation, Cole slipped his hands under her knees and back and hauled her off the bed. Before he'd straightened, Charlie had rushed onto the balcony. The doctor let out a sharp whistle much as Jane used to get an unruly crowds attention.

Shockingly, every single noise outside quieted.

Charlie leaned over the balcony. "Tommy. Ice. Now. Lots of it. The tub is downstairs. James, Mike—get enough water to fill it. *Fast.*"

Cole followed Charlie to the door and ran down the hall. Jane didn't react to the brutal jarring of his pace, not even a flutter of an eyelid.

It hadn't taken a minute to get downstairs, but there was a line of four men through the waiting room and hall, transferring buckets of water and ice between them in a bucket brigade he'd not seen the likes of since the fires set by the renegades.

Tommy came barreling in the back door hauling two large buckets Cole recognized from the Inn. Both were full with chunks of ice.

Charlie didn't stop, walking right past the bucket brigade to the room it led to. He pointed to the tub as he passed.

While he stood there, Tommy dumped the ice into the tub, then turned to bolt out the door. A minute later, Chauncey carried in two equally full buckets.

"What? How? Takes forever to chip those ice blocks." Cole stared at the tub filling fast with water and ice.

Chauncey hefted the empty buckets. "Tommy's been having us hack at it for days."

Charlie pointed to the tub. "Put her in."

Cole hesitated. "What?"

"Get her in. Now. We have to get her temperature down immediately." Charlie grabbed a couple empty jars and a mug, tossing out the coffee inside.

Cole's stomach twisted, but he did as he was told. The ice water burned his flesh as much as Jane's feverish body had. He held his breath and kept her descent steady despite the cold so she wouldn't fall. The second she was in he ripped his arms out. "Are you insane? That's freezing."

"Exactly. Her fever spiked too high." Charlie handed the jars and mugs around. "It's making her heart work too hard."

"Meaning?" Cole turned the jar in his hand in confusion.

"Simply, it means she could die." Charlie tugged him toward the head of the tub and shoved him into a chair. "Make yourself feel useful. Just like this."

Cole wrinkled his nose when Charlie dumped a cup of the cold ice water over Jane's hair. Still, he followed suit. If it meant Jane not dying, he'd throw himself under a stampeding horse again.

"Try to get her to drink some when she starts to come awake, James." Charlie turned his attention to the medicine on the counter and began to mix some.

James filled the mug he held with ice water and held it gingerly to Jane's mouth. Not a word was spoken until Tommy dismissed the men that had helped once the tub got full. Cole nodded his thanks to the men that all popped in to wish them the best of luck before silence fell.

"The ice is already melting." Charlie murmured as he handled the mortar with medicine. "I don't think we need to worry about hypothermia, Cole."

Cole ground his teeth together when James mixed the medicine in with the ice water in his mug and tried to get Jane to drink again. With a sigh, Cole lifted another cup of ice water and poured it over Jane's head. "How long does she gotta stay in here?"

"Until we get her heart under one hundred beats per minute." Charlie set his hand on Jane's shoulder when she shuddered.

Her blue eyes fluttered open and darted between Charlie and Cole. After a moment they rolled back to reveal the whites before closing again.

"Jane?" Cole ran his thumb over her forehead.

Charlie kept his hand on her neck, one eye on his pocket watch. "She's doing better. I wouldn't count on steady consciousness. It's going to be a while before we reach that."

"She never has that." Tommy muttered, adding more ice to the water.

Cole chuckled and nodded. "Not much steady here."

James smirked when Tommy nudged him. "Don't try to get me involved. I'd prefer she not beat me up when she does waken."

"Yellow." Tommy snorted. "Jane'll tell you when she wakes. You're yellow."

Even with his focus still on his watch, Charlie grinned. "Be careful—getting her mad could get her heart going again, too."

"That's not the only thing." Cole laughed when James almost dropped his cup with the force of his guffaw.

"Hey. We're her brothers. We don't need to hear that." Tommy's nose wrinkled.

"She'd say the same thing, and ya know it." Cole stopped pouring to eye Tommy.

"Damn it. You're right."

*The sorrow for the dead is the only sorrow
from which we refuse to be divorced.
-Washington Irving*

"Jane?" Through the fog and clinging oblivion of sleep, Charlie's voice stirred her toward consciousness. "Jane. Can you hear me?"

Jane wrinkled her nose against the pull away from the comfort of sleep. She cracked one eye open. The sunlight was blissfully blocked by curtains, so she felt safe to open her other eye. She nodded, but immediately regretted the simple action when the room spun. "Yes. I think."

"Easy." He set a nice cool hand on her forehead. A smile lit his previously strained features. "I need you to listen to me, all right?"

"Jesse?"

"He's fine. Healthy as a horse."

"Lizzie." She tried to push herself to sitting, but her arms refused to work. Every word and question she needed to ask or say waited in the back of her painful throat. She wanted to say so much, but she was sure the fires of hell burned in her throat.

"She's doing much better. There is a lingering fever, but it's as low as yours has finally become. The infection spread to her ears and is holding on tight."

Her repeated attempts to sit stalled when his words sank through the fog in her mind. Her eyes widened and she met his eyes. "Ears?"

"Yes. We're pretty sure she isn't going to hear again."

Tears rushed forward at the revelation so fast she twitched her nose against them. One escaped to slip down her cheek. She sank back onto the bed and took a shuddering breath. "How…long…" Each word hurt, but she had so many questions.

"You've been down about four days now. You've needed two ice baths." He set his hand on hers. "Jane, I need you to stop asking questions and listen to me."

She knew she should, she understood, but she had to ask. "Mrs. Broder."

"Clara Louise. You listen to me now."

Reluctantly, she drew her gaze to his. There was a bit of embarrassment to note that her chin quivered. She gave him a small nod to show she'd listen.

"The infection is clinging to your tonsils. Your rash has dissipated and other than your tonsils, you aren't showing any other signs of lingering infection." Charlie held her hand gently. A cool sponge ran along her arm. "I'm going to need to remove your tonsils. If I get rid of the worst of the infection, you might just heal faster."

Jane frowned at the diagnosis. She sighed. "Whatever you need to do."

"Good girl."

"Where's Cole?"

"Right here." Cole spoke from somewhere out of her sight line.

She turned her head toward the sound. When she spotted him finally, she narrowed her eyes. "Damn fool."

"I know. Ya told me already." Cole took the chair beside the bed and leaned so far forward the chair creaked. "So far I ain't sick, so stop looking at me like I'm the one dying."

Charlie laughed. "And you'd best not start feeling guilty now. There's no need. We've been lucky. This has shown no signs of becoming an epidemic. We managed to keep it well contained. It's been over a week since you found the Broder's and there's no sign of anyone else in the camp getting sick."

"Thank heavens." She allowed a brief smile, but felt it tremble. "Mrs. Broder?"

Charlie lowered his eyes. A slow shake of his head preceded his deep sigh. "I'm sorry, Jane. We couldn't help her. Caroline had a stroke several days ago and was catatonic until the infection won."

"Oh no." Jane's lungs grew tight, the air not filling them as it had a few minutes before. The little girl was now all alone; the Broder's had no family left. Jane herself had promised to help care for the girl in case of the worst. Now the worst had happened. "Lizzie."

"She is being well cared for, and we will continue to do so." Charlie wiped away a few of her tears with his finger. "Please, Clara. You need to remain as calm as possible. I'm going to operate in a few hours. Now that you're awake, spend some time with the idiot that figured he was stronger than this infection."

Jane pulled her hand from Charlie's and reached over to grasp Cole's where it lay on her forearm. She let her eyes fall shut when Charlie kissed her forehead. "Thank you."

"Don't thank me yet. You won't be able to talk for some time after the surgery. You'll be cursing me soon enough, might as well not be sweet before that." Charlie rose. "I'm going to check on the others and prepare for your surgery."

"Thanks, doc." Cole set his other hand on top of hers. "We'll see ya in a bit."

The moment the door clicked shut she gave Cole's hand a squeeze. "Why are you here? I didn't want you risking yourself."

"Did you really think I wouldn't be here once I knew you were sick?" Cole chuckled when she wrinkled her nose and shrugged. "I'm gonna be fine. So are you."

"I'm impressed."

"By what?"

"That you managed to curb your impulse for as long as you did. I didn't think you'd last three days before you tried to barge in."

Laughing, he shook his head. "It was easier when you were healthy. Much as I enjoy getting slapped by you, I really wasn't in the mood. Besides, I knew you were focusing all your energy on the girl. You wouldn't have had no time for me."

"I always have time for you."

"No ya don't." He snorted. Her attempts to look wounded only increased his amusement. "Don't go getting all hurt. You know it's true. You got the library, and Kat, and your Tuesday's. You do plenty on your own time. Ain't complaining, just stating facts. We each got our own time."

"You would grow tiresome if I was always around you."

"Feeling's mutual."

She managed a smile, although it didn't feel too strong. It faded after a moment and she stared at their joined hands.

"Well go on. Get it out."

"If you get sick…" She swallowed against the thick lump, and winced at the burning flash of pain. "It won't be the infection that kills you. I'll do it myself."

"I know."

"But I'm glad you're here. I don't remember much of the past few days, but I knew you were here."

"Only one thing I ain't been able to do."

A smile tugged at her lips, but she sighed out the exasperation. The man had a one track mind. "Cole."

"No. Not that." His lips twisted into a frown, but then he hesitated. "All right, that too. But it ain't what I meant."

A weak giggle escaped, and she winced again. She squeezed his hand and raised a brow expectantly.

He met her gaze and shifted off the chair he perched on. After he'd detangled their hands, he stretched his long body out next to hers and pulled her close. He waited until she'd settled in against him. "You been too feverish. Charlie pitched a fit if I did more'n hold your hand. Then again, I had incentive to stay away."

"What's that?"

"You took a swing at anyone that got too close. Walloped Tommy and Charlie both real good a few times."

"They probably deserved it."

"Tommy sure was trying to earn it. But he's been keeping a good eye on the Inn for us. Even found another bartender."

Jane snuggled closer with a sigh and listened to his heartbeat. The steady, strong beat soothed her lingering worries until she'd relaxed. "You've been here for four days?"

"Since Tommy told me ya got it."

"What have you done with yourself? It must have been awfully boring for you."

"Wasn't so bad. Ya got pretty entertaining when you were delirious."

"You are not endearing yourself to me."

Laughing, he snuggled closer and let his fingers dance along her arm. "Ain't worried about that. You aren't going nowhere."

"Don't be so sure."

"Oh?"

"Plenty of options." She smiled against his chest when he shifted beneath her, most likely an attempt to meet her eyes. Focused on his bicep, she didn't give him the pleasure. "Al is still in town."

He tensed. The light touch of his fingers stopped on her forearm. The heartbeat she still focused on skipped and sped up. "Last I checked he was."

The immediate reaction Al's name always got from him annoyed her. As if she hadn't made it quite clear where her affections lie. A wicked thought jumped to the forefront and she bit her cheeks to keep the laughter at bay. "Of course, Mr. Hamm has always been so kind and adoring. I'm sure that—"

"Hammy?" Cole whooped, all tension leaving him. The bed shook with his laughter. "Now I know you're teasing me. You'd make his head spin if you even brushed up against him right. Ain't no way he could handle a woman like you."

"That so? Well, who could? You?"

"I get by—but I can't handle ya neither."

Her fingers laced with his and she snuggled closer with a pleased smile. "On the contrary. You handle me just right. In every way. Always did."

"Not always. There've been a couple of times ya didn't speak to me for weeks."

"Ah yes." She fought against the rising chuckle, knowing it would cause her worse discomfort than just talking quietly did. "That's because I was handling you."

"That so?" His hand ran along her back. "You do realize that every time you get mad at me, I mean real mad, you stop speaking to me. Cut me right off."

"When you're not distracted you think remarkably clear. Sometimes it just takes longer for you to see logically that I am right."

"What if you ain't right?"

"But I always am."

"Uh-huh."

She patted his stomach and nodded. Out of the corner of her eye she noticed something on the table beside the bed, something she'd suspected was there, but now had confirmed proof of. Her brow quirked up and she propped herself up on her elbow. "Maybe I'm still delirious."

"What?"

"Is that an open book?"

He shrugged, his lips pursed. "So?"

"You were bored."

"Nah."

Humming suspiciously, she laid back down on his chest.

"I was reading it to ya. All right?"

A smile curved her lips. "I know."

"Then why did you—no."

"So you'll only read to me when I'm unconscious? That's not very fair. I do love the sound of your voice…"

"No."

She sighed and nodded. "I suppose it's for the best anyhow. With what you were reading, I was already having rather intriguing dreams. You went back to Whitman."

"Never left."

"You wouldn't."

"Don't mean I like it." He smirked when she looked up.

"I wouldn't dream of accusing you of such a thing."

"Good." His chin rested on her head when she curled closer again.

"Cole."

"Hmm?"

"Don't you dare get sick."

His arms went around her and he held her tight. "Ain't gonna."

She buried her face in his chest and let her fear escape in another long shudder. The warmth of his arms and the soothing touch to her back worked against the burgeoning fear. Little by little she relaxed until she hovered on the edge of sleep.

A knock on the door prevented her from falling and Cole twitched above her with movement. His voice stayed low in what she guessed was an attempt to not wake her. "She ain't fully asleep. Just waiting for it to take hold."

"She doing better?" Kat sounded tired.

"Been yelling at me a fair deal. Think she's just fine."

"Good."

"The girl?"

Kat released a heavy sigh. "Her fever is almost gone. I think she wants her parents, but it's difficult to explain what happened. It just seems wrong to write it down and force her to read something like that."

"Ain't no other way if she can't hear." Another movement from Cole, probably a shrug. "It's better she know, rather than thinking they could walk in any second."

The man had a point. Kat knew it too; Jane figured she just didn't want to be the bearer of bad news. Kat's footsteps drew her closer to the bed. "I know. I just hate breaking the girls heart."

"'You must submit to supreme suffering in order to discover the completion of joy'." Jane whispered. "John Calvin."

Kat burst into laughter. "Oh goodness. You didn't really just say that, did you?"

Jane rolled to face her friend. Why the woman was laughing, Jane had no idea. Her brows knit together. "What?"

"Your brother said the exact same thing a few days ago." Kat squeezed her hand.

Cole chuckled. "Think your family needs to work on your act."

Jane smiled. "Sometimes it just works."

"Lizzie." Ida's panicked voice echoed down the hall.

All three of them turned toward the door. Jane tried to push herself to sitting, and couldn't have been more grateful for Cole's help to achieve it. She offered him a smile and swung her legs over the side of the bed. At that moment a streak of pure blond hair rushed through the room and hid behind the bureau.

"Lizzie." Ida burst in and scanned the room. She stopped at the sight of Jane. "I'm sorry. It's wonderful to see you awake, but Lizzie is a bit—"

"It's all right." Jane interrupted. She bit her lip and glanced at Kat. After a moment of indecision, she tried to rise to her feet.

"Jane. You shouldn't get up." Ida protested. "Katherine and I can take care of it. You need your rest."

"I know you can, and I know I do—but I haven't seen her since I fell ill." Jane struggled to get her limbs to respond.

"Sure you're strong enough?" Cole was beside her before she'd half risen, his hand placed firm at the small of her back.

"I've got you here. I'm sure I can make it five feet." She gripped his arm and sighed in relief when he helped her stand instead of arguing. It took a little doing, but she made it to the corner where Lizzie hid.

Lizzie curled up with her knees to her chest and rocked back and forth. When Jane sank down the wall, she startled.

Jane smiled and waved, not bothering to try to speak. After what Charlie said, she figured Lizzie wouldn't hear anyway. Seeing everyone talking and not hearing it probably scared the daylights out of her.

Lizzie's eyes shifted over to the legs beside Jane, and then rose up toward the ceiling, her already pale skin almost white.

After following the path of Lizzie's gaze, Jane's brow popped up and she smirked. With a grin she turned back to Lizzie and made a scary face. She laughed when Lizzie nodded. Jane wrinkled her nose and pushed on Cole's legs to make him move a few feet away.

Lizzie sucked her lips into her mouth. She wiped at her tears and rested her chin on her knees.

Jane turned completely away so Lizzie wouldn't see she was talking aloud. "Kat, would you get me a pencil and paper, please?"

At the movement, Lizzie's head lifted again. Not one movement was missed, and by the time Jane had the paper in front of her she opened her mouth to speak. "Mama." The word was a little drawn out, but Lizzie's brow furrowed and she clasped her hands over her ears. Tears slipped down her cheeks.

Jane squeezed her knee and moved closer. After a minute, she shifted so she was lying on her belly on the floor, the paper in front of her. It wasn't comfortable in the slightest and she almost gave into Cole and Kat's protests, but when Lizzie moved to join her she was glad she had.

With the paper between them, Jane remembered the hand she'd broken before she got sick. It still wouldn't let her write, so she could only hope Lizzie would be able to read her writing. She gripped the pencil in her right hand and began to write. *Apples and bananas. Monkeys in a tree. The monsters cannot get you. They only come for the flea.*

Lizzie perked up, a smile growing.

The dark is naught. The stars still shine above. No evil enters in a home so filled with love.

Lip trembling, Lizzie shook her head and buried her face in her arm with a sob.

Jane wrote a little more, and then tapped Lizzie's hand with the pencil.

The girl looked up with a sniff, turning toward the paper.

I know you want to know. I want to tell you. Will you talk to me?

Lizzie hesitated, but offered a weak nod.

You can still talk, but the world is quiet to you. I can hear the world, but it is annoying.

A weak smile crossed Lizzie's lips for a moment. She nodded and took the pencil. Her tongue poked out while she concentrated on writing neat and careful. *Why is the world quiet?*

Jane sighed and pulled the paper close to write it down.

"We've tried notes before." Kat whispered. "What's different?"

"We used to practice writing together when I visited." Jane didn't budge from the paper or writing. "We made up a little poem when she got scared of sleeping in the tent with the winds and all. I figured she was still scared and it might help."

"Is that what you two were doing?" Kat chuckled. "I should have known. How many children were you secretly tutoring when we went to the village?"

Waving off the question, Jane turned the paper back to Lizzie. *Your family and I got very sick. When I came by your house, I found your Ma and Pa and you all very sick. I had Miss Kat get the doctors and we came back here.*

The sickness we had is very, very bad. It hurts other parts of us, and it hurt each of us different. It is in your ears and in my throat. It hurt your Ma and Pa much worse.

The tears that had slowed began to stream down Lizzie's cheeks again. Sorrow laced through the words she managed to form. "Ma. Pa."

Jane shifted, but with her hand still weak couldn't quite sit without Cole's help. Once she was sitting, she urged Lizzie close. She pulled the paper closer and wrapped one arm around Lizzie's shoulder as she wrote. *I'm sorry, Lizzie. The sickness took them away. I'm so sorry."*

With a loud sob, Lizzie flung the paper away. She fought against the arm Jane had around her shoulder for a moment before she spun and wrapped her own little arms tight around her neck. She clambered into Jane's lap and cried into her neck.

Jane sighed and held her close. Her lip trembled and she held Lizzie tight.

Cole crouched down next to her and managed to gather them both close. Once he had them secure he rose and carried them back to the bed.

Once he'd set them down and they were settled, Kat perched on the edge of the bed. She smoothed a hand over Lizzie's hair. "Sure it was wise to tell her already?"

Jane shook her head. "Absolutely sure? No. But she needed to know. Now the healing can start, and she won't be alone. She'll never be alone."

Character is like a tree and reputation like a shadow. The shadow is what we think of it; the tree is the real thing.
—Abraham Lincoln

A sharp slap to Jane's face startled her awake. Her attempted gasp only resulted in a pained wince. Her throat was in worse pain than she'd been in before the surgery. She blinked against the grogginess in an attempt to get her bearings.

The last thing she remembered clearly was Charlie preparing the chloroform so he could perform surgery.

She assumed the fiery pain in her throat was the result of her tonsillectomy, and the lingering grogginess likely came from the chloroform. The weight against her left side seemed terribly out of place, though. The very un-pillow like form beneath her head she assumed to be an arm that had to be attached to the warmth at her right, which held the exceedingly familiar sensation of Cole.

She lifted her right hand slowly so she didn't startle Cole, and moved the limb to her chest to find the source of the weight. When her hand closed around a smaller one, panic set in as her mind immediately flew to her son, Jesse.

He wasn't supposed to be there, shouldn't be there. The moment before she moved to kick and wake up Cole to yell at him for allowing such a horrible thing, reason set in. There was no way it could be Jesse. Cole might be a damn fool in some ways, but he'd never let her son be at risk—and neither would David for that matter.

As her brain became more alert, it dawned on her. Lizzie.

The girl should have been in her own room. Jane had no idea how Lizzie could have ended up in her bed, but that was the only person it could be.

The fear and worry slipped away, which allowed her to relax once again. Within minutes the door creaked open. Kat's harsh whisper sounded in the room. "Lizzie? Lizzie, where did you go this time?"

Jane's whole body trembled with painfully concealed laughter when Kat's face peeked around the edge of the door. The fact her friend had lost track of the child once again was funny enough, but to have Kat was whispering as if Lizzie would hear made the whole situation funnier. Jane lifted her hand and wriggled her fingers in a semblance of a wave.

"Oh dear. Charlie won't be happy about this." Kat chuckled through her whispers. "But isn't this an adorable image? Wish I had one of those fancy cameras. No one would believe me if I told them what Cole looked like right now."

"Shut up," Cole mumbled. Though he complained, his eyes remained closed.

Jane's grin grew broader until she winced from the pain. She closed her eyes and took a few steady breaths to ease the pain. Once she felt better she attempted to chastise Kat with a look.

"I'll get her back to her room." Kat moved closer. "I fell asleep and she must have decided to check on you. Although it looks like she's comfortable, even with scary Cole."

Jane furrowed her brow, and she shook her head in confusion. At Kat's point, she shifted enough to see that Cole, having wrapped his arm under Jane's shoulders, had his hand resting on Lizzie's back.

Her bright smile returned at the sight. She held out her hand to Kat. When she mouthed for *help* and sat as carefully as possible. The action of pulling her still-tender left hand out from under Lizzie weight brought about another flinch, but she managed to free it fast enough to escape great pain.

Kat gave one strong tug to help Jane climb out from between the two. She assisted Jane until both feet were square on the floor. By the time they turned around, Lizzie had snuggled closer to Cole. The girl remained asleep, and Cole himself hadn't yet opened his eyes.

Jane rubbed her hand over her sore throat, attempting to hush Kat's laughing with a wave of her hand. She pushed her friend toward the table and took a seat beside her.

Kat poured a glass of water for them both, then leaned in close. She kept her voice low so as to not wake the sleeping pair. "I know you'd prefer coffee, but Charlie said nothing hot."

A sip of the water felt like rocks going down her throat, but she nodded. She set down the glass with a shaky breath. It would take some time to drink a full glass at this rate.

"Are you sure it's smart to leave them like that? Cole might scare her."

Jane attempted a glare, only to realize she was holding back her amusement again. After she'd slid her notepad across the table she wrote quick as she could with her right hand. *He is not fully asleep. He knows she's there. No harm will come to her.*

Kat giggled. "Even after all this time, what with Cindy, Jesse, and even Isaac around; I think Daisy would faint if she saw him being so accommodating of a child. She still thinks he only tolerates them because of you."

Most of the town thought the same, Jane knew. Cole wanted it that way, too. Considering she'd spent most of her known life being rather anti-child herself, she understood. Even now there were only a small group of children she felt tolerant of. She still wondered how her predecessor Clara had tolerated being a school teacher with a classroom that, by all accounts, fairly burst with children from all over the area.

Jane smiled warmly. *And on that note, do not tell Norman. Cole would never forgive you—we'd not be allowed to speak again.*

All Kat gave her in reply was a wicked grin.

How was she after I went in for surgery? Rather than fight, which would lead Kat into doing the opposite of what Cole wanted, Jane quickly changed the subject.

"It took a little while. She warmed up to Ida once we were all together and she saw me interacting with her nice and friendly. Obviously, she's still quite distraught, but we were able to distract her and keep her calm." Kat sighed and offered Jane a sad smile. "I should have told her sooner. I just hated the thought of breaking her heart. I couldn't imagine what it would be like for someone to tell Cindy..."

Jane clasped her hand on Kat's and shook her head. *Don't feel bad for wishing the child some peace. After what she's been through, it was the last thing she needed to hear.*

"But you told her."

Because sometimes the last thing we need to hear is exactly what we need to be told. Jane looked back at the bed. Tears stung the back of her eyes so she turned away. *She will hurt, but now she can heal.*

"How are you feeling this morning?"

Throat hurts like the devil, tired, but better. Where's Charlie to check on me every five minutes? It's all he's good for, it seems.

Kat snorted, covering her mouth at the loud sound. "He's probably asleep. He was awake half the night looking in on you and Lizzie constantly."

On the bed, Cole shifted and mumbled something under his breath. Jane smiled when he opened his eyes and she gave him a wink.

Cole frowned down at the shock of white hair under his chin and shook his head. "This ain't how I went to sleep."

Jane's smile widened when Kat giggled next to her. After a shrug, Jane turned back to pick up her water. Painful as her throat was, she was so thirsty she was willing to suffer.

Kat didn't avert her gaze, her shoulders shaking with barely contained laughter. "But you are such a good pillow."

Jane nodded enthusiastically and set down her glass to write fast.

Once Kat had read Jane's words, she laughed out loud. "She says that even Jesse thinks you make a great pillow. So is this normal for you, Cole?"

His eyes narrowed at Jane, a frown tugged down his lips at her silent laughter.

Tears formed to course down her cheeks when her silent laughter sent sharp spikes of pain through her throat. She rubbed her throat, not even the pain able to still her laughter completely.

"Kathy." Cole's voice rumbled in quiet warning.

"Don't worry. It's our little secret. I wouldn't dream of spreading around a rumor like this." Kat sighed. "No matter how amusing it might be, no one would believe me."

"Jane." Cole beckoned, a brow quirked.

With a smile, Jane stood shakily and walked over to the bed. She sat down with a heavy sigh, her laughter finally sated. *Sorry.* She mouthed and squeezed his hand.

"Yeah. Ya better be." Despite the dark frown, his eyes sparkled with humor.

She brushed her fingers along Lizzie's cheek. A soft sigh escaped and she managed to bring up a smile she didn't quite feel.

Cole gave her waist a small tug until she caved and lay back down at his side, opposite Lizzie.

Kat stood and carried over the pad and pencil. "It's still pretty early. When Tommy gets here with breakfast I'll make sure everyone gets up." Once the writing materials were on the bedside table, she squeezed Jane's shoulder.

"Thanks Kathy." Cole murmured.

Jane set her hand on top of Lizzie's and sighed.

"Get back to sleep. I ain't moving." Cole's hand ran along her back, soothing her until she couldn't keep her eyes open any longer.

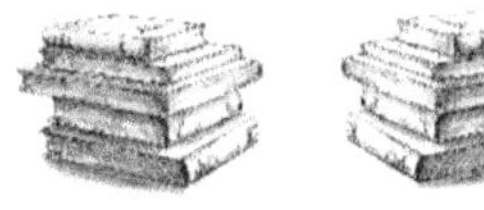

Family connections are always worth preserving, good company is always worth seeking.
—Jane Austen

A cool hand to her forehead woke Jane a few hours later. It took Jane no time to realize that she lay in the bed alone. She stuck out her lip in a pout when she opened her eyes to glare at Charlie.

"You are still a little warm. I need to take your temperature again and do an exam."

Jane smacked away Charlie's hand. Laughter outside the room captured her attention. She narrowed her eyes at the door.

"Cole is helping Kat keep Lizzie distracted. I'm not certain what they're doing, but I heard Cole grumble something about you owing him big time." Charlie didn't quite succeed in hiding his amusement while he grabbed some items from his bag.

She huffed and sat before he could try to help. The thermometer hovered in her face. Childish though it was, she was so tired of being poked and prodded, she clamped her lips against it. At her brother's quirked brow, she sighed heavily. She obliged him by opening her mouth to allow him to check her temperature.

"You must be feeling better, you are being far more obstinate." He pulled his watch from his pocket as he pressed his fingers against the pulse point on her wrist. "Though you might be feeling more cantankerous, I would appreciate honestly when I ask you how you're feeling today. Will you tell me?"

She nodded quietly, though she was loathed to tell the truth. Once he'd stopped checking her pulse, she wrinkled her nose. She pointed to her throat as well as her ear.

"All right. If I understand you correctly, your throat hurts—which is to be expected. Are you saying that your ear hurts now as well?" His brow furrowed at her nod. "Well, then. Let me have a look."

As obedient as she could be, she remained still while he checked her ears. When he'd finished without saying much of anything, she snatched the pad from the table. *Well? Has it spread to my ear?*

"Yes. It appears as though the infection has settled in your right ear." Charlie set his magnifying glass back in his bag. "Your case does not look as severe as Lizzie's, and it appears to only be in one ear. I think that's a good sign."

For you, maybe.

He chuckled. "Well, just be glad it isn't likely you'll lose your ability to speak. I think you'd be lost without your voice. Not able to yell at Cole and all."

Plenty I can do without words.

"Now I know you and Cole belong together. You're both despicable."

'There is no one thoroughly despicable. We cannot descend much lower than an idiot, and an idiot has some

advantages over a wise man'. Hazlitt. It was messy with how fast she'd written it with her right hand, but it would do.

Charlie didn't have any trouble reading, as his lips pursed. "'Those are only despicable who fear to be despised'. Rouchefoucauld. Isn't that what you were going to say next?"

She frowned and shook her head. *Cole is not despicable. Frustrating. Incorrigible. Obstinate. Rowdy.*

"You talking about Cole, or you?" He grunted when she smacked him in the stomach. Before she could smack him again, he took a step away. "One hundred almost exactly. Much more acceptable. I think you and Lizzie are both going to live."

How much longer until we know if Cole, Ida, or Katherine are sick?

"Kat and Ida have been exposed, so I'm not as worried about them. However, I'd like to keep Cole another week." He set the thermometer back in its case and put it in his bag. "Another three days would normally be the maximum, but there've been cases where it was almost two weeks for the illness to strike and I'd like to err on the side of caution. We might be sick of each other by the end of this."

I'm already sick of you.

"I know."

I'll never tire of Cole or Kat. And Lizzie could never get on my nerves.

"Glad to know I have the singular distinction of annoying you." Charlie picked up her broken hand and began to unwrap it carefully. "You've been here for a couple of weeks, sick for at least one. How is your hand feeling these days?"

Still pretty sore when I try to use it. Jane shrugged. *I'm just glad I can write with my right now, however illegible it might be.*

"It never rains…"

She shook her head and sighed heavily. The exam of her hand drew a few flinches and a groan of discomfort before he finally finished and began to wrap it again. *Well?*

"A few more weeks in the wrapping, I think. It's healing well, but if you try to use it too soon, I'm worried you'll just damage it again. Will you please not use it, even if you think I'm a stuffy old fool trying to keep you from having fun?"

With a twist of her lips, she sneered. *If I must.*

He laughed. "Yes, you must. I'll tell Cole your restrictions if I have to. Just remember what happened to your ankle, Jane. It still gives you trouble because you pushed yourself too hard. First while it was nowhere near ready to be used, and again by going to your cane before Daisy thought it wise."

She offered a begrudging nod and bit her lip to keep from wincing as he rewrapped the injured appendage. More laughter drifted into the room, loud and strong. Cole's laughter mixed into the sounds of Kat and Lizzie. She smiled. *He is a good man.*

"Well, it's rather clear how he feels about you. So I can't fault him anymore than I can fault you. He's family now— and he fits right in with Tommy."

A silent laugh made her shoulders shake and she nodded fiercely. *And the rest of you. You may talk a good game, but you're all as despicable as we are.*

Charlie snorted. "Yes. Yes, we are."

"What are we?" Tommy entered without knocking, moving into Jane's line of sight quick enough to keep her scowl away.

"She says we're all as despicable as her and Cole." Charlie tied off the wrapping and set her hand back on her lap.

"Of course we are. Ma and Pa didn't raise fools. Life is far more fun when you're despicable." Tommy let his laugh boom through the room until it spread to Jane and Charlie. He gave Jane a kiss on the cheek "How are you doing?"

Annoyed.

"Can't blame you. Charlie gets that way." Tommy winked. "But before you ask, the Inn and saloon are running smooth. Been keeping a close eye on that Warren character when he comes in."

Any more funny business? The girls?

"Violet's sick as a dog, but manages to pull herself together every night. I offered to let her off the hook, but she wants to stay." Tommy shrugged. "She says she owes you."

Jane's brow furrowed. Why in the world Violet thought she owed Jane anything was beyond her.

"Of all the discussions I thought I'd be in the middle of with my sister—discussing the whores she owns was not one of them." Charlie muttered with a rueful tone.

"She doesn't own them yet." Tommy smirked. "But I knew she'd be fine in a job like this. Just didn't think she'd actually do it. The girl's smart and great with people. What better job for her?"

Neither of them paid attention to her waved attempts for their attention. Charlie bristled and got in Tommy's face. "Plenty of jobs that'd be better suited for a woman of her station. I mean, she was a teacher and a damn good one. She could have been a writer. Or worked at a real hotel. Then again maybe she could have been the first woman in congress."

Jane blinked in surprise and did a double take in Charlie's direction. She huffed and tried to gain their attention again. At their continued ignorance she started to write while the discussion continued right beside her.

"The Hangman's Inn is a real hotel—it just employs entertainment. Makes it no less than anything proper. Doesn't take one lick away from how smart she is, or how good she is at what she does."

"'It is not enough to have a good mind, the main thing is to use it well'." Charlie tapped Tommy on the shoulder. "Descartes."

"'The person born with a talent they are meant to use will find their greatest happiness in using it.'" It seemed like Tommy grew to cover their three-inch height difference and got nose to nose. "Goethe."

"'To sentence a man of true genius to the drudgery of school is to put a horse on a treadmill'." Charlie adjusted his glasses and pushed up his sleeves. "Coleridge."

"'The true genius shudders at incompleteness—and usually prefers silence to saying something which is not everything it should be'. Poe."

Both men grunted in pain when she clunked their heads together hard and they flinched back with their hands to their foreheads. Jane glared at them both and picked up her pad to whack them both hard on the head before she shoved it into Tommy's chest.

"Did she just knock our heads together?" Tommy kept rubbing his head. "That brings back memories."

"Got that did you? And it might bring back memories, but not for her." Charlie chuckled when she stomped her foot. He resumed rubbing his forehead. "Damn."

Tommy read the scrawled note with a smirk. He passed the pad off to Charlie and pulled off his hat to rub his forehead again. "Damn girl gave me a headache. You still got a hard head, Charlie."

"She hasn't done that since we were teenagers." Charlie muttered. He turned his attention to the pad.

Jane glared at him as he read what she'd written.

You stupid fools. I didn't ask for your opinions. I am content in my life and use my 'talent' and 'intelligence' plenty.

Charlie—go jump off a cliff. Glad to know what you really think of me.

Tommy—shame on you for getting pulled into such a menial argument.

'Choose a job you love and you will never have to work a day in your life'. Confucius.

'I know who I am and who I may be, if I choose'. Saavedra.

It is my *choice. It will* always *be my choice. Do not try to make my choices for me. You may have book smarts, but even Cole is smart enough not to speak for me. Look to him for wisdom for a change, you buffoons.*

Before Charlie could look up from the note, she spun on her heel and stormed toward the door.

"I think she's mad at us." Tommy chuckled. "More mad at you than me, though. You insulted her life."

"You tried to speak for her."

"You—*ow*." Tommy cringed when the shoe she'd just thrown at him hit him dead square in the forehead. "All right, woman. We get it. We'll shut up."

Jane nodded and stepped out of sight. Before she could get out of hearing range, the last of their conversation hit her.

"I think she's gotten more violent since she lost her mind." Charlie made no effort to be quiet.

"You mean her memory."

"No. I mean she lost her damn mind."

Life consists in what a man is thinking of all day.
-Ralph Waldo Emerson

"*Ma.*" Jesse's excited voice echoed through the street. Several passers-by paused to find the source of the commotion.

Jane stopped fussing with Lizzie's new dress the second she heard his voice. She held out her arms the moment she spotted her son barreling toward them. His arms flew around her, and she clutched him against her. When they broke apart, she cleared her throat to put her hoarse voice into action. "I've missed you."

"You all better Ma? And Lizzie?" Jesse grinned at Lizzie. "Hi!"

"We aren't sick or contagious any longer, however 'all better' is a relative term." Jane smiled at the shy wave Lizzie gave Jesse. She pulled the girl closer and met Jesse's gaze. "My throat still hurts, and if you want to tell me a secret, you'll need to use my left ear."

"Why?" Jesse's eager bouncing slowed.

"Because my right one doesn't hear so well anymore."

Jesse frowned. "But why?"

"Well—"

"Jesse. Don't pester your ma too much," David's soft laugh interrupted. His warm hazel eyes sparkled down at her. "Sorry, Jane. He saw you from down the street and just took off."

"It's all right." Jane pulled a small pad of paper from her reticule to write a note to Lizzie. *Do you remember sheriff Schaffer?*

Lizzie nodded and smiled shyly at David.

"Why ya writing that Ma? Ain't she—"

"Isn't she."

Jesse huffed in frustration. "Isn't she listening?"

Jane pursed her lips at Jesse's ignorance of Lizzie's state. She knew word had spread, and David had to know. She cast a glance in David's direction, but he wrinkled his nose and became fascinated with the horse tied up at the hitching post. She sighed. "All right, well your pa told you we were sick, right? The sickness we had caused complications."

"Complications?" Jesse's face scrunched. "What's that?"

Jane laughed softly, letting it grow when David's joined hers. "A complication is a difficulty or an adverse reaction. For Lizzie and I, it means that different parts of us got hurt because of the sickness. Lizzie can no longer hear anything."

"Nothing?" Jesse's jaw slackened.

"Not so far. It would be like if you stuffed your ears with cotton. So until Lizzie can learn to talk with her hands, we need to write."

Jesse frowned and stared at the boards of the porch. He kicked at a crack. "I ain't good at writing yet."

"I'm not good. And you do just fine. Here." Jane handed him the pad and pointed toward the bench. "Lizzie and I were going to take a walk, but I'm sure she'd like to spend time with a friend. Why don't you both have a seat and you can write notes back and forth while I talk to your pa."

Jesse snatched the pad and raced to the bench. When Lizzie joined him, their heads leaned close together as they started to write quickly.

"You didn't tell him?" Jane rose to stand next to David. "Why in heavens not?"

"I tried." David gave her a sheepish smile. "You're just better at explaining stuff like that. I did think I'd see you before he did, though. I wasn't expecting you out so soon."

"Cole is still trapped inside with Kat and Ida, but Lizzie and I broke our fevers. So Charlie gave us the clearance to take a walk and get some sunshine so long as we didn't go too far and rested when we returned." She pursed her lips. "You are hopeless sometimes."

"So Cole's still trapped inside? Must be going stir-crazy."

"A change of subject won't help you." Jane laughed. She glanced over her shoulder to see Lizzie and Jesse still writing. "She's going to need a home. We have to make sure she's taken care of. I promised Caroline long ago that I'd care for her if anything happened. I just can't imagine. She has no one, and nowhere to go. I don't think I'm helping her much."

"Sure you are. Somehow you always do." He draped an arm across her shoulders. "We'll figure out a way to help her. You want me to start looking?"

"Yes, please. We're probably going to visit Reverend Greene, so I'll ask him as well. She needs a good family to take her in. I won't let just anyone have her."

"Understood. I'll keep in mind your high standards."

"And someone willing to learn hand-speak. I've already contacted the American School for the Deaf to learn the best way to help her. I think learning some hand-speak will help for certain. I'm going to try to order a few books."

"I thought they didn't want to teach that anymore." David's brow furrowed. "I thought I read something about that."

"Well, Bell is an idiot. Learning to express yourself using your hands doesn't make you a lesser being. It only aids in communication. Lizzie can still speak for now, her throat and mouth seems to remember what she can no longer hear. I just don't know if that will be permanent if she doesn't keep trying to talk."

"I'm sorry." David pulled his arm away and turned to lean back on the hitching post. Once he'd met her eyes, he smirked. "Did you just call Alexander Graham Bell an idiot?"

"Yes I did. You know who he is?"

"He's the one that's trying to make a telegraph that will send talking instead of just the clicks we hear now. Right?"

"Yes." Jane's eyes grew wide. "But that's in its infancy."

"Charlie mentioned him last month." He snorted at her continuing shock. "He'd just read an article in the paper he gets from New York."

"I read that same article." Jane shook her head to clear away the shock. "His theories on that aside, I disagree with him on manual signing. He is a strict oralist and goes so far as to say all deafness should be eradicated. You can't make the deaf hear—you can help them understand and communicate better. Oralism is fine to an extent, but you must allow manualism as well. Bell is an idiot that would tie a child's hands behind their back rather than allow such 'subhuman' communication."

"I'm guessing you feel strongly on this." He grunted when her elbow hit him right in the ribs. "Hey."

"Sorry." Even though she wasn't, she made the allowance. It wasn't fair to take out her annoyance on him. "I've been trapped inside so long I'm feeling short-tempered."

"I bet everyone is."

"Cole is very grumpy." She took a deep breath. "Lizzie and I should get on with our walk. I promised Charles we wouldn't be gone long."

"I'm real glad you feel better. It's been awful quiet around here with you locked up like that." He winked and squeezed her elbow. "Once you're feeling better I expect to meet you for coffee. Got something I want to talk to you about."

"I promise. Once I'm feeling better and things with Lizzie are more settled we'll sit down." She kissed his cheek and moved over toward the bench. Once the sway of her skirts caught Lizzie's eye, Jane spoke. "Jesse? Lizzie and I are going to take a walk and then we need rest. We're still recuperating."

Jesse's lower lip stuck out and he mumbled. "All right."

Lizzie took the pad from Jesse once he'd scrawled a final message.

He hopped off the bench and rushed up to hug Jane tight again. "Will you spend the night soon, Ma? I've missed ya."

"I've missed you too. I promise I'll spend the night soon. Now go on with your pa and let him finish whatever task he was set to before you ran off." Jane ruffled his hair.

Lizzie slipped under Jane's arm when the boys took off toward Cora's. She clutched Jane's hand as they started their leisurely stroll through town. A few wary glances were cast in their direction, but everyone seemed to trust the doctor's assessments that they were all right to be out in the open.

When they reached the meadow, Jane urged Lizzie toward the flowers. Jane took her time crossing the meadow, enjoying the laughter from Lizzie. It would be fleeting moments of laughter the girl would be able to enjoy for some time.

By the time Jane reached the church steps, Lizzie was beside her with a fist full of wild flowers. Jane gave her a smile and knocked on the door. A quiet voice bade them enter, so Jane pushed open the door. "Reverend?"

"Good afternoon, Jane." Reverend Greene rose from the front pew and turned toward them. "Oh, and Lizzie."

"Good afternoon. Sorry for the surprise visit. We were allowed some time out of the clinic." Jane stepped further in, waiting for Lizzie to close the door.

Lizzie peeked around Jane's skirts, her gaze fixed at the far corner.

Jane frowned and followed her line of sight to the piano sitting in the corner. She crouched down beside Lizzie. When Lizzie looked her way, Jane moved her fingers like they were working a piano.

A smile lit the girl's features and she nodded fiercely.

Jane waved her toward the piano and rose when Lizzie tore across the church. "I certainly hope you don't mind if she plays on the piano while we talk. I hope she won't insult our ears too badly."

"I don't think she will." Reverend Greene smiled, holding up his hand until a simple melody began to fill the church. "I haven't had a chance to thank you. Your fast action to protect Katherine and myself was very kind."

"Sometimes it doesn't feel like enough, Reverend. Lizzie is still without a home. Her parents are gone. Her hearing is gone." Her weak voice faltered, and she rubbed her throat as if to pass it off on the pain instead of her tears.

"And yet, she can still play a very beautiful melody."

"I never knew she could play."

"Mrs. Broder was always quite sad that the attack on their original home destroyed their piano." He gestured to the pew beside him and waited for her to sit before he joined her. "She said that she and Mr. Broder brought it here all the way from Indiana. That Lizzie had been playing since she was very young."

"I had no idea." Jane whispered. "I would have given them the piano Nick sent me. Mrs. Broder never told me."

"She felt it was a luxury. When you need so many basic necessities, the luxuries are irrelevant. All she asked was that I let Lizzie come and play on the church piano from time to time. Of course, I wouldn't ever say no to beautiful music."

Jane fell silent. The melody filled the church, pulling at the heart Jane kept guarded against its desire to do anything she needed to in order to take in Lizzie herself. "How do you help a child that has suffered so much? First her home is lost, her pa loses his job, and now she falls ill, only to wake up having lost both her parents and her hearing. What could possibly comfort anyone that has been through so much?"

"Says the woman who faced death itself."

"This is different. I was a grown woman. She's a child."

"Romans five. Three and four."

A tear she'd tried to hold back slipped down her cheek. "'And not only so, but we glory in tribulations also: knowing that tribulation worketh patience; and patience, experience; and experience, hope'."

"Psalms thirty-four, eighteen."

"'The Lord is nigh unto them that are of a broken heart; and saveth such as be contrite of spirit'." Sighing, Jane closed her eyes. "Psalms thirty, fifteen."

"'Weeping may endure for a night, but joy cometh in the morning'."

"It is difficult to remember when you look upon her face, into those eyes that expect you to have the answers. There is little I fear after the life I've lived, but always the innocent souls of the children bring a certain fear and pain. I don't wish to do wrong in my answers to them."

"You'll do well as long as you do what you have always done, Jane."

She shook her head and turned to him in confusion. "What is that?"

"Be honest."

"Tell her I don't know why this had to happen? That I can understand my own suffering, but not hers?"

"Do you truly understand your own?" The reverend squeezed her hand gently. "I don't think you still believe you deserve suffering as you once did."

"No. I suppose I don't. But I still am not faultless by any means."

"No man is."

"How many times have we had this discussion?"

He smiled warm and bright. "And what do we always return to?"

"First John, four-eight. 'He that loveth not knoweth not God, for God is love'." Jane matched his smile.

"Among others." He chuckled. "We won't continue to debate what you have done and continue to do in attempts to right past wrongs. Not the least of which is your current care for this young life."

"I fear that I'm limited in what I can do for her." Jane sighed and played with the hem of her bodice. "But I will do all I can."

"That is all any of us can do."

"Thank you, Reverend." Jane rose as Lizzie finished a song and started another. "I hope you don't mind if I bring Lizzie here every few days to let her play. It seems soothing to her."

"Of course I don't mind. And if you feel the need to talk again, the church is always open. I'm very glad you're feeling better."

"As am I. Convalescing is not much fun." She walked beside him toward the piano.

"Daisy told me you've also experienced some hearing loss yourself?"

"My right ear. I hear almost nothing out of that side any longer. It's a bit disconcerting—and any whispering will need to be done in my left ear." Jane laughed. "It's just as well, I suppose. For whispering is often gossip anyway."

"Very true." He smiled, his kind brown eyes sparkling with hidden laughter. When they got to the piano, he set his hands on it and listened quietly.

Jane sat beside Lizzie as the song ended and picked up the pencil Lizzie had set on the music rack. *Are you ready to take the flowers to Miss Katherine? I asked Reverend Greene and he said we can come back any time so you can play.*

Lizzie perked up and scribbled a fast note. *Can we come back tomorrow?*

Of course. I'm glad you still enjoy playing.

Lips pursed together, Lizzie took the pencil and wrote slower this time. *I can feel the music. I can't hear if I hit a bad note—but I feel the vibrations.*

"Wonderful." Jane sighed in relief. "She feels the vibrations. It still gives her joy even though she can't hear it." *Then you are learning as you play, as you do something you love. There's no better way to learn.*

"That is wonderful. She's welcome any time." Reverend Greene held out his hand to Lizzie and walked toward the door. "I look forward to seeing you again tomorrow."

Jane grabbed Lizzie's flowers and quick-stepped after them. "Thank you for your candor, Reverend. You've been very helpful, as you always are when it comes to my spirit." Jane tried not to wince when Lizzie snatched the flowers from her bad hand.

"It's good to see both of you healthy. You gave us all quite a scare."

"So I've been told on numerous occasions by those that wish to chastise me." Jane chuckled. "But I'm glad to be feeling healthy again."

Lizzie waved and stepped outside. They headed back toward town, but kept their pace slow and steady. Lizzie took the opportunity to pick more flowers, the bouquet in her hands growing rather large.

On their way down the street, Jane had to guide Lizzie out of the way of a few approaching horses and wagons as the girl focused on the flowers in her hands. As if counting them, her finger touched just about every flower. It wasn't until they were back on the boardwalk in front of Kat's, and just a few doors away from the clinic that Jane relaxed her vigilance.

A few greetings came her way this time, and Jane returned each one, but didn't linger to talk. Charlie would probably already be upset that they'd been gone as long as they had, although they hadn't overexerted themselves in the slightest.

Inside the clinic waiting room, Lizzie split the flowers carefully into three sections. She handed one to Jane and said. "For you."

A smile broke through her grumpy and negative thoughts toward her brother and she took the small bouquet. She inhaled the sweet perfume and sighed. She touched her heart and then reached out to cup Lizzie's cheek. "Thank you."

Lizzie gathered the other two bundles and tore up the stairs, calling for Kat and Ida much louder than Jane suspected she thought she was being.

Jane followed at a slower pace, reaching the top of the steps in time to hear the pleased exclamations of Kat and Ida over their flowers. She paused at the girls' room and leaned on the doorframe. "She's quite talented. She can play the piano. I'm sure she'll tell you about our day, but she should get a little rest, too."

"Don't worry. We'll take care of it." Kat chuckled. "You should do the same. I think Cole's back in your room. Said he had something to talk to you about."

Curiosity got the better of her and after a quick goodbye to Lizzie; she darted the few feet to her door. She pushed open the door and headed straight for the table to put the flowers in water. "It was so nice to get outside today."

"I'm sure it was." The door shut and the distinct clink of the key turning reached her good ear. In a few seconds his warmth filled the space behind her, his nose brushed the edge of her ear, his lips grazed her neck.

Her whole body trembled at the contact and her breath caught in her throat. "Cole."

With careful footsteps he moved them until she was pressed against the wall. "Was talking to Charlie. Found out something interesting."

"Oh?" She arched back when he tugged on her hips. Even with her bustle between them, her whole body came alive at the direction his actions were leading them. A different sort of heat than the fever she'd been dealing with rushed through her veins.

He spun her quick, so they were nose to nose, his body flush against hers.

"Cole, I don't think…"

"Apparently once you've had the fever, you ain't likely to get sick again. So even if I still get it, I ain't gonna make you sick." He brushed his lips along her jugular, right down to flick his tongue in the sensitive dip in her neck. "And you aren't contagious no more."

One by one he began to pop open the buttons on the back of her bodice. Heat pooled between her legs when he nipped at her neck. A yelp escaped when one jerk ripped opened her bodice. She sighed, gripping the front of his shirt in her good hand. "So?"

"It ain't been that long." Cole's warm breath brushed across her neck and ear as he chuckled. "Did you already forget what I'm doing here?"

A small smile formed and she looked up at him through her lashes when he pulled back. "I highly doubt my brother gave permission for you to rip my clothes off."

"Not in so many words."

"But I suppose." Her breathing slowed and she leaned toward him. "When you look at it like that. I mean—if you're certain you aren't feeling ill in any way?"

He pushed her bodice from her shoulders and she let her arms drop so it could fall to the floor. With one step he had her pressed firm against the wall again, his hands coursed along her waist, his lips seeking out her neck again. "Ain't much else to do around here. I'm getting bored."

"Oh. We can't have that."

"No, we can't."

*I enjoy convalescence. It is the part that
makes the illness worthwhile.
—George Bernard Shaw*

"I do not believe this would fall under the proper definition of convalescing." Despite her words, Jane's whole body relaxed snug against Cole.

His breath warmed the back of her neck as he chuckled low and deep. Gentle kisses along her shoulder set her nerves tingling. "Don't see why not."

"The proper definition is 'to return to strength after illness'." She wondered how she could remember anything with the way his very touch drove her to distraction.

"Yeah? So?" A gentle nip to her jugular sent the modest tingling into full-fledged electricity that shot right between her legs.

She let her eyes drift closed, doing her best to stifle the moan caused by his wandering fingers. "I feel a great many things right now, but strong is not one of them."

"You don't?" He rolled her toward him. As he did, his lips never left her flesh. Inch by inch he moved lower, until his tongue flicked across her erect nipple. "Ya feel plenty strong to me. At least ya did when you made them scratches across my back."

A throaty chuckle burgeoned despite her still painful throat. She did her best to hold it back, lest she begin coughing. Before she could fully calm her throat, he sucked her taut nipple into his mouth. She arched toward him, a whimper of a gasp slipped free. "However, you have sufficiently relaxed me. I doubt I could walk now if I tried. My limbs are jelly."

"No matter. Walking is over-rated."

She hummed in agreement. With a strong tug to his shoulders she brought his lips to hers in a slow, searching kiss. Her fingers danced eagerly along the strong muscles of his back. She wrapped her legs around his waist to tug him closer.

A knock on the door drew a deep groan from them both. Cole glared toward the door. "Get on outta here. We're convalescing."

Jane giggled despite their intimate embrace. The glare he cut her did little to stem the flow. If anything, her laughter grew bolder. Before she could do a thing to stop him, his touches went from teasing to full on tickling. She laughed so hard she soon found herself gasping for air. Her throat protested the activity with a series of harsh coughs.

"Jane," Charlie shouted through the door. "That is *not* convalescing."

She pulled her lips between her teeth to curb her laughter. Instead of succeeding, a pig-like snort erupted.

Apparently dissastisfied with the distraction from their pleasures, Cole's fingers stopped the tickling. Rather, he began teasing and taunting. His hands slipped expertly along her flesh to her core until he had worked her back into a heated fluster.

Charlie's voice broke through the haze of pleasure with a hint of a snarl, "If you don't eat, I'll make you stay here for another three days." He pounded on the door.

"Go the hell away Charl—oh, Cole!" Jane gasped as his fingers dipped deep into her moist heat. Her back arched half of the bed.

A crash of glass made them both jump. Jane propped herself on her elbows to stare at the door. The tingles of excitement poured out of her from the mix of distraction and Cole's lack of attention. "I think Charles is upset."

Cole crept back up her body to press a sound kiss on her lips. "He's just mad 'cause he ain't been home in over a week and wants a little convalescing of his own."

Jane chuckled. "I suppose you're right. Of course, the fact that I hardly speak to him is likely not helping. He has just been so terribly annoying since I became sick."

"Think we should apologize?"

While fully aware the proper thing would be to do just that, she wasn't quite ready to end their afternoon of pleasure quite yet. "Not until we're done. I think I could use a little more of your version of convalescing."

In a heartbeat, the tray of food was left to get cold. The world became dark outside before they sated their enthusiasm.

"Still worried I'm feeling poorly?" Cole snuggled closer. His thumb trailed along her spine.

"Goodness, no." Jane would have snuggled closer if her body hadn't already been flush against his. "I would say you're feeling quite good."

"I am now." He chuckled low. "Don't think I affected your proper convalescing, do ya?"

She released a contented sigh. "No. Definitely not. I have not felt so well in quite some time. You always seem to know what I need."

"Think that was more about what I needed."

"Perhaps. I might even call you selfish if your needs hadn't satisfied my own so completely." Contented, she relaxed fully against him. In the quiet that fell between them her eyes wandered the room. When they came to rest on the pad she'd left on the table, her mind immediately drifted to Lizzie.

"You're already gone, ain't ya?"

"Hmm?" She knew she should pay attention to what he was saying, but her mind dove deep into the problem of the young girl too fast for her to stop the fall. Her heart longed to help the girl, take her in and help her—but in their life it didn't seem possible.

"Yeah. You're gone, all right."

Her attention snapped back to him once she'd realized what he'd said. She furrowed her brow. His hand kept her firm against him despite her attempt to prop herself on her elbow. Frustrated, she studied his features. "Whatever do you mean?"

"Long as I known ya, your mind hasn't ever stopped working long. The minute it gets quiet, ya get to thinking."

Since he wouldn't let her rise to sitting, she lifted her head to rest her chin on his chest. When his fingers brushed along her cheek, she leaned into them with a smile. "I suppose. Yet, you are always part of those thoughts."

"I can guess which part."

She stuck her tongue out. "No. Not just that."

He shifted when she did, his body turning so she could fit closer against him. When her head rested on his shoulder, he tightened his arms around her. Kissing the top of her head, he sighed and rested his chin against her head.

"Sorry about embarrassing you in front of Kat the other day."

"It's just Kathy. Not like you don't tell her everything anyhow."

"True…"

"It wouldn't ever work." His tone carried a pang of regret, his voice quiet. "You do know that, don't ya?"

She didn't have to ask, even if she wondered how he knew where her mind had drifted a few minutes ago. How she'd been trying to figure out if they could ever make it work. Tears strained against her sore throat. Somehow she forced them back. "I know. I just want to help her."

"Things being the way they are…"

"The hotel the way it is." She could elaborate, but they both knew what she meant. Though their tiny room might be enough for them, a family would be too much for such a small space. The hotel itself still operated mostly as a saloon, brothel and all. They had changes to make, changes they had not the means to make happen. "It's just not plausible. I know this, I truly do. In my head, I do."

"Ya know we'll make sure she's got a good home. One that ain't so messed up."

"And small."

"You never complained before."

She sniffled against the lingering sting of tears. A smile tugged her lips. "I'm running out of room for my books."

"Keep 'em in the library."

"And my clothes."

"And I'm getting tired of using the public bath for our private pleasures." A laugh rumbled deep in his chest. "Sure wouldn't mind one just for us."

She giggled. "You are so single minded sometimes."

"Can you blame me?"

"Not at all."

Silence fell between them again. Their laughter settled down and he tapped her hip. "You're thinking about it again."

"And it's stupid to think about. A judge would never approve it. We aren't—"

"What in heaven's name?" Kat's confusion filtered through the door moments before her knock. "Jane? Cole?"

Chuckling, Cole winked. "We forgot about that food Charlie dropped."

Her stomach rumbled, and Jane groaned. "Hmm, I wish we hadn't. I'm starving."

"Jane?" Kat knocked again.

"Just a minute, Kat." Jane slipped to the edge of the bed, yelping when Cole tugged her back against him. "You've had me all afternoon. It's time to share. Make yourself decent, she might have Lizzie with her."

"Right." He stuck his lip out in a pout, but rose to grab trousers.

Jane paused to admire the view as he slipped them on. After a sigh, she flew out of the bed and snatched up her dress. Not bothering with undergarments, she threw on her skirt, and then frowned at her bodice. "Another bodice that needs mending. You're the reason I have so many clothes."

"I'd rather be the reason you got none."

She threw the bodice at him with a snort and grabbed another. In a rush, she awkwardly tried to hook it together as she ran toward the door. Flinging it open, she smiled brightly. "Kat."

"Oh—Jane." Kat covered her mouth in a failed attempt to cover her laughter. "I'm glad Lizzie isn't with me. You forgot to straighten your hair. Not to mention your bodice is crooked. I'm guessing your current state has to do with this mess?"

Jane took in the tray with a broken plate and food spilled across the floor. "That's my brother being a child. Step over it, I'll clean it up in a few minutes."

Still chuckling, Kat stepped over it and smirked when Cole turned up the lamp. The man hadn't bothered with a shirt and the casual mess of his hair dropped into his eyes. "The two of you couldn't have waited two more days for our complete clearance and freedom to leave the clinic? Impatient."

"When have we ever waited for when the timing was right for others?" Jane brushed her tangled hair until Cole took the brush from her hands. She gave him a wink and turned back to Kat. She took a seat and indicated for Kat to join her. The first stroke of the brush through her hair sent tingles along her scalp and Jane sighed. "So what brings you up here?"

"Just came to see if you wanted some popcorn." Kat sat up eagerly. "Tommy brought some over and we're doing a little music-less dancing with Lizzie."

Cole laughed when Jane's stomach rumbled at the mere mention of popcorn. "I think Jane's gonna need more than popcorn."

"I think you already handled that." Kat's lips thinned in her attempt to keep the laughter at bay.

"Sure did." Cole's hand rested on Jane's shoulder, his warm chuckle filling the room.

Jane rolled her eyes and giggled. The protest died on her lips when Cole resumed brushing her hair. "And you act so shocked when I speak like that, Kat. Really. I think being cooped up in the same place with me for all this time has made you even worse. Norman will never forgive me."

"Nah. It'll be Cole he'll not forgive. You've been unconscious at least half of the time—so we can blame Cole."

"Oh good. I'd rather be allowed to send a telegram again."

"Neither of you are funny." Cole set aside the brush and squeezed her shoulders.

Jane twisted in her chair and offered him a bright smile. "Not funny, hmm? You thought it was plenty funny when it was my brother we were making fun of instead of your good buddy Norman."

"Buddy?"

Kat snorted. "Oh, would you two quit for a few hours? Get your clothes on proper and join us downstairs."

"But I'd love to have Cole sitting around shirtless all night." Jane set her hand on his abs. A soft sigh escaped. "But there is a young girl that thinks you're scary enough, so shirt on."

"She don't think I'm scary." Cole set his hand on hers and quirked a brow.

"If you say so." Jane rose and looked back down at her bodice. The hooks were misaligned, so she popped them open and tried to reclose them one handed.

"Ya really don't play fair." Cole muttered before reaching out to help. Quick as a wink he got them fastened.

"Just think how much easier these hooks will be than buttons once we're done playing nice." Jane winked and smacked his rear when she walked past him toward the door. "Now go with Kat. I need to clean up the mess Charles made."

When they passed, Kat was practically dragging him like a child. "Behave yourself for a couple hours, Cole. You can do that, can't you?"

"Not sure. Not knowing she don't have no corset on." Cole's laughter echoed down the hall after he'd disappeared from view.

Jane shook her head, not bothering to hide her smile as she gathered up the broken plate and spilled food. With care she used the napkin to wipe every last drop and crumb from the floor.

With that accomplished she realized the pickle she'd put herself in. It would be impossible to pick up the tray with her hand still out of commission. She sighed and pushed it against the wall next to the door. Somehow she'd get Cole, or maybe Tommy, to grab it for her.

She brushed down her skirt when she rose and started for the back stairs that led to the kitchen. The minute she passed through the door dividing the halves of the building the muffled noise she'd been ignoring became much louder.

A raucous beat, loud thumping that almost shook the stairs she crept down. Halfway down, she paused and peeked through the bars. From where she sat she could just see inside the door of the wide open room they usually used as an operating room.

Tommy and Lizzie performed a boisterous dance of their own creation. The 'music' was the stomping feet of Charlie, James, and Ida—an idea that impressed Jane.

The vibrations of each beat reverberated through the building, and she had no doubt that Lizzie could feel it as well as Jane could hear it. When Cole and Kat swung past in a poor imitation of Lizzie and Tommy's dance, Jane had to cover her mouth to keep from laughing aloud.

After observing the party for a few minutes, she stood and slipped past the door toward the kitchen. She wanted to join the fun, but the lure of food was too much. The pounding beat followed her all the way there and back, where she poked her head into the room. A good-sized roll in her hand, she nibbled on it when she slipped inside the room.

It was mere moments before Tommy grabbed her and pulled her into the dance so fast her roll went flying. She yelped, but fell into laughter as he spun her in crazy circles.

James began to sing a raucous tune along to the beat. Ida's protests were met with him pointing to his ears and shrugging. His point made, he continued the inappropriate tune, and Kat joined along.

Cole and Charlie soon joined the singing until the room filled with the pounding of feet and lively song. Switching partners, Jane managed to dance with Cole, Kat, Lizzie and Tommy until Charlie was in front of her.

She pursed her lips and dropped her arms. The step she took to get away was the only one she made. He grabbed her arm and spun her fast. Although initially against her will, the brevity of the evening soon won out and she laughed and danced with him as freely as she had the others.

The noise level kept increasing, the party showed no signs of calming down.

"What is going on here?" It wasn't until Daisy's cry broke through that Jane even knew she was there.

Cole winked at Jane before stepping in front of Daisy. To the woman he'd once owned a contract on, and had since had a rather coarse relationship with, he bowed low. He offered his hand and gestured to the floor. "Would ya like to dance?"

Daisy's brow furrowed and she scanned the entire room before stopping again on Cole. "Excuse me?"

"He's a good dancer, Daisy. It won't kill you." Jane laughed. A screech slipped out when Tommy yanked her back into the dance.

The pounding on the floor resumed, and Kat kept dancing. She called over the music. "It's something to help brighten spirits, Daisy. Doctor's orders."

"Which doctor?" Daisy still eyed Cole's hand suspiciously.

"Depends." Cole's booming laughter filled the room. "Are you dancing or not?"

Daisy couldn't stop her smile and she shook her head before setting down her bag. Once she was free of her medical bag she took his hand and let him sweep her into the dance with the others.

After almost an hour things started to settle down and Lizzie rested near Ida as the woman sang a sweeter song. The quiet melody filled the room in Ida's sweet soprano voice, and stilled even the most raucous of the group.

Lizzie set her hand on Ida's shoulder, staring intently as Ida continued to sing.

Jane nudged Kat and started for the door. She tapped Daisy on the shoulder as she passed, and led both women into the kitchen. Together, Jane and Kat began to gather the supplies for popcorn.

"What exactly did I walk into?" Daisy pulled down the kettle to make tea.

Kat's soft laughter filled the space before the popcorn started. "When Jane mentioned that Lizzie played piano, and then Lizzie herself mentioned feeling the vibrations of the piano, we started to think we needed to make a little music of our own."

"It really was a wonderful idea." Jane nodded. "I wish I had thought of it."

"Well you might have if you hadn't been so preoccupied this afternoon." Kat shrugged. "We thought Lizzie needed a little lighthearted fun after all the pain and suffering. She's been so very sick, and lost her parents. Not to mention that we've all been cooped up in here for over a week. We all needed the fun."

"It's only a couple more days until you're set free." Daisy grinned. "Is everyone getting a little impatient?"

"It's a long time for the whole lot of us to be stuck in here." Jane admitted. "Charlie and I are on each other's last nerve. I think a little brevity was well in order."

"I have to admit it was fun. It's been quite a while since I've had a night of just—fun." Daisy leaned against the table with a sigh. "Once I got out of the saloon and back to doctoring, I wanted everyone to take me seriously, but…"

"There's nothing wrong with having fun." Jane quirked a brow. "You clung to your clothing and mannerisms from being one of the girls, and then once Mike's hotel opened you became just the opposite. I have to say I'm happy to see you having fun again."

"I agree." Kat nodded. "It's about time. Look at Jane and I. We have plenty of fun and don't mind what gossip goes about. We're still taken seriously by the people that matter. You don't have to be one or the other, Daisy."

"Life would be boring if you were just one or the other." Jane chuckled. "Look at Ida. She could be every bit the prim and proper woman, but she had fun tonight."

"I would hope so, it was her idea." Kat grinned. "And I'm glad she had it. She has a lovely voice."

"Just as well that she does—I'm tone deaf." Jane snorted and tugged her ear. "And half deaf now. I think with my voice I could even make Lizzie cringe and she is deaf."

"How are you adjusting, Jane?" Daisy tilted her head curiously. "With the loss of hearing in that ear?"

"Quite well, I think. It's not as difficult for me. It's just the one ear, after all." Jane frowned and tugged on her earlobe. "And I haven't lost all hearing in this ear. Things don't sound the same, or as loud—but it hardly affects my daily—"

"Um, Jane?" Kat straightened. "The popcorn is popping. Are you trying to burn it?"

"Oh, blast! I didn't hear it."

"What was that you were saying about it not affecting your daily life?"

*Business, you know may bring money,
but friendship hardly ever does.
-Jane Austen*

The moment Jane walked into the saloon, Hammy almost fell off his barstool. "Lady Jane! Ya came back."

"Mr. Hamm." Jane hugged him tight, her laughter ill-contained. After a bold kiss to his cheek, she grinned at the deep blush that bloomed across his ruddy cheeks. She warranted a brief scan of the saloon. With everyone seemingly in order, she nodded in satisfaction. "It would appear Thomas and Cole have kept things in order while I've been staying at the clinic."

"Ain't been giving me no free beer—but things have been calm."

Jane gasped, her attention back on the older gentleman. "Oh my! We cannot have that, Mr. Hamm. I won't have you without your daily free drink. We must rectify this immediately."

"Aw, shucks. I was just teasing."

"Nonsense. Edgar," she addressed the bartender. "Mr. Hamm's next beer is on the house."

"Much obliged, Lady Jane."

"Any time, Mr. Hamm." Jane squeezed his shoulder briefly. She turned her attention to the saloon. With practiced precision, she made her way through the semi-occupied tables to greet customers and re-attune herself to the place.

Even though their quarantine had been lifted the week before, Jane remained behind at the clinic. Taking care of Lizzie had taken much of her focus and time. Of course, Cole didn't like that much time apart from her any more than she did, so he'd spent every night and several days at the clinic with them.

Their original time table for her purchase of the Inn had been pushed back. James and Ida had finally left to return to their home in New York. As for herself, Jane felt hopelessly out of touch with reality.

For the past week she'd spent so much of her time with Lizzie and Kat, learning hand speak, helping the child deal with her deep grief. The only time Jane got out to enjoy the day, she spent it with children so that Lizzie might have some company.

Her musings were interrupted by the door to the storeroom slamming open. Graham barreled out, complaining loudly.

"The shipment was short by five barrels. It isn't—oh, Jane. It's about time. You finally gonna take over here? Becky's getting real impatient." He stopped short. "And then there's this guy. He's driving me madder than a March hare."

"Looks like the feeling is quite mutual, Graham." Jane pursed her lips. Behind Graham, Tommy appeared as if he were ready to kill. She sighed deep. It sure hadn't taken long for the quiet to dissipate. "What is this about the shipment being short?"

"He's getting all worked up over a minor incident, Lou. Don't you worry none. I already had it covered, without any added expense, or any loss." Tommy glared daggers into Graham's back, his fists clenched. "Where's Cole?"

"He went to Turner's for me to pick up some items I ordered from Lizzie." Jane approached the pair, unable to stop her brief admonishment. "Graham, really. You look as though you're going to explode. You're supposed to be relaxing now, remember?"

"I'll relax when it's over," he mumbled.

"Nick is making some final adjustments to the contract. Your father-in-law's lawyer thought he could trick us with words, the silly man. The new contract will arrive any day now for another round of arguments between Brooks and Nick. Besides, as far as the hotel goes, Tommy has handled things well enough, and we will continue to handle it with or without you." She pinched the bridge of her nose. "Do we have coffee?"

"I'll bring it out for you." Tommy tipped the brim of his hat.

"One for Graham too, please," Jane called as he disappeared back through the storeroom door.

Graham remained tense, his fists opening and closing. He danced on the balls of his feet, still bright red up to the top of his bald head.

"Graham, please." She edged closer to test his mood. When he didn't react, she took his tense arm. "Come sit down. You're making *me* anxious, and I've just arrived."

His nostrils flared, but in a moment, the tension dissipated. He allowed her to lead him to a nearby table. Once he'd dropped into his seat, he rubbed his hands along his scalp.

Jane wanted to ask, but the approach of Tommy gave her pause. She smiled gratefully when he handed off the coffees. When he'd left, she turned her attention to Graham. "What is it now? I won't apologize for breaking your nose, so don't bother starting there."

"You could apologize to my wife for the embarrassment you caused her."

"I did nothing but speak the truth. I hardly think I embarrassed her." She took a sip of her coffee while she gave him a minute. "Of course, I do not think you really care a bit about your wife's embarrassment at this point. Maybe you're only beginning to realize your mistake."

For the briefest flash of time, his mask of anger disappeared. In its place a stark pain paled his rough features. For all the pain that she'd seen, it took him no time to get a hold of his anger again. "You always had it in for me."

"I never have. I don't hate you. I never did. I didn't even hate you for threatening me so often before my hanging. Or for your increasing levels of threats in recent months—although I certainly don't appreciate how close you've come to truly injuring me on a few occasions."

His eyes narrowed at his mug, but he remained staunchly silent.

"I was angry at you for the destruction you caused to the saloon, I won't deny that. However, you cannot deny that I attempted to help you that first time. You were Cole's friend for many years before I came along, and I thought that friendship should be encouraged, even if it was at times destructive."

He snorted. His mouth opened to make some sort of comment, then slammed shut.

She sighed. "I do have to admit, you also thought I'd hurt your friend, and acted toward me accordingly. It was understandable then. However, nothing I've done since has worked to change your prevailing opinion of me."

The muscles in his jaw twitched with each grind of his teeth. "How long have you really had your eye on this place? You wanted it from the start, didn't you? Is that why you dug your hooks into Cole like you did?"

"What?" Jane clasped her hand over her mouth to keep from spitting out the coffee she'd just sipped. The mere idea was so ridiculous, she couldn't even fathom. When she'd first arrived she'd been half-dead and couldn't even remember stepping foot in the saloon until she'd become familiar with Cole. "What in blazes are you talking about? I have never had designs on owning the saloon."

"Seems like it's been your game all along."

Jane closed her eyes against the ridiculous notion. "Don't be ridiculous, or keep listening to whatever nonsense your in-laws are spouting. The only thing I have ever had designs on was a man, and that man was Cole. Even before I knew I had designs on him, actually."

"You've just always been acting like you own the place."

"I've only ever tried to help you both out to make the business more profitable. A happy Cole means a happy me. I was as shocked as you were that Cole suggested I buy your half." The annoyance she'd felt over his suggestion faded. Something about the idea continued to nag in the back of her mind. She couldn't quite put her finger on what about his insane idea had caught her attention.

"Becky don't care none about that." He'd said it so quiet, she almost didn't hear him. Still staring into his mug, Graham's body tensed once again.

Jane brushed aside the nagging thought, prepared to focus on it later. "Graham. Your marriage has been one of convenience from the very start. You knew that going in. Unfortunately, in your marriage she holds all the cards. That's what happens when you are the poorer of the two in such a relationship."

His lip curled into a sneer. "Her pa holds all the cards." In one gulp, he drained his coffee.

"True. His wealth and power are what's going to win every time until he dies." Jane dared to set her hand on his wrist. He flinched, but didn't react otherwise. She leaned closer in the absence of a negative reaction. "You need to accept things as they are, or move on."

"I was here first."

She snorted. Her full laughter spilled free at the hint of a smile tugging his lips. "Fine. If you wish to be a child, you may remain miserable and go pout in your corner."

"There's nothing else to be done. I'm good and married now."

"True. You are married. Then again, I was once, too. Not so long ago, if you recall." She tapped his wrist. "Based on what I know of him, I'm not certain her pa would have any desire to see the scandal of a divorce to mar his daughters' pristine reputation."

Graham scoffed. "God forbid."

"Then again, my brother Nick is an accomplished lawyer. From what he tells me, Tommy also knows a very skilled lawyer in Laramie."

"Good for him."

Jane did her best to keep her smile hidden from the clueless man before her. She leaned in close again. "Graham. Do you have any clue what is in Laramie right now?"

"Not much. Dead end town with nothing."

"The town is fairly new, so I'd hardly call it dead-end. Although the population is small, it is growing. These days it even includes a few Chinese families. There's even one that runs a successful laundry."

Graham straightened, tension coursing down his arms until his fists clenched. She could almost see the thoughts spinning through his mind. After an extended silence, his near-smile faded as he shook his head. He cast her a wary glance. "I don't get it. You said you'd never help me if I went through with the marriage."

"I had no intention of ever doing so, either. Then the loss of the love of your life turned you into a bigger bastard than I imagined possible."

"I don't love her." He snarled, casting a furtive glance around the half-empty saloon.

"Liar."

He stood so fast his chair clattered to the floor. "Crazy. That's what you are. Stay the hell out of my business."

Jane saluted his retreating back as he stormed off. A sigh welled from her belly, so she released it into the quiet air.

"If I were to wager, I'd say that was not a happy conversation," Al's voice interrupted her brooding. A bright smile creased his features when she looked his way. "It's good to see you."

"Al." Jane rose to accept his hug, which she returned with one of her own. She gestured for him to join her. "I'm afraid I've missed much of your trip. I hope you'll forgive me for that. Honestly, I'm not even certain why you've lingered in Dominion Falls so long. I laid in that clinic for a month. Even my own brother left two days ago."

He shrugged. "I'm in no rush. I've got nowhere to be with any expediency."

"If I remember correctly, you said you planned to go home. You haven't been there since before the war, not to mention seeing your family." She leaned on the table to study him closely. "Selfish as I am, I'm more than happy to spend more time with you. However, I don't wish to keep you away from what family you have left."

"I haven't got much family left any longer, you know that well enough." He smiled. "Besides, like you said, you haven't been around to spend time with. I did stop here on my way through with the intention of seeing you, after all. I had to see if you've improved your poker game at all."

She snorted. "I haven't."

"It never hurts to try—,"

"Oh my goodness!" Jane flew to her feet in surprise as the nagging through caught up to her. Graham's words once again echoed through her mind. *Seems like that's been your game all along.*

"Jane?" Concern creased Al's brow when he rose to meet her gaze. He touched her shoulder when she failed to respond immediately. "Jane, are you all right?"

She blinked at him, not able to answer his question, afraid she'd lose her train of thought. "I can't believe I didn't think about it before. *Thomas!*"

"Quit your yelling," Tommy chastised from the back room.

"Al, I apologize. I hate to part ways so quickly, but I must speak with Tommy. We'll have supper. Tonight at Turner's, five o'clock. Will that be all right?"

"I-I suppose so." Al's confusion sat clear in his puckered brow.

"Wonderful." She spun away without so much as a farewell to race into the back room. "Thomas. Have you heard word about this Gus Warren character yet?"

"Still waiting. I had to go through a few connections, but I expect it will be any day now. Why?" Tommy wiped the straw from his arms back into the box he'd been unpacking. He stepped over the crate to get face to face with her.

"Graham said something earlier in his little fit of anger. I've heard it before, as has anyone that will listen to his drivel. You know he believes I have had designs on this business since the beginning, and manipulated my way into it."

"Bunkum."

"Of course it is, but it just hit me. We are losing girls left and right, Mel was killed, it seems like every week we end up losing money to some sort of destruction or property or other crisis."

Tommy's brows lifted with every word. His gaze drifted as if he were thinking. "Building isn't much, but it has potential. This lot, however, is one of the best in town. With all the new business coming in, someone could want it for their own."

"Whether they take the business, or simply take the land, it could be a tremendous profit if our hotel goes under."

"Who's your investor?"

"I haven't the foggiest." She glared in response to his exasperated growl. "In the past I have always intentionally remained out of the financials. Graham didn't need any further fuel added to his fire, not to mention Cole is excellent at numbers."

"But you are buying in."

"Right after that decision I fell ill, remember? I had only begun to get such in depth information in the days before we went out to the Broder's. Since I've been released, I have been busy with Lizzie."

"Where's Graham now?"

"If I were to wager a guess, I'd say sulking in his office. I mentioned that Linh's family had been located."

"Did you tell him I couldn't confirm whether or not Linh herself is there?"

"No. He got pissy and scared himself right on out of here much too fast to give him details."

Tommy's eyes narrowed. "I doubt Graham could be causing this. He's the one trying to sell, he wouldn't want to decrease the value. He's getting little enough out of it after he pays back what he still owes Cole for his various drunken feats of destruction."

"I also think that while Graham might have a modicum of intelligence, he isn't quite so smart." Another possibility emerged. "What about Becky's father? Only person I've known greedier than Brooks Carrington is Jackson Krenshaw. With Jackson's death, perhaps he would have reason enough."

"Could be. I need a lot more information to figure it out, though. Namely, the investor."

"Cole and I planned to sit down in a couple of days to go over all of the financials. Now that Lizzie has begun to adjust,

I have more time to focus on the inn. I suppose we could arrange to do so sooner, all things considered."

"I'll get the information. Don't you worry."

"Thomas—," She hadn't even finished his name before he stormed past her. Considering only a short while before Tommy and Graham had been ready to come to fisticuffs, she knew Graham wouldn't be in a listening mood. The only likely outcome of the confrontation would be an all-out brawl.

Rather than wait for the inevitable, she hightailed it out of the inn. She ran down the street to Turner's as fast as she possibly could. Cora Turner, the owner, was wrapped up in customers in the restaurant side of the store, so Jane felt no obligation for greetings.

She turned her attention to the packed aisles of the store on the left side of the mercantile. Cole had come to obtain a few supplies for them, and for Lizzie, at Jane's request. Unsure where he might be in the maze of products, she quick-footed across two aisles. A quick glance down each revealed no Cole.

As she hit the third, Cole emerged at the same time. She all but barreled into him, though he didn't falter in his hold on the pile of items in his arms. Damn man never would bother with a basket to carry anything.

Amusement slid across his features in a slow grin, and creases at the corners of his sparkling blue eyes. "Where's the fire?"

"The inn. No, actually right now it's likely at Graham's." She paused to catch her breath. "I'd wager a bet Graham is pitching a fit right now, giving Thomas all sorts of trouble."

"That ain't no different than normal."

"Oh, but it is. Thomas is trying to find out who the Inn's investor is. It's something we need to know, but you know Graham will never willingly part with information to me or my brother."

"Why? What happened? What's so important he knows now, when you haven't known before?"

"If you want to save the Hangman's Inn, you'd best make sure Thomas gets the information he needs. I think, and he agrees, that someone is attempting to decrease the value so they can come in and take it."

The amused crinkles disappeared into deep lines above his brow. Confusion flickered in his gaze, but her words had their intended impact as he tensed all over. He shoved the items he held into her arms in such a rush she stumbled briefly under the surprising force. He muttered a quick apology, made sure she stood upright, then tore out of the store even faster than she'd entered.

Jane did her best to rearrange the packages in her arms without knocking an item to the floor. Once she felt more secure, she took a quick stock of what he'd grabbed. On her way back toward the front of the store she picked a few more items he'd not yet collected.

Though she didn't need them, she snagged several books from the shelves as she passed that section. By the time she reached the counter, she had to all but drop the pile in her arms onto it. She grabbed a few pieces as they threatened to topple to the floor.

"Jane." Cora laughed as she helped to make sure everything settled on the counter. "You have quite a bit today."

"Afternoon, Cora." Jane sighed as she took in the lot. "Yes. I'm quite sure between the two of us we probably still forgot something, though."

"Well, you know where to find me should that prove true." Cora wrote down prices on a list that had already been started under Jane's name. "I have to say, I was rather impressed with the dresses Cole ordered for Lizzie. They were rather stylish."

"Cole bought her more dresses than I ordered?" Jane's concern washed away into a bright smile at the thought.

"Yes. I believe so. You had told me you had four in mind, the order totaled ten after Cole and Kat had their say in the matter."

Jane wasn't surprised that Kat had added to the order, for she'd said she would, and pay Jane back. It was easier to order them all at once, after all. "Well, then I can't wait to see what he ordered."

Cora wrapped two of the books, then looked over the lot again. "This is a big load, and it appears your hand is still wrapped."

Jane ran her hand along the wrapping still around her appendage. Daisy had assured her that she'd have full use again soon. Sometimes she forgot it was even there as the pain had decreased. "For another week, then hopefully I'll be free of the dreaded thing."

"Should I have Arthur drop them off for you instead?"

"Would you? That would be a great help." Jane picked through the items to separate what would go to the inn, and what would go to the clinic where she still slept while they sought out a home for Lizzie.

"What're ya doing with all this stuff?" Norman muttered behind her. "You don't plan on taking that little girl to the saloon, are ya? It ain't the place—"

"Norman!" Kat squeezed Jane's shoulder even as she scolded her husband. "I told you that Jane was staying with Lizzie at the clinic while we try to find a home for her."

Jane bristled despite Kat's comforting squeeze. She turned to face Norman, her chin lifted in defiance. "So what if I did decide to take that child in?"

"That saloon ain't no place for her. Besides, you and Cole aren't married. No judge'll let you adopt her with those strikes against you." Norman grunted when Kat poked him in the side. He grumbled. "What? Just being honest. She likes honest, remember?"

"Well. Thank you for reminding me of those points, Norman. I simply didn't have the intelligence to figure that all out on my own. Not that you cared to know if I was aiming to, anyhow." Even though he'd spoken the truth, hearing the finer points out loud stung. Jane dug into her purse to grab some money. She handed Cora enough to pay for her purchases as well as part of her balance. "Please see that it's all delivered to the clinic."

The whole way to the door she could hear Kat chastising Norman quietly. Once out in the open air again she took a deep breath to steady herself. Rather than linger where she might possibly run into Kat and Norman again, Jane took the stairs into the street quick as a wink.

It seemed that any time she got herself good and settled in her heart that taking Lizzie in was not a possibility, someone like Norman came along to drive the point in deeper.

When Jesse had first come into her life, she'd been to afraid to even be a mother. Thus, the question of him staying with her had never come up. Even though at the time she'd lived in the homestead Jesse and David now lived in. When she'd moved into what had then been the saloon, before they'd officially named it an inn, she still hadn't felt right being his ma. With her own life in danger, she didn't want to hurt him that way.

Jesse and David had moved into her homestead, and only in the past year with the nightmare of her forgotten past behind her had she begun to feel the true pain at the separation. They'd made the compromise of her staying at the homestead relatively often, and Cole even joined her on many occasions. He'd surprised even her with how well he and Jesse got along, and David even let Cole take Jesse on rides with a small horse Cole had trained just for Jesse.

Jane knew Jesse was safe and content with David. He had a warm and loving home with his pa, and Jane had a feeling that soon David would finally take the step to marry the woman he'd been courting for over a year. Lee had been a joyous presence in Jesse's life and Jane certainly had no objections.

But Lizzie was all alone. Jane wanted nothing more than to give Lizzie what she knew Jesse had. A good home, and a large family to love her. Jane paused outside the Inn and stared up at the sign above the doors.

After a long sigh, she turned and kept walking toward the edge of town. While Cole had taken the move to call the saloon a hotel now, and they took on guests, the saloon was still the main source of income. The brothel aspect didn't help matters. As it stood now, the Hangman's Inn wasn't somewhere to bring a child to live. Jane had no shame for her life, and could bear whatever talk or opinions were directed her way. She wouldn't put Lizzie through that, any more than she would Jesse.

Her mind again set, Jane stopped in the middle of the road. She'd passed her destination and had to turn back. Across from the jail a new café had opened to compete with Turners. While Jane still preferred Cora's cooking, she was always happy to support any new business in town. Too many families were struggling for her to ignore any opportunity to help, even by the simple matter of patronage. Plus, Cora still had the general store, which Jane made far too much use of. Rumors of a new mercantile had buzzed through town during her illness, but she had yet to see proof of it.

Inside David sat in a corner, his knee bounced nervously as he sipped his coffee. Soon as he saw her, he rose and offered a nod.

She joined him, glad to find she could place a smile on her face that felt genuine. After a kiss to his cheek she sat, waiting for him to do the same. "You're early."

"I work right across the street. It's tough to be late." He pushed up the brim of his hat, a sharp gaze on her features. "What's wrong?"

"Nothing," she sputtered quickly, astonished that he'd picked up on her frustrated state. After a deep breath, she attempted to reassure him. "I am just having a very busy day."

"Is everything all right with Lizzie? I thought you said there was no shortage of assistance to make sure she's never alone."

"Oh, goodness, no. There's no shortage of assistance. There is simply a shortage of families able to take her in.

Certainly no shortage of temporary help." The words came out more biting than she'd intended. She sucked her lips between her teeth to steady herself again. "Sorry."

"No apology needed." David's shoulders relaxed visibly. The cause of his tension dissipating was beyond her. Perhaps she'd distracted him, or even just amused him enough to ease his nerves. He took a sip of coffee, his attention returning to her again. "How are you feeling?"

"I am fairing quite well. My throat is still sore, but that doesn't stop me from talking."

"Does anything?"

She fought the urge to stick her tongue out at him like a child. "I didn't talk for three days after the surgery—and for almost a month after my hanging. I think you've managed to obtain all the silence you can ever expect from me."

"And here I thought you'd be in a good mood." His brow furrowed.

She pursed her tips at the tension returning to his shoulders. With a sigh, she leaned forward to set her hand on his. "I am. I apologize. I am already appreciating the solitude and isolation we had in the clinic. Things were far less complicated."

"Maybe we should talk later, then."

"David. What is it?" She kept an eye on him and the other on the waitress at a nearby table. Soon enough they'd be interrupted. "Please hurry and tell me before Teresa interrupts us to take our order."

"Well…"

Thanks to him dragging it out, or simply because Jane had said the girls name, Teresa did arrive to take their order then. Jane rushed through their requests, glad to see Teresa didn't linger. Jane leaned on the table, her eyes narrowed on David. "For goodness sake, just tell me."

"I wanted to tell you because it sort of indirectly affects you. Through Jesse."

"Is there something wrong with him?"

"No. No, it's nothing like that." David gripped her hand. "There's nothing wrong. I just—I wanted you to know what I was planning. So it wouldn't be a surprise. And. Well. With what you've got going on with Cole, I didn't think you'd really mind, but I wasn't for sure. I never really know—"

"David." She snatched her hand away for the mere satisfaction of smacking him with it. "Get on with it, already."

He clamped his mouth shut, his eyes downcast on the table. A heavy sigh blew out of him. His knee bobbed rapidly under the table.

"I apologize, but I am very short-tempered today. I do not have patience enough for you to tell me everything except the whole point of our meeting. So please, say it already."

"It's about Lee."

"Oh." There it stood before her. Exactly as she'd suspected for months. He was going to ask Lee to marry him. Oddly, she noticed a faint ache in her heart. She wondered if Clara still lingered in there, aware of what was happening.

He remained silent, his eyes fixed on her for several minutes. When the silence continued to drag out he whispered, "Jane?"

In a heartbeat the echo of pain faded away, the fleeting glimpse of Clara gone into the shadows as she always did. A rush of joy filled her heart. All along she'd wanted David to find happiness again. She reached out to take his hand again. "I love her. Jesse loves her. You did not need to tell me first, or ask permission, or whatever it is you were doing here. Lee makes you happy, and that is all I have ever wanted for you. I told you that you would find someone."

Relief relaxed the lines of stress from his forehead. "I did need to tell you. I knew you'd tell me if you thought I was having an error in judgment."

"Really, David. I would have told you over a year ago when you finally got up the gumption to court her proper." Jane laughed. "And you know I would have."

"I suppose so."

"So?"

"What?"

"When are you going to ask her? Do you know yet?"

"Next week…"

"Stop looking so incredibly nervous. There's no reason. She'll say yes. I'm certain of it." She scooted her chair closer. Once he met her gaze, she winked. "From what I've read in Clara's letters, you're rather impossible to say no to. Just don't give her an option like you gave Clara."

"No." He chuckled low, his hand squeezing hers. "I'll just be asking her to marry me, I won't be offering a walk instead."

They both laughed together at the memory. One of the few she actually had of Clara. Once the food arrived, they separated. Jane didn't waste much time in further talk. Her appetite was too big. Mix in her curiosity over what might have happened with Cole, Thomas, and Graham, and she was anxious to get back to the inn.

She set down her fork on her empty plate before David had finished half his meal. "Congratulations in advance."

He grinned when she rose and kissed him on the cheek. "Heading off already?"

"I told you it's been a crazy day. I need to go make sure there are no new patients in the clinic with the force of the argument I left behind."

"Wait." His laughter was barely controlled when he grabbed her elbow. "You walked away from an argument?"

"Ha. Ha. You're so funny." She hit him playfully in the shoulder before he released her arm. "Have a good day, David."

"Good luck, Jane."

She let his amusement carry her out to the street. The elation faded quickly once out of his proximity, though. Who knew what might have happened in the interim. She'd never done well with curiosity, but this was about her home and business.

If she'd eaten at Turner's, she could have stopped by the undertakers to see if the battle still raged before returning to the inn. Instead, she had to go straight to the Inn in hopes the argument had already concluded. Preferably with success to her brother and Cole.

To her surprise, instead of a still raging battle elsewhere in town, she found Graham himself behind the bar. She scanned the room for signs of Cole or Thomas, but they were nowhere to be found. The only help Edgar provided was a shrug before he turned his attention back to the poker game he was heading up.

She tried to keep her tone light and airy as she approached the bar, not daring to step behind it where she might get trapped again. "I thought Edgar was behind the bar."

"Someone wanted a game. I came back here so Edgar could run it. Cuddy isn't due in until six. That all right with you?" Graham set down the glass he'd been cleaning, his dark glare fixed on her over the bar. If looks could kill, his would be wrapped around her throat choking the life out of her right about then.

"I was just curious." She chose a seat on a stool, still wary of approaching the angry man. More than anything, she wanted to determine the situation before she proceeded further. After their chat this morning, she couldn't be sure where Graham's head could be. "What of Cole and Thomas? Where'd they get off to?"

"Sending telegrams." He moved toward her end of the bar. Though his glare remained dark, his moves were non-threatening, so she remained where she sat. He leaned on the bar across from her. "How'd you figure it?"

"Hmm?" Jane eyed him, unsure of his exact meaning.

"The whole thing."

"Oh. Do you mean the idea that someone might be trying to lessen the inns value?" Jane shrugged when he nodded an affirmation. "Goodness, I can't take all the credit. It was actually what you said to me this morning about having my eyes on the saloon all along. That got me thinking about what had been going on."

"Guess it doesn't matter anyway. It's not my concern anymore, right?"

"Would you stop? This is growing so tiresome."

"'Scuse me?"

Jane met him glare for glare. "This whole thing. You're angry over the wrong thing, and your constant complaining and digs are little more than annoying now."

"I'm not angry over the wrong thing."

"You most certainly are. You're angry that I'm buying the inn, but that's not what you're really angry over. You're angry that you have to sell at all." She held up her hand at his protest. "You're selling because you need to get away from the alcohol. You're selling because Becky is insisting, or rather, forcing you to do it. Or her father his. You don't want to. I know that. Cole knows that. But you *are* selling. Deal with it."

Graham grumbled a few curses under his breath. "I need to get away from the alcohol? What d' you mean by that?"

"I mean that is your wife's convenient, perhaps accurate, excuse to make you sell. She wants to get you away from the 'negative influences'. You know, alcohol, Cole, and I. Whatever is her most convenient weapon at the time."

His lips twisted in a grimace until he flinched away from her assessment.

She dared to set her hand on his where it remained on the bar. "I know this isn't easy for you, Graham. I know you have no desire to sell, but you have had plenty of time to adjust to what's happening. Several weeks, in fact, while I was trapped in the clinic, although that might have made you see what you missed because you were needed to work."

He grunted, but didn't pull away from her hand.

"I really wish you'd stop trying to blame me for everything that's gone wrong for you, but I'm beginning to think that may be impossible."

"You changed him."

"Cole? No. I don't think I did." She frowned as she thought it over. Then again, didn't everyone change over time, with help from those around him? "I suppose I can understand why you'd see it that way. In truth, though, he's always been like he is now, hasn't he? Strong. Loyal to those he cares about. Not a man you want to cross. He hides his feelings from the world. He's stubborn, proud. What, exactly, did I change to your way of thinking?"

"You make him do whatever you want, just by ignoring him."

"I manipulate him?" Jane snorted at the idea. "If that's the case, he manipulates me in the exact same way. I'm just as easy for him to coerce in most cases."

The dark scowl he'd been wearing eased a smidgen. "I've never seen it."

"Trust me." She chuckled. "It's happened more than enough."

"It's different. He's different."

"So are you. Changed by what happened with Linh, by your marriage, by having to sell this place. It's made you angry, and bitter to have lost so much." She met his gaze. "You and I could argue all day and night for years. It wouldn't change the fact that things now aren't how they were when you both became best friends, or when you went into business together. Either you adjust to what your lives are now and find a way to keep that friendship, or you part ways."

"You'd like that."

"Actually, no. I would not like that one bit." Her grin grew at his double take. "What? I have no idea how many ways I can tell you. I don't hate you. I have never liked your attitude toward me, and I do not appreciate the way you manhandled me last month."

"Sorry about that." The apology might have been mumbled, but he appeared properly reticent for his actions.

"You are Cole's friend, or at least you were at one time. He does not make friends, or keep them, easily. Not good friends like you were. It means something to him to call you friend, and therefore it means something to me. Besides, if he doesn't have friends so he can get out of my hair once in a while, I might just kill him."

Graham guffawed, the last of the menace dissipating. "Is that so?"

"Being around the same persona all day, every day, can really get under your skin. I have an escape or two so I might get out of his way. He deserves the same."

"I don't get you."

"Neither does Cole half the time. Just ask him. Without vilifying me, ask him." Jane rose, secure she'd made her point. "I don't hate you, Graham. I never did. I got damn mad at you, but I never hated you. If you wish to regain your friendship with Cole again, you're free to try. However, if you screw with me again, a broken nose will be the least of your worries. You're so worried about me hurting him or taking advantage, you can't even see what you've done."

His head hung; his shoulders drooped. "I know."

"It's easier to blame me."

"Yeah."

"Becoming, and staying, sober isn't about taking the easy way. It's about facing the truth—not just the alcohol, but your life. Start being honest with yourself. Be honest with your wife, and true to your own heart, and be honest with your friend. Stop blaming me and look at where the problem truly lies."

*How paramount the future is to the present
when one is surrounded by children.
-Charles Darwin*

From his vantage point on the porch of the Hangman's Inn Cole had a good view of most of the town. That's why his business was in danger, supposedly. For now, the view afforded him a perfect view of the church. Out past the depot, across the meadow the white building stood tall. As the townsfolk spilled from the church after Sunday service, he kept his gaze fixed on the activity filling the meadow.

As frequently happened on warm Sundays, picnic baskets emerged from wagons, blankets spread across the grass of the meadow like a wild patchwork quilt of people, food, cloth, and grass. Cole sipped his coffee, remaining where he was. Of all the things he didn't mind Jane roping him into, church had never been one of them.

Long ago he'd given up on church, figuring God had given up on him. Jane's arrival in his life might have left him doubting that, he still was far from ready to return to Sunday service. He did have a reputation to maintain.

As per usual, Jane drew his attention immediately. The bright green dress she wore was easy to spot in the sea of browns and blues. Instead of joining the adults to set up picnics or chat, she took the mass of children, playing games with them.

For years she'd avoided children, but today she held court with a growing number of them. He wondered if perhaps this was how Clara had been. The easy way she moved through the sea of children, how they all listened to what appeared to be orders.

Even from the distance he stood at, he could tell she wasn't uneasy despite the growing crowd around her. Lizzie, Cindy, and Jesse were, not surprisingly, right on her tail.

She most likely picked a game that Lizzie could join in without trouble. One that wouldn't require shouting, or even words at all, except for whatever laughter might happen. Jane tended to think of things like that, especially for that little girl. Her attachment to the orphan rivaled her love for her own son, so that Cole sometimes worried he would lose Jane.

Cole's jaw clenched when a male figure waded through the children to Jane's side.

Al Webb.

The way that man looked at Cole's woman drove him to madness. He knew that no matter how much he might trust Jane, he didn't trust Al for nothing. It seemed like in the month since they'd been released from quarantine Al's yen for Jane had become stronger still.

Without a doubt Al had his eye on Jane, and Cole didn't like it one bit. He wasn't about to let another man take his woman, but Cole didn't know how to make Jane see what Al was after. She declared him no more than a friend, and wouldn't hear a word against him, swearing that Al felt nothing more than friendship.

Lechery and lust were Cole's specialty, so he couldn't ignore what he saw.

Worst part was, he wondered if Al might just be a better match now that she wanted to help Lizzie, perhaps even take her in as her ward. As much as they may have talked about it, and both agreed it wasn't right or possible, he wasn't a fool.

Four weeks ago they'd been released from quarantine, and she hadn't returned to their room for even one night to sleep. Not one night had been spent in their own bed, together. While she'd not neglected him, and his desires had never been left cold, her main focus was the towheaded child.

Cole couldn't believe how difficult it was proving to find a home for Lizzie. Then again, there were very few people that could meet the brutal standards Jane expected in caring for the little girl she'd grown so attached to. Not to mention the number of men still searching for jobs since the closing of half the silver mines. Things had begun to pick up, but not enough to find families willing to take in another child.

Jane's brother James and his wife Ida were among the very few to meet Jane's tough standards—but the idea of them taking the child all the way to New York where she'd only see her once or twice a year killed Jane.

To be honest, he was damn surprised Jane hadn't said another word about taking the girl in herself once quarantine had been lifted. He shouldn't have been so surprised—once Jane made up her mind it usually stuck. Never mind if she was happy about the decision, which he knew she wasn't, she would keep to it.

Although he'd never admit it to another soul, he'd spent more time than he cared to admit considering their own options with the girl. Long before Lizzie's orphaned state had entered their lives he'd considered making things legal with Jane.

Lizzie only added to the argument that getting married would be the right thing. Hell, with this development Jane might actually want marriage now.

Still, Cole was loath to ask for the sole purpose of the child's sake. If he asked now, that's what Jane'd accuse him of in a heartbeat. That he was asking just because he assumed she wanted it—for the girl or whatever reason the latest rumor held.

Truth was he'd been thinking on it for a while, but the idea of being married again, and immediately having a child—a child with difficulties to boot—was almost too much to bear. His first marriage and its tragic ending, not to mention the truths Jane would learn when she went through his financial records? Well—marriage scared the devil out of him in more ways than one.

Squeals and laughter from the meadow echoed through the empty streets to his place on the porch. He pulled from his thoughts to focus again on the activity in the distance.

Al performed an elaborate fall that drew a round of laughter from Lizzie and Jane that echoed much louder than the laughter he'd just heard.

Children filtered away from the game as parents rose to call their children to blankets. Cole could picture the way Jane's lip likely stuck out in a pout, disappointed her game had ended. His eyes narrowed when Al drew close enough to Jane to put his arm around her waist. When Lizzie and Jesse lined up beside her, they all headed toward a blanket.

Almost like a family.

Cole's stomach turned. He spun on his heel to head into the Inn so he could dump his coffee. He needed whiskey now. Lots of it.

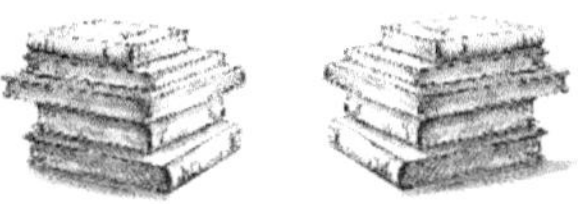

Do not spoil what you have by desiring what you have not.
—Epicurus

Jane got the children settled on the blanket. Once they'd snatched up food, she glanced back toward town. Though she would've sworn she could feel his gaze on her earlier, now all she managed to glimpse was the hint of a shadow moving into the saloon.

Odd, she thought. Most Sunday's he lingered on the porch for the duration of the picnic as the saloon didn't open until quite late, so he'd await her return. She often wondered if he really could see this far, or if he just spent his time in indecent thoughts. Perhaps it was both.

"Not hungry, Lou?" A biscuit hit her stomach to accompany Thomas' words. The man nearly busted his gut laughing at his own cleverness.

"You would rather eat, I would rather play. Shoot me." Jane sank to the blanket, her nose wrinkled at the idea of food as it had a few days that week.

"Don't tempt me. We could've been eating half an hour ago if you hadn't gone and gotten those kids riled up." Tommy winked.

Jane shook her head, a laugh seeped through her attempt at scolding. The distraction of Cole drifted away in the mirth. "You didn't have to wait for us, silly man. My goodness, I would hardly dare to stand between you and your stomach. You are both so obviously happy together."

"His stomach's the only thing that won't leave him." Mike joined in the fun, a wicked grin planted on his lips. "It puts up with him because he fills it so full, it couldn't leave if it tried. The poor thing is weighed down and tired."

Laughter made its way through the large group spread across three joined blankets. Food passed from hand to hand around the haphazard circle. Once all the plates were full, everyone settled in to eat in relative peace. Soon as the food was before her, Jane realized she was starving and ate heartily until she thought she might burst herself.

Once the plates were clean, Jane flopped onto the blanket to stare at the sky. She sighed heartily, rubbing her now full belly. Nearby, Tommy drew a squeal from Lizzie before the two rushed from the blanket. The unmistakable sounds of another game filled the air.

"Are you joining us again?" Al stopped beside her, the sun backlighting his features until they were imperceptible. He held his hand down toward her. "Maybe you could play away that large meal you just ate."

"Are you calling me a glutton?"

"I wouldn't dare."

She laughed and took his hand easily. The man didn't wait for her to pull herself up, lending his own strength to the grip so she was on her feet in not time. The moment she became upright, the world spun around her.

"Jane?"

"Woah." Jane gripped his arm to steady herself. "I believe I stood too fast."

"Are you all right?" One of his arms circled her waist to support her.

The spell passed so quick, she already felt right as rain. Rather than tell him, she took advantage of his concern. With a shove to knock him off balance, she ran off to join in the fun. A small shriek burst free when Al caught up quick enough to catch her. They both stumbled at the impact until the tumbled. She laughed and slipped from his grasp.

This time around the game grew even larger. More adults joined in the fun until the meadow was overflowing with life and laughter. For almost two hours the revelry continued, then slowly began to break apart. One by one families peeled off until only their own large party remained.

"What are you doing for supper?" David approached with Jesse tugging on both his and Lee's hands. The laughter he'd hardly kept contained burst free. "Jesse wanted me to ask."

Jane chuckled along with him. She waved Lizzie closer to their group. "I'm not certain. I picked up an extra basket from Cora yesterday, so I suppose Lizzie and I will enjoy some cold chicken at the clinic."

"I think, perhaps, that Jesse might be all right with you and Lizzie joining us for supper."

To that, Jesse hopped up and down eagerly. "Oh, yeah. Yeah! Please, Ma?"

"Lee put on a stew for us last night to slow simmer today. That would mean a hot meal instead of a repeat of your picnic." David tilted his head. "There's plenty if you want to come and eat at a real dinner table for a change, Al."

Jane hesitated, and cast a glance at Lizzie—who was in the middle of a rapid exchange of notes with Jesse. While she would enjoy the hot supper, and the company, she hadn't seen Cole much today. There was also the factor of Cole's increasing distrust of Al. All of her insisting to trust her fell on deaf ears over Cole's long standing jealousy.

Lizzie tugged her sleeve and held up her note pad. *Please?*

Unable to say no, Jane smiled through her sigh. "All right. It seems Jesse has already invited Lizzie and she'd like to go."

"Good." David smiled at Lee. "It's a full house, then."

Lee nodded. "Yes it is. Which is wonderful. The more, the merrier."

"It's a little more than a full house." Jane laughed. "You forget I know how big that house is. Still, we appreciate the welcome. I think Lizzie gets pretty bored at the clinic sometimes. She'll have fun."

At that moment, both Jesse and Lizzie took off running full tilt.

"I think we'd better catch up." Lee gathered her skirts with a giggle and tore after them both.

"Jane." Kat's voice echoed across the meadow. She raced toward them from the depot. "Jane."

"Go on." Jane waved the men on. "I'll catch up."

Once they'd headed off toward David's, Jane turned back toward the oncoming redhead. They clasped hands the moment Kat grew close.

"He said yes." Kat whispered. A bright smile lit her features.

Jane's eyes grew wide and she squealed, giving Kat a big hug. "So she can stay at the old boarding house with you both until we find her a home?"

"Yes. Isn't it wonderful? I know you've been feeling homesick." Kat nudged her.

"Perhaps a little, but I don't mind caring for Lizzie. I think Cole is getting a wee bit paranoid about the whole situation." Jane sighed. "Even though we already agreed she couldn't stay with us, he thinks I'm still plotting to keep her."

"Have you told him otherwise?" Kat walked arm in arm with her toward the edge of the meadow. "You know Cole is possessive of you."

"I do know, but this past month has been rather busy. Between taking care of Lizzie and the ongoing contract negotiations for me to buy the business, life has been busy."

"What is the delay?"

"Becky's pa is trying to pull strings so Graham has to ask for more money. Graham himself told me he doesn't want that. If anything he wants to lower it after all the damage he's done. We've had to arrange to have Nick send a false contract to Brooks, with Graham's real contract disguised as mail to Tommy from a whore in New York in order to get everything finalized without any further delay."

"No." Kat stopped short, wide-eyed. "You didn't tell me that."

"When have I had time?" Jane laughed. "If I'm not at the inn, I'm at the library where we pass like ships in the night. I return to the clinic to care for Lizzie. You and I both have been too busy to meet even for tea. The only time we've talked it's been about your efforts to get Norman to agree to Lizzie staying with you all until we find a good home for her."

"I suppose that's true enough. Norman has been so busy at the depot that I've had to step in and help him when I'm not at the library helping you on your off hours." Kat frowned. "This will never do. We have to make a point to get together twice a week again. We have too much going on not to."

"Agreed. I should go to supper now, though. I'll tell Lizzie this evening, she'll be so excited." Jane hugged her tight. "We'll talk tomorrow. Promise. I'll tell you all about Graham's recent and newest changes in behavior."

"I am dying of curiosity." Kat waved and ran back toward town, her red curls bouncing behind her.

*Love will enter cloaked in friendships name.
—Ovid*

After their hearty supper, Jane and Al remained at David's for a few hours, talking and sharing stories. By the time Jane realized how late it had become, Lizzie was already sound asleep in Jesse's bed, while Jesse was curled up on the floor just as asleep.

Al picked up Lizzie so David could get Jesse back in his own bed. When he stirred and woke the slightest bit, Jane lingered to say goodbye. After a few good strong hugs and promises for a ride in a couple days, Jane bid farewell to David and Lee.

She met Al's pace for the walk back to town, a comfortable silence settling between them for a good portion of the walk.

Almost at town, Al spoke in hushed tones to keep Lizzie sleeping. "I thought you told me you didn't like kids. Didn't want any. Looks to me like that's changed."

"No one is more surprised than I am." Jane laughed. "Then again, having a special place in my heart for a few select children hardly means I like all children."

"You looked pretty loving today. I think it was about fifteen of them you were keeping happy and occupied."

"Games alone, fun and frolicking is all." She admonished. "That's easy. I still couldn't be a teacher for a classroom full of children."

"You really think so?"

"Playing games with them is one thing. Making them sit in a classroom and learn something is far different."

"Sure it is. I've seen the way you teach Jesse and now Lizzie with her hand-speak. I believe a few other children have learned at your hip the past couple of years." He smirked. "I don't think any class of yours would be sitting in desks learning lessons by rote."

"One on one teaching is far different and easier."

"Of course. How silly of me to think otherwise."

She jabbed her elbow into his ribs and wrinkled her nose. "It doesn't matter anyhow. I'm not about to become a teacher, nor am I about to have a brood of children. Such a thing is a ridiculous notion. Things will remain much as they are."

"I have something to tell you." He sighed as they got to the clinic. "But first I want to ask you something."

Something in his tone made her stomach twitch and unease settled into her heart until her hand shook when she pushed open the door. "Sounds serious."

"We should get Lizzie tucked into bed first. Then we can talk more openly."

Eying him curiously, Jane nodded and held open the door. While he stepped inside, she cast a glance toward the Inn. No sign of Cole, even though he usually emerged when she passed by. All of his words of warning about Al raced through her mind.

He believed the man wanted more than friendship. Though years ago their brief attempt at anything more than friendship had come to a rather hysterical conclusion. Cole insisted Al wanted more, more than she'd be willing to give him. Her reassurances that he was reading too much into it, and she had no such desire never touched his jealousy.

After a minute she shook it off and cursed under her breath. She was letting Cole's paranoia get to her. Not once had Al made anything resembling an overture since his disastrous first attempt years before. He'd always been a friend and a complete gentleman.

She shut the door and made her way through the darkened building upstairs to Lizzie's room. Al already had her tucked in and comfortable, so Jane leaned down to kiss her forehead.

Once Lizzie was settled, Jane led Al from the room and into hers. The summer air hung thick in the room, so she didn't stop until she'd pushed open the balcony doors. "There. It was a bit stifling in here."

"Now that summer is here, the heat is oppressive."

Jane kept her back to him, her nose wrinkled at the small talk. It wasn't like Al at all. She poured them both a glass of water. Handing him his, she took a seat at the table. "Now. What is it you wished to speak to me about?"

"I wanted to let you know my plans."

"All right." She tapped her finger on the edge of her glass. A smile formed and she took a sip of water. That was easy enough to talk about. "Well, considering your original plans were to be in Dominion Falls for only a few days— should I count on your adherence to these new plans?"

Al leaned forward on his knees. "To be honest, that depends a great deal on you."

Her stomach twisted back into knots so tight she swallowed reflexively. She took another sip of water to cover the brief falter. Unsure she wanted to dare try to decipher that comment, she found herself at a loss for words.

"I would like if you allowed me to finish what I'm going to say before I get your arguments." He lifted his head to meet her gaze. "Know that I'm not a fool, nor am I ignorant."

"I would never accuse you of such things, Al."

"Before I start, do you agree to bite your tongue while I explain?"

"Consider it bitten."

He rubbed his palms on his trousers before clasping them together again. "I've known for some time how your feelings lie. You've been a fool over Cole for as long as I've known you. Our brief flirtation aside, it was obvious where your eye always fell at the end of the day."

Jane's brow furrowed and she turned her focus on her glass. The intensity of his stare made biting her tongue increasingly difficult. Even as the pieces of the puzzle fell together and suddenly Cole's warnings didn't seem so paranoid.

"We couldn't ever have a great love, that much is true. But we're comfortable with each other—"

"Al. Don't."

"You agreed to bite your tongue. You don't even know why I'm saying this."

She rose to walk away from the table. Each beat of her heart rushed through her ears; her hands clenched into fists around the fabric of her skirt.

"It's been breaking your heart since you got out of quarantine, probably before. You want to take the child in, but you don't have a home or a husband. I know you're happy with that—at least you were until Lizzie came along. Jesse gave you pause, but he always had David. She's got no one."

Words she'd thought herself, repeated from a man she'd counted as a friend. A good one, if he knew all this without her saying it aloud. Logical arguments to what she feared was coming flew out of her head. He'd caught her so off guard she had nothing to offer.

"We're good friends, and that's a good basis for any lasting relationship. I could assist in getting the adoption approved despite your lack of a past with my connections. I would care for you both."

"I..." Her throat was dry, and she swallowed against the lump in her throat. Unable to face him yet, she kept her back turned. "I cannot believe you are suggesting—"

"I know it isn't a thought that even crossed your mind. I know you love him, but I think you feel trapped by lack of options. For the first time I think you want to be asked, and you aren't sure he would."

Tears blurred her vision. She turned toward him now that he was little more than a watery blur. "No."

"No, what? No to me? Or no, you aren't sure he'd ask?"

"I—I don't know, I..." Her eyes fluttered shut and she tried to rein in the tears. Charlie's taunting that she always lost arguments when it came to matters of the heart reared its ugly head. "It's not often I'm at a loss for words."

"I'm not going to pressure you. I sprung this on you, but I wanted to let you know the option is there." He crossed the room and set his hands on her arms. When she opened her eyes, he smiled. "I made plans to leave in a week, and until that time I won't expect an answer until you're ready."

Jane's jaw twitched and the tears threatened again. All she could do was nod weakly in reply. If she dared open her mouth, she'd lose control. She couldn't do that now, not here, not in front of him.

"Take your time. I'll be around. Good night, Jane."

"Good night." She whispered, not moving an inch when he kissed her temple. It wasn't until he left the room that she let the trembling that had started in her belly out. Her breath left in a shaky gust and she sank to the edge of the bed. "It's crazy. I can't even think it."

She hadn't thought of it, not even for a moment. Not until Al had suggested it. Now it wouldn't leave her head. Not until she'd thought it through and figured out what would be best. Cole would be furious if he knew, but she had to tell him, he was the one she needed to talk to. To see.

"I am happy." She whispered, "I love Cole, he loves me. That's all that's supposed to matter. It is all that matters, it is all I need to know."

She bit her lip and straightened as the chaos Al had caused began to settle. The confusion and doubt disappeared, although she could curse herself for not immediately saying no as she should have. She smiled. "Besides. I never wanted marriage—certainly not one of convenience and that is all this would be. A marriage of convenience. That isn't fair to Al or me, and it wouldn't be fair to Lizzie. It's ridiculous. Why did I even consider it for a second?"

Burying her face in her hands, she took a deep breath. The trembling and worry eased. She rubbed her hands over her face and rose. Lizzie was going to stay with Kat the next day, and they would find her a home. The thought and suggestion, while made with good intentions and a warm heart, had been unnecessary.

Jane had known all along she wouldn't be able to care for Lizzie in that way. It was why she was so determined to find her the best possible home. In the end, it might mean sending her to New York with James and Ida, but if that was what was needed for Lizzie, then it would happen.

She sighed and nodded. "I won't think of it again. I just need to talk to Cole. Kat was right; this has gone on far too long. And now I need to apologize for telling him all along he was a jealous fool."

Of course, she also needed to stop talking to herself. That's what happened when she didn't have Cole there to talk to. While he'd be furious at first, he had always been the best person for her to work out the chaos in her head with. He always cut right though the ridiculous thoughts and got to the truth. Despite his anger, he'd do that this time.

Already her heart felt more settled in the matter, but she wanted that last bit of comfort of the knowledge that she could tell Cole what had happened and her decision. Her initial confusion had been caused by shock, not a desire to do what Al had suggested.

Not really.

It hadn't been more than a fleeting thought.

I have to talk to Cole.

She paced to the door and stared toward The Hangman's Inn. Helplessly she waited and hoped to see some sign of him. She wasn't about to leave Lizzie lying there alone, and Cole was nowhere to be seen.

"Don't linger too long tonight, Cole. I must see you. I have to."

She rubbed her hands on her arms against the sudden chill that settled in her soul and went back inside. Restless, she paced the room until she decided to just get herself ready for bed. After getting settled in bed she picked up the book she'd left beside it the night before. Unable to focus, she read and reread the same page many times before being able to move onto the next one.

Finally she slammed the book shut and looked at the clock.

Nearly three in the morning. Where was he? Every day that month since their release he'd joined her at the clinic when the saloon closed. Sometimes before, but never long after. She rose to her feet and rushed out onto the balcony.

The town was silent, the saloon was silent.

He hadn't come.

Pain lanced her heart and she tried to resist the urge to blame him for not coming when she needed him so desperately. After all, he didn't know. There had to be another reason he hadn't come.

She stared at the quiet inn, her heart pounding an uneasy cadence. "Oh Cole. Where are you? I need you."

The secret of happiness is not in what one likes to do, but in what one has to do.
-James M. Barrie

Cole paced the storeroom, whiskey in hand. From the moment he'd left the balcony of the clinic, he hadn't been able to speak, to think straight.

Rather than return to the crowded bar, he'd come into the storeroom to wrestle with his thoughts. He might have gone to his room for more privacy, but he wanted to talk to Tom the second the doors closed.

While he waited, he stewed, he paced, and he drank. A lot. Once in a while Tom would come into the storeroom for something. Each time he eyed Cole curiously but said nothing. Probably good for him, Cole would have gone off and the whole saloon would have gotten an earful.

For hours he remained there when he had half a mind to go shake Jane for not immediately saying no. How dare she even think a minute.

After all they'd been through.

Worse, the pansy ass soldier had beaten Cole to the punch. Said the words Cole hadn't managed to string together. Worse, he pointed out that Cole was unlikely to ask—not having the foggiest who Cole was or what was really going through his head when it came to Jane.

The noise outside the room died down, then became silence. Doors closed throughout the building.

Cole stopped his pacing. Whiskey bottle in hand, he glared at the door. A few chairs scraped the floor, glasses chinked together.

Tom was actually cleaning up the saloon instead of coming in here? Cole stormed toward the door, stopping short when it opened.

He snarled at Jane's brother. "It's about damn time."

"I grabbed a few things on my way here. Got a lot to clean up, the crowd was lively tonight despite your absence." Tom didn't flinch under Cole's glare. He folded his arms across his chest. "What put the bee in your bonnet?"

"Webb." Cole could barely form the word through his gritted teeth.

Tom waved his hand as if to brush off the word. He moved past Cole to pick up the empty bottles Cole had left scattered on the floor. "Jane told you he wasn't a problem. If you don't get it through your head, she'll kill you."

"I was right."

"Doubtful."

"The asshole proposed to her tonight."

Tom froze where he stood. Back to Cole, three bottles in hand, he didn't move for a long minute. Then he shook his head. "No matter, Jane wouldn't say yes."

"She didn't say no."

For that Tom turned to face him, brow raised. "You've got to be joking. How do you know, anyhow?"

"Went to see her." Cole slugged back the rest of the bottle in his hand as if it would burn away the memory. He used his whole forearm to wipe away the dribbles. "She left the doors open."

"I need more information."

"He proposed, she didn't say no. What in hell else could you need to hear?"

"How did he propose?"

Cole stared at Tom, confounded at his calm nature. "Didn't you fucking hear me?"

"I did."

Cole tossed aside his empty bottle in frustration. When he reached to grab another, Tom's beefy hand clamped on his wrist. "Let me go."

"No. You're drunk enough and riled enough to spit fire. Don't need any more help. Tell me how he proposed. With flowery declarations of love?"

"No. The girl." Cole's lip curled against the rising bile. "Said they couldn't have a great love. Friendship is…uh…"

Tom still hadn't let go of his hand. He held his silence while Cole struggled to remember.

"I don't remember."

"Coffee."

"What?"

Tom set aside the empty bottles to attend to the fire in the small stove. "You need your wits about you."

"I need to go kill the bastard."

"Wouldn't recommend it. He's in his room upstairs, and everyone would hear."

Cole glared in the general direction of the room Webb was renting as if he could see through the wall right to the door of the room. "It would be so easy, though."

"Probably." Tom kept busy with the coffee pot, throwing in grounds and the water from the kettle. "Doubt it would be worth it. Jane would never forgive you. Then where would you be?"

"She'd understand."

"Sure. Sure. She'd match you kill for kill for hurting her friend."

"Friend," Cole spit the word as if it would remove the bad taste it left in his mouth.

"Yes. Friend, even if you don't like it, that's what he is. Although after Al asking her this, I imagine such a friendship would be irrevocably altered."

"It best be over and done with."

"Have you met Jane? I doubt it. She has even forgiven that ass Graham several times over."

Cole's hand settled on his pistol, the sick pit in his stomach growing stronger. "She didn't fucking say no."

Tom handed him a mug of coffee. "Drink."

Rather than take it, Cole stared the man down.

"Before you do something rash, take it."

"Gonna go give your sister a shake."

"Drink up. That would be stupid."

"Nah. We're good at fighting."

"Precisely. You'd wake the town with your fighting. You really want the world to hear that another man asked your woman to marry her? Even more than that, whatever crazy thoughts are running through your head after it? All your actual feelings on the matter?"

Cole met him stare for stare for several minutes. He didn't like admitting the man had a point. The whole town would know what he was thinking on the matter of marriage. Finally, he took the coffee.

"I get that you're upset he'd ask, but I doubt Jane would say yes. She's a fool for you, and oftener led by her heart than her head."

"She hesitated." Cole drank the bitter liquid, wishing it was more whiskey the whole time.

"Again—she'll say no."

"You don't know that. She ain't your sister, not like she was, anyhow."

"True. That's why I'm more sure she'll say no. So you'd best stop your ranting."

"No. He asked her."

"Yeah, so?" Tom took a seat, this time his gaze fell fully on Cole without distraction. "Man, you are pissed. You're the one that suspected he wanted more. What has you so upset about this? You know she'll say no."

"I don't."

"You do."

Cole's lip curled in his frustration. He set down the mug, rage making his hands shake. "That bastard fucking asked before I could, and now no matter what it ain't gonna ring true if I do the same."

Silence lingered after his statement. Tom said nothing at all while Cole remained turned away, leaning against the shelves for support.

All his rage had blown away when he'd admitted that he'd been thinking of asking Jane to marry him. In the prolonged silence, he closed his eyes. Why the hell had it taken him so long to get up the gumption to even admit his feelings, and now for this? He'd ruined it himself by delaying.

"How long?"

"What?"

"How long have you been thinking this? Is it just because Webb proposed, because she won't stand for that."

"No. It ain't because of him." Cole rubbed his hand over his face. "Been thinking it for a while. Only now got up the courage to tell her how I feel."

"She knew anyway."

"But she ain't heard it."

"She still knew."

"I don't…" Cole's hesitation lingered. Much as he'd liked Tom from the start, admitting certain things wouldn't ever sit well. Parts of his past he couldn't help but hide away.

"I know about them, if it helps."

That could mean any number of things. From those dead, to those living. Cole met his friend's gaze. "Who?"

"All of them. Mostly the one's you're probably thinking of. Ella. Lydia."

Tension raced through Cole. He could be furious. "How?"

"Pinkerton, remember?" Tom leaned forward. "You're involved with my sister. I did a little digging. I can assure you I didn't go deep, once I learned about the other two, I dropped it. I knew you were a better man than you seemed after that."

The other two. That was something Jane would need to know about. Especially if she was coming onto the business and paid the slightest bit of mind to the books. "Jane doesn't know about those other two."

"She will. Not worried." Tom slurped his coffee noisily. "I know your baby died, and shortly after, your wife. I know she lost her mind when she lost her child."

Cole closed his eyes against the memories. "Jane didn't."

"Clara did."

"Clara lost everything."

"Don't I know it." Tom sighed. "Now, what are you going to do about the pickle you're in?"

"No idea." Cole stared at the door, still longing to go to Jane and hear her assurances that she'd never say yes to Webb. That she still loved Cole, and no one else. That she'd never sacrifice that, not even for the child. He still wanted all of her as much as he ever had.

"You still want to marry her?"

"Scares the shit out of me, but yeah."

"Jane isn't Ella."

"Not even close. Ain't no one like Jane."

Tom chuckled. "She's got five living brothers that are a little like her, or a lot in some cases."

Cole chuckled when Tom snapped his own suspenders as if to say it was himself he spoke of. "I still want to ask her, but it won't mean nothing after Webb. Especially with the girl involved. She'll say that's why I'm asking."

"Maybe, but she loves you. That would be enough for her to say yes."

"Nah. She won't want asked now."

Tom rose. "I got our grandmother's ring you can use. It'll need sized, grandmother was a big woman."

Cole stared at Tom. "I just said she won't want asked now. Why you talking foolish?"

"She will, once she's had a few days. What were you planning to celebrate getting into business together."

"Nothing."

Tom shook his head. He heaved himself to his feet with a grunt. "Fool. Take her to Denver to celebrate."

"Denver."

"You said she doesn't know, so what harm will it do?"

"You're plotting to make her see about them."

"I'm not. Denver is a big town, she doesn't have to know about your remaining family until she's ready."

"They aren't family."

Tom's brow rose as he stared Cole down again.

"Not really."

Tom harumphed, but said no more. "Take Jane to Denver. Ask her there, better yet, ask her before. Get things arranged now so you can get hitched in Denver."

"I can't. Whole town'll know. Jane'll know if Kathy's around for the answers."

"Then don't do it here. Geez, you can be an idiot. Head to Pueblo, get the ring fixed, reach out to your contacts in Denver and set everything up, then be back before Jane can complain at your absence."

"Pueblo."

"Less than a day by horse. Worst part is the mountains."

"You really think she'll say yes, and not think I'm asking because of the girl?"

Tom grinned. "My sister's an idiot that loves you."

"That didn't answer my question."

Nothing is more capable of troubling our reason, and consuming our health, than secret notions of jealousy in solitude.
—Aphra Behn

After a long, fitful night of tossing and turning, somehow Jane managed to find the sleep that eluded her. She only knew this because she woke, keenly aware that someone stared at her. The sensation seemed especially jarring, as the empty bed beside her told her Cole had never bothered to arrive.

Jane drew her eyes open, a grin sliding into place when she found a sweet, smiling face peering down at her. Lizzie bounced on the bed, then shook Jane's shoulders. A squealing giggle slipped out of the young girl.

"All right, all right. I'm awake." Jane laughed as she tried to sit amidst the eager bouncing of the child. She grabbed the pad beside the bed to scribble. *Are you ready for today?*

Lizzie's enthusiastic nod got punctuated by her strong pull on Jane's hand. The night before, Jane had taken a few minutes after dinner to inform Lizzie of her new temporary living arrangements with Kat. The young girl had been over the moon at the idea of staying in the same home as her good friend Cindy all the time.

Jane allowed Lizzie to drag her to the next room where a satchel already lay out on the bed. Lizzie threw open the armoire, then climbed all the way inside. Dresses flew out one after the other into an ever-growing pile on the floor.

The troubles that had plagued her sleep slipped away at the sight of small feet poking out of the armoire, and the pile of clothes beside it. Pure laughter that could only be caused by a child's antics pushed aside her grumpiness into an outright giggle. Lizzie's contagious levels of excitement could not be ignored. When Lizzie emerged finally, she was dressed in the same dress as she'd worn the day before—her Sunday best.

Jane didn't dare chastise Lizzie for wearing her Sunday best on such an exciting day. Instead, she moved to help Lizzie pack every item as careful as they could through the impatience of the young ward.

Somehow within half an hour Jane managed to pack Lizzie's things. In that time, she also managed to get herself dressed and ready to face the day.

Hand in hand, each of them with a satchel in the other, they made their way down the street the two buildings to the old boarding house. Jane only bothered with a brief knock before pushing the door open, as Kat was expecting them.

Norman's voice echoed out from the kitchen the moment they entered. "Too old to have two young ones running around here."

"Oh, you aren't too old, Norman," Jane countered. Before she made it two steps toward the kitchen to greet her friend, Lizzie squealed beside her. The young girl yanked her hand free in order to dart up the stairs. A matching squeal from Cindy explained Lizzie's quick departure from her side.

Kat popped around the corner, her arms held out for a hug.

Jane abandoned the satchel she carried to welcome the hug of her friend. She spotted Norman emerging from the kitchen and offered him a wink. "If you can live with Kat and Cindy, I think you can handle a nine year old girl who is far more well-behaved than your wife. The biggest problem will be if we have to separate the pair of them."

"Well, she'd better be," Norman groused. At the rapid dash of footsteps above them, he glared toward the ceiling. "Just get on upstairs and get her settled in before I change my mind."

"It's just a few days." Jane slipped from Kat's side to give Norman a fierce hug and a kiss on the cheek. "You are a dear man, Norman. I can't appreciate you accommodating for Lizzie this way enough. But if Lizzie truly is a terrifying creature to have around, I'm certain I can find some other arrangement."

"Yeah, yeah." Norman's voice took on a gruff note as he waved them off.

Kat grinned, dragging Jane toward the stairs. She lowered her voice to a hush. "He keeps trying to protest, but you should see what he has done to your old room."

"You will be putting her in my old room?" Jane smiled. "That's lovely. It is such a good sized room. She might get lost compared to where we've been staying."

At the top the stairs the women paused to a peal of giggles from the direction of Jane's old room, which preceded both girls racing into the hall, then into the room next door. Cindy was about two years younger than Lizzie, but the pair had proven to become fast friends when Cindy first arrived in town.

Cindy's lack of a 'real' pa, not to mention the rampant rumors of who her pa might really be spread fast, even among the school children. Lizzie had been the one girl that didn't listen. Jane couldn't be certain if it was because she already knew Kat, or because she was friends with Jesse, Isaac, and Arthur, all of whom supported Cindy.

For the moment, the tight friendship only served to make their laughter louder than ever.

Kat chuckled. "I have no doubt that they'll settle in quickly so we'll be breaking up arguments in no time. I'm glad that we're off to a good start, at least."

"Oh, you definitely are. We—oh, my."

"I told you." Kat stepped into the room that had been Jane's when she'd lived in the boarding house several years before.

Back when Jane had known nothing of herself or her past, the room had ben simple, barren. The only signs of her own existence had been some books on the tables, and her perfume on the dresser.

The room seemed softer without the cheap decorations Martha had used to adorn the boarding house. The walls were painted white; the old wood bed replaced with an iron bed Jane knew mirrored the one next door in Cindy's room.

Little touches like a low shelf for Lizzie's favorite books, and armoire already half-filled with clothes before Lizzie had touched her bags to unpack, and a bell rope installed in case Lizzie needed to call Kat and Norman finished off the room.

"It's perfect." The words choked in Jane's throat. The room was everything Jane knew she couldn't give to the young girl, no matter how attached to her she might have gotten. It was everything, and the opposite of what her betraying heart might have wanted, no matter what her logical brain told her.

"Jane? Are you all right?" Kat touched her arm gently.

"Yes." Jane tried to wave off the concern with a laugh. She knew how ridiculous it was to be so upset. This room left no doubt that Kat's attempts to sway Norman to adopt Lizzie were working. She should be nothing less than happy. "Sorry. I honestly did not expect Norman to go through all of this trouble."

"He's not as curmudgeonly as he acts."

"I've noticed." Another squeal from the balcony drew Jane's attention. Lizzie waved her over, gesturing madly about being able to see so much. Compared to the small window into the alley she'd had at the clinic, it was a world of difference. The hand-speak they'd been working on was proving to have taken root.

Jane stepped onto the balcony with the young girl. She knelt down as Lizzie once again exclaimed that she could see everything. Jane nodded in agreement, signing that she knew. She withdrew the pad from her pocket to write, *When I first moved to town, I lived in this room. Do you remember coming to watch over me?*

Lizzie's excitement faltered. Her hands flew to reply. *Ma. With ma.*

Jane cursed herself from bringing the memory to the forefront and ruining the day. When Lizzie had visited Jane, she'd come with her ma to take care of her after being shot.

Jane pulled Lizzie into a tight hug meant to soothe them both. After a small sigh, she released Lizzie to write again. *Do you like it here?*

A fierce nod preceded the bear hug Lizzie wrapped Jane in. Lizzie spoke, her tone low and controlled as she formed the words she could no longer hear. "I'll miss you."

Tears Jane couldn't control spilled free, so Jane held Lizzie tight until she thought she could control herself. She was glad she'd made sure Lizzie kept talking so the girl could say it aloud, but at the same time, it still brought an ache to her heart.

After a shaky breath to pull herself together, she released Lizzie from the hug. She managed to smile. She wrote quickly. *That is silly. We will see each other all the time. I live right across the street, and we still have your lessons, right?"*

Lizzie nodded before she gave Jane another near-brutal hug. The second she released Jane, she grabbed Cindy's hand to run through the rooms again.

Jane hauled herself to her feet. The girls burst onto the neighboring balcony, eliciting a smile from Jane as they grabbed hands to spin in a circle. Jane turned from the sight, her own conflicting emotions bringing almost as many tears as smiles. The Inn across the street appeared empty. No sign of Cole on the porch, or in their room. Not even Tommy appeared to be getting things set for the day.

"Jane?" Kat touched her shoulder.

"Hmm?"

"Jane. You haven't heard a word I've said. What is going on?"

"Nothing." She said it too fast for it to be believed. Kat's furrowed brow proved to Jane her friend hadn't missed that fact. Jane sighed. "I just—it's not something I can discuss quite yet. I really should go see Cole."

"Again? Didn't you two just part company?"

The smile Jane had forced forward faltered at the comment. She cleared her throat to cover. "Right. I, um…"

"Jane?"

"I really must go. I have to check on the Inn, and then the library."

"Are we still on for lunch?"

Jane couldn't know what would happen to her day when she finally saw Cole. She shook her head. "Supper. Tonight. I promise. Something has come up that I need to take care of."

"Are you certain you're all right?" Kat's grasp on Jane's hand didn't loosen at first. Only Jane's wince freed them.

Jane flexed and closed her still sore left hand. She managed a nod. "I am fine. I will be. I have just had a very long night. Excuse me."

Before her friend could protest or ask any further questions, Jane darted around her toward the stairs. She tried to get a handle on her emotions all the way down the steps. Lack of sleep hadn't ever made her this off-kilter before. She could only put her state of turmoil on the combination of Al's proposal, and Lizzie no longer being under her care.

The moment she closed the door behind her, a familiar voice spoke. "Mrs. Mitchell."

Several curious, and amused, eyes turned their way. All the tension she'd tried to release came rushing out toward the nearby target. "Mr. Hamm. I will not tell you again. You must cease calling me that. I am certainly *not* Mrs. Mitchell."

"Janey. I didn't mean—"

Jane stormed off before he could finish his apology. The pang of guilt over yelling at the interminably sweet Mr. Hamm only fueled her emotional upheaval further until she slammed open the doors of the inn. Behind the bar, Edgar startled out of his bored stupor over wiping the counter.

The nearly empty room didn't boost her mood any. Quiet and dull meant no income, and certainly no Cole. She turned an accusatory gaze on Edgar. "Where is Cole?"

"Ain't seen him." Edgar leaned his head on his hand, his other resuming the wiping off the bar.

In a huff, Jane stormed across the room. She pounded up the stairs loud enough to rouse the quiet customers into conversation, likely about her. Her behavior might be childish, but her nervous energy had to go somewhere.

Something had to be wrong. Cole would never skip coming to her bed if he could help it. He also never missed opening the doors of the saloon.

At the end of the hall she grabbed the knob to their room, but found it locked. A nearly animal-like growl sounded low in her throat, her frustration, nerves, and worry all mixing together to leave her in close to a panic. She dug into her purse for the key. The minute she found it, she threw open the door. "*Cole.*"

Silence greeted her in response. A few steps in showed her just how profoundly empty the room remained. As if mocking her empty bed last night, the silence settled into her belly with a deep twist of her gut.

Where in the hell could he be? The temptation to blame him for her emotional upheaval, certainly for not being there when she needed him, reared its ugly head again.

She slammed the door shut hard enough to shake the wall. The ten steps it usually took her to reach Tommy's door got cleared in four, long, furious strides. She pounded on the door. "Get up, you lazy sod."

Tommy pulled the door open, only one of his eyes open, and a grunt of initial greeting. His hair stuck out from his head in several directions. The night shirt he wore creased into a rumpled state that rivaled his own. "What the damn hell, Lou? I was up late playing poker. I need my beauty sleep, you know."

"I could not care less about your damn beauty sleep." Jane shoved him aside hard enough that he thumped into the wall. She tossed some clothes his way from his dresser. "I have no idea where Cole is. The train should arrive any minute, and someone needs to maintain an eye on this place while I go try to drum up some business before I head to the library. Get your shirt on and get the hell downstairs. Business is dead, and we need it."

"What crawled under your skin?"

"Just do as I say." Jane stomped down the hall. It wasn't until she was halfway down the stairs that Tommy bothered to stop sputtering and slam his door shut. She couldn't deny that her initial concern at Cole's absence had morphed into an ugly branch of anger.

Not truly believing he might be there, but fearing it none the less, she threw open the door to one of the whore's rooms. No sign of him there didn't alleviate her anger in the slightest. Instead, she moved to the next room to throw open that door.

Still no sign of Cole, so she turned her wrath toward the startled Iris. "Where in blazes has Cole gotten to?"

"Ain't seen him since we closed last night. He was acting sore, so we left him be with his whiskey." Iris yawned wide. "Last I seen, he was heading outside with his bottle."

"Wonderful," Jane grumbled.

Violet hung over the edge of a bed, a bucket held tight to her face. The heave of her body was enough to shake Jane from her anger, even if for only a moment.

"Are you all right, Violet? Sickness getting the best of you?"

"I'm fine." Violet's voice was weak, but at least she was able to speak. "I'm right tired of getting sick, though."

"I've no doubt. You keep resting. Stay in here until you're certain you won't be relieving the contents of your stomach on the customers. Understood?" At Violet's nod, Jane turned to Iris. "I expect all of you to be cleaned properly and dressed in the good dresses I gave you. Be prepared to do more than offer company. Look your absolute best. I need to go meet the train."

Jane shut the door and strode through the saloon, with far less childish stomping than before, though her frustration still bubbled near the surface. Once outside, she gathered her skirts to run fast as she could to the depot. If on time, the train would arrive at any minute. Her best hope at this point was that Cole might be there.

The whistle sounded in the distance at the same time she stepped on the platform. A quiet curse slipped out under her breath when she found no sign of Cole there either. She now had no idea where he could be, or why he'd gone.

Iris had mentioned he'd been acting sore, but why? Tommy in his freshly waken state had been of no assistance. Stress over her own dilemma, the question of where Cole might be, and the loss of Lizzie all raced through her head until her eyes pounded with a headache. She pinched the bridge of her nose to stave off the headache while she paced through the small crowd.

"Would this not fall under false advertising?" Mike's voice broke into her thoughts, his bright smile not easing her fired nerves in the least. He paid no heed to her glare, instead kissing her cheek. "Getting dressed in your Sunday best might give off the wrong impression to the customers you approach—"

Jane clamped her hand over his mouth. "One more word and the only impression you'll be showing your customers is a broken nose, even if I have to break my hand again to do it. You understand?"

His eyes were wide as he gently pried her hand from his mouth. "Jane? What's wrong."

"I can't talk to you right now. It's nothing."

"Why are you here, by the way? Shouldn't you be at the library at this hour?"

"Not another damn word." She straightened her shoulders against his questioning gaze, relieved the train had arrived. Though it took some digging, she found a smile to plaster on her face as people began to disembark. This was for business, and for that she'd smile no matter what her current state.

With Mike nearby competing for customers, it took some doing for Jane to gather together several guests to take back to the Hangman's Inn. The couple that stood near her had needed more convincing than the two men, including a bribe of free meals. Thankfully in recent weeks, Jane had managed to strike a deal with Cora over the cost of meals for her customers that made such a deal possible.

Introducing the guests to each other, Jane struck up a conversation and kept them all chatting on the walk back to town. She roped the younger of the gentlemen into the five-dollar-in poker game that afternoon, and one by one sent each patron to their room with the assistance of a dressed-up whore.

Jane ignored Edgar's curious glance, walked right past him into the storeroom, only to keep going right into the ice house. She sat on a block of ice, and leaned against the wall of stacked ice behind her. The cold soaked through her dress into every muscle until the heat of her anger faded somewhat.

Her mind raced with every possible scenario of what might have happened to Cole, where he might be. Perhaps he'd finally spooked as she'd always feared now that they were business partners. Maybe he'd even heard Al's proposal, but that didn't seem possible. After all, there'd been no word of Al being on the business end of Cole's fists.

Since the clinic hadn't come alive with one of its doctors having to treat Al after a beating, it seemed infinitely unlikely Cole had heard.

So where could he be? Her heart clenched tight in worry, anger, frustration, and grief. She wanted nothing more than to talk to him, to tell him what had happened. The thoughts that had raced through her head immediately after, the feelings that had torn her apart. To have him hear it and know where her heart remained.

The door opened, but she chose to ignore it. It was taking all her energy to keep the ridiculous, foolish tears at bay.

"Lou? You all right?" Tommy's presence filled the small icehouse. "You're not feeling poorly again, are you? Feverish?"

"It's been over a month, Thomas." She swatted at the hand that reached toward her forehead. "Leave me the hell alone. I feel fine."

"Bull."

"I'm not talking to you."

"To be frank, you actually are." Tommy frowned at her lack of reaction. He sat beside her, his hands folded in front of him, his forearms on his knees. "What's going on, Janey?"

"I have no idea—except that I'm late for the library."

"What can I do?"

"Nothing."

"I think I can handle that." He wrapped his arm around her shoulders and pulled her into a hug. "I'm pretty good at nothing."

Despite her state of mind, she managed a weak laugh. She hugged him in return. For several minutes, she let herself soak in the comfort until she'd managed to relax somewhat.

She sighed deeply as she pulled back. She brushed the straw from her skirts when she stood. "Mr. Gibbs in room four will need to be retrieved for the five-dollar-in game at three. I should be back around then. Kat is working at the library this evening."

He brushed her back, sending several more pieces of straw to the floor. Once she finally met his gaze, he opened the door. "We've got it covered here if you wanted to eat supper with Jesse, or whatever you need to do."

"Thank you, Thomas. We'll see how the day goes. I promised supper with Kat, but Jesse is coming by for a few hours today. He wants to start a new book; he's been reading fast these days."

"Just like his Ma." Tommy grinned. "And all of us, I guess."

"I guess."

"Hey." He set his strong hand on her shoulder to hold her still. "I know this is not solely about Lizzie, although that would be enough. If you need anything, you know where to find me."

"You would think I would, wouldn't you?" She ignored his questioning gaze to place a kiss on his cheek. "Thank you."

"No need to thank me, it's my job."

"No. For what you're doing right here. For being good to me."

Tommy shrugged. For the barest of seconds his eyes flicked away, a hint of a guilty grimace crossing his features in the motion. "Told you a long time ago. You're family, no matter what damn fool thing you do."

She brushed off the sense that he seemed guilty as her own anger at Cole being redirected his way. A small, weak but genuine laugh emerged. "The feeling is mutual."

*Delay always breeds danger;
and to protract a great design is often
to ruin it.
-Miguel de Cervantes*

Cole paced in front of the telegraph office. Already a full day had passed. He'd had to spend the night in Pueblo. Worst thing being, he couldn't even get a message to Tom to let him know of the delays he was having.

That afternoon he'd finally be able to pick up the ring. The man had promised it would be ready by four.

In the meantime, he was still waiting on two responses from Denver. He'd needed to make arrangements for them to visit so the one they were visiting would be aware. She didn't like surprises.

The other telegram was to one final minister that might be willing to do the ceremony as he wanted. Rather, how he imagined Jane would want.

Of course, all of this was assuming she'd say yes.

Though Tom had seemed confident in the notion, the longer he stayed in Pueblo, the more doubtful Cole became. There was a lot riding on the faith of a brother that hardly knew Jane compared to his sister Clara.

He would have asked Mike, but the fewer people that knew about Cole's potential humiliation, the better.

Honestly, already too many people knew. Tom knew, and his contact in Denver had been utterly curious about why he needed a minister with an open mind.

It would cost him to shut that woman up, but hopefully it would be worth it in the end. If she didn't owe him a lifetime of favors already, he would be in debt up to his eyeballs with the assistance she'd been providing.

At the sound of his name, Cole strode back into the telegraph office.

"A response from The Wellman School, Mr. Mitchell." The clerk handed him the paper.

Mr. Mitchell,

Alma will be delighted to have a visit. I will apprise her of the company that will come with you. When you are certain of a date, please send a telegram.

Yours,

Mrs. Wellman

Cole let out a breath of relief. One task handled, at least partially. He still had to explain to Jane—somehow. She'd likely be angry about the secrecy.

Damn, he'd be lucky if she said yes. Extremely lucky.

He needed a drink. Bad.

"I'll be back for the other telegram in an hour or two." Cole nodded to the clerk on his way out. He strode over to the closest saloon to get some whiskey.

He tugged the small notebook out of his pocket, flipping it open to the page with Tom's notes.

Ring. He'd pick that up in two hours time.

School, contacted.

Reverend, contacted four of them. First three were no good. He hoped the fourth would work. Otherwise he'd have to go to Denver himself.

Then he'd really be screwed. Maybe he should have sent Tom for the tasks. Then again, he didn't trust no one to reach out to Alma's school, even on his behalf.

For the lawyer, he'd put his own neck on the line and reached out to Jane's brother, Nick. He was already working on the contracts for the sale of Graham's half of the business. All Cole asked him to do was make an alternate version with a different name in case she said yes.

Unsurprisingly, Nick's response had been short and to the point. With the exception of what Cole was sure was a snide *It's about damn time* slipped in for good measure.

"Need some company?" A young whore with strawberry blond hair leaned forward, her ample bosoms nearly falling out of her corset.

Cole lifted a brow, then shook his head. "Not interested. Got a hell of a woman back home. No need for whores."

"Everyone has a need, mister."

"My woman fills mine, has for a long time." Cole turned his attention back to his notebook. He needed the response from the minister so he could get back home.

It would be so much faster by train, but the last one to Dominion Falls had left that morning. Either he rode all night, or took the morning train. He'd likely get home around the same time either way, but sitting around doing nothing wouldn't help him feel any better about his extended absence.

He had no idea what Jane had told Webb during his absence. What if she'd told him yes? What if his absence had spurred her to say yes out of spite?

His nerves got him back to his feet and heading toward the office. The clerk assured him his telegram still hadn't arrived.

He pondered sending a message to Tom, but again word would spread. Norman wasn't the quietest, and if Kathy was at the telegram she'd be awful curious why he was in Pueblo.

"Damn it."

"Sir?" The clerk turned at his outburst. His brow pursed in confusion. "Did you need something else?"

"No. No. Just my response. I'll wait outside." Cole strode to the bench outside, staring down the bustling street.

Jane was going to kill him.

He never should have left.

But then again—what did he have to worry about? She wouldn't say yes to Webb. How many times had she told him to trust her?

How many times had she professed her love for him?

Many, many times. Even before she'd used the words, she'd let him know how she felt. He only hoped he'd been able to do the same.

If she had any doubts, then Webb had a leg up.

No. He couldn't think that way.

"Mr. Mitchell."

Cole hopped to his feet to grab the next telegram. A confirmation of his wishes for the ceremony, along with a request for a date so the Reverend could confirm availability.

It took some self-control not to whoop in excitement. Soon as he got the ring, he could go home.

Then he'd make his own proposal.

One Jane wouldn't hesitate to accept.

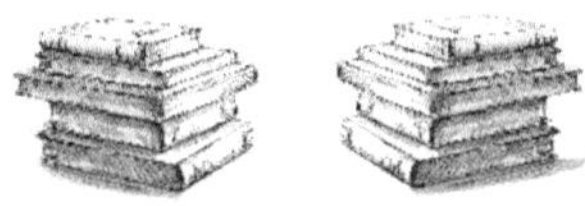

You are in a pitiable condition if you have to conceal what you wish to tell.
—Pubilius Syrus

Jane worked all afternoon, if staring at the books could be called work. Her best companion had been distraction. When Kat arrived, she'd forced herself to go through the motions of tea and conversation. Somehow she'd managed to avoid the topic of Cole, grateful Kat had plenty to tell her.

She indulged in conversations about Lizzie, Kat's friend Patrick, and a sordid tale about a rumored affair between the Widow Billery and the new school teacher, John Withers. If Kat sensed Jane's utter distraction, she was kind enough to not let on until the end of the afternoon.

A gentle hand on hers before she could make her escape pulled Jane's full focus to Kat. Kat's brows pursed in concern. "Are you certain you don't want to talk about what's bothering you?"

In many ways, she did, but Jane shook her head. "Not right now. I think I need rest."

"I'll be here to talk when you're ready."

"I know." Jane squeezed Kat's hand. "I do. Thank you."

Kat's concern relaxed into a warm smile. With the release of Jane's hand she offered an understanding nod. "Go on, then."

Jane didn't wait for further permission to dart from the room. She crossed the street in a daze. Upon entering the saloon, she returned warm welcomes with more instinctive reactions than full involvement like usual.

She finally made it to her room, only to find it still empty. The night before she'd returned to her own bed for the first time in weeks.

Alone.

There wasn't the welcome home she'd expected, the sheets cold beside her. All she'd wished for was to talk to Cole, but he remained absent. It appeared as if once again she'd be alone.

The ache of his absence tossed and turned with her until it roiled into a bubbling pit of anger. Not only was he not there, but there was no explanation. No note left, no message with Tommy. He was just gone.

For two whole days.

If she'd taken her love for him too far, he could have told her. Had he truly just disappeared without a word? She couldn't fathom it; he hadn't seemed like that sort of man in the past year.

When the sun rose through the window, she could officially call her restless night over, but she remained in the bed, lying about for no reason other than to wait.

After an hour, she grew disgusted with herself. Why pine for him? It wasn't as though he was good at conversation anyhow. She'd have to figure things out on her own, then.

With that though, she leapt from the bed to dress fast as she could. A good ride would clear her head.

"Jane." Tommy called as she descended the steps. "Hey, Jane."

She ignored him, not even offering a wave on her rush through to the barn behind the inn. Tempest seemed eager as she was to run, so she let her go free. The wind whipped across her face, tore several curls loose from her hair, and sent the ribbons on her petticoats flying about. Still, for all its power, it didn't clear her head as she'd hoped.

As they returned to town, she didn't know what else to do. She wasn't due to open the library until one. Kat, Lizzie, and Cindy had roped Norman into a picnic. His protests of needing to work had fallen on deaf ears since they'd already managed to get Norman's new apprentice, Byron, to agree to watch the depot for several hours. Not that Kat had managed to distract her enough the day before.

She stopped by David's on the way by in hopes of seeing Jesse, but no one was home. A quick stop by Cora's proved fruitless, for Jesse wasn't there either. Jane could only assume David and Jesse had gone fishing, or on some other adventure.

Jane put Tempest in her stall. To spend more time, she gave her a thorough brush down. When she passed through the saloon again, Tommy didn't bother with a greeting, though he eyed her carefully as though she might attack.

She stepped onto the porch to fill her time with taking in the hustle and bustle of the town. Right as she decided to go ahead and open the library despite the early hour, she spotted Cole. Relief raced through her tense body that he was all right.

He guided Faro through town at a slow, easy gait. From what she could tell, he had yet to see her under the shadows of the porch. He wore a lazy grin, tipping his hat to passersby. No, not a lazy grin. More like the wicked grin of the Cheshire Cat from Wonderland.

The rush of relief she'd embraced turned over quick as that. All of the worry she'd lived in over the past two days, not knowing where he'd gone, why he'd left, if he was even all right. If he was angry, or if he'd somehow heard Al. All of it crashed into a hurricane-level tidal wave of anger. He hadn't even had the decency to leave her a note.

She gathered her skirts, ready to storm forward to unleash the gale-wind force of her fury. The moment she stepped into sunlight, she changed her mind. He wanted to leave her alone, so be it. She'd help him in the endeavor.

No longer caring if he'd even saw her, she turned her back on him. She let her fury fuel her forward motion to the library. She had no idea if he expected a cheerful greeting, but he was not going to anything of the sort. Not after what he'd put her through, whether he knew it or not.

She no longer cared if her state of mind had been made worse by Al, who'd also been avoiding her for the past couple of days. No, Cole didn't know about that so it was irrelevant.

Al's sweet, unromantic proposal rang through her head with every step across the street. The only reason she even bothered to give it a moment's thought had been because of Lizzie. Without that factor, the answer would have been an immediate no.

Especially now, after her two days of solitude where she'd been able to run over the events more time than she cared to count, she was not truly entertaining the idea of marrying Al. Though she knew her heart, the memory continued to nag because the one person she'd wanted to talk about it with had disappeared without so much as a bye or leave.

I think you want to be asked, and you aren't so sure he would. The words pierced her heart as she heard them again in her head, accompanied with the image of Al's kind smile. Could he have been right? Did she really want to be asked?

No.

She sat down hard in her desk chair, not remembering unlocking the library, or entering the room at all. A pile of books sat on her desk awaiting her attention. She ignored them.

No. I did not want to be asked. Not because of this. I did not want to be asked for the sole purpose of adopting that child.

Part of her was curious if Cole had even considered it for a minute. Not that such a thing would matter in the long run, for she would have turned him down as well. It wasn't what she wanted.

No, perhaps she did want it now, but it wasn't *why* she wanted it.

The blasted curiosity that always pushed forward still wondered if he'd thought of it.

Her gaze drifted to the window where she spotted Cole's familiar form striding closer. Her thoughts grew dark again. It wasn't as though she'd been able to ask him or talk about it at all. No one deserved to know what had happened before Cole did, but he'd been gone.

She couldn't even admit to him that for one fleeting moment she'd considered it, only to dismiss it as something she could never do. Not to him. Not to her. If she hadn't had Cole in her life, perhaps she would have truly considered it, but she did have him. Or she had.

Logically she knew his absence shouldn't have been so vitally painful—she was a grown woman, after all. A tear slipped down her cheek. She swiped it away quick a moment before he darkened her doorway.

She rose, determined to ignore him. A grown woman, yes. One that loved the infuriating man that remained hovering in the doorway rather than entering.

"So what'd ya say?"

Every limb went numb. The book she'd just picked up dropped back to the desk. *Thump.* Like the sound she was certain her heart made as it hit her stomach. Her jaw slackened to open. She struggled to process what she'd just heard him ask.

He had heard?

Worse. After hearing another man propose to her, he'd walked away. He didn't wait for her answer, or bother to confront her, or Al, or speak to her at all? Fury slammed her jaw back shut. "Where the hell here you? I *needed* you."

"Sure didn't sound like it."

Every breath struggled against her corset. The white hot lava of anger appeared to have seized her lungs until she couldn't quite remember how to make them function. The room spun. She clenched her jaw. Her hands balled into fists. She pressed them into the desk. "I needed you."

"I'm here now."

"Now? Well, you're too damn late."

*But love is blind,
and lovers cannot see
the pretty follies that
themselves commit.
-William Shakespeare*

His hands were already balled into fists, but Cole clenched them tighter at her words. After what he'd been doing, he'd never expected her to say that.

Sure, he'd worried over it. He didn't dare imagine she would actually say yes to Al. Especially not after Tommy's reassurance. Jealous as he was of the man, this cut him to the core. "Too late? Did you tell that bastard you'd marry him?"

Not once did she look right at him after her declaration. She slammed her chair back under her desk. She gathered the things she must have just set down together. "You're too late to discuss any of this with me now."

"Jane," Cole barked. He strode closer to the desk. She wasn't answering him. He *needed* her to answer. He had to know that he'd been right, that she'd never truly say yes to the man she swore was nothing more than a friend.

"If you really wanted to know, you would have been there that night when I really needed you. Now get out, I need to lock up."

"Ya just got here." He folded his arms across his chest. She still hadn't answered his question straight. He had to know. Eyes narrowed, he watched her every move.

She stepped closer, a deep glare darkening her eyes to a stormy grey. One step closer, she was near enough to grab, but he held back. Inches away from him, she darted around him quick as a wink. Before he'd made it two steps out the door after her, she spun around. Without warning, her arm whipped out, the keys in her hand flying right at his head.

The sting of pain in his forehead made him curse, but he didn't give chase right away. He had no idea what the hell her problem was. She'd been the one proposed to, and apparently agreed to that proposal. He was the one with the right to be angry.

Once he got his anger in check, he ignored the keys on the ground in favor of chasing after her. He caught up to her right at the edge of the new café two doors down. This one had outside tables, now half-full with the lunch crowd. Jane stood right inside, scanning the tables.

"Jane." When she ignored him, he wrapped his arm around her arm and held fast. Not tight enough to hurt her. Hell, his hand didn't even close all the way around her small arm. No, he just kept it there to stop her. "Damn it, Jane."

Her nostrils flared. She tugged against his grasp. "Let me go."

"You're mad at me? Ain't that a bit backwards? You're the one that said you'd—"

"*Yes.*" She shouted over him. "I'm mad at you and I have every right to be. Now release my arm, you obtuse fool."

A stab of pain raced up his shin from the hard kick he received. In a knee-jerk reaction, his hand relaxed on her arm while he tried to shake away the hurt. She yanked free easy as pie. After a hop and a curse he followed right behind her. The wide-eyed stares of the diners didn't bother him. He leaned down next to her where she'd sat. "I'm obtuse? Do you have any idea what I've been off doing?"

She turned toward him, eyes flashing. She rose to shove him away. "If you're going to insult me, you son of a bitch, use the ear that isn't deaf."

"Jane. Cole." The café owner Maude raced toward them. "Please. Stop."

"Fine." Cole ignored Maude. He got in Jane's face. "You crazy jezebel. I shoulda known that you—"

"That I would *what*? Are you going to *dare* accuse me of doing something tawdry when you're the one that disappeared for over two days?" Jane didn't back down an inch.

"I'm not the one considering other offers." A bitter pain ripped through his chest every time she failed to deny it. Both he and Tommy had been sure she'd say no. They'd discussed it at length, so that by the time they were done Cole's mind and heart were set. Now she wouldn't deny she'd done what he'd been sure she wouldn't, she'd gone and said yes. "You sure know how to line them up and use them when you need 'em, don't ya?"

"If you had bothered to stick around and talk to me, you'd know *exactly* what was going through my head. But you didn't did you? No, you decided to be an ignorant *ass* that acts as though he's never met me before." For a brief moment the fire left her eyes, and he could have sworn he thought he saw a tear. "You left."

It was almost enough to crack his ire, but not quite. "You sure didn't seem to want me around."

"*How would you know?* You imbecile. You didn't even ask. You assumed."

"You don't know *what* I was doing."

"No. I don't. That is half of the damn problem."

"No. The problem is you can't get it through your head that ya can't keep jerking so many men around. One of them lassos you use is bound to break."

She scoffed. Her small hands shoved him back again. "You're a fine one to talk."

"I ain't running around accepting proposals."

"And you sure as hell aren't making any either. It's much more fun to keep it easy to end, right? That way the *second* you get tired of someone you can stop letting them in. Letting yourself feel anything."

Cole continued to ignore Maude's rising attempts to intervene. He gripped Jane's wrists when she shoved him again. This time it was easier to keep his grip loose and still hold her there. She stilled, even though she could have easily yanked free. Maybe her fight was finally leaving so they could talk rational-like. "Least I don't *lie* about what I want."

"I've never lied about what I want."

"You sure have a funny way of showing it." Wrong tactic. He could practically see her anger rising again.

She tugged against his hold. "You blind sod. All I ever *do* is show it. If I'd had the option, the first thing I would have done was talk to you. But *no*. You chose to assume that I'm a lecherous jezebel, and you left. You walked away. Disappeared without one word. Not even a damn note."

"Well, you're a woman, ain't you? That makes you deceitful."

She stilled for a moment before she moved like lightning. Cole didn't have a second to realize what she was doing to protect himself before she jerked her knee straight up. Colors swam in his vision, the pain cutting so deep he almost hit the ground. He gripped the chair, trying to come to rights again.

The moment he managed to recover enough to take a solid, deep breath, she spoke again. "By that account, all men are fatheaded pricks."

Graham grabbed Cole's arm when he stumbled. "You two should go somewhere else and calm down."

Cole shook his head. His focus returned enough to see Jane skirting away through the tables. He shoved aside Graham to dart after Jane.

When he caught her wrist, she spun and slapped him. "Let me go."

He wrapped his arm around her to tug her close. "Tell me what you said to him."

"Let me go." She snarled, her normally bright blue eyes now dark as slate.

"Cole." Al's voice was close, too close. Cole had no idea when he'd arrived. "Let her go."

Jane's eyes widened, a note of concern pinching her brow. Whether for Cole or the bastard nearby, Cole couldn't be sure, which annoyed him further.

He smirked. "Well, well, well. Lookie there. Maybe you should run to him?"

Jane narrowed her eyes. "You stupid son of a—"

"Cole." David's voice interrupted Jane's protest. He stood nearby, one hand on his gun, ready to draw. "Don't make me take you both in."

Somewhere in his brain, he knew Jane had no designs on her ex, but his presence only fueled the fire of anger. He sneered down at Jane. "And another. You've got a collection. Or am I wrong?"

"If you have to ask, it no longer matters, does it?" She managed to take a step back. "I already told you. You're too late."

"Too late for what?" All Cole wanted was a damn straight answer.

This time when he tried to draw her closer, he got shoved aside.

Jane let out a yelp some distance away, but Cole's focus was on the man that had shoved him away. Al.

Cole charged the ex-soldier, who met him with equal ire. Every bit of pain Jane had made him feel changed into anger that easily, and he let loose on the man making moves on his woman.

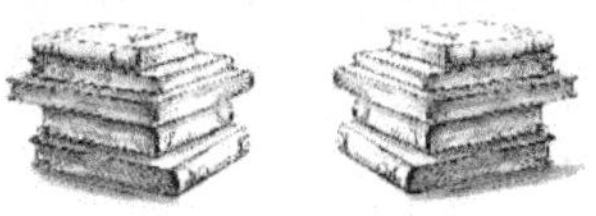

Not to be provoked is best; but if moved,
never correct until the fume is spent;
for every stroke our fury strikes is sure
to hit ourselves last.
—William Penn

Mike heard the commotion before he ever saw it. The new café had a large crowd gathered around it. Shouts, jeers, and feminine shrieks grew louder with every step. Among those came the familiar voice of his sister yelling above the ruckus. "*You're too late.*"

What the hell was going on with Jane? He darted toward the throng blocking the entrance. As deputy it might have been his duty, but he was damn curious what the issue was anyway. Using elbows and strong language to get through the crowd, he broke free of the entangled group in time to see Al tackle Cole away from Jane.

She stumbled backward into David. Neither of them looked too happy over the turn of events. She struggled against the grasp the Sheriff kept on her arms. "What the hell are you doing, David?"

David's brow twisted at her struggled. "What? You want to—"

"You let Al go after him?" She broke free only to spin on David. "Are you *completely* insane? They'll kill each other."

"Jane!" David reached for her too late, she took off toward the fight.

Mike knew that had 'bad idea' written all over it. Not even Cole's swinging fists slowed her down. "*Cole, stop.*"

Al crashed into a table, sending plates of food flying. Half the crowd scattered away from the mess. Jane finally froze, no longer heading toward the fray. Her eyes grew wide. She turned in place as if seeing the growing crowd for the first time. Although how she'd missed them, he had no idea.

"Jane." Mike ran to his sister's side the moment Cole launched himself at Al again. David yelled for more help, so

Mike pulled Jane back a few steps from the battle. "What in blazes is going on here?"

Jane gripped his hand so hard, he was sure she'd break the skin. "Please. Please help David separate them. Cole will kill him if he has the chance."

"Pretty sure he always would have."

"Just do it." She shoved him toward the fight.

Mike circled behind Cole, not quite sure how he ended up with the bigger brute in the fray until Archie took a place next to him.

Cole and Al remained locked together in a tight stance. Both of them swung an arm, landing a punch on the other. Al stumbled back, while Cole stood tall, blood streaming from the formers lip and nose.

"*Stop*." Jane's shriek was desperate when both men moved toward each other. She took a step toward the battle, adding a level of desperation to Mike's own worries.

"Jane. Stay back." Mike held out his hand, not that it would stop her. Just as they were about to move in to separate the men, Al took another swing at Cole. The pair fell into another series of blows until Al landed a solid hook to Cole's jaw.

The second Cole stumbled back, Mike and Archie moved to grab him. Across the impromptu battlefield, David grabbed Al.

Cole fought tooth and nail against them. "Think you can just come in and take her away. You were just *waiting* for the perfect chance. She called ya honorable." He spat blood on the ground, a dark sneer on his features.

"At least someone was willing to give her what she needed to get her what she wanted most." Al was more fired up then Mike had ever seen the normally quiet man. Whether it was the battle or Jane herself, he was ready for this fight. "You aren't man enough—"

Everything happened at once. Jane's protest was drowned out by Cole's primal shout. Every fiber of muscle tightened to strain against Mike's hold. Cole broke free of Archie's hold.

"No, Cole." Jane's hands flew out, she took several steps forward.

Mike guessed she was trying to regain the man's attention, but Mike had no time to let out a warning, his own struggle to hold back the infuriated barman was faltering. He grunted a final effort, but Cole burst free a heartbeat later.

Time itself slowed down. Mike tumbled back. Jane leaped forward to block Cole's path toward Al, desperation lining her face as it yelled at the man she loved.

Cole never saw her until it was too late. His fist was already swinging, his eyes grew wide when he saw Jane the split second before his fist made contact. Jane dropped like a sack of potatoes. Cole's whole body jerked back. Torment ripped away the dark fury in an instant. His body sagged, his hands reaching toward her. *"Jane. No."*

"You stupid bastard." Tommy burst through the crowd toward Cole.

"Tommy, wait." Mike tried to grab him, but Tommy moved like a steam engine toward the shocked, and now lax Cole. Clearly his brother had missed the whole scene, and Mike knew if he hadn't witnessed it himself, he'd react the same damn way. It looked much worse than it was, though it was sure as hell bad enough.

Problem was, they'd just stopped one fight. Then again, Cole wasn't exactly putting up a fight. As his focus was on Jane, Mike wasn't even sure he'd seen or heard Tommy coming. He dropped with Tommy's first hit, and took several blows before he'd bothered to respond. Even then, he only defended himself.

Mike, Archie, and three other men converged on Tommy to pull him off Cole. Mike grunted when Tommy tried to fight them all off. They managed to drag him back several feet from the two prone lovers. "Thomas. Enough. He didn't mean to hit her."

Tommy had always liked Cole, but Mike knew the past ten years had made them all more sensitive over Jane's hurts. They'd lost their sister once, and not one of them wanted to do it again. Tommy didn't seem to hear him, though. He kept struggling, more so when Cole managed to get on one elbow, reaching a bloodied hand toward Jane but pulling it back before he made contact.

"Tommy. Stop." Mike planted himself in front of Tommy while the other men tried to keep him back.

Tommy's fight lessened incrementally. He remained tense enough that no one dared release their hold on him just yet. He snarled toward Cole. "Stay away—"

"Thomas Eugene. Look at me. It was an accident, but that's no matter. We've got to get her to the clinic. We can't do that if you're being an idiot."

Nostril's flared, Tommy glared at Mike. At least he'd stopped arguing.

Mike turned in time to see Al heading toward Jane.

Cole tensed immediately. The torment in his features echoed in his voice, though the underlying threat of anger bubbled under the surface. "You stay the hell away from her."

"David," Mike started to suggest. Immediately, Cole's wrath turned toward Jane's ex-husband. Mike sighed. "Fine. What about Archie and Wills? Are they acceptable?"

Cole's jaw twitched, his gaze back on Jane. He offered a short nod of reply.

"Archie, Wills. Would one of you get Jane to the clinic? The other escort Al to a separate room so Cole doesn't feel the need to follow. I believe Dr. Pearson is there. I think Tommy can control himself now." Mike turned back to his brother. He set a firm hand on Tommy's chest. "Isn't that right, brother?"

A low growl emanated from the man, but he said nothing.

Once Jane had been carried off out of sight, Mike smacked Tommy on the side of the head. The nasty glare he received in return didn't faze him. Mike met Tommy sneer for sneer. "How does Clara try to stop a damn fight every single time? How many times have *you* hit her for doing the same thing?"

Tommy's glare shifted to Cole. "Why the hell didn't you just tell her? She's been nothing but a mess since you left. I was about to tell her why you were gone so damn long."

"Because she said yes," Cole barked right back.

That stilled all Tommy's fury. His features slackened in shock. "Wait. She what?"

Mike glanced between the two of them, confused as hell. He cast a glance toward David in hopes he had a clue. The sheriff shrugged a reply. Mike shook his head. "What is going on? Would the two of you care to explain?"

"No," they both replied in unison.

"Then someone had better come up with some money for Maude for damages. Then you'd better help clean this place up before you get medical attention of your own." Mike frowned. "You made a mess of the café for no apparent reason in the middle of a rush."

David folded his arms across his chest. "If you have a problem with that, you can all go to jail for disturbing the peace. Hell, at this point I may still do that."

"Jane." Cole's voice cracked. He bowed his head, though not before Mike caught a glimpse of fear he was trying to hide.

"You let Daisy worry about Jane." Mike tried to maintain a glare on the man. "Once you're done cleaning up this mess, you can see about cleaning up that one."

At Cole's first rumbling of protest, David pulled out his shackles. He waited until Cole and Tommy began to clean the mess with help from Graham and a few others before he nodded to Mike. "I think things are handled here. Go check on her."

Mike gave him a grateful nod. He edged through the lingering crowd. The moment he got free he jogged toward the clinic. He didn't bother knocking, just stepped inside. "Daisy?"

Archie stood outside a door nearby, but his gaze remained down the hall on another closed door. He jerked his thumb behind him to the shut door. "She's in there stitching up Jane."

"Thanks, Archie. David has them cleaning the mess at Maude's. Threatened them with jail, which he might still follow through on." Mike frowned toward the door Archie had been watching. "What about Al?"

"Got a towel on that lip. You know what this is about? Do I need to be worried about more trouble?" As Mayor, Archie kept as close an eye on these things as David did as Sheriff. He worried about the town on more levels, though. "Mrs. Daugherty's bringing in some people to talk about all those new businesses she wants to build. She'd be awful unhappy for something like this to ruin things."

Mike snorted, for despite the way the words might have expressed concern, the tone was completely different. "Why do you sound almost hopeful that could happen? Are you among those that wish the Daugherty's would remain in Denver?"

"Of course not," Archie muttered. Though his arms remained still, his fingers crossed.

"So sorry I even dared to suggest such a thing." Mike chuckled as he clapped him on the shoulder. "Honestly, I have no idea what it was about. Tommy seems to have an idea, but he's not talking. So, I can't make any promises that it won't happen again."

"A mayor can hope."

"He certainly can." Mike offered a smile. He knocked softly on the door. Daisy's voice beckoned him in, so he went in. Jane lay on the exam table, still unconscious. A row of neat stitches crept across her hairline like a caterpillar. "How is she?"

"She needed a few stitches." Daisy kept her voice low, her entire focus on the thread while she tied off the final stitch. "Hopefully other than the headache, she'll be all right. I would ask what happened, but Archie said Cole hit her."

"It was sort of accidental."

"Sort of?" Daisy's head snapped up. Fury flamed across her pretty eyes before she retained control. "This is not a *sort of* sort of injury. Honestly, I'm shocked. In all my years I've never known Cole to hit a woman. They've always fought so strongly, though. I just don't know what to think."

"He meant to hit Al. She kind of got in the middle."

"Oh." She huffed. "Is that supposed to make it better somehow?"

"Jane has a horrible habit of stopping fights by jumping between the pair of fighters. I've hit her a few times. Tommy's hit her—a lot, James, and Nick, too. Of course, Nick's the only one that did a good amount of damage."

"How wonderful," Daisy muttered in a droll tone.

He chuckled, despite the seriousness the situation called for. "I know. It sounds terrible, doesn't it? When you grow up in a house full of boys, there are a lot of fights. If Clara wasn't the initiator, she was usually the one trying to break things up—which usually caused her far more damage than it did any of us."

"Well, she took a good blow today. I have little doubt she has a concussion. I'll need to keep an eye on her to make sure there isn't further damage."

"She's not going to be happy when she wakes. Then again, she's been fairly miserable the past few days."

Daisy wiped her hands off, her brow furrowed. "Does anyone know what brought all of this about today?"

"Well, like I said, Tommy seems to have some idea. Neither he nor Cole seem inclined to discuss the matter. I'll be damned if I know. When I arrived at the café at the end of that epic argument, Cole and Al were already in fisticuffs. All I know is Jane told me they needed to be separated or Cole would kill Al."

Daisy finished setting aside her equipment. "Am I to wager a bet there are more injuries to patch, then?"

"Oh, yes. Al's in the back room. Cole and Tommy will need looked over when they're done cleaning up Maude's place." Mike moved next to Jane. He scooped her in his arms. "I'll get her settled upstairs. If she wakes, I'll try to keep her that way until you can get upstairs."

"Thank you." Daisy's lips twitched in a wry smile. "I guess that's one good thing about growing up in your house—you already know what to expect from certain injuries."

"What can I say? I've had a few blows to the head myself. Of course, I'm sure you noticed that already." He winked.

Daisy laughed. She opened the door and shooed him from the room.

Mike got Jane upstairs, into a front room where she'd have plenty of sunlight. He pulled a chair next to the bed. "What was that you said about wanting a boring life, Jane? I don't know what you were thinking, but this is far from boring."

A soft sigh slipped free from Jane. "Cole."

"Jane." Mike leaned forward. "Wake yourself up. You need to tell me what in heavens led to this. I'm dying to know."

She groaned. "Biddy."

Mike laughed softly. He took her hand in his. "Not a biddy. That was one hell of a fist fight Cole and Al were caught up in. This is beyond gossip, Jane. Not to mention the mood you've been in the past few days. Would you care to explain?"

Her eyes cracked open. She winced, a hand flew to her head. When her fingers brushed along the stitches, she frowned. "Sleep."

"Nope. Not allowed to after how hard you got it. So stay awake, and explain."

"Al proposed."

"Oh."

"Cole heard."

"Uh-oh."

"Exactly."

*Nothing is more wretched
than the mind of a man conscious of guilt.
–Titus Maccius Plautus*

Cole sat on the edge of the bed hard. A drop of blood hit the floor between his feet.

He stared at it as another drop hit the same spot, splattering across the wood surface.

His hands shook violently before he plastered them against his knees. The scene replayed over and over in his head. Jane's face, mouth wide in protest, then eyes in fear as his fist made impact.

The sound of her body hitting the dirt.

He'd hit her. The woman he loved. The woman he'd had designs on marrying.

It would never happen now, and he didn't blame her one damn bit. He wasn't cut out for this. He never had been.

How could he have been such a fool?

"Jane," he whispered to the quiet room.

The silence echoed back in a way it hadn't since after her hanging when he'd thought her dead.

Fitting, seeing as he'd likely just killed any hope of a relationship with her.

She'd hate him. With good reason.

Once before in his life he'd felt this guilt. After Ella's death, when he'd killed her defending himself from her. What he'd done to Jane was no better.

He'd left after Ella. He'd have to leave Dominion Falls now. Everything was Jane's. She deserved it, far more than he'd ever deserved her.

A knock came on the door. In the absence of his reply, the door opened. The only person to brave crossing his threshold came into view.

Tommy. Probably come to finish him off.

"She's awake," Tommy said in quiet tones. "Mike said she asked for you."

"Liar." Cole wrung his hands together to hide their trembling.

"No. Jane asked for you."

Cole closed his eyes and shook his head. He couldn't hear her end things. It was too much.

"Don't go running."

"Get the fuck out of my room. No one is allowed in here."

"Except Jane."

Grief compacted the words of anger into a thick knot in his throat. Unwilling to let Tommy see, Cole kept his gaze on the growing spot of blood on the floor.

"Go see her."

Cole shook his head again.

"You'll regret it if you don't."

"I've got enough regrets for a lifetime. What's one more?"

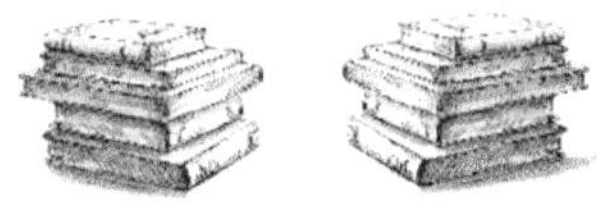

But our love it was stronger by far
than the love
Of those who were older than we—
Of many far wiser than we—
-Edgar Allan Poe

Jane's head felt like it was flooded with water. Her thoughts muddled together in a sickening swirl that churned her stomach something fierce. Then it pounded and pressed against her eyeballs.

Every move left her dizzy, and though she'd begged for sleep, it now eluded her. Even as her guardian for the night, Mike, had drifted off when he was supposed to be keeping watch over her.

Slow as molasses Jane rose to her feet. The floor tilted beneath her. A steadying grip to the chair Michael sat in righted her again.

Her memories fluctuated in a way that always struck her deepest fear. She'd lost all of her memories once; she hated losing any now. Even those like what had caused her concussion.

She knew in her heart Cole would never have struck her intentionally. Even as a brothel owner, most of whom didn't mind keeping their whores in line with a slap, he'd never once hit one of them.

Worse, she knew with the accident that had killed his first wife, he'd carried that guilt for years. Though this blow hadn't been meant for her, she knew his remorse had to be immeasurable right then. The fact he hadn't visited when she'd asked for him told her as much.

Somehow she made it to the balcony doors without stumbling or vomiting. Both accomplishments, but she didn't trust herself to go any further yet.

She pushed aside the curtain to look toward the saloon. The streetlamps were the only lights she could see. The saloon was dark, even their room.

"Cole," she whispered into the darkness. The headache returned to pound behind her eyes, but she didn't remove her gaze from the room they lived in.

Perhaps Tom could drag the stubborn man to her.

No. Cole would be in fight mode, unwilling to listen to anyone but perhaps her. Then again, perhaps not.

This was her fault. She'd allowed him to believe she'd accepted another man's proposal because, why? Because he'd made her mad? He did that all the time.

Because she'd been wounded by his disappearance? Yes, but more so by his admittance he'd left after hearing the proposal. Without any explanation to his departure.

What was it he'd said? The thoughts swirled and churned again. She groaned, clutching her stomach in hopes it would stave the rising nausea.

Do you have any idea what I've been off doing? Cole's words came back to her through the muddled memories.

What *had* he been off doing? Where had he gone? Why?

Answers she might never get if she didn't speak to him soon. In the past his all-consuming guilt had led him to leave his life and form a new one in Dominion Falls. She feared he'd do it again if they didn't clear this mess up.

"Jane? Jane!" Mike's panic voice hit her injured brain like a steam engine.

"Oh, don't." She pressed her forehead to the glass pane at the next wave of nausea. "Your voice pains me."

"Sorry," he spoke softer now. "I thought you'd run off."

"I'm barely capable of walking. I doubt I'd run."

"You'd run to the fool that put you in here."

"If I could, you're probably right."

"Come sit down before you fall over." Mike guided her back to the bed. He pushed her to sit, but no further.

"He didn't come."

"No, he didn't."

"He must be so distraught."

"You're the one injured and distraught."

"So is he."

Mike sighed heavily. "Jane."

"Annabel."

"What? No. You're Jane. Don't tell me you've forgotten again."

She pursed her lips at him. "No, you dunce. Annabel Lee. 'And neither the angels in heaven above, nor the demons down under the sea'."

"'Can ever dissever my soul from the soul of the beautiful Annabel Lee'." Mike squeezed her hands.

"But what if fool human actions can?"

To Be

Continued...

In Book 5 of the
Dominion Falls Series

Runaway
Train

About the

Author

Sarah Cass, author of over twenty novels in 4 series, is devoted to giving her readers well-crafted, emotional stories, with depth to even her secondary characters—to give readers a full world to explore. Stories that explore not only the labyrinths of the heart, but the nightmares of the soul. A RONE finalist, she is also owner and creator of Redefining Perfect. By day, she's a nurse, a mother, wife and cat-mom to 4 mischievous beasts. By night she crafts stories that take her across centuries. From the old west of Dominion Falls, to the small town of Lake Point for the holidays, and even into the paranormal land of Shifters and Magic in The Tribe. She loves hearing from her readers. Visit her at www.authorsarahcass.com

Other Books in
The Dominion Falls Series

Independent Brake
Changing Tracks
Derailed
Dark Territory
Runaway Train
Home Signal
Red Zone

Coming Soon in
The Dominion Falls Series

Dust Raiser
Chase the Red
Blizzard Lights
Dead Man's Switch
Bird Cage
A Highball Arrangement
Douse the Glim
Blood
Grave Digger
Bad Order

Books by Sarah Cass

The Tribe Series
The Tribe
The Wolf
The Chief
The Raven

The Lake Point Series
Santa, Maybe
Deep-Fried Sweethearts
Stalled Independence
Witch Way
A Thorough Thanksgiving
Eve's New Year
Heartstrings & Hockey Pucks
Luck of the Cowgirl
Stars, Stripes & Motorbikes
Free Falling
Love for Hire
Haunted Hearts

Stand Alone Novels
Masked Hearts
Leap